THE *Night* MEDICINE

JODY A. KESSLER

Please visit:
www.JodyAKessler.com

ISBN: 978-0-9862406-2-1
E book ISBN: 978-0-9862406-3-8

Edited by

Missed Period Editing services
kyla.stein@gmail.com
and
Nancy Segovia

Cover Art & Design by

Laura Gordon
www.thebookcovermachine.com

Manufactured in the United States of America

First Edition

To Nancy and John.
This novel would not exist without the two of you.

Prologue

The stories of my ancestors are all true. We believe that a story holds its own medicine. That the listener will swallow the pieces that are meant to be absorbed into the spirit and then the spirit will use the knowledge to make the listener a more honorable person.

When I was a kid, I could not believe the tall tales. Animals do not talk. Gods do not walk the earth among us to marry women and take them up to the clouds. People do not transform into wolves and crows and bears, and our people did not travel to ghost villages to find our lost loved ones.

I would often go to bed after long nights of listening to those stories with dreams of being chased by painted warriors on horseback and then being scalped as I lay dying in the grass. Other nights, I would dream of becoming a talking mountain cat or a wolf and go hunting for deer or innoka or moose. Grandfather wouldn't wake up to tell me it was only a dream and to go back to sleep, but Grandmother would come and sit next to me in the dark. Only, she didn't comfort me in the way I needed. I wanted reassurance that my dreams were not real. Instead, she would rub my back and sing a song under her breath until my heart stopped pounding and the sweat from my panic dried. She would always stay by my side until I went back to sleep. The next morning, she would ask me about my dream, and if I told her about the horrible things I saw or the great adventure I had as a red-tailed hawk, she would only nod like it was very important and then she would turn back to whatever food she was preparing and start humming another song, keeping her hands endlessly busy.

In the summer before I turned fifteen years old, my grandfather took me to the ceremonial place high in the mountains beneath the Thunderbird Peaks, and next to the beaver ponds. It was in that place that I became fully aware of my smallness in the world. That my insistence to make assumptions had kept me ignorant, and all the stories I heard growing up were more than just fables. There were valuable lessons to be learned from them and there were layers of understanding built into the stories that could only be uncovered when my small mind was ready to expand. As it did, I began to understand more about my life and about the Blackfoot people. That the world extended past my school and our small town and my grandfather and his tribal council. The plains reached farther than I, or even the eagles, could see from the summit of Chief Mountain. I learned that the universe existed beyond the Seven Sisters in the night sky. My complaints about the reservation where I lived became meaningless. Grandpa Two Eagles shared the summer with me where I grew up and became a man. He took me on a journey filled with medicine, songs, dancing, and ceremonies. It was an adventure of wilderness and horses and sleeping next to the fire wrapped snugly in a buffalo hide robe.

When we returned from the mountains, I slept once again in my bed at Grandmother's house. I put away in the back of my mind all of those tall stories, everything I didn't want to listen to or believe, because if what had happened to me and Grandfather was real, then every word of every story I have ever heard would have to be true.

Chapter One

The smell of the place was perpetually stale and sour. Its source could have been the wood planks of the creaking floorboards, where beer had been spilled for decades, but more likely it was the aroma wafting off of the patrons that frequented Growler's Tavern. Hank Williams or Dwight Yoakam were usually singing out of the jukebox, which was wedged beneath the single high window that faced the main street through town. Someone was always plunking quarters into the machine and punching buttons in search of more modern music, but they weren't going to find it in this joint.

The potpourri of odors, the low lights, the sorrowful twang of classic country music, and the ever-flowing tap were part of Growler's dingy appeal, but none of these reasons were why Dean Wolfsblood sat at the bar drinking bottles of Corona until someone insisted on giving him a ride home.

More often than not, he wouldn't speak to anyone. He was there because the bartender was his cousin and she would serve him until Morning Star had risen. He never talked about his problems unless they had to do with broken equipment at the mine or why the parts didn't show up on time. Occasionally, the subject changed to who'd been fired or walked off the job. The conversation had to stay neutral so that any man sitting at the bar could contribute his two cents, and Dean could leave all of his sharp-edged memories buried where the haze of alcohol dulled the gleam of the proverbial knife twisting in his heart.

"I can't cart your sorry butt home tonight," the bartender told him as she wiped the bar top in front of Dean. "I have a date."

Dean sucked in a deep breath and wagered in his mind how he could get out of hearing about his cousin's latest victim. "Your caring heart is the eighth wonder of the world, Gena, but I didn't ask for a ride."

"I'm not about to let you drive anywhere."

"I wouldn't dream of it," he muttered and took another swig of beer.

"You promise?" She cocked a brow skeptically.

"Don't give me that look. I'm meeting up with an old buddy from the Corps. He'll take me home."

"Not if he's been drinking too."

"Cut it out, Gena. He doesn't drink. Never has. Thinks it's snake venom for us N-D-N's."

"Sounds like a decent guy," she said as she rinsed the towel out in the sink.

"He might be. He might be an ass. I never paid much attention. We were too busy making sure we didn't get blown up."

"So you were stationed in Iraq together?" She paused in front of her cousin, speculating about how loaded he already was.

Dean didn't look up to meet her gaze. These days, making eye contact with anyone meant that he would have to see the worry lines etched around their eyes and the sympathetic half-smiles that just made him feel worse.

He stared at his hand wrapped around the bottle instead. "Iraq and Afghanistan. We shared a few tours. Badger's a hell of a shot. Quick with intel, and saved my rear end more than once."

"You said he's a Blackfoot too? You'll have to introduce me."

Dean risked looking up at his cousin and saw the undeniable expression of an interested woman. A coy smirk touched the corners of her mouth as she tucked her hair behind an ear.

"Listen lil' 'cuz," he warned. "I'll have no part in hooking you up with Badger Lowell. Didn't you just tell me you have a date tonight?"

He'd gone and done it. He could feel himself being sucked into her black hole of male drama. Dean bit down on his tongue, forcing himself not to get any deeper into this firing hole.

She shrugged like it was inconsequential for her to be inquiring about a man when she's currently dating another. "It's always good to have a backup plan. So, since your friend's a Marine…"

"Former Marine," Dean interrupted.

"Is he all ripped and muscular like you?" Deviousness twinkled in her dark eyes.

He glanced down at his biceps, frowned, and shook his head, wondering again how he ended up in this absurd conversation. "I have no clue."

Dean could remember Gena planning her future wedding all the way back in middle school. Her teeny-bopper appraisal of every male specimen within a three hundred mile radius drove him nuts. Not much had changed since she'd grown up. She still wanted the whole package: marriage, a house, and kids. Dean thought she wanted it too much, and that it was her longing that kept her from acquiring it. He had seen too many people caught in the trap of wanting it all and not being able to see what was right in front of them as they looked too far into the future. He never voiced these thoughts aloud, however. Gena was a good cousin, more like his sister, and they had always gotten along well. He didn't need to ruin their relationship with his own unwanted opinions.

But the thoughts about his lonely cousin continued to nag at him over the buzz from the beer. Maybe he should be easier on her. She could just be taking advantage of the situation at hand. She worked all the time, between running the local daycare center and managing the bar on the weekends. How else was she ever going to land a guy if she didn't go after opportunities where she saw them? He certainly wasn't the one to consult when it came to life plans. He once had the life she wanted so badly, and look where it had landed him.

Disbelieving how far he'd let this train get away from the station, he said, "Turn on a baseball game, will 'ya?" He stared up at the television suspended from the ceiling. The game mattered little to him, but he wanted a believable way out of this conversation.

A woman Dean didn't recognize walked behind the bar and grabbed the remote control. "I got it," she said.

Gena turned to her replacement and flashed a wide smile. "Hey, thanks again for coming in."

As the girl pointed the remote at the T.V., Dean stole a look at her. He appraised her long, braided hair and narrow figure appreciatively. She wore dark jeans that reminded him of something his ex-wife might wear, but this woman had plain tennis shoes on, whereas Marissa would have worn something with deadly points and heels that no one should ever walk in. He never could understand where her toes were inside those awful shoes, but he had enough sense to know that she liked them, so he didn't question her choice. Once again affirming that it's better to keep his mouth shut.

"I don't see a listing for any games tonight," the mystery woman said as she scrolled through the guide.

"It was my attempt at shutting down Gena's man-dar."

The two women exchanged a look that told Dean that he should definitely stop talking. He hid behind his beer as the new bartender asked, "How about Sports Center?"

"Sure," he answered and pretended to look toward the door, wondering how long it would take Badger to show.

A couple of weeks earlier, Badger had found Dean's grandmother listed in the phone directory. His Marine pal was coming all the way from Newfoundland where he had been contracted to maintain equipment for a gold mine during the last two years. Badger told her that his contract had ended, he was done with Canada, and was coming back to the States. Grandma Rosemary invited Badger out to Montana for a visit. That was all it took, and now Dean was faced with having to confront his past.

He finished his bottle of beer and contemplated how numb he'd like to be for the meeting. Beer may not be sufficient for the task.

His Marine days were part of the time in his life that he no longer thought about. That experience was securely tied in with meeting his wife and starting his family. He buried those thoughts two years ago, but he couldn't tell Badger not to come. They had too much in common to ignore and throw away. Badger claimed to be a full-blooded Kainah Blackfoot; a Blood. He said his parents left Montana to find work in Colorado years before he was ever born, and then ended up in Butte when his father started working for a copper mine. That's where Badger had grown up.

Dean was an Amsskaapipikani, a South Piegan, but they were both Blackfoot, and it was rare to find anyone from home in the service. Strangers in their youth, sheer luck and synchronicity landed them in the same unit in the Marine Corps, deploying to Iraq. Badger was a few years older than Dean, but no one could ever tell because of his baby face and broad smile. Everyone in their squadron assumed they would be fast friends, including Badger. He was always eager to talk about home and tribal councils and the summer pow-wows, but Dean didn't understand Badger's motivations and remained cautious around the man. *At least at first.*

Dean grew up on the reservation and Badger had never lived on one. It was hard for Dean to understand why Badger wanted to know so much about life there. It was home and nothing all that special, but Badge acted like he had missed out on something great. Dean tried to convince him that all he was missing was a bunch of boring nothing, but Badger never believed it, and pumped him for information constantly.

During their five tours together, Dean began to trust and even like the opinionated, hot-headed Marine, and they eventually did become friends. Dean knew that after eight years in the military and all of the deployments with Badger, he should have kept in touch with his buddy. He also knew that he should have done a lot of things that he'd neglected, but life had taken a crushing turn for him, and he wanted to forget everything. He had to; otherwise, he was going to be singing his death song a lot sooner than his grandmother would approve of.

Dean stared at his fingers resting against the bar and noticed how his hands looked like they belonged to some fifty-year-old roughneck, not the twenty-eight-year-old that he actually was. The grime and grease from running the drill rig and working on his truck wouldn't leave the cracks in his skin for at least a week. By then, he could be on a new job drilling or be out repairing some broken part. Available work was there for him when he wanted it. *He was lucky like that.* So many others on the Reserve never knew steady work, and probably never would.

He flexed his hand and felt the ripped skin tear open where he'd scraped his knuckles ten times too many. It's too easy for his body to forget that he's still a young man. The work at the mines made his knees and shoulders ache. It made him look older too, but that didn't bother him. For all anyone else knew, he was just a cranky old bastard. It helped people stay away.

Working the rigs paid well. The last contract had been decent, and his living expenses were so low that his paycheck would see him through for a few months. Now all he needed was regular sleep and time off from the ear-splitting machines. He was somewhat happy to be home, and grateful that Gena was working tonight before he holed up in his cabin. If he could endure this reunion with Badger quickly, he would then be free to disappear on his land until he left for his next job.

"Will you grab me another Corona?"

Gena was out of her apron and had her purse in her hands, but she leaned down and opened a cooler to retrieve yet another beer.

"I don't see your friend," she accused as she opened the bottle and set it down in front of him, stuffing a wedge of lime into the top.

"I'll walk if he doesn't show," Dean said, placating her.

"Twenty miles?" The dubious look was back.

"Yes, ma'am," he said, and took a drink.

"What's going on?" the new bartender asked.

She was inquisitive, but only just, with nothing particularly friendly in the straight line of her mouth or the cool gaze behind her doe-shaped eyes.

Dean chanced a steady look at her face. Even in his drunken stupor, he could observe and assess a target in seconds. It was a desirable trait to have in the field, and he had often been consulted by his Commanding Officers for his keen vision. He decided that she was definitely Native, but looked different from the girls he was used to seeing on the Blackfoot Reserve. Her face was slimmer and more angular, kind of like her body. Her eyes were deeply set, or maybe it was just the way that she looked back at him. There was a shield behind those dark eyes, and it felt awfully familiar. He didn't want to see any more, and looked at the T.V. quickly before he noticed too much, or she did.

"Kai, this is my cousin, Dean. I take care of him because he's a good tipper, and he's family. Plus he's usually not too big of a pain in my ass," Gena said.

"Don't listen to her," he said without looking at them. "I am."

Unable to help himself, he glanced at Kai for the second it took to see her raised eyebrows and lack of enthusiasm.

"Dean, this is my friend, Kai. She's working here during the tourist season while she's out of school for the summer. Don't give her a hard time." Gena said this last part in a playful way, but he knew she meant it.

He swallowed. His mouth felt dry. Dean couldn't remember ever having felt like he'd swallowed his tongue because of meeting a woman for the first time. "Hey," he said, and gave a brusque nod.

"Now give me your keys." Gena held out her hand expectantly.

"I thought you were leaving," he grumbled.

"I am. Right now. So hand them over. Kai can hold them for you until Badger gets here. I'll find out later if you've lied to me about your fake ride."

Knowing she wouldn't give up, he dug out the key to his truck and then watched Gena hand it over to her friend. Kai slipped it into her apron pocket, and he knew he'd just been swindled out of his key for a twelve pack of beer.

"He'll be here," he said.

Gena gave him an evil smile and turned to Kai. "Stop serving him whenever you like. Especially if he gets out of line."

"Oh, I will," she said with a sobering glance at Dean.

"You're the one out of line, Gena. Without me, this dump would shut down. You'd be jobless, and we can't have that."

Dean could hear the alcohol starting to warp his tongue. *He hated that.* Despised himself for being drunk in public, but it was the only way that he'd been able to handle the reality of his life.

"I mean it. Don't be afraid to cut him off," Gena said to Kai as she walked out from behind the bar toward the door. "There's a list of numbers next to his name on the phone pad. Anyone you call will come pick him up if his ride doesn't show."

Kai watched Gena as she gave her an encouraging nod and then hustled out the door, excited for her date.

She went to the sinks and began washing glasses before moving on to restock beer bottles. The couple of patrons sitting at the bar weren't of the chatty sort, and her one waitress on duty tonight was taking care of the floor. With virtually nothing to do, Kai thought about spending her summer in this place, and almost walked right out. It wasn't ideal, but it should be easy cash, and she needed all she could get. Working with Gena part time at the daycare was her better job, but the hours were minimal and so was the pay. She and Gena had become trusted friends quickly, so when Gena offered her the summer position at Growler's, she took it. She decided that she could give up one summer working both days and nights to build her savings, especially since her aunt was willing to watch her son. She needed to have a few dollars saved up before the fall and winter semesters began. Bartending would have to hold her over.

Now that she had been through her first week, Kai could see why Gena always looked so tired after a long night at the bar. The customers could drain the life out of you with one dreadful drunken story after another. That, and she'd already been asked out a half dozen times by belligerent and loathsome old men who made her want to gag.

Now she found herself behind the bar trying not to stare at Gena's cousin while wondering just how many beers the guy could drink before floating off his bar stool and drowning in his own watery piss. It's really too bad that someone with such an amazing body and ruggedly handsome face could waste it by dating *Senorita Corona*.

Half an hour before last call rolled around, his supposed friend had still not arrived, so she stood in front of Dean and asked, "Can I call someone for you?"

"No thanks."

His eyes were unfocussed, and she thought again about the unfortunate commitment she'd made in agreeing to work at the bar through the tourist season.

"We're closing soon."

"How about another beer then?"

"I don't think so," she said while tapping her fingers on the bar.

"The injustices of the world never stop, do they?" he slurred. "Someone always thinks they know what's best for you."

"You know what I call an injustice? Making your server responsible for taking care of you because you're too drunk to do it yourself. That seems a bit unfair to me."

"You're absolutely right." He paused, attempting to focus on her face. "What's your name again? Leah? No, that's not it, is it? I have a terrible memory when I've been drinking."

"Really? I wonder why that would be." Her sarcasm was probably lost on him in his drunken haze, but she didn't care.

"Kai. Right? I got it," he said, sloppy pride tingeing his voice. "I can't put my unfortunate state of being on you. I've got buffalo chips for brains. Excuse me," he apologized, and then pushed himself off the sticky vinyl barstool.

Surprised by the unexpected response, she watched him shuffle over to the restroom and disappear inside. Not knowing what he may or may not do next, she kept an eye on the door to make sure he didn't just pass out on the floor. This was her first night to shut down the bar by herself, and it would be embarrassing to have to call Gena to come back in and help her. Her friend was giddy with excitement over having an actual date, and Kai wasn't about to ruin it. When Dean didn't reappear after ten minutes, she grudgingly knocked on the men's room door.

No answer. She sighed and then berated herself for telling her waitress that it was okay to leave an hour earlier. She dreaded having to handle a drunk man twice her size by herself, but she gritted her teeth and gingerly pushed the door open.

Dean turned at the sound of the creaking door and embarrassment flushed her face as she saw that he was only slouched over the sink washing his hands, not passed out next to a vomit-filled toilet. She backed out of the restroom and let the door close in her face. Mortified that her suspicions had proved unwarranted, she was about to go hide behind the bar when something odd occurred to her, and she slammed the door back open.

"Are you bleeding?" Kai strained to get a good look at his head.

Dean's hand rose to his forehead and she rushed forward. As she passed the trashcan, she noticed soiled paper towels that were bright red with blood.

"What the hell did you do to yourself?"

Dean tried to step around her and leave the bathroom, but she wouldn't let him. Not until she got a look at the injury.

"It's nothing," he said, and stumbled back into the sink.

She gripped his arm, partly to steady him and partly so she could turn him around and look at his head. She recoiled as she stared at the split on his skin and the rising lump just above his right eyebrow.

He ducked his head away from her so she couldn't see it and then pulled free of her loose grasp.

"The damn door bites. Now back off. It's nothing." He walked out of the men's room, leaving an astonished Kai standing inside with her mouth hanging open.

Collecting herself, Kai followed him into the bar and then decided to call someone on Gena's list. Looking around though, she realized that Dean had walked out into the late night and he was no longer her problem.

Uneasy relief settled over her shoulders as she realized that she was at last completely alone and could now finish shutting down the bar. She wished Gena's cousin would have just let her call someone, but she already knew not to argue or confront a drunk. If he could put himself in this situation, he could get himself out of it. With that in mind, she cleaned the bar top, the taps, shut down the jukebox, and closed her register.

As Kai walked to her car, her brain told her that her son would be awake in five hours or less. Could she really handle working such late hours? The brutal reality that sleep had become a precious commodity felt like another drain on her spirit, but Kai knew it could be a lot worse. She could be broke, hungry, and homeless. She had firsthand experience with even worse fates than those. Sleepy was the lesser of the current evils, and if she had to remind herself a thousand times a day that she was working to make her and her son's lives better, then she would keep it up like a mantra. She yawned as she turned the key to start the engine and dreamed about what it will be like after she graduated nursing school, started working at the medical clinic, and could get her own place.

She drove across the lot toward the empty street, but as she passed the only other parked vehicle, she happened to see a pair of boots dangling over the edge of the open tailgate.

"Why me?" she asked the sliver of moon hanging over the western horizon.

Unable to ignore her natural tendency to nurture and take care of the needy, she stopped her car and climbed out. The thought of him lying there with a concussion forced her to drag her sorry, exhausted self over to his supine body.

She approached with caution. "Yo. You alive in there?"

"I wasn't until you started screeching at me," he said, and sat up.

She crossed her arms over her chest. "I am not screechy."

"No. You sound more like a bawling, sultry cow." He covered his forehead with his palm, winced, and then lay back down in the bed of his truck.

"A cow?" she asked, insulted and disbelieving the craziness unfolding on her first night alone at the bar.

"A key stealing cow," he said.

Right. She touched the pocket on her apron and felt the foreign object. She started to toss it over, but remembered Gena threatening him about not driving. *And what happened to his buddy?*

She wanted to go home. Unlocking the bar to call strangers in the middle of the night to come pick up some drunk Indian wasn't happening either. She could call Gena, who was probably back from her date, but it didn't seem fair to do that to her friend on a much needed night off. Her mind imagined calling the cops and letting law enforcement teach this enormously inconvenient man a lesson, but she knew she would never ruin a man's reputation and record for making unwanted comments while lying in the back of his own truck.

"Can I have my key, Kai? Or do you just want to stare at me a little longer first?"

"You're a serious douche. And the answer is no. Now get up and get into my car before I change my mind."

He pulled himself up once again and she noticed that the strain of his movements had opened the cut on his face. In the shadowed light of the parking lot she watched a trickle of blood seep from the wound, drawing a thin black line down his forehead.

"I'll quit bothering you if you just open my truck. I'll sleep it off in the parking lot."

It was a good alternative to her idea, but Kai had already made up her mind to take him home herself. Sleep could wait, and Gena wouldn't have to know just how out of hand the night had gotten. Besides, if she could get a better look at his head, she could take him over to the emergency room if needed.

"Get down from there and tell me where you live. Do it," she ordered after he merely stared at her, unmoving.

"I never could say no to a demanding woman," Dean confessed and finally did as he was told.

Kai felt her misfortune escalate after she learned how remote his house was. She took yet another single track trail in the middle of nowhere Montana. This one led over a rolling hill and down the other side into a shallow valley. She passed a small pond and found her headlights shining on a tiny log cabin next to a white tipi in the middle of a grassy meadow.

Dean had passed out after his last instructions to turn right, so she shook his shoulder and said, "You're home, jackass."

Luckily, the trickle of blood on his face had stopped almost immediately after getting him into the car, so Kai wasn't going to concern herself with it any longer.

"A sweet talker, too. That's special. It matches your suspicious eyes."

"Just get out."

Before he closed the door, he threw some bills on the seat and mumbled, "Sorry to keep you out so late. This is for your gas."

She watched him walk inside his teeny, ancient-looking house where the timbers leaned to the left, the roof sagged to the right, and the trim needed a new coat of paint about twenty years earlier. Then she realized that she still had his key. Frustrated with herself, she opened her door and stepped into the brisk star-lit night. She jogged up to the door, hoping she wouldn't have to see him again for even one more second. The way he called her a cow and then topped it off with more insults. It was unbearable, and she wouldn't take any more of that. She laid his key on the stoop, happy to finally see the night's monkey business come to a close.

Chapter Two

Over the next couple of weeks, Kai saw Dean exactly three more times. Always at Growler's Tavern, where he drank Coronas until his friend, Badger, escorted him away. Kai played indifferent to both of the former Marines, and neither she nor Dean brought up the night that she drove him home at three in the morning.

Each time they came into the bar, Badger tried flirting with her. He was decent looking enough, she acknowledged. Skinny, but muscular, and she had to admit he had a great smile. But she disliked him. Mostly because she noticed how he acted the same way with Gena and one of the waitresses they worked with. There was a cynical edge to some of his comments that made Kai uneasy. She didn't like to think of people as shifty, but she'd had enough personal experience with underhanded men, and Badger reminded her of some past dealings. His behavior felt devious and slimy, but Gena didn't seem to care. When Kai mentioned that she thought he was a man-whore, all Gena said was, "At least he's fun." And, "Lighten up, Kai."

If Gena had asked Kai to be honest, she would've admitted that Dean was more her type. He was thoughtful, and had a sense of humor that made her smile, even though she usually hid it from him. He was also a little too easy on the eyes, and all of the muscles were definitely a bonus. None of her private thoughts about Dean or Badger mattered because she'd already decided that they were too military and too unsettling. Not to mention Dean's glaring fault that couldn't be dismissed. She would never allow herself to have a relationship with someone who drank. Alcohol had ruined her family, and she would never get over it.

On their three nights together sitting in the bar, Dean and Badger spent most of the time talking over the history of the Native tribes in Montana. They would work themselves into a couple of foaming rabid dogs over the details of the Lame Bull Treaty in 1855. The shrinking reservation lands during the 1880's. Treaty 7 in Canada. Kai had to tune out the entire conversation when it eventually turned to the Marias Massacre of 1870. Mercifully, Dean changed the subject from the murder of children and the elderly in Chief Heavy Runner's band camped on the river that unforgettable winter day to modern politics. That led to gun rights, comparing weapons, and mining operations. They may as well have been aliens discussing space travel at that point. She would have definitely been more interested if they were.

They left the bar at closing one Saturday night, and she hadn't seen either one of them since. *She was glad.* Even if they were her best tippers, their distraction wasn't needed. She didn't like the way they attracted sleazy women to the bar, looking for free drinks. And she kept catching herself looking for Dean when he wasn't around. *That was unacceptable.* She didn't want to spare an ounce of concern for an ex-Marine who made her worry that he was drinking his life away, even if she did laugh at his jokes.

So when Friday evening rolled around and she was getting ready to leave her daycare job and embrace another weekend slinging drinks at Growler's, she was taken off-guard to find Dean standing at the door, having an in-depth conversation with her five-year-old son, Trevyn.

"The best horses for roping are quarter horses."

"How does a five-year-old know so much about ponies?" Dean asked as he grinned down at her boy.

"Oh, I know everything about horses. My daddy's a famous bronc rider. He's good at calf roping, but the saddle bronc event is his how he makes his money. Do you ride, Mr. Dean?"

Her son's enthusiasm made her chest swell with pride, even though she was inwardly cringing at the topic of conversation. Dean didn't need to hear about her ex-husband. He didn't need to know anything about her or her family.

"Of course I do," he said with a wink. Then he squatted down in front of Trevyn, and pulled the neck of his T-shirt open, exposing the front of his shoulder. "See this scar?"

Trevyn's eyes went wide as he stared at the white line on Dean's bronze shoulder.

"That's from dislocating my shoulder riding bareback."

"Wow," Trevyn ooohed. "My dad has lots of scars too. You'd like my daddy. You should go to the rodeo this summer and meet him."

Kai cleared her throat. "Hello."

"Mom, this is Dean. He's really nice. And big, too."

Kai watched Dean swallow hard and rise to his feet. In the daylight, and unobstructed by the bar, Kai noticed a lot more details about Dean that she missed before. Like how tall he was, and how wide his shoulders were. Trevyn spun around and wrapped his arms around his mom's legs. She squeezed him back and kissed the top of his head.

"Did you sneak out of your room?"

"Yes." He gave her the sheepish grin that melted her heart enough to get him out of trouble.

"Why?" she asked.

"I wanted to see who was ringing the bell," he answered with the simple honesty characteristic of small children.

"Trevyn, you know you're supposed to wait for an adult."

"I get tired of hanging out will all the babies. I want to be the doorman now."

"Next time, wait for an adult," she warned.

"Sorry." The boy whined the apology, and Kai squeezed him in another hug.

"Trevyn's your son?" Dean asked. His eyes widened with what looked like surprise to Kai, but also had a hint of respectful approval.

"Yes." She felt her protective instincts rise. It happened more these days, after the divorce. Insecurities came with the territory, she guessed, and she was powerless to stop them. Trevyn was her life, and she would do anything to keep him safe. Including keeping him away from alcohol, or persons under the influence.

"Well, he was just telling me all about horses."

"Mr. Dean rides bareback, Mom. Do you think we could watch him at Dad's next rodeo?"

"Thanks, big guy, but I used to ride. In high school, for fun. I don't anymore," Dean started to explain, but Trevyn was already bored and was looking around and fidgeting like he had to use the bathroom.

Right on cue, Kai said, "Please go use the restroom, Trev."

"I have to go potty now. Bye." Trevyn skipped down the hallway and disappeared into one of the daycare rooms.

She watched her son do the potty dance and smiled to herself. Her boy could always bring a much-needed moment of warmth to her spirit. Then Kai remembered why she was standing by the door and turned back around to see Dean staring at her. Her smile dropped. There were lingering shadows behind his oddly light colored eyes, and it suddenly felt too intimate in the entryway.

She stepped back and erased any feelings about her son from her face. "What are you doing here?"

He looked down at his boots, and when he glanced back up, he had his guard up, too. Kai could feel the drop in the temperature around him, like clouds had just moved over the sun.

"I've come to see Gena."

"She's with the afterschool kids. It's the last room on the left."

"Where Trevyn went?" he asked.

"That's right. Do you want me to go get her?" Kai gave him an inspecting eye. She was looking for cracks in his story and smelling the air for whiffs of beer. Kai didn't want Dean in the room with the kids if he was drunk. She didn't smell alcohol on him, and his eyes appeared unusually clear. Shining, in fact, and the most golden color of brown she'd seen in a long time on an Indian. She did pick up a faint trace of woodsy cologne, mixed with something that reminded her of diesel exhaust. Berating herself for having taken such a close look, she stepped back again.

He must have been aware of her visual overhaul, because he said, "I don't drink if I've been working."

"I really don't need a playbill," she lied. "Besides, it's none of my business."

His forehead creased in surprise or disbelief — she couldn't tell — but he didn't take the conversation any further. "I'll go back and see my cousin."

He started toward the room, but Kai was blocking his way. She jumped to get out of his path, as if she was afraid he might touch her. He gave her another one of his looks; partially mysterious, but mostly speculative. She cringed inside knowing how nervous she was, but she hoped it didn't show.

"Hey." He paused in front of her. His hand rose and he placed his fingertips to her elbow.

She was so confused by her reaction to him that she didn't know if he was trying to steady her jumpiness, or just giving a friendly touch.

"I wanted to thank you again for the ride home a few weeks back. You didn't have to do it, and it took time away from your family. That was nice of you."

She averted her gaze and pulled her arm away. She gave a dismissive shake of her head and turned into her own childcare room without saying another word.

Half a dozen toddlers were busy listening to a story read aloud by the other teacher, and she was glad that she had a minute to compose herself. Dean shouldn't have touched her, or have been so nice. It disconcerted her, and her response was even more unbelievable. She couldn't even speak. She disliked him for drinking, but she really detested him for confusing her.

When she heard a cheer in the room next door, she raised her head to see what the commotion was about. Dean was being mauled by a handful of the older kids through the open doorway between the rooms. It perplexed her even more. She watched his face transform from the secretive fire that he holds at bay to one of entertained joy as he received multiple hugs and high fives from the children. She hurried over to the reading circle and sat down with the kids, making sure she was out of sight of the other room.

Chapter Three

"The Lynx Clan is dying out," Dean said in answer to another one of Badger's questions about his family.

"Better find yourself a new woman and solve that problem."

Dean heaved a four-foot long section of log into the back of his truck. "I'm not looking for a solution."

Badger lifted the next block of cottonwood into the bed, and they worked with each other like they were back on duty.

They had woken up before dawn and set off to collect the firewood that Dean would use to heat his cabin. By the time they arrived at the spot where a massive section of a cottonwood tree had broken off during the winter, the sun was just peeking over the eastern hills.

Badger was on again, talking about clans and destinies. It was an endless subject for him to dwell over and reiterate on for hours. Dean humored it because Badger was a reliable source of horsepower and didn't seem to mind the hard labor.

"I hear you, bro. What happened with the wife, anyway? I thought you were in it for the long haul with Marissa."

Dean dismissed the question with a shake of his head as he chugged water from a bottle. "Don't want to talk about it," he said as he wiped his mouth with the back of his hand.

"Sure. Sorry it didn't work out." Badger bent down to grab another log. "So, have you ever heard about the Dragonfly Clan and their traveling pipe?" he asked conversationally.

Dean's blank expression yielded no clues as he stared down the length of the creek bank. He watched the cotton fluff float gently on the surface of the water. It would be carried downstream, where it would meet the Two Medicine River and eventually roll out into the distant prairies. One tree, touching miles of river. Dean felt the urge to take to foot and head downstream with the cotton, and never come back. He thought his cabin would give him solace, but anyone could find it with little more than a question. *Badger was here.* He was proof enough that Dean wasn't as far out of the way as he'd hoped.

The Dragonfly pipe. He knew about it. He knew it was stored with the other belongings that his grandfather wanted him to have. His grandma hadn't forced him to take care of those things. It was too soon. Grandpa Two Eagles had passed to the Sand Hills a few months earlier. *Or maybe it had been almost a year.* Dean didn't like to think about it. The man was more like his father than his grandfather. It was another memory file that Dean never opened. But the bundle Badger was asking about was there. *It should be donated to the museum*, he thought. He wouldn't take care of it or honor it the way that it should be honored. The way his grandfather did. He told his grandma that he didn't think he was the right person to carry on the traditions, but she had given him such a look of disappointment that he took it back immediately, and didn't bring up the subject again.

The ceremonial pipe was his now, waiting in a box, along with Grandfather's watch and his tools. Dean wasn't a carver, or a flint knapper like Grandpa. He knew it, but there was something personal about the antler-handled chisels and awls that couldn't be given away to just anyone. He would keep the tools stashed in a closet somewhere, nestled in with the memories of the man who raised him.

The sway of grass, the trickle of water, the floating wisps of cotton in the air, and the memories of his grandfather's steady-handed technique of making arrows all made him think about his pencils and pads of paper. *Jesus, how had he gotten so far away from everything that ever mattered to him?*

Damn it. If only Badger hadn't opened a lid that couldn't be resealed. He had even convinced Dean to try going without beer for a month. It had become a challenge, and he wouldn't let Badge win the argument that Dean had turned into an addict.

"What's up with you?" Badger asked.

Dean suddenly realized that the sound of thumping and tumbling logs has stopped.

"It's the Dragonfly pipe, not a clan, and it's at my grandmother's."

"Right. I knew that," he corrected and then asked, "It still exists, huh?"

It was unlike Badger to mix up important details. The man had everything under the sun committed to memory. Dean watched him closely for a second, looking for a clue of what he was up to. "It does. Why are you asking about it?"

"Curious," Badger said with a shrug of his shoulders like it wasn't all that important.

"That's frightening," Dean said only half joking. "Wasn't it curiosity that led the dragon to fall for coyote's tricks and ended up changing him into the shape of a dragonfly?"

"I've never heard it put that way before."

"Hmmph," he snorted.

Dean thought that the storytelling he had grown up with from his grandfather and the elders was a way to teach him about life. When he was younger, he suspected he was being punished for misbehaving, and listening to the stories was their way to show him how to be more respectful. He realized later that it wasn't only for his benefit. The adults were often so enraptured in the story that it was a common occurrence to leave the gathering with a sore ear from being pinched for interrupting or not paying attention. The elders would make the kids sit with them and listen to stories of the long-ago times for hours upon end. Times that seemed so distant, they were difficult to even imagine. He was forced to sit on the ground or the floor and smell the burning of their pipes as they taught the kids about what happens to horrible people for lying and thieving, or just being an overall turd.

"Let's go," Badger said, interrupting Dean's unwelcome memories. "I got the last of the wood, and I'll tell you what I've heard about your pipe on the way back."

Dean checked the load of firewood, packed up his chainsaw, and climbed into his truck, thinking that he was still being punished for being the aforementioned turd, and that he should probably try to be more respectful. But, since he was an adult now, he decided that he didn't have to. He rolled his eyes toward Badger and wondered how he was going to accomplish that one-way trip down river.

Badger started in as soon as they drove away from the creek. "About the time I turned sixteen, my ma became really ill. My sister was supposed to be taking care of her after school, but she didn't show up on time one day, and Ma needed help. She was weak and feverish, and I'm pretty certain, close to dying."

"That's pretty rough, man," Dean said, and glanced over at his friend. Badger was staring straight ahead, focused on his story.

He continued without responding to Dean's acknowledgment. "She needed help getting to the bathroom, and then she asked me to get her a drink and sit with her until my sister arrived. I don't think I realized just how sick she was until that afternoon, but then it hit me like a fist to my throat. When my sister finally did come home, I wouldn't leave her side."

They were both quiet for a minute as Dean maneuvered the truck over a minefield of potholes.

Badger continued. "I'm not telling you about my mom for sympathy. She recovered after a few weeks and is still living outside of Butte. I'm telling you because this was when I found out about my family and heard the rumors about the Dragonfly pipe."

Now it was Dean's turn to be curious. He wasn't sure where Badge was going with this. He waited for his friend to continue.

"Have you ever seen someone with fever dreams?"

"I don't think so," Dean said.

"Well, she had them. It could have been the whacked-out medicine the doctor gave her. I think it was a narcotic, but in any case, my mom started saying things that I couldn't believe. She kept talking about the big boss of the mine where my dad worked, and how she couldn't go back to work there.

"She was a mess. I thought she was completely out of her mind, but I kept listening anyway. How could I not, even if I thought it was crazy talk? She kept going on and on about begging to quit her cleaning job for the owners of the mine. That was a surprise to me. I didn't know that she had ever worked for the mine. She had never mentioned it before. I kept listening to her moan and heard her praying in her sleep for some Dragonfly medicine pipe. She kept asking that she be allowed to travel with the pipe. She prayed and asked me to find a member of the clan who kept the Dragonfly pipe."

Badger looked over at Dean to see if he was still listening.

"As soon as I could find a time to ask my dad about it, I did. He said that the Dragonfly ceremonial pipe was a story about illusions. Then he told me the story, or at least the parts he could remember. This is what he said.

"In the very old times, during the thunder moon, a great flying beast came over the prairie. It was large enough to darken the entire sky. The people hid in their lodges and waited for it to pass, not understanding what had come to visit them, and not liking the unwelcome darkness.

All but one brave warrior hid. He wanted to fight this unknown enemy and take its scalp so he could count the largest coup anyone had ever witnessed. His fearlessness would earn him great respect and many eagle feathers for his bonnet.

He shot his arrows into the sky, but nothing happened. He threw rocks and spears, but no one died or cried out. All of his weapons simply disappeared into the great void blocking the stars and the moon. After four days of fighting against the black enemy, he sank to his knees and gave up. But instead of admitting defeat and returning to his lodge, he began to sing.

It was a song full of challenge and daring. He wanted the great beast to show its face and fight back. He sang for another day and an entire night until his voice gave out, and he collapsed from exhaustion.

He had fought and sung to his death. Or that's what he thought. But death was not what he thought it would be. On the other side of life, there was a camp very much like his own. They were his people. The painting on the chief's lodge could only be a Blackfoot design. He rose from the grass and entered the camp to find many people in mourning. The dead people had spears and arrows sticking out of them and others had gaping wounds, as if they had been mauled or struck with stones. As he approached a woman wailing over her dead husband, he recognized his own red markings on the shaft of the arrow and the orange and black flicker feathers he used for flights.

'What has happened here?' he asked a passing stranger.

The old woman stared at him and then answered, 'The Above Ones have punished them, and the medicine men did not understand why. They were struck in the night for four days by weapons from the sky. They had been afraid to fight back because they didn't want to anger the Gods and lose everyone in their camp.'

'And what camp is this?' he asked the woman.

'This is a Piegan camp. I am of the Lynx Clan,' she said.

He thought the woman was lying to him, because the Lynx Clan were his own people, but he didn't recognize a single person. How had his arrows traveled the great distance to another camp? Why was he being punished for trying to protect his people? The ghost village was a place of terrible confusion. He began to suspect that the Above Ones were involved and that they had tricked him, so he ran away from the camp, not wanting to bring them any more misfortune.

The warrior ran far into the mountains, not stopping until he was at the top of the Backbone of the World, for surely the great beast who had caused all of this trouble could be seen from there. He did not find the beast, so he again began to sing. The same song again, only this time adding in a verse calling the creature to him on the top of the mountain.

When night came, the sky darkened and the warrior knew that his unknown enemy had returned.

'Who are you?' he screamed. 'Show yourself!'

The warrior was struck down. He fell down the face of the mountain and when he awoke, there was a warm fire and a visitor watching over him. His fear consumed him, because he knew the creature had condensed itself into human form to sit with him there by the fire.

'You are brave and foolish,' it said. 'Why do you battle with something that you do not first understand?'

'You frightened my family. I thought you were going to harm us,' he said as he found his tongue. 'What are you?'

'I am the space around your stars. The great distance beyond your blue sky. My reach is farther than that of your mighty Sun.'

The warrior believed it. The dark creature was nothing he could ever have imagined. It was dense like stone, yet moved like wind. It shimmered in the firelight, and the warrior could see that every color existed inside it. 'You shimmer like frost in the first light of day, but you do so in the dark of night. Like a dragonfly's wings.'

'That is a kind way to describe me. When I came to visit your people, I did not mean for so many to perish. We have caused great harm to your ancestors, brave warrior.'

'I don't understand. Those people were not my ancestors.'

'But they are. You saw the lodges and their clothes. You know that those are your relations.'

'I've never seen them before,' he said. 'It is not possible.'

'It is the truth I speak. They are the relatives of your past. I see I have made a mistake by coming here. I wanted to see what life was like on this green and blue Earth, but I have brought suffering.'

'My wife will be in mourning for a long time,' he told the God. 'We love each other very much. She is carrying a child who will now never know his father.'

'You think you are dead, but I assure you that you are not in the Shadowlands,' the God of Night and the Void told him.

The warrior rose to his feet. 'I must return to them. If I am not dead, how have you brought me to this place? I wish to go back.'

'It was a mistake. On the far side of the Sun, where I come from, time does not move the same way as it does on your Earth. Now you must sing your way back to your family, Lynx warrior. I will gift you a pipe. It will have the dragonfly carved onto it so your clan will always know who it was from. Smoke, pray, and sing the song you used to call to me. Think only of your family, and when the Sun rises, you will be with them once more.'

The black creature disappeared. Where he sat lay a ceremonial pipe with a dragonfly etched onto the stem."

Dean waited another minute to make sure Badger's story was finished.

"Are you telling me your mom wanted to run away to be with her family?" he asked.

"She didn't just want to be with her family. She wanted to go back to another time. One without copper mines and white people ordering her around."

With these last words came a weighted stillness in the air only disturbed by the drone of the engine and the rattling of the truck as they drove down the rough backcountry road.

"Sounds like the fever dreams messed with her head pretty good." He glanced over at Badger and saw resentment and something akin to hatred on his face.

"That isn't what screwed her up," he said, staring out the window.

He could tell that Badger wasn't able to lighten up on this topic so he shut his mouth and quit thinking about his friend's inner turmoil. Dean was shocked that Badger had shared a story with him that he thought no one else knew. Badger's version of the story was slightly off, but it was close enough. Grandpa had never been more serious than when he repeated the warning that accompanied the legend of the Dragonfly pipe. Do not share the knowledge with anyone other than male members of the Lynx Clan. Dean was the last living member of the clan, so it hadn't been a problem. He was fairly certain his grandmother Rosemary knew everything about the pipe, but he also knew she was an honorable woman who would take her husband's secrets with her to the Sand Hills.

Secrecy didn't come naturally to Dean. It felt wrong to hide things like stories, but he understood why this particular tale shouldn't be shared. He thought of it like levels of security clearance. If you couldn't be trusted, you shouldn't have the information. He knew firsthand the power of the ceremonial pipe that was kept by the Lynx Clan. He didn't want to talk about it. He didn't even like thinking about it. The memories he had with his grandfather and the pipe were in a vault that he'd lost security clearance access to. Badger had once again shoved at a door that Dean wanted to keep closed.

Unfortunately, now it stood wide open.

Badger may know the story of his ancestors, but he would never know the songs. Only Dean and his grandfather knew them and his grandfather was gone. He wasn't even sure if he could recall them or not. This was Lynx Clan business, and he wasn't at all sure how to tell his friend, his fellow Marine, and a Blackfoot, that he couldn't or wouldn't talk about it.

He dodged around a plump prairie dog in the road and said, "The story is about illusions. It's about doing what it takes to makes things right. Including facing your fears."

"Doing what's right is exactly my point."

Dean noticed Badger's clenched fist. He didn't want to ignore his friend's torment, but he didn't want to escalate it either. "It's only a story about bravery and standing up when no one else will. An allegory like so many of the stories are."

"Stop blowing smoke over this. You know that time is the illusion in the story. The warrior went back in time, by accident. The black creature is the powerful unknown. The dark matter. The all-knowing. The manipulator of space and time. Don't sit there and pretend that you don't know anything," Badger spit out. "You're holding out on me. I've seen you make that face before. You think you can turn off what you don't want to look at, but you can't."

In response to his friend's accusation, Dean narrowed his gaze and stared down the road. They would be pulling in front of his cabin in a few more minutes. *How was he going to get Badger to change subjects?* His tenacity to drag up the past and linger on every wrongdoing that ever happened to the Plains tribes was second to none.

"Sorry my joe-schmoe face disturbs you. Your mom was sick and having weird dreams. Did your dad tell you where he heard the story?"

"Yeah. From my mother. She had relatives in the Lynx Clan."

"Huh," Dean said noncommittally. He ran his tongue around his teeth, buying him a few seconds. "This isn't the best time to bring it up."

"Because you don't like thinking about anything that happened before yesterday," Badger accused, and shot Dean a glaring look.

"You know it." Dean didn't deny or defend his actions. He'd asked Badger to leave his personal demons alone before.

"You don't give a rat's ass about where you come from, do you? You just take it for granted that you have generations of history in your family. That you have more family and band members watching out for you than you can count. You know what I had growing up?"

Dean parked his truck next to the cabin and turned off the engine, not responding to Badger's fury. *Maybe the man needed to get this off his chest.* It was obvious to Dean that his friend had some deep-seated resentments that needed to be released. He could use a couple of rounds anyway, so he was willing to see where this was headed.

"I had a fucking father who worked himself to death. And a mother who walked on eggshells her whole life, and a sister who couldn't give a crap about anything except how her hair looked. You have the ability to honor your people and your family, but you choose to drink until you're a worthless shit pile. And don't lie to me again that your damn pipe is nothing less than a gift from the Gods. I know what it is. I know the stories are true."

Dean felt buried emotions swell inside him. They moved through his blood like an angry swarm.

He threw open the door. "Outside. Now."

It didn't take Badger but a second to meet Dean face to face in the dust of the driveway. Dean swung his fist at Badger's jaw, landing a solid blow to skin and bone. Badger had been ready, and feinted enough that his jaw wasn't broken, but the contact was still substantial.

"That's for telling me what it's like to grow up without parents," he spat. Badger may have had a dysfunctional family, but at least he had a chance to know them. Dean didn't have one memory of his mother or his father.

Dean also made the mistake of forgetting just how wily and fast his friend was, and took a jab to his nose before he could duck.

Needing to release pent up frustration and anger over the unfairness in his life that the world had delivered to him, especially what happened to him after he left the Marines, he threw his weight into Badger's middle, toppling them both to the ground. Rolling over the gravel and grinding dirt into their clothes, they pounded each other until Dean escaped Badger's chokehold and tumbled into the grass. He rolled to his feet.

Badger being more of a scrapper than he realized, Dean barely got his feet under him before his friend was charging toward him again.

"Stop," he gurgled through the blood dripping out of his nose and down his throat. He raised a hand. "You've beaten the shit out of me, Master Gunny. We're done."

Badger, fists ready, feet spread and leaning toward Dean, stopped just before his next attack. His breath was ragged and a feral snarl curled his lip, but he managed to control himself. "I outrank you, remember? I call it."

"Good thing our Jarhead days are behind us then."

Badger laid into Dean with a quick left hook to his ribs and then stomped off behind the cabin saying, "Now, we're finished."

Some space was exactly what they both needed. It had been cramped quarters inside the one-room cabin, even though Badger slept inside the tipi by the pond. Dean had been away, working at a mine for a couple of weeks, but he still felt the strain of the lack of privacy and lack of beer on his land. *Badger had this coming.* He'd been pushing his buttons and making Dean face reality. Dean had made himself comfortably numb over the last two years, and Badger was determined to not let Dean get away with it any longer. It pissed him off to be so deeply intruded on. He also knew he had only himself to blame for not making Badger leave shortly after coming to town.

Dean's liver ached from the blow, and his nose throbbed, but he had to admit that he felt some weight had been lifted from somewhere inside of him.

As he considered searching for a hunk of ice from the cooler to put on his face, he saw the dust trail of an approaching car rising from the grassy hills. Wishing he could go inside and pretend he wasn't home was at the forefront of his thoughts. That was pointless, since he knew his family would let themselves inside to check on him. So he stood in front of his cabin, ready to face the music.

He spat a glob of blood onto the ground, grimaced, and then wiped his nose with the bottom of his shirt. His face wasn't going to be pretty tomorrow, but he wasn't out to impress anyone. When he didn't recognize the car, he thought it must be a lost tourist. His sense of humor enjoyed the thought of scaring them off his property with his bloody and bruised face. Then he noticed the long black hair and the delicate angle of jawbone. He saw the sweet curve of soft lips as the sun shone through her windshield. His eyes drew lower and he saw the beaded necklace lying against her chest. He'd seen her wearing it before. As she parked, he thought he saw displeasure in her dark eyes, but also determination. He didn't want another argument or more judgmental glares from the woman. He wanted an icepack and a six-pack. The latter wouldn't be happening, no matter how his body craved the alcohol. Dean was determined to prove that he could cut himself off at any time, and stay off.

What the hell was she doing here?

Kai didn't notice Dean standing on the far side of his pickup until she was about to step onto the porch. She startled at the sight of him, but recovered with hardly an outward flinch. Her gaze landed on his nose.

"Hurt much?" she asked.

"Doesn't matter," he said with a shrug, and didn't move from the grass.

She took in the heaping pile of logs in the back of his truck, and then without speaking walked back to her car. She opened the trunk and found the small red case she kept inside, mostly for Trevyn, because young boys often need a first aid kit. Before she returned to Dean, she walked out into the meadow and picked a plant she saw growing near the driveway.

Dean walked toward the porch, and Kai saw the brooding scowl across his brow.

Now that she had driven all the way out there, Kai was determined to get through this meeting. *Did it matter that he was bloody and covered in dirt?* It should, but she was pressed for time, and wanted to follow through on her intentions.

"Sit down," she said, and pointed at the bench on the porch.

He sat without argument, and leaned back heavily against the wall of his cabin.

She stepped in close enough to see the sweat drying at his temples and smelled the sawdust in his clothes, mingled with the copper scent of blood. Kai angled his head up with gentle fingertips against his jaw. She inspected his nose and appraised the forming bruise on his cheek. The cut above his eyebrow from the night at the bar was nothing but a small faint line now. She looked everywhere except into his eyes. "Your face isn't supposed to be a shield," she said as she stuffed the fern-like leaves of the yarrow plant into his nostrils.

"That tickles," he said as he tried to pull away.

She kept her fingers firm against his jaw not letting him escape. "It will stop the bleeding."

He let her finish and said, "I know. The flower is a favorite of my grandma's. Couldn't you use it on a scraped elbow or knee like she did?" He gingerly touched his nose and the leaves hanging out of his face.

Kai stepped back and opened the first aid kit that had been tucked under her arm. She sorted through the packets and the gauze, taking a long time to look inside the little case. She was stalling in order to keep her emotions in check.

"I would have if your elbow was bleeding as bad as your nose," she said.

"The devil's in the details," he acknowledged, and leaned his head back against the house.

"There's not much that can be done for your nose. It's straight. An ice pack would be the best, and maybe some painkillers. I'm looking for an anti-inflammatory to give you."

"Nursing come naturally to you?"

"Not really. I was kind of thrown into it when I was younger. Once I graduate from school, it'll be a way to pay for a roof over our heads."

"You and Trevyn?"

"That's right." She handed him a square package of pills and then turned to face the pond and the stream. She noticed a second truck parked near the tipi and wondered if Dean had company.

"Do you always wrestle tree trunks with your face?"

"Nah. I was kind of thrown into it when I was younger. Once I graduate, I'll be able to use axes and chainsaws. I may even build a roof to go over my head."

She rolled her eyes and suppressed a smile as Dean watched her. Then he stood and walked to the door.

"I better get on that ice pack. Nurse's orders. Want to come in?" His voice was muffled and congested from the swollen nose, but she understood him well enough.

She glanced over her shoulder at him. He didn't wait for her to go inside.

Kai had come to visit him, and if she wanted to stand on his porch all day, he wouldn't stop her. He wasn't going anywhere. Badger hadn't come in the back door of the cabin, and Dean wondered if he had stalked off to walk the land and brood. Leaving the ibuprofen tablets on the counter, Dean bent down and opened the cooler in search of ice. The cabin didn't have electricity, so if Dean wanted anything to stay cold, he kept an ice chest stocked. He wasn't very thoughtful about cooking or shopping for food, so all he found inside was water. He dipped in a finger. *At least it was cold.* He reached across the counter for a hand towel and soaked it, then wrung it out. He applied the cold cloth to his stinging nose and cheek and then gently unplugged the leaves from his nostrils. Leaning forward to catch leaking blood, he somehow managed to dribble a red watery mess down the front of his T-shirt instead of into the towel. He should have left the leaves alone, he realized too late. Already sweat stained and covered with wood chips, the blood and cold water added unwanted pizzazz to his disheveled look. He stripped off the dirty shirt and tossed it over to the laundry basket in the corner. Feeling like hell, he eyed his bed and contemplated lying down for the rest of the week. If he had a case of beer, there would be no hesitation. But without it, he knew he was going to be restless.

That's when he noticed Kai standing in the doorway. He suspected she had been watching him, but she was courteously keeping her gaze on the framed drawing hanging on the wall. She had a hand tucked into the back pocket of her shorts while she fiddled with the beads of her necklace with her other hand.

"You want to fill me in on what you're doing out here?" he asked as he leaned against the counter, instead of crossing over to his bed. "Is my cousin and the daycare kids doing all right?"

"They're fine. If you can call Gena pulling her hair out over the increase in rent, fine. She's working really hard on getting the loan from the bank to buy the building. It's been tough on her, but I think she'll pull it off." She pointed at the pencil drawing of painted Blackfoot horses racing across the prairie. "This is nice. Did you draw it?" she asked, but Dean could see her studying his high school signature in the corner.

"It's from ages ago. Something my grandmother saved," he said, trying to blow it off and hoping Kai wouldn't notice the sketchpad on his bed. The desire to draw animals and landscapes had all but deserted him once he left high school. There wasn't time, or inspiration, for drawing during his years as a Marine. Then a wife and a baby entered the picture, followed by an affair with Corona and Mrs. Lime. Since the desertion of his last mistresses found him with a lot of time to kill, he found that pencil and paper had a way of keeping his head on straight. Seeing Kai's interest in his work made him want to bury the habit back on the shelf where it had been for the last decade.

"Gena mentioned the loan to me," Dean continued. "Dealing with banks is about as frustrating as dealing with the government. They want you to fill out a million pieces of paper right now, and then sit around and wait until your hair is gray and every piece of information is too old to be of any use."

"Sounds about right. Gena's handling it better than I could, though. Her credit's good. I think it will happen for her."

Kai did a half-turn and rested her back against the doorjamb. The toe of one shoe pointed out the door like she was ready to sprint back to her car at any second. Staring outside she said, "I noticed the kids at work all seemed to like you. Trevyn talked about you for the rest of the night. Am I in the wrong age group or something?"

Dean dipped his towel in the cold water instead of looking at Kai. "I've known most of the older kids since they were born. I always stopped in at Kinder Place when I was home on leave. And I grew up with a lot of the parents. It's nothing." The cold felt good on his face, but he lowered the cloth and turned back to his uninvited guest. "Why did you drive all the way out here, Kai? I'm sure you could just ask my cousin why all the kids hang on me the moment I walk in the door."

He watched her struggle before answering. She pressed her lips together before speaking, and couldn't meet his eyes for longer than a fleeting glance.

"I just… Well, I needed to apologize."

"That's the last thing I thought you were going to say," he said, and looked down at the cooler, still wishing it was filled with beer bottles.

"I was really rude to you the other day. I'm not sure it was justified. I'm sorry," she said with such a formal tone that Dean didn't know if she was being for real.

"Your rudeness comes across as being indifferent. I thought you must be that way with everyone. So now you're telling me it's just me. That makes me feel *much* better."

"All the kids think you're the greatest, but I think you're intolerable," she huffed, and stepped out the door.

Dean liked the way her voice sounded when she was irritated. It showed her personality better than her flat, formal approach.

"Goodbye, Dean."

"That was fast."

Dean recognized Badger's voice from outside. Kai whipped around to see who had spoken.

Badger continued. "Imagine holding the key to great change, and all you ever do with it is stuff it in your pocket."

"I don't know what you're talking about," Kai said, and retreated a couple of steps across the porch.

Dean moved to the door.

"Dean thinks inaction is a solution, whereas I believe it's the same thing as betrayal."

"Don't drag her into our argument," Dean said.

Kai jumped at the sound of Dean's voice, as if he were suddenly too near to her.

"Your jaw looks terrible," she said to Badger. Then she turned to Dean. "You two were fighting. You didn't have a wood cutting accident," she accused.

"I never said I did."

Badger wasn't done. He never was.

"Our people live on these Reserves like caged animals. Your own families have suffered for generations." He waved a hand at Dean. "And you do nothing. We're supposed to be warriors and hunters. Our land should stretch far into Canada and down to the Missouri river. How have you lived with yourself? With the information you have, how can you not do something to change things?"

Badger's eyes bore into Dean's. He saw Kai watching him as if waiting to see his reaction. Dean returned Badger's cold-hearted glare and hoped that it warned his friend to be silent. Then Dean noticed Kai swallow and take another step across the narrow porch.

"What about you?" Badger turned on Kai. "Could you stand by and do nothing about the circumstances of our people if you had a way to make great changes? Unemployment. Poor housing. Crime. Drugs. The statistics for living on a rez are sickening."

"You're asking the wrong person. I'm not a member of the Blackfoot Nation," she said as she stepped down off the porch.

"Crow, Assiniboine, Salish, Kutenai, Gros Ventre, Cheyenne. It doesn't matter. We've all had our land stolen from us. Sergeant Wolfsblood stands over there like he knows nothing. Can do nothing to help the tribes."

Kai appeared visibly shaken by Badger's ferocity and passion. She mumbled, "My family is Cree. I'm really leaving now."

Badger stood near her car and she hesitated approaching him.

"You're a Liar. Doesn't that just figure," he said as he glanced up and down the length of Kai's body. "Whatever. All of us, including the traitorous, lying Crees, deserve a chance to right the wrongs of our past."

Dean saw her narrow her eyes at Badger. He wondered if she was biting her tongue to keep quiet over the insult to her tribe.

"Move out of the way, Badge," Dean said. "Kai wants to leave, and who can blame her? You're ranting. And don't address me like I'm still in the service."

"You're a self-serving prick," he shot back, but he stepped out of her way.

"You think you know everything, but the truth is, your mouth is too loud and your brain is too narrow. If the situation were as simple as you're making it sound, things would have changed a century ago."

"You speak just like a politician. No balls to back up your beliefs. Is that it? Are you buying the bullshit fed to us about equal rights and doing what is best for the greater good?"

Kai scooted around to the driver's side door and opened it.

Dean jogged over to her before she could climb inside her car.

"Now I get to apologize. We're having a gentlemanly disagreement."

Kai's look of skepticism at Dean's description almost made him smile, but it wasn't funny. *Badger needed to shut his trap.*

She looked up at him with her cool mask back in place. "It was a mistake coming here. Sorry again."

He nodded. *There couldn't have been a worse time for her to show up.* "It's probably best you get out of here, Nurse Kai. We may use up the rest of your first aid kit with round two."

He held the door for her and then closed it gently after she sat down. They shared one last look at one another, and Dean thought he saw regret in the depths of her dark chocolate eyes. Then Kai stared straight ahead, and Dean was left feeling that regret as well.

There was a deep scowl etched across his brow as he watched her drive off.

With Kai safely away from the conversation, Dean turned back to Badger. "Drop it, asswipe. History can't be rewritten, no matter how hard you try."

"How do you know?"

"Because my grandfather told me it was so. The major events won't change. Our family legends say it over and over again."

"I don't believe you. I think you lie out of convenience. Maybe you and the Cree girl can get together and make your own little lying bastards."

"I only see one bastard around here," he said calmly.

Badger's jaw throbbed with clenched muscles, but he held back his readied fists. "Take me with you. This summer, during the thunder moon. We can prove that history can be changed. And when we do it, we'll return to a better Blackfoot Nation."

Dean shook his head with more than a little disdain and walked back into the gloom of his single-room house.

"You grew up here. You know that the people are surviving on almost nothing. There's no work. There's nothing to do besides drugs and alcohol. The poverty is atrocious. We are better than what our historical circumstances have forced us to become, and you know it."

Badger followed Dean inside and stood, staring at him. Dean lay back against his pillows and crossed his ankles. He quickly decided that the pressure in his nose was far greater in that position, and he sat back up again.

"Come on, man. You've traveled to the past before. Don't deny it any longer."

"I'm not talking about this anymore," Dean said firmly.

"So what if we can't make a huge change. What if we can just help a few? Educate them. Tell them how to prepare for the changes. How can that hurt?" Badger cut the air with his hands, accentuating his fervor as he spoke. Then he began to pace.

Dean watched him with wary eyes. He suspected Badger was named incorrectly. It should have been Stalking-mountain-cat or Fire-that-smolders. His suggestion about meeting with only a few bands of people reminded him of his travels with his grandfather. *Hadn't the trip been just that?* He explored, made new friends, rode horses, and hunted while his grandfather sat in endless council meetings. *What words had been exchanged between the chiefs and his grandfather? Did he warn them of the future for the Niitsitapi — The Real People? Did he make any attempt at changing the future?* Dean couldn't answer any of his questions. At the time, the trip had seemed like an educational adventure. *How naïve he had been.* A young boy going along for a ride. Grandpa had talked to him about a few important matters, but Dean couldn't remember the conversations the way he thought his grandfather would have wanted him to.

"I don't know, but I'm not willing to find out."

Badger stopped pacing and said, "How does a coward look himself in the mirror every day?"

"He doesn't own a mirror," Dean said.

"Incorrect answer, smartass."

"It's the only answer I've got." Dean sighed, or attempted to, through the obstruction of his clogged and swollen nose. He looked around for his discarded cloth. His nose needed something cool laid over it.

"I can save Gena's daycare."

"Stop it. You're taking this too far. I've already told you the story is about illusions. The great leaps of faith it takes to cross them."

"No. It's about traveling into the past," Badger argued. "We should do this. I can fund our trip. I can pay for all of our provisions, and for that daycare center, too. I've saved thousands of dollars."

"This isn't happening."

"You need to consider what I'm offering."

"I've considered it, and I'm telling you no."

"All those kids will be stuffed into someone's living room, crying and wanting their teachers back. Or worse, they'll be babysat by Nickelodeon. It's a good center. It will be a huge loss to the community when Gena can't afford the rent any longer."

"You need to step outside."

"What's she need? Fifteen thousand? Twenty? Thirty? I've got it. All you have to do is go camping for one month. Find your own people. Go to a place where none of this wretched town exists. You could hide out in the mountains for the entire time, and Gena's daycare will be all set when we return."

"Get out!"

"Coward." Badger slammed the door behind him.

Dean thought about his 9mm semi-automatic nestled it its case, but he didn't follow the impulse to do something regrettable, like shoot Badger in the foot. Badger needed to leave. *That was all.* Dean wanted to be left alone. He wanted a damn beer. He wanted to rewind his life and see his daughter's face again. Wadding the pillows into a heap, he leaned back and shut his eyes.

Chapter Four

"A deal's a deal, bro."

"I don't have to be reminded," Dean said, and gave Badger a look of contempt.

Badger sported an eager grin. "Nah, don't make faces like that. You get to camp out for one month, which is pretty much what you've been doing anyway. And you're helping out your cousin. It's a win-win, for everyone."

"Except I'm not a hundred percent certain this is even going to work," Dean responded as he switched the bundle under his arm from his right to his left side.

"There's no doubt in my mind we'll make it fine. Your grandfather taught you what to do. You should grow a pair like his. Strap'em on, and quit worrying like a woman."

"Don't talk about my grandpa again," Dean warned.

"Man, you are one touchy broad."

"I want you to be clear on the fact that we may not go anywhere tomorrow night without another medicine man. That's all I'm saying."

"Well, you've been clear about it all along. So I get it already. There isn't anyone else to sing or drum for us, so if it works, it works, and if it doesn't, then I'm out twenty grand."

"You got it, jerkface."

"If you're bad-mouthin' me, you must be feeling better about our plans."

"Like you said, I'm hunting and camping for a month while you do whatever it is you think you need to do in 1868."

Dean and Badger continued hiking up the mountain trail through the spruce and pine forest until they saw the log hut. They stepped off the ancient trail that continued deeper into the mountains and eventually rose above the tree line to touch the sky at the very pinnacle of the Backbone of the World.

Dean inspected the old cabin for signs of inhabitants, current or recent, human or animal, and saw nothing that alarmed him. Spider webs were undisturbed under the eaves and fresh deer tracks could be seen near the door. No one had been here recently, and Dean felt comfortable with the knowledge of solitude. The single-roomed log structure had been built around the same time that living in tipis had become the old way of life. The hut sat near Dancing Bear's Pond beneath the peaks, and despite the lack of his grandfather's lodge, it still felt like a good place. His grandfather preferred the tipi, but Dean thought hauling the tipi to the sacred site was unnecessary. If all went well, they were only going to be camped there one night. The small building would be a good place to leave their modern belongings behind once they were traveling.

Nothing made or manufactured after 1868 would be able to survive the trip. This was what the family legends said, and Dean would abide by the rule. The trips always went back one hundred and forty-four years. Dean thought it was an unusual number, but nothing about time traveling felt normal, and that was the length of time originally traveled by the very first Lynx Clan warrior.

His memories refused to stay concealed any longer. Grandfather was in this place as much as the balsam trees, the willows, and the juniper berries. The cooing of a mourning dove seemed to confirm Dean's growing suspicions that Grandpa was there with him now. It was one of his favorite birds. When he was little they used to watch the doves from the kitchen window as they pecked at the ground beneath the bird feeders. Grandpa told him the birds cooed their sorrow for lost loved ones. It was only now that Dean wondered if by listening to those doves, Grandpa was remembering Dean's mother.

Was Grandfather Two Eagles watching over him and directing him back to the truck with that stern look he gave so well? The look that needed no words to say everything he wanted to say. Or was

Grandfather leading the way? He was the one who brought Dean to the sacred site and made him sing the songs. Grandpa had wanted him to learn the Night Medicine ceremony all those years ago. Telling Dean he was the last one to carry the Dragonfly medicine bundle and making him memorize the story of how his many times great-grandfather received the sacred pipe that travels through time. Grandfather never said not to use it.

The summer before he started high school was the strangest time in his entire childhood. So strange that Dean convinced himself that he had made up the part about time travel, and forced himself believe that he and Grandpa had only found some extravagant rendezvous. The kind where no one was allowed to have anything modern in camp. He blocked out every memory that said he had gone back one hundred and forty-four years in time.

With Badger pushing him to take the journey, and his grandfather's recent passing, the memories were back. Very real, and fresh in his mind. Returning to the mountain was a bath in memory acetone for Dean. Carefully applied layers of denial were being stripped away with every passing minute as they came closer to performing the ceremony. *Would Grandpa Two Eagles approve of taking Badger to the People to warn and help them? Didn't they do the same thing all those years ago?*

Dean shrugged out of his oversized pack and laid it down on a bench inside the hut. He placed the medicine bundle with his Dragonfly pipe next to it, being careful that it wouldn't fall onto the dirt floor. Badger stood by the open door, his body blocking most of the evening light.

"We'll need a fire to last through the night. Check the woodpile. If there isn't a stack up to your ass, start gathering and chopping. I'll check the sweat lodge and make sure it's in good shape."

"Are you sure we can't have dinner before we start this?"

"No. If you want to travel tomorrow night, you'll be cleansed down to the last pore in your body. No food until we get there."

"That's pretty rough, isn't it?"

"No," Dean repeated as he slipped past Badger, ducked under the doorframe, and stepped back out into the pine-scented mountain air.

"I don't see what difference it will make. Having food in our stomachs before we travel will give us a boost."

"We've been over this. Do it my way, or forget about it. You've had the same training as me in the Corps. You can go hungry for a few hours. Or, are you going soft in your old age?"

Badger followed Dean out of the rustic cabin. "Never liked traveling on an empty stomach. Starving for an entire day before we even leave seems harsh."

"It's not that kind of traveling. Besides, as soon as we get there, you can eat whatever you can catch."

"Now you're just being a jerk," Badger said, as he fiddled with the knife sheath at his waist.

"Get the wood, and leave the damn rabbits and trout alone until we're a century and a half away from here."

As Badger stockpiled firewood, Dean looked over the old sweat lodge. It resembled an oversized beaver lodge, except that it wasn't in the water. It sat in the grass near the pond and looked untouched for years, just like the cabin. The bent willow branches were still strong, and the ties that held it together were mostly intact. It needed to be repaired in only one place that Dean could see. He thought both the cabin and the sweat lodge were holding up well considering the long months of freezing weather in the Rocky Mountains. He walked over to the red willows growing near the outlet of the pond and cut fresh flexible stems. He breathed in the tart, earthy scent of the branches as he bent, weaved, and tied the willows over the gaps in the lodge.

He would conduct the sweating ceremony for him and Badger, as well as the Night Medicine. Badger had been studying and he was a fast learner, but he had no real experience to speak of. At least not in the way Dean did. Badger wanted what Dean had growing up. He longed for a past filled with pow-wows and tribal council meetings. He wanted what Dean always took for granted. Not that he didn't appreciate having his grandparents, aunts, uncles, and cousins, but the tribal gatherings, feasts, and celebrations were normal for him. Not particularly special or unique, the way Badger seemed to think they were.

Dean had to keep reminding himself that Badger didn't have a big family stuffing traditions down his throat his entire life. Dean thought that the lack of tribal members must have left a hole inside his friend. An emptiness that Badger needed to fill with knowledge. He thought the answers Badger wanted didn't come from inside a book, or from a friend's mouth, but he couldn't say exactly where the answers could be found, either. In Dean's opinion, anyone's truth was a singular quest, not to be handed out for free. Badger would find what he needed, or he wouldn't. Dean wanted Gena to keep her business running. Too many families depended on her child care center. Badge had the solution. Cash, and plenty of it. Dean had come to the tenuous decision that it was a good trade.

After Dean threw a tarp and a wool blanket over the willow branches, he crawled into the narrow opening of the sweat lodge's east facing door and took a look around. The lodge needed to hold in as much of the heat and steam from the hot rocks as possible. They would sweat until the impurities poured out of their bodies. The lodge appeared to be sealed well, with only the bare minimum of light peeking in the cracks. Dean crawled back out and began to gather the stones that would be heated in the fire before being brought inside the lodge.

Working side by side, their efficiency showed as the wood was stacked high and the fire blazed a short time later. Dean and Badger alternated poking the fire with long branches and adding fresh split wood to build up the heat. With the evening settling into night around them and the fire radiating a good amount of warmth, Badger put his stick aside and walked over to the cabin. He returned with his pack and placed it on the ground near the fire.

"Before I'm too loopy from starvation and sweating, I want to go over everything in my bag one last time."

"Gear inspection," Dean affirmed.

"Yeah. Tell me if you see anything you think won't make the trip. We can leave it stashed in the shack until we get back."

Dean nodded and looked at the spreading pile of mid-nineteenth century tools and clothes. Badger was careful in the selection of his traditional clothes for the time they would be with the Piegans, but he also had breeches, shirt, a pair of wool socks, leather shoes and a decent coat. The coat would pass as middle class white man's attire, not a miner or logger's jacket. It was similar to what Dean had packed, except he skipped the jacket and shoes. He preferred moccasins and if it was colder than he suspected it would be, then he could use his Hudson Bay blanket over his hunting shirt for warmth.

They planned to travel in their buckskins. The leggings, moccasins, shirts, and breechclouts were hand stitched and authentic. They should travel fine, and not disappear with the passage of time. Everything else needed to be double-checked. Nothing would cross with them if it didn't exist in the time they walked into. Nothing, that is, except for themselves. Grandpa had been clear about that. They couldn't take anything from the present time to the past.

Badger began to unpack the weapons. Five knives, with antler or wood handles, all in their respective sheaths.

"Two are mine and three for trading or gifts," he explained.

Next, he laid out the pistols. Dean raised his eyebrows at the pile. He didn't realize how much weight was inside Badger's pack. The collection of guns would be extremely valuable anywhere. Dean packed a revolver and ammunition, but he had only one, and what he thought was enough ammo to get him through the month. Badger must be counting on using the guns to buy him a lot of clout with the tribes. Either that, or he was more paranoid than he let on.

"Planning a war?"

"The war has been going on long before we show up," he said as he spread out three Colt revolvers in various conditions, two other pistols of a different make, a large pouch of gunpowder, boxes of cartridges, two lead ingots, and a bullet mold. He also had an antique cleaning kit.

Next to his knives and guns, Badger set down a length of rope, a hatchet, mess kit and canteen, a compass, two straight razors, a bar of soap, tobacco, and some wrapped packs of dried meat and fruit. He also had matches in a small tin box, a leather-bound book, and a small pouch of gold nuggets. Dean's own gear was similar. The only difference was that Dean had brought a lot fewer weapons and no gold. Dean had packed a pound of ground coffee, a three-pound bag of salt, some unprocessed sugar, and multiple tobacco knots. These would be easy to trade and were valuable giveaway items. He also had flint and steel, in case something happened to the matches.

They would both be carrying rifles, in addition to the pistols and knives. Everything, including the weapons, had been researched carefully and paid for by Badger in preparation for their trip. Badger had a Winchester repeating rifle made in 1866, and Dean carried a Spencer. Dean enjoyed hunting with a bow, but his modern version wouldn't travel through time. The guns provided a level of security unmatched by a bow against the unknown dangers they could face during their journey.

Dean was bringing packages of dried medicinal plants: Bistort, Echinacea, comfrey, pipsissewa (a natural antibiotic), and a variety of S. purpurea from Canada, which had once been used to treat smallpox. He hoped he would be able to find a medicine man or woman willing to use the medicines he brought. It was his way of contributing to Badger's plan. He would gift every bit of it. It was something his grandfather had taught him so many years ago, and Dean had not forgotten. He knew in his gut that he couldn't stop sickness from spreading. There would always be a new outbreak of some flu or cold, but this was one way he could ease some suffering and discomfort, and maybe even save a life.

Their plan was to try to get their people interested in raising sheep and possibly cattle if they could find breeding stock to give to them. Some of Badger's weapons and the gold were meant for trading or buying the animals. They hoped the chiefs they encountered would be open to the idea.

It was all up in the air at this point. Dean and Badger could end up in the wrong century and lose everything they had meticulously packed, due to an error during the ceremony. They also could arrive in the desired time frame and not find anyone. They could travel to the past and be killed as an outsider by either the natives or the homesteaders. There was so much unknown about their journey that it was probably sheer insanity to even attempt such a crossing. But Dean believed that man had been courting insanity since the very first voyage ever taken. The unknown risks were part of the appeal. Traveling to the past wasn't entirely different from when he joined the military. At least that is what he kept telling himself.

Dean and Badger had many things in common, and this intrinsic desire was one of them. They had both sought to travel into unknown territory since they were young boys. Dean knew long before he took the journey with his grandfather that he wanted to see the world. The Marine gig had sent him into unforgiving landscapes, and he didn't enjoy all of them, but he didn't hate them either. Badger wasn't as willing to accept without complaint the rough conditions of the desert or the brutality of the sweltering jungle, but he liked to explore, and to know what was out there. The two of them had seen much during their time in the Corps, and they had both returned to Blackfoot land afterward. Between the vast, rolling plains and the mountains rising on the western horizon that was where each of them ultimately wanted to be.

After high school, Dean knew he had to get away from the place he'd grown up, but he never stayed away long. After the divorce, he ended up back in Montana either because he didn't have any better idea of where to go, or he was seeking the comforts of familiarity, or it was just the easiest way to hide from the troubles in his life. Hiding out on his native land had eventually become vital to his survival. His family would have said he was out there in his cabin drinking himself to death, but Dean thought that by living apart from the rest of the world, he was surviving the only way he could.

Dean stared across the pond. The moon's reflection shimmered over the surface of the water with silver highlights. His daughter would have loved it here. And it would have been hell trying to keep her from drowning herself. She loved to splash and explore and chase the bugs. Dean remembered the days on the beach at Camp Pendleton, when he and Marissa took turns chasing Ellie in the shallow waves of the Pacific. He thought she was a maniac, and swore that his daughter would have dived in and swum away with the seals if he took his eyes off of her for even a second.

Ellie loved being outside more than anything in the world. From day one, if she was crying or fussing, all they had to do was step outdoors and let the air wash over her skin and the sun shine on her little round face, and she would be soothed instantly. Babies understood that the wonder and beauty of nature took away all grievances. He understood it, too. He and Ellie needed sky and light and air for all to be well in the world. When she was dying in the hospital, Dean would open the window in her room to let the light in and try to catch a breeze for her. Then a nurse would come in and close the window, telling him that the temperature outside was too cold for her. Those last days, Dean wanted to take her away and tell the doctors that they were the ones killing his daughter, with all of their injected drugs and sterile this and that. He wanted to bring her to his grandfather and grandmother, to let them sing and pray over her. He wanted so much to bring her to the mountains and let her walk beneath the towering trees and find a moose eating grass at the edge of a lake. He wanted to see her face light up at the sight of an elk or a mountain goat, and be with her when she saw her first bald eagle.

Instead, he had sat next to her hospital bed on some military base, holding her hand, surrounded by strangers, in a city a thousand miles away from his family. Grandpa and Grandma had come, but they looked equally out of place there, and the songs they sang for her didn't have the healing power of home.

Ellie was braver than the toughest Marine during that battle. How could one tiny body withstand all of that torture? All with no air. No sky. Dean had completely shut down by the time she died. As if he died with her that day. But it was all a blur now. He didn't blame Marissa for leaving him; he had already left her. Not in body, but in his mind. She needed him to be stronger. She needed Dean to help her with the doctors and the never-ending paperwork. She needed Dean to hold them together, but there wasn't anything left for him to grab onto. He gave everything he had to Ellie. There in the hospital room, he gave his spirit to save her, and it hadn't worked. She left anyway. Did she find her way to the Sand Hills? That's where Grandmother said she was. But how does the spirit of a little girl find her way across the desert and mountains to a place so far away?

Dean reached to his right, grabbing for a bottle of beer that wasn't there. He came back to himself as his hand wrapped around emptiness. Shaken that he'd allowed himself to visit the cemetery of grief buried inside him, he glanced at Badger, wondering if his friend had noticed his temporary lack of presence.

Badger's gaze darted to the fire and then at the pile of supplies in front of him. He saw Dean's slip, but he didn't mention it. Sobriety had been a burly battle, and they both knew Dean was still riding down a rough road.

The mountain was already dredging up more than Dean bargained for. First about his grandfather, and now the memories of Ellie. He grabbed a log and placed it in the flames.

"How long until we climb inside the sweat?" Badger asked as he stared at the dome-shaped lodge.

Dean rose to his feet and turned to face the pond. Marissa's angry face swam in his mind's eye. She wouldn't stop yelling at him after Ellie had died. She yelled that he was a weak bastard. She yelled because they didn't have enough money for her to fly home to her parents, and pay for the house, and the car she drove, and all the bills on his single military income. She yelled because the washing machine needed to be repaired, and she yelled because she couldn't get pregnant again. And that was mostly because Dean wouldn't touch her after so much yelling. And also because of the unbelievable fear that if she were to get pregnant again, it meant that there was the possibility that they could lose another child. Marissa was hurt beyond repair, and Dean couldn't fix that, either. The divorce was inevitable, and to Dean, so was his alcohol consumption. Drinking became the natural, unspoken solution to his problems.

He stepped toward the water, not looking at Badger. "Soon," he muttered.

Was Dean finding a better place to hide? He hadn't had alcohol in six weeks. It was a start, but Dean now held the thought that he was disappearing in another way. *Was this journey into the past another blatant escape from his misery?* He kept walking out of the circle of firelight and away from the sweat lodge and cabin. He needed a minute in the dark. He needed to clear his head of his past. The mental focus he was going to need in the next twenty-four hours had to be absolute. He couldn't forget any part of the ceremony. The money was already on its way to Gena, and Badger was counting on him. He wanted a month of solitude. He needed a dose of reality that wasn't his own. Dean wanted to get away from the mournful faces of his family. The looks of sympathy over the fate of his daughter and Grandfather. The looks of disgust that came from knowing Dean had turned to alcohol to solve his problems. He wanted to take Badger back to the past probably more than he had previously been aware of until right then.

After his moment in the woods, Dean returned to their camp and walked into the hut for his bundle. He would smoke now. Not because he enjoyed it, but in prayer. The way his grandfather had shown him.

Badger joined in, and they shared the pipe by the fire. Taking turns puffing and passing the long-stemmed pipe, the men were each lost in their own thoughts. It surprised Dean when he heard himself say, "Can you fill the gourds with water and place them inside the sweat lodge? I'll move the rocks inside."

Badger looked a little too self-satisfied to be starting the ceremony at last. The smugness under the surface was hard for

Dean to be around. It had always been there, ever since they met. Dean eventually got used to his friend's personality and lack of humility. He knew Badger was excited for the trip. Dean took a deep breath and retrieved the forked branch he had set aside to lift the heated rocks out of the coals.

By this time tomorrow night, they would be crossing the void of space, and traversing one hundred and forty-four years back in time.

Chapter Five

"Thanks for riding with me," Gena said.

"It's no problem. I'm just glad I was able to get away for a couple of hours. I needed something to do to get my mind off of Trevyn being with his father."

"Where did you say they were going, again?"

"All over," Kai said, balling her fists against her jeans. She stared hard out of the passenger side window, not wanting her friend to see her gritting her teeth.

Although Gena didn't see Kai's face, she could hear the bitterness. "He's with your ex's parents too, right?"

"Yes," Kai conceded, and finished answering the question. "They're taking him rafting and camping for almost a week. Then they're flying to southern California for some big beach vacation and a trip to Disneyland. I swear Gabe's doing this on purpose because he knows I can't afford this type of thing."

"Probably, but don't go there, Kai. Your ex-hole will be out to get you forever. Don't waste your brain cells on him. And besides, once you finish school you'll be able to take your little man on vacation every summer."

"Thanks. It's just that when we were together, I couldn't even get him to go to a movie with us. Now that he's gone, he's doing everything I wanted to do while we were married."

"And proving exactly why you're no longer with the loser."

"True," Kai said, and finally looked forward toward the approaching mountains.

Gena slowed her car as she entered the turn lane.

"What's your idiot cousin doing out here, anyway?"

"He wants me to pick up his truck so it doesn't get broken in to or stolen while he and Badger play some weird commando survivalist hunting games."

"Maybe they're actually a couple and keeping it a big secret. I didn't think your cousin was *that* way, but it would explain why he's always with that dipstick, Badger Sneers-a-lot."

"Hey, I think Badger is sort of cute," Gena said, feigning offense.

"I know you do, but there's something seriously wrong with that guy. You should stay away from him."

"Oh, I can't. The more damaged they are, the more I want them. And the whole ex-military thing is so hot. You know, he makes really good money mining up north somewhere, too. He's cute and rich. And my cousin is definitely straight."

Gena smiled at her own admitted shortcomings and drove down the long straight dirt road.

"You're messed up, you know that?"

"I know," Gena said as her grin widened. "And you must be, too. Why else would we get along so well?"

Kai pressed her lips together, seemingly not amused by Gena's observation. Unfortunately, she knew there was some truth to it.

"He's slippery is all I'm saying. Dean deserves the messed-up bromance, but you could do a lot better than Badger."

"I doubt it. The selection of decent horny twenty-somethings, or even thirty-somethings, is all tapped out around here. But it doesn't matter. Badger isn't looking for anything permanent. He already told me."

"He told you?" Kai asked incredulously. "Like, he actually just told you that he doesn't want to be in a relationship?"

"Yeah. He said he's too busy with work and blah blah blah, and doesn't want to get serious with anyone."

"Just confirms my first opinion about him. He's a selfish, arrogant meathead, and even if you do like that sort of thing, I don't think he's trustworthy."

Kai hadn't told Gena about her run-in with Badger at Dean's house. Badger's temper and haughty rant was worth noting and filing away in a category not to be forgotten, but she didn't feel the need to talk about it.

"Jeez, I got it already," Gena said. "I think you have more issues than I do when it comes to men. We're going to be alone forever. The daycare center isn't going to be around much longer since I can't afford the rent, so it will just be me, you, and the bar."

"Shut up. You are not. And I'll be more than happy if I'm without a daily dose of smelly testosterone."

"Speaking of Dean. When he returns from this hunting trip, could you go easy on my big cousin?"

"Seriously? I was going easy on him," Kai said, shocked. Hadn't she let Dean talk to Trevyn and even tried to smile at him? And she had driven him all the way out to his house when he needed a ride, and then went back there again to apologize for acting so strange. But if Dean hadn't said anything to Gena and neither had she, then Gena didn't know the lengths she had gone to keep an eye on her cousin. "Believe me, I could have been a lot bitchier. I've been holding back."

"Hey," Gena softened her tone. "I shouldn't have brought it up. It's just that he doesn't like anyone to talk about it. He made me swear I wouldn't tell anyone who didn't already know."

"Is this about the fact that he drinks like a lush, or because his grandfather passed away recently? I know he was raised by his grandparents so it's more like his dad died, but come on. You want me to go easy on a sorry-ass, ex-Marine drunk? He wears stereotypes like a neon sign."

"Dang, you can be nasty when you want to be."

Kai swallowed some pride and acknowledged yet another obvious truth from her closest friend. She supposed it was one of the reasons she liked being around Gena so much. She could count on her friend to be honest and take none of her crap.

"Sorry," she mumbled. "I can overlook a lot of things, but alcohol is a hard one. It really gets to me. Your cousin seems like he could be a nice guy when he's not drinking. I just hate seeing anyone mess up their life like that."

Gena had no way of knowing just how personal alcohol abuse was to her. Her father had gone crazy from drinking more than once. But it was her uncles who scared the piss out of her when she was a girl. One uncle in particular had been the instigator in changing her life, and her family's lives forever. It was strange that she ended up serving alcohol on the weekends for a living, but somehow she had managed to separate her feelings from her work. *At least most of the time.* And her life had changed so much. Everything was different now. Maybe that's why seeing Dean intoxicated set her off so thoroughly. She had let her feelings get involved.

"Dean's issues aren't about his grandfather or drinking too much," Gena said. "He's been through some serious drama in his life. He needs some space right now and doesn't need a judgmental comment every few seconds."

"He pretty much earns the comments. And I don't have to serve anyone I don't want to at the bar."

"You're right about the bar. I'll take care of him if he ever comes back. I kind of think you scared him off, though. He hasn't been in for over a month."

Kai had noticed. She couldn't seem to stop herself from looking for him when she showed up at work. She would scan all the heads for Dean's short, shiny black hair and his too perfect ears. How did she decide that Dean had perfect ears? *Who thinks that?* It was because they were nicely curved and not too big or too small, and they didn't stick out. *Blasted man.* The ears just went right along with the rest of his perfect body, and those light brown eyes. She wished she hadn't seen him half-naked that day at his cabin. The image of his smooth chest and toned abs haunted her, and there was no forgetting beauty like that.

Kai snapped herself out of her distracting thoughts. "Maybe he's coming in during the week to avoid me."

"He's not. I asked."

"Well, he probably switched bars or is drinking at home," she added with a barbed tongue. She just couldn't handle the fact that

Dean had somehow gotten under her skin, and it was now causing a rash. *Sort of like ringworm. Dean had become her own personal ringworm, and she needed to find a pill to make him go away.* "Why is he so damaged, anyway?"

"He lost his daughter, Kai. She died from cancer," Gena finally said. "I swear if you tell him I told you, I'll write your name and phone number inside the bathroom stalls at Growler's and I'll leave it posted there until the end of time."

"You're not going to work there forever," Kai said as she rolled her eyes.

"I will if I don't come up with the money to keep the doors open at Kinder Place. It's crazy how much the lease has gone up. I swear the landlord is using taxes as an excuse to raise our rent. It's so unfair. When my mom started the daycare, the rent cost half of what it is now."

Kai could see Gena gripping the steering wheel so hard that her knuckles were white.

"And you didn't qualify for the loan to buy the building?"

"I did, but I need a bigger down payment. If I'm paying the slum lord all my extra cash in rent, I won't ever be able to save enough to buy the place."

It sickened Kai to think of all the families in town that were going to be without affordable child care in the next month when Kinder Place's lease expired. Kai knew not to bring up the idea of the families paying more for the daycare. *That was pointless.* So many of the parents couldn't afford it already and were being subsidized by the government, or scrimping to make ends meet. The staff was already being paid the bare minimum, and Gena's mom didn't even take a salary. She was a full-time volunteer.

"I think Dean gave me another check," Gena said.

"He gives you money?"

"Yep. For the daycare. He keeps enough of his paychecks to buy food and gas and usually gives me the rest. Drunk or not, he's the man, Kai. No one else does that for us. More than half of what I have saved up is from him. The problem is, it still isn't enough. I haven't even opened the envelope I just got from him, because I know I'll just get depressed again."

Gena reached into the door pocket next to her side. She held up an envelope for Kai to see and then lowered it to her lap.

"Why does he do that? Where does he work that he can be home for weeks and away for weeks at a time?"

"He does contract work for the mines. It's good money. He only works when he needs to. Or wants to. He spends the rest of his time making himself suffer."

"Because of his daughter?" Kai asked tentatively.

Gena nodded and made a left turn onto an even smaller road that was more of a trail through the grass than an actual road. They had been slowly climbing in altitude since they left town, but now it was obvious to Kai they were headed to high country. Towering bluffs lay before them, and sweeping buttes caressed the landscape to the north and south. The car climbed, leveled out, and then climbed again. Then Kai saw trees at the end of the road.

"Sorry, I got sidetracked thinking about Kinder Place," Gena continued. "Dean's daughter died of leukemia about two years ago. She was only four years old. Dean and his wife couldn't hold it together afterward, and she divorced him. He was still in the Marines back then, but his enlistment was just about over, and he didn't re-up. So, he moved back home and has been hiding out in his family's summer cabin ever since."

She made a pained face that Kai interpreted as, *That's his story. Isn't it sad?*

"So he's been drinking like that for two years," Kai said. "I knew he was a loser as soon as I saw him."

Now it was Gena's turn to roll her eyes at her friend. Kai was a tough nut, and forgiveness wasn't her forte. What Gena didn't know was that Kai's heart felt like it had shrunk in her chest. It ached for Dean, and the pain made it hard for Kai to breathe.

Two years ago, Trevyn was only three years old. She couldn't even begin to imagine what it would be like to watch her son die of cancer. *Only that wasn't entirely true.* Kai had nightmares about losing her son. Her imagination liked to hijack her thoughts and emotions, and play out the most terrible images and ideas of all the ways he could be injured or harmed or taken from her. It was her greatest fear. And she, of all people, knew what it was like to have your closest family members die. The fear she had of losing her son was a big part of the reason why she was freaking out about the three-week summer vacation Trevyn was on with his father and grandparents.

"He's not perfect, but we're giving him his space. And if you think about it, he's only hurting himself."

"I guess you can't take away a fool's right to self-flagellate."

"Where do you come up with this shit?" she asked.

"I spent my entire adolescence reading," Kai said dryly.

"Why do I think you're lying right now? You're way too pretty to have been hanging out in the library for four years of high school."

"I'm not lying. Ask my aunt. I had absolutely no social life until I met my ex."

"Well, I guess you just answered my question about why you have so many issues."

"So what's your excuse?" Kai teased and grinned. She wanted to lighten the mood of the conversation. Her mind was dredging up past pain, and she didn't like the way it made her feel.

Gena ignored the bait and pointed ahead.

"There's Dean's blue beast."

The pickup truck was parked a hundred yards ahead in a turn-around at the edge of the forest. Gena pulled her car around and parked next to it.

"Are you sure you can drive that back to town?" Gena asked again.

"I can't believe you don't know how to drive a stick shift."

"I've never had a reason to learn how," Gena said with a nonchalant shrug. "Who buys a standard transmission?"

"I guess your cousin does," Kai said as she reached for the door. "And it's no problem. I learned to drive in a big old ranch truck."

"Maybe you can teach me in Dean's truck while he's off camping."

"I think you'd better ask him to teach you."

"Yeah, in all of my spare time."

"Sleep is so overrated," Kai said, matching Gena's sarcasm. She opened the door. "Where's the key?"

"I've got his spare."

As she dug in her pocket, the envelope from Dean slipped off of her lap landing in the space between the seats. Kai grabbed it and they traded the key for the envelope.

"Let me get it started, and then we can follow each other back to town," Kai suggested.

Gena agreed, so Kai shut the door and walked over to the truck. She noticed the green gate in the fence and the trail alongside the creek beyond, leading into the depths of the forest. *How long had it been since she had taken a hike or visited the snow on the peaks?* It must have been years. Motherhood had more or less stripped her of time outdoors reserved just for the experience of exploring or hunting. Over the last five years, any time she'd spent under the sun was playing in a sandbox, or pushing Trevyn in a swing. She used to like digging for crystals and gemstones, or wading in a stream. She hadn't foraged for food or plants since she was a teenager.

Trevyn would love coming up here and learning about life in the woods. She could teach him more about living in the wilderness than anyone else she knew. She had pushed all of that knowledge aside when she moved to western Montana with her recently married aunt. She spent much of her time and energy assimilating to her new surroundings. *Her new life.* She tried hard to be a good student, and then a wife, and to forget about her previous life. Now Kai could easily visualize herself taking Trevyn camping and showing him things that she hadn't thought about in years. She would have to ask her aunt and uncle if they could borrow a tipi from a friend so she could teach Trevyn the old ways. Teach him what her parents had taught her. *Maybe it would be good for them both.*

She turned back to the task at hand and noticed the oversized tires and the lift kit Dean had added onto the Ford. It was a stretch for her just to place her foot on the side rail. She unlocked the door and climbed inside, tossing her purse onto the passenger seat. She had to adjust the seat to be able to push the brake pedal. Dean must have some really long legs, she thought as she started the engine. It turned over immediately. The rumble was obnoxious in the quiet of the wilderness, but then she was suddenly aware of an even more alarming sound.

Kai looked over and saw her friend jumping up and down. Gena was screeching like a lunatic. Kai opened the door and hopped out. Gena jumped on her and squeezed her so hard, she felt like she was being choked.

"Whoo-hoo! It's a bloody freaking miracle!"

"What? What is?" Kai asked as she peeled Gena off of her.

"Look!"

She's waved a slip of paper so frantically in front of Kai's face that she couldn't see what was on it.

"Hold still," she commanded.

Gena could hardly contain herself for the second it took to stuff the check into the neckline of Kai's shirt, but she managed. Then she danced away, jumping and spinning in circles. It resembled a Smoke Dance, only faster and without the drumming.

Kai rescued the paper from disappearing down the front of her shirt and read the numbers on the check. Twenty thousand dollars. Dean Wolfsblood's signature was on the bottom. Gena snapped the check out of Kai's fingers before she could close her mouth.

"I don't know how he did it, but I'm dancing to great Napi, and the Sun, and the Moon, and the Morning Star. Whoo-hoo!" she screamed again. "Dean wrote a note too. All of it is for the daycare center. My cousin may be a drunk, but he's the most fabulous drunk I know."

Gena dashed to her car, yelling, "I have to tell my mom. And call the bank. And tell all the parents to quit looking for a new school."

She threw open the door and jumped inside. Then she apparently remembered Kai. The window lowered. "You coming?" she yelled.

Her eyes were bright with exhilaration, and all of her teeth flashed in a toothy grin.

"Go on." Kai shooed her off with a wave. "I'll be right behind you," she called and smiled, feeling Gena's contagious excitement ripple through her.

Chapter Six

Back inside Dean's truck, Kai shifted into first gear and pulled away, fully intending to drive straight back to her car, currently parked at Gena's house. She wanted to go home and bury herself beneath the covers of her bed and not over think about what Trevyn was doing with his father. It would be a good hour's drive back to town, and then another ten minutes to her aunt and uncle's house. It was just evening now, and it wouldn't be dark until around nine o'clock this time of year. Kai had gotten used to staying up late at night because of tending bar, and she knew her chances of getting to bed early were next to none, but she was going to hide out and brood in bed anyway. She knew it was ridiculous to waste a perfect summer night, and her only day off this week, sulking, but she didn't want to bother anyone else with her problems. Maybe she would get a head start on some of the required reading for her fall classes. She had two semesters left before getting her bachelor's degree. Then after that, she would be on to her clinicals and considering furthering her education by pursuing a Master's program. She was so close to reaching her goals. Her aunt and uncle were giving her and Trevyn a place to live while she earned her degree, but she didn't want to live with them forever.

Completely lost in her thoughts, it took longer than it should have for her to realize the truck's engine and battery lights were glowing a ferocious and unwanted shade of orange. She had a vague, unconscious awareness of a loud thump a minute before, but with the rough road, she hadn't given it much thought. The suspension bumped and thunked regularly as she drove down the cow trail. Suddenly cognizant of the problem with the engine, she let the truck coast over into the swaying grass. Kai muscled the oversized truck to a stop as she realized the power steering and brakes were out. A sigh of resignation escaped her lips as she quickly came to terms with her predicament. She should have known anything involving Dean would come back around to bite her in the ass.

She scanned the road, but Gena was nowhere in sight. Her car had disappeared over the crest of a hill almost as soon as she had left Kai. She thought her friend would notice Dean's big blue truck missing in her rearview mirror sooner or later and would come back for her, so she wasn't too worried.

Being the independent and resourceful type, Kai didn't sit and wait helplessly for very long. She grabbed the lever to pop the hood, and then climbed out of the truck. The height of the bumper was above her knees, and she felt mildly absurd having to heft herself up and hang onto the frame just to look at the engine. It took her only a second to spot the broken serpentine belt. She knew she wasn't going any further in Dean's pickup.

When Gena's car didn't reappear over the horizon, Kai began to think about the possibilities of how she would be spending her evening. Every image her brain could conjure involved a lot of walking. *How many miles was it to just get back to the pavement?* She had memorized the turns, but hadn't paid particularly close attention to the distance. Gena had a way of distracting her that she didn't care for. Or perhaps it had been the subject of their conversation. Dean had a similar affect on her mind. Maybe it was in their blood. The walk back to civilization would take hours. It would be well past dark, and possibly not until morning, before she found another living soul. She had no water and maybe a pack of fruit flavored gummies or a granola bar in her purse that she liked to keep ready for Trevyn. That was it. The only other logical plan was to wait inside the truck for Gena to come floating down off of her twenty thousand dollar cloud and realize Kai hadn't come back. *She had to notice eventually, right?*

Ransacking the truck for emergency supplies yielded a couple of treasures, but mostly brought disappointment. The search revealed a flashlight from the glove box and a tool kit and jumper cables from under the back seat. The tools weren't much help without a new belt. But she did find an empty water bottle, which she counted as a treasure along with the flashlight. Dean's truck was clean and uncluttered, and definitely smelled like him. It reminded Kai of his cabin.

Thinking about spending the night in the foothills of the reservation, which was beginning to look like a definite possibility, she decided to walk the mile back to where she saw the stream, near the gate. She could fill her bottle with water and look for some wild strawberries to snack on. Maybe even forage for other edible plants.

Kai left a note wedged into the rubber seal around the window, telling Gena that she would be at the end of the road getting water from the stream. She guessed she could walk there and back in less than an hour, and would still have time to forage before night set in. Gena better come pick her up long before her night turned into an unplanned truck cab sleep over, she thought as she started hoofing it toward the forest. If her friend forgot about her, then she would walk back to town in the morning. Gena would definitely notice when she didn't show up for work at Kinder Place in the morning.

The emerald shadows beneath the trees were cool and welcoming as Kai walked along the bank of the stream. She relished the patches of soft moss beneath her shoes and the comforting babble of the flowing water. She wished she had worn her moccasins today. It felt strange to be so disconnected from the earth through the rubber soles of her tennis shoes. She kept her ears tuned for the sound of an approaching car, but never heard one as she wandered farther from the road. Her eyes searched for edible plants, and she found some plantain leaves. She recalled the Native name of white-man's-footprint and smiled to herself. The plantain herb came with the first Europeans and could be found virtually anywhere on the globe because of its versatility. It could be eaten like salad, or used for healing wounds. While picking the tender leaves that were best for eating raw, she saw some huckleberries.

Feeling fortunate about her easy finds, she suddenly became overwhelmed with memories and emotions tied to her childhood. Cupping the berries and leaves in her hand, she began inspecting every plant around her and recalled the many uses her mother and aunt had taught her. White flowers on a dense shrub of rusty twigs pulled her attention straight to the familiar plant. Muskeko-pukwan. She hadn't thought of the name in so long, it brought tears to her eyes. Kai didn't even know the non-Cree name for the plant.

It was powerful medicine that could be taken for fevers or colds, but what she remembered the most about it was when she and her sister had picked up head lice from visitors, and her mother had washed her hair with a strong batch of the tea made from this plant. Her aunt always kept the dried leaves stored during the months that it didn't grow. Kai didn't pick any. She wasn't sick, and she definitely didn't have lice, but the memories were strong nonetheless.

Kai stood, just now realizing that she had been kneeling next to the plant for a long time. She ate a berry and chewed at it absently. Her aunt would probably be setting the table for dinner about now. Before Kai left, she had mentioned something about pork chops and corn on the cob. Kai had only been half listening, too caught up in her own thoughts that Trevyn liked macaroni and cheese with his pork chops, and how he wouldn't be there tonight to ask for it.

She took a deep breath and looked around for the trail. It was about thirty feet to her right, and she started toward it. When she stepped onto the path, she looked back to the dead end road and wondered if she could hear Gena calling her from so far away. Deciding she could, she stared up the trail, wondering if Dean and Badger were close enough to find so she could tell him that his worthless truck had left her stranded in the middle of the nowhere, below the Thunderbird Peaks. They would have food. They may even have a radio, or an idea of how to get her out of there. Kai made up her mind to hike up the trail and have a look around. *What could it hurt?* The night looked like it was going to be a clear one, so even in the dark she could make it back to the truck without difficulty.

She ate the leaves and berries and kept looking for more. It wasn't smart to eat too much of an unfamiliar food. Not that these were unfamiliar to her digestive system, but it had been over eleven years since she'd eaten foraged meals. Along the trail, she made mental notes of the places where there were more edible plants. The knowledge came flooding back, and Kai enjoyed the mental hunt and search for food. Caught up in the game, it was nearly dark when Kai started paying closer attention to the time. Fortunately, she had brought the flashlight along just in case. It was stuffed into her back pocket like a battery operated beam of security.

Despite being alone in the woods, and what seemed like endless miles away from civilization, Kai felt at home in the forest. She was relaxed and invigorated. It felt great to be out of town. Away from traffic and work and responsibilities. It was unexpected, and something she didn't realize she missed quite so much until she was standing out there, by herself.

She took a quick break and gratefully drank pure mountain stream water with the assistance of the plastic bottle. It was cold and nourishing, and she could hardly believe how much better it tasted than city water. After emptying half the bottle, she looked down the trail. She'd been steadily climbing higher and higher into the mountains. She told herself she should head back, but after coming so far, she couldn't resist the urge to make it to the summit of the pass between the two steep hills on her right and left. She thought that anyone wanting to make a camp would do so at the top, where the land should level out.

With the last light of dusk falling around her, Kai left the flashlight off to conserve the battery and moved quickly up the trail, watching the crest of the hill come closer and closer. She both was and wasn't disappointed when she reached the top. Endless trees spread before her, instead of the meadow she had pictured in her mind. Trees, trees, and more trees. Thick trunks, soaring branches, and dense brush surrounded her. She didn't see Dean or any sign of campers or hunters, but she wasn't totally discouraged. It wasn't the end of the world, after all. Kai clicked on the flashlight as the forest engulfed her in full darkness. It was a new moon, the darkest night of the month. The stars shone through gaps in the branches, winking at her from distances unimaginable.

Kai brushed her hair back over her shoulder and turned around to start back toward Dean's truck. She was going to have to sleep in the cab. Gena would owe her for the rest of her life, Kai thought as she followed the trail down the mountain. It was like winning the guilt trip lottery, she decided, and she was already devising ways to cash in her ticket for a night off at the bar. Maybe when Trevyn returned from his father's.

A snap of a branch made her stop walking. On instant alert, she turned to the direction of the sound. She heard the soft crunching of pine litter, followed by a heavy huffing sound. She knew the sound. It wasn't a huffing as much as chuffing. Kai's heart thumped and her blood began to roar in her ears. She sniffed the air expecting the stench of bear but didn't smell him yet. A crunch of smashing wood got her mind reeling. The bear was tearing something up. It sounded like a log or a stump, but Kai didn't need to see a close-up verification of her imaginings. She had to get away from the animal, just in case it was in the mood to defend its territory, or its cub. Most black bears didn't like encounters with humans, and would scare off with a yell or would simply ignore intruders. Unfortunately, most wasn't all, and Kai believed it was best to leave all bears, black or grizzly, alone.

The chuffing sound continued from somewhere over her left shoulder. Ever so carefully, she looked to see if she could pinpoint its location in the black shadows beneath the trees. What she saw was so unexpected that her surge of adrenaline sent her into panic mode. The bear lumbered out from between two tree trunks, head down and sniffing the ground. She turned on her heel and ran to the nearest tree she could launch herself into. Her fear caused her to react without thinking clearly. She jumped and caught the scratchy bark of a branch just above her head and kicked her feet up, wrapping her leg around another branch. In a flash, she scrambled up the massive tree, ignoring her scrapes and scratches. She only stopped when she couldn't climb any higher. It wasn't until she swayed on the thin trunk that she realized how ridiculous she was. The bear was the much more adept climber in this horrifying scenario.

Feeling the press of fear, she stared down at the ground, expecting to see a mouth full of sharp teeth and long claws reaching for her. Instead, nothing greeted her but a million fragrant and spiny needles. She immediately focused on her other senses. Her hearing reached out into the night. Her nose sought the musky stench of bear. Her sense of location within the universe in comparison to where one particularly fuzzy bear roamed groped for an answer. When she heard or felt nothing that alarmed her, she finally let herself take a dozen deep breaths. Wedging herself in next to the trunk, while balancing on an impossibly skinny branch, she reached for the flashlight in her back pocket and found it empty. She had dropped it. The stupidity of her overreaction began to gnaw at her. *Why did she do that?* That bear hadn't even seen her, and she had run. Now her flashlight was gone, and so was her water.

Waiting was a tenuous exercise that strained her resolve. Her mind worked like a machine, thinking about all of the possible outcomes of her predicament. She could still walk back to the truck. Starlight was better than nothing. Maybe she could even stumble across her water bottle and the flashlight. *The trail was close to her tree, wasn't it?* Her dash to safety had happened so quickly that she wasn't entirely sure which direction the trail was anymore.

Kai groaned inwardly and berated herself one more time for reacting so badly. Wind whispered through the trees and hit her spruce. The top of the tree bent with her weight in it, and the shift gave her a whole new concern. She attempted to move down a couple branches, but found the climb down in the dark to be exceedingly more challenging than the upward trek. She swallowed hard as a branch cracked under her weight, but it didn't snap completely off. She shifted to another branch, hugging the trunk. She held her breath and listened for the bear. *Did it hear her up in the tree? Did it smell her fear-tinged sweat? Could it be on the ground, waiting for her to fall to her death?*

With eyes closed, she stopped insulting herself and her error in judgment and began to assess her situation with a clearer perspective. Climb down, find the trail, and stay calm, she told herself, but she couldn't get her body to cooperate. The memory of when she hid in a tree eleven years earlier was so strong that it muddled her thinking. She couldn't block out the memories that wanted to be seen right now. She didn't want to see them ever again. It had been a miracle that no one found her that night. When she did finally climb down from her place of safety that night so long ago, she had almost died from terror and grief. Somehow, she had found the strength to help her sister get away, but it had been a living nightmare. Something no one should ever have to endure. Especially a fourteen-year-old with her sixteen-year-old sister. She guessed that the intruders thought Nadie was dead, but she wasn't. They were eventually found by an elderly man, and it was because of him that she was here now, living with her Aunt Sue and her Blackfoot uncle on the reservation. *But Nadie hadn't survived in the end.*

The shaking in Kai's limbs reminded her to be strong. Her mother always told her how strong she was. When she was forced to say goodbye to her mom and leave her home with her father and uncle to help earn some money, her mother had said, "The strength of a bear lives in your heart. His courage is in your limbs, Anna-kai. You will be of great help to the men, so listen to them and interpret for them. Only show your strength when you must, otherwise you may intimidate the men." Then she had kissed Kai's forehead and sent her to follow the others. That was the last time she saw her mom.

What did it mean that a bear was the reason she was up this tree now? What would her mother say to that? Was a circle in her life coming around? She didn't want to think about her past any longer.

It had turned over and over in her mind a hundred times too many over the years. *Be strong and brave.*

Kai lowered herself to the next branch and another breeze rustled the trees. She could hear it coming, moving in from the northwest this time. Holding the trunk and waiting for it to pass before continuing her climb down, she was stunned when she smelled the fresh smoke of a campfire. Turning her head, she peered into the forest, looking for any flicker of flame or light. She couldn't see any, but she knew the source must be close. Dean and Badger, she thought.

Encouraged, she climbed a little faster, and only hesitated when she thought she was about ten or fifteen feet from the ground. Pausing, she listened again for any sounds from the bear and heard nothing but the normal soundtrack of the night. Silence, with an occasional brush of wind, a creak of wood, and the distant croak of a frog. She thought she could hear the stream tinkling somewhere to the north. Then she realized that Dean was probably camped by the water.

Uncertain of how long she'd been up in the tree, she hung from the lowest branch and finally dropped to the ground. She quickly searched for the flashlight beam and the water bottle, but couldn't find either one. The light wind continued to come from the northwest, and the smell of camp smoke was unmistakably growing stronger. Feeling positive about finding them, and soon, she followed her nose, and a few minutes later caught a glimpse of a flickering orange flame through the shadows of the forest.

Chapter Seven

Dean unwrapped the lynx fur from around the Dragonfly pipe. He laid it down next to the other items from the bundle, on top of a large piece of red flannel. Every movement he made during the ceremony was precise and with purpose. Every thought that entered his mind had to be in alignment with his intentions. The songs must be sung in the correct order. The dance would be last. For now, he took some of the prepared tobacco mixture out of the elk skin pouch and filled the bowl of the pipe.

He and Badger had sweat and prayed all through the previous night. Sleep had come only after dawn, and they rested in their blanket rolls until Dean woke Badger up to begin the next part of the Night Medicine ceremony.

With the fasting and the purifying of his mind and body, he was probably clearer in his thoughts than he had ever been in his life. It was as if he could see each step he needed to take to complete the ceremony without thinking about it. His hands moved automatically, and his voice rolled through the chanting and singing with a pure heart.

He raised the pipe and addressed the four directions, then handed the pipe to Badger, stem first. Badger lit the pipe with a burning twig from the fire. He breathed in the sacred mixture, and Dean approved of the reverence and respect on his friend's face. With care Badger handed the pipe back to Dean, this time bowl first, as a sign of respect.

"Great Spirit, watch over us and our families. Grant us long, healthy lives. Earth Mother, provide us with the food we need to stay strong. Morning Star, guide us toward a good and honorable life. God of the Night and the great and vast unknown, take us on the journey we seek. Take us to the place where our ancestors wait. Give us safe passage, and allow us a safe return." Dean repeated the prayer four times.

He laid the pipe on top of the bundle and addressed Badger with a solemn nod. Taking his cue, Badger began the song Dean had taught him. He closed his eyes and let the rhythm sway his body. They knew this would be the tricky part. Badger wasn't part of the Lynx Clan, but Dean wanted him to perform part of the ceremony. When he was fourteen, he sang this same song while his grandfather danced. Now it was his turn. The steps were never taught to him, other than by watching his grandfather. Two times. One time to get there, and once more to return. He prayed his memory wouldn't fail him on this night.

With the only light coming from the dying fire, Dean was a dancing shadow around the glowing embers. He conjured the image of a powerful bear in his mind and imitated its lumbering movements with his steps. The chirp of crickets and the singing of bull frogs from the shores of Dancing Bear's Pond added to the night music. His body moved with the highs and lows of the song. Each step was an orchestra of movement, a pivot of heel and toe. The bend of his knee, the dip and rise of a shoulder, the turn of his hip, all in perfect time with Badger's inflections. He danced counter sun-wise for traveling into the past, one circle for each verse, and repeated four times. This was the method Grandfather had used to take them back one hundred and forty-four years.

The unknown outcome of the ceremony hung over the pair like a storm cloud. They knew it held great power, but they didn't know exactly what was coming down on them. With the passing of Grandfather Two Eagles, the chance to have his questions answered was gone forever. Dean did his best to imitate every part of the ceremony the way he remembered it, but with just one misstep, their likelihood at success could be diminished.

At the end of the song, Dean faced the fire with the western horizon before him. Badger rose and began the last steps of their plan. He grabbed the two travel packs and put his on first, then helped secure Dean's over his back. Next, he retrieved the Dragonfly pipe and placed it Dean's hands. He rolled the furs, feathers, talons, claws, and other sacred items inside the bundle, and packed it all under the flap of Dean's backpack, so they would have access to it on the other side.

As Dean concentrated on the pipe, and on the past, he could already feel the shift in reality beginning. The tenuous threads began to shimmer and vibrate. The concentration of the physical world softened like icicles melting under the winter sun. He was vaguely aware of Badger's movements around him, but his focus was centered on finding the place in history where he wanted the ground to hold him up again. He knew that history was there, waiting for them. The story from the God of Night and the Void told his people that all existence ran in spiraling parallels. Movement along the parallels is guided only by willpower and the strength of the cause. Breaking through the illusions, put forth for one's own survival, was the hardest part. The Night Medicine ceremony was a gift to mend the chaos that the god created. It was a way to fracture the illusions of time and space, and slip through both with ease.

Dean heard the hiss and crackle of the fire at his moccasins. Smoke and fragrant steam rose into his face as Badger finished emptying the water skin over the coals. He felt Badger take his place on his left, and then Badger's hands connected with the pipe stem. Four hands held the smooth stem above the spitting steam that rose up from the sizzling coals. Dean sensed Badger's tension grow a little as he became aware of the shift in time, but then his friend relaxed and he was no longer distracted.

The song came from the depths of his spirit. He repeated each verse four times, letting his voice rise into the moonless sky. He kept up the tones and rhythms and sent the call to travel into the inky blackness of the void that surrounded each of the stars. The smoke circled around him and moved in and out of his lungs. A memory of riding a swift pinto on a buffalo hunt called to him. The terror and joy and the exhilaration. The sun glaring in his eyes as he hollered and whooped with the other hunters, in order to scare and torment the herd over the jump. It was the highlight of his last journey. Hunting the buffalo with his friends, his family, and his ancestors. He was ready to do it again.

Dean heard shuffling coming from the underbrush near him. The uncertainty of what time period the sound originated from altered his meditative state of mind, and his eyes opened. If he remembered correctly, as soon as the last verse was sung and the smoke from the fire had cleared, he and Badger should be in the past. But he could still smell the burning pine and cedar. He was losing the efforts already gained by letting his focus shift, and he knew it. The sound came nearer, and he stared harder. The bushes rustled and he saw the black nose, the fur-covered face, and the hulking shoulders of a bear as it approached his fire.

Great God. The beast huffed at him. Its chest puffed as it stared straight into his eyes. Badger must have been far gone mentally, because he didn't even stir. Dean wondered if the Gods had made a decision to be rid of him at last. He stood his ground to accept whatever punishment was coming for him. His arrogance was being struck down. *Who was he to take the Dragonfly pipe back in time? What purpose was he serving by doing so? Was his heart taking the path of selfishness?* He had been struggling with these questions since the moment he accepted Badger's proposition, and it seemed that all of his fears were now being affirmed in doing so.

The bear huffed again, this time rising onto his back feet at full height. He then let his upper body pound the ground not once, but twice, as he threw his paws back to the earth, nostrils flared and mouth chuffing. Dean held perfectly still. The bear raised its head, matching Dean's stance on the opposite side of the fire. A standoff between man and beast, dual spirits of strength and introspection. Dean wanted approval for this journey. *Would the great bear give it?*

A shift in the air breathed life into the dying cinders at his feet. Papery ashes rose from the edge of the fire pit and blew into his face. He felt a sting like a wasp as the ash landed in his eye, and it made him act on reflex as he reached up to press a fingertip to the corner of his lid.

Halfway between the past and the present, the jolt of Dean letting go of the pipe alerted Badger, and his friend became semi-aware of the changes happening in the ceremony. With the two of them agitated, the bear decided this was the opportune moment he had been waiting for to teach Dean a lesson.

The bear charged, crossing the dozen steps to the fire. Badger ducked and swung his pack around, probably in search of a gun, but Dean knew this was *his* test. It was a false charge, and the bear halted before stepping over the fire pit.

With the honor of taking care of a ceremonial pipe came great responsibility. Dean stood his ground and held the pipe before him and the bear. He was letting Great Spirit know he was brave, and he held his place in the Lynx Clan with honor and without fear. In that moment, he felt his personal demons finally lay down to rest. He was ready to move forward, at last.

The bear rose to its full height again and looked at Dean, eye to eye. He could smell its oily fur, and heard the animal breathe. With a swipe of a paw, the bear struck the pipe out of Dean's hand and sent it flying. After a deep huff and gush of hot, musky air from its lungs, the bear lowered to all fours. Badger rose from his crouched position, having given up on retrieving a gun, but instead held a knife in his hand. As he swung in defense, Dean grabbed his arm and stopped him. The bear leaned to its right and twisted halfway around, muscles bunched, before he galloped off into the night.

Dean stood motionless, processing what he'd just witnessed.

"Is this a pipe?" a familiar voiced asked. "Why are you..."

Right on cue, Dean and Badger turned to see who was walking out of the trees. The new moon and the nearly extinguished fire barely revealed the outline of a body.

Badger blurted, "There was a bear."

Fright quickened the intruder's steps. As she neared the fire ring, she asked, "The bear was just here?"

Dean stared at the pipe in Kai's hands. It appeared undamaged.

"It batted that right out of Dean's hand," Badger mumbled.

Dean thought Badger was as muddle-brained as himself. *Were they still in the same time? What was Kai doing here?*

She raised the pipe slowly between them. "You two look really strange. What were you doing, anyway?"

Dean and Badger reached for the pipe together. Their hands gripped the stem. Then the three of them heard the unmistakably gruff roar of the bear. Absolutely petrified, Kai was unable to move as she waited to see if the bear was coming. Dean and Badger exchanged a look just before the last coal in the fire died. The stars blackened, as if a great blanket was laid across the sky, and a vast stillness overtook their very existence.

Chapter Eight

Slightly disoriented, Dean watched as Kai dropped the pipe's stem and placed protective arms in front of her body. She wasn't completely naked. She wore a T-shirt and white socks, but her pants, underwear, and shoes were gone, as history hadn't yet discovered synthetic materials.

Backing away from the others, Kai stumbled over an unseen log and landed hard on her rear end with a shriek.

"Look," Badger said, and pointed at the empty space where the shack should have been.

"We did it," Dean said definitively.

"What's going on?" Kai asked. "What did you do to me?"

Dean was aware of the panic in Kai's voice, but also acknowledged her attempt to suppress it. He stared at the empty space where the old hut would be built sometime in the future, instead of at a half-dressed Kai. He was fairly certain their journey was over. Or just beginning, depending on how he wanted to think of it. He needed a minute to let the truth sink in, but it was a minute he didn't have. He swung his leather pack off of his back and set it down at his feet, reassured that it had also made the trip. His supplies gave him a small sense of security. What triggered his insecurity was scrambling to her feet while trying to hide her bare backside.

"Send her back before she gets us killed," Badger muttered as he set his own pack next to Dean's.

"Send me back?" Kai asked. "What's that supposed to mean? Back to where?"

Dean heard her buried hysteria rising with the tone of her voice. He decided a calm approach would be the best way to handle things.

"That's not going to happen," Dean said to Badger. "Give her your extra pants."

"Give her yours," he snapped back.

"Mine will be too big. You're closer in size. Just do it. Shoes, too. How would you feel if your ding-dong was hanging out in front of her?"

"Proud," Badger answered, but he tossed the clothes over to Kai. "I want those back," he warned.

She slipped on the pants and shoes and walked up to Dean as he squatted down to start a campfire, much like the one they had just been burning in 2012. He thought it was even in the exact same spot. He had a second to marvel at the thought of a century and a half-old fire ring, before he felt his ear being pinched.

He swatted at her hand, and then promptly tipped over from trying to get away from the pain. He caught himself before falling into the grass and forest debris.

"Hands off, woman," he said as his ear flared with stinging pain.

She glared at the pipe bundle sitting on top of his pack.

"Explain everything. Right now!" she ordered.

Dean righted his body and continued to start the fire. He placed a lit match to some dry pine needles and punk wood and blew gently, staying focused so as to not waste a single precious match.

"Settle yourself for two seconds, would you? We'll be here for the rest of the night, and we need a fire."

He wouldn't look up at her, knowing the futility of his words. He could all but see the angry fumes oozing out of her.

"This is a disappointment, Wolfsblood. She's a complication we didn't plan for."

Kai turned on Badger. "Shut up, you stupid pig. What did you do to my clothes? Where is the bear?"

"Can we just put her out of her misery and save us some trouble?" Badger mumbled, more to himself than to Dean.

Dean didn't want to get in the middle of these two, but how could he avoid it? They were standing there because of him.

"Your damn truck broke down, and you need to fix it right now and get me the hell out of here," Kai said, crossing her arms over her chest.

"My truck?" Dean asked, feeling confused for a second.

"That's right. I was driving it back to town, following behind Gena, and it stopped running. The belt is broken," she said, waving a hand through the air. "Now give me my pants and shoes back. I have to be at work in the morning."

"Kai, you need to sit down and let me try to explain some things. And believe me when I say that the truck is the least of your worries, woman."

"I'm not your woman. If you say it again, I'll cut your ding-dong off. Since you like that word," she snapped back at him.

She shot a hostile look at Dean's crotch, and he doubted that she was lying. Feeling the fearful retreat of his cojones, he stepped back from the awakening fire and cleared his throat. Running his tongue around his teeth to moisten his suddenly dry mouth, he settled one hand on the grip of his knife and started again.

"Kai. You're not going to like this, just as much as we don't like having you here."

"This isn't happening. You know what? Play your weird little warrior games on your own. I'll sleep in the truck, and walk back to town in the morning." She shook her head at them as if in denial, and turned for the trees.

"Does time travel cause women to lose their marbles?" Badger asked, sounding almost genuinely concerned. Almost, but not quite. "I mean, didn't we all just feel the darkness come over us? Could she have gone insane without having the time to prepare for this kind of journey?"

"Maybe," Dean said.

"Screw you both," Kai tossed over her shoulder before disappearing into the forest.

"Stop," Dean said, but Kai didn't.

The next sound had Dean rushing blindly after her. Her scream was suddenly cut off with heart-stopping silence. Before he saw her again, the weight of what felt like a tree trunk crashed into him, and he collapsed to the ground. Everything went black.

When Dean awoke, he found himself bound at the wrists and ankles. He heard Kai speaking a language he didn't recognize. He looked for her and saw her sitting cross-legged with head bent in a humble fashion, talking to three Natives.

He met the cold glare of one of his attackers, and saw hatred etched in the hard lines of his face.

The man spoke, and then they all looked at Dean. Kai's eyes tried to tell him something, but it was indecipherable. He wrestled against his restraints. The warrior closest to him raised his tomahawk. The butt end was poised above Dean's head, ready to knock him out again.

Kai reached forward waving both hands, and said something quickly, urgency and panic obvious in her tone. The man lowered his hand to his side.

Dean wished he could understand what they said, but he could only pick out a few words that didn't connect well. The sounds were Algonquin, but different from the Blackfoot of his time. He thought he would be able to speak his native language here, but it looked like he was mistaken once again. *How many ways could he botch this mission? Where was Badger, and why was Kai free? What could she possibly have said to keep herself alive and unharmed?*

Dean wasn't used to failing. He was accustomed to completing assignments with self-confidence and victory. Kai threw him off kilter. A complication, like Badger had said. It was because of her that he lay on the ground, unable to move. But it was also because of her that he was conscious. He quieted his brain and took in the scene with a fresh perspective. Time to analyze the facts.

Three warriors. All armed with knives. He saw two tomahawks, two bows with arrows, and a one rifle. They looked the worse for wear, but in the dim light of the low burning fire, and in a different century, he could have been mistaken. He noticed their buckskins appeared soiled with dirt and possibly blood. He began to see more. One man's shirt had a tear at the seam and a gash on his face, while another one had a bandage tied around his arm. Dean had seen wounded and defeated men before, and these three had the same worn look in their eyes and a drag around their mouths.

Kai started moving her hands as she spoke. Dean recognized the old, universal kind of sign language. Shocked by what he was seeing, he missed the first few signs, but then caught one or two. Traveling and family were the only ones he recognized before she lowered her hands back into her lap.

The man who Dean suspected was in charge looked at him, and then back to Kai. They were silent for a long pause, and then everyone's attention turned as a warrior stepped out of the shadows and into circle of firelight.

He shook his head as if in answer to an unspoken question and then spoke fast. Dean couldn't understand a word the man said. Then Dean noticed what he held in his hands: his medicine bundle. So that meant that Badger had gotten away with the packs, but somehow had forgotten or dropped the medicine pipe. The warrior handed the bundle over to the compact and sturdy-looking man in charge. He placed it down before the fire and hastily removed his hands from the fur wrapping.

Dean controlled his rage with the practice of years of turning off his emotions while in combat. His thoughts turned to action as he planned his escape and the recapture of his family's medicine pipe. He couldn't allow the sacred bundle to be taken. His life meant nothing if his pipe was lost. Dean glanced at Kai and saw the shock in her eyes and her trembling hands. He thought she understood the meaning of this loss as well. Maybe not in the context he did, but at least to some degree.

She began to speak again. The sound of her words and the appearance of the men came together at last in his mind. Nehiyawak. Plains Cree. In Dean's mind, the designs on their buckskins, their hairstyles, and their smaller stature confirmed their membership to the warring tribe of the Piegans. They definitely did not have the physique of Blackfoot warriors. Kai had mentioned her ancestry to Dean and Badger, but he now saw that she was incredibly adept at conversing in the old ways. She held her body with deference to the men and waited for her turn to speak. Dean warned Badger about some of the nuances that would be very different for them, and hoped they would be forgiven for their ignorance. He hoped they could pick up mannerisms and customs quickly by imitation, but Kai seemed to have it down already. He was in awe at her mental strength and fortitude. She was going to need it when they escaped from these four.

She gestured to the pipe and then to Dean. He started picking up some of the words, now that he realized who these men were. He thought Kai was insisting that Dean was a medicine man and that great tragedy would befall them if they didn't let them go on their way.

Like an omen from the spirit world, an owl hooted for all to hear. Dean didn't know what the Cree thought of owls, but he was raised to be wary of them. Owls were often spirits of the dead, and their appearance did not bode well on the psyche. Dean noticed a collective shift away from the bundle laying on the ground.

Dean said in Blackfoot, "Let us be on our way before bad luck falls upon you. The owl has spoken."

He didn't think any of them knew exactly what he'd said, but they grasped the general idea.

The one in charge with his short brow and long beaded earrings spoke to Kai.

After he finished, Kai turned to Dean. "He does not wish to anger the spirits but is afraid if he lets you go, you will kill him and his friends. Because I am Cree and also a translator, he had already decided to let me untie you at first light after they have a head start to leave this area."

"Tell him he doesn't have to worry about me killing anyone as I don't have my weapons to do it with."

Kai translated and waited for a response as the four men came to a decision.

Kai said, "They say you are strong and powerful in body and in medicine. Your magic could easily overtake four tired and weary men. They believe that by showing you good will and letting you go, you will be obligated to give them a chance to get away from here. He said they are in desperate need of rest, and will wait until sunrise to leave."

Dean thought he understood their leader say, "It is settled."

Kai then rose slowly, picked up Dean's bundle, and placed it by his side. She returned to where she had been sitting by the fire.

After three of the warriors settled onto their blankets and furs, and one sat up to keep guard, Dean whispered to Kai. "Do they speak any English?"

She shook her head.

"Who are they?"

She kept her voice low. "Failed Cree warriors. They are trying to return home, but misfortune keeps finding them. I think that is the reason they are afraid of hurting us. They don't want anything else bad to happen to them, especially now that they know what a powerful medicine man you are."

Dean gave her a small nod and shifted positions. His muscles were cramping and ached to be released. The guard watched him closely, but Dean wasn't trying to escape. He would wait and see if they followed through on their promise. Morning would be here soon enough. *Another hour, maybe two.*

"And you're a Cree-Blackfoot-English translator?" he asked with questioning brows.

"Not Blackfoot, but yes. I speak multiple languages."

He could tell she was holding information back, but he wouldn't ask about it right now.

"Do they know about Badger?"

"Yes. They saw him run away, but couldn't catch him. They suspect I am not telling them everything."

"As they should."

He watched as she closed her eyes and breathed. When she looked at him again, he saw fear deep inside her like ice in the bottom of a cavern cracking under the pressure. With cold detachment, she looked away from him, focusing on the eastern horizon.

With the first birds calling from the trees, but before the transformation of the night sky into dawn, the group stirred from their blankets and packed up their sparse belongings. The one Dean thought of as Long Earrings approached Kai and handed her Dean's bone handled knife. Without further exchange, he and his friends disappeared into the clutches of the forest.

Kai scuttled over to Dean and began to saw at the cords binding his wrists and ankles. Unfortunately, she wasn't quick enough. A shot blast, followed by muffled yells, made Kai dive to the ground.

"Faster," Dean said as he struggled to free his wrists.

She almost had his feet free when they heard a whooping victory cry through the underbrush. A second shot made Dean think Kai was going to make a run for it, but she held her ground long enough to finish cutting the straps. She grabbed the medicine bundle and tucked it under her arm.

Stiff and numb from holding the same position, Kai had to help Dean clamber to his feet. Not knowing if it was Badger doing the shooting or someone else, they weren't going to wait around to find out. They made a dash in the opposite direction of the gunfire.

Dean sensed the attack coming before hearing it this time. He shoved Kai out of the way with one arm as he dove under a swinging bludgeon. He tucked, rolled, and immediately came back up on his feet, ready to pounce.

His assailant was swift, and did not allow Dean any chances to pick an angle or strategy before the club was sailing through the air, aimed directly for his head. Dean raised his arm to block the blow as he hurled his body into the knees of the man. He surged upward, throwing the attacker onto his back.

"We are Aamssáápipikani. Name yourself," he spat in Blackfoot as he spun and readied for the next move.

The warrior rolled over in the forest mulch and pulled himself onto his feet. The dimness of approaching daybreak had lightened the sky just enough to see the warrior taking in Dean's muscular build and glance quickly over at Kai, then his face relaxed and he grinned.

"I am Aáattsishaa Mohtóókis of the Aamssáápipikani."

Dean translated in his mind and recognized the words. *Rabbit Ears of the South Piegan.*

"My chief is Running Fox of the Spotted Calf Clan," he said, head held high.

Dean returned the smile. He remembered Running Fox from his previous journey and hoped the chief would also remember him. *Luck had found them.* Rabbit Ears was a member of his tribe.

"I am called Dean Wolfsblood of the Lynx Clan. This is my," he hesitated, not sure how to explain Kai. He hadn't had time to think about it. He could call her his slave, but knowing Kai this would only result in more threats to his genitals. He continued, "She is my wife, and a translator."

Kai coughed and sputtered, as if the mean streak inside her needed any possible exit. Dean feared she would kill him before giving him a chance to explain his reasoning to her. He also noted that even though she said she didn't speak Blackfoot, she obviously understood some of what he'd said.

"I know members of the Lynx Clan and have not seen you before. Tahkáa kinóóhkiitsistowahsina?"

Who are your relations? Dean translated again.

Rabbit Ears had more to say. "Your dress is odd. Your wife wears Napikwan clothing." He looked at Kai with suspicion. "How can I know that you are who you say you are? Do you lie like the Crees we just killed?"

"We have come a very long way. My wife is in need of women's clothes. If you take me to Running Fox, he will verify who I am and who my relatives are."

This seemed to satisfy Rabbit Ears, and he cocked his head in a way that had the universal meaning of *follow me*.

They approached the southern edge of Dancing Bear's Pond, where their passage through time had begun. When the three of them had arrived only hours earlier, the group of Crees had been fifty yards away. No wonder they had come to see what all the noise was during the night. And with Kai making such a fuss, she must have sounded like a bellowing troll.

Dean's wandering attention was smacked back to the present when he heard a struggle going on. He looked over and watched one of the four Cree warriors lose their scalp to a tall Blackfoot warrior. Dean shifted his gaze away from the bloodshed and immediately noticed his pack full of supplies, and Badger's, lying on the ground. A different warrior appeared to be guarding the pile of loot.

He could still hear a scuffle happening somewhere else nearby. He rushed past the trees and into the grass, searching the faces of the men for Badger, dead or alive. He saw a couple of the dead Cree men, and other braves he assumed were with Rabbit Ears. Then he finally saw the struggle going on behind a clump of shrubby cinquefoil.

"Stop!" he yelled and charged the warrior, who was currently holding Badger down.

The man had a knee gouged in Badger's back, and a blade clutched in his raised hand.

Dean's tackle came by surprise, and they rolled in a tangle of leather and fists. He heard Kai screaming something at Badger and then he was consumed as they toppled over into the icy pond. He tried to pull away, but his opponent didn't have the same idea and he felt his face being smashed under the water, into the muck and silt. With strength that only comes from life threatening circumstances, he threw off the man holding him down and launched himself back onto the bank.

"He is a friend of Running Fox," Rabbit Ears proclaimed as he walked over in time to stop further attack from the dripping Blackfoot fighter.

The warrior stopped advancing and plodded out of the pond.

As he passed by Dean, Rabbit Ears added, "The two others are his friends."

"Why were they with those filthy Crees?" the man asked, looking unsatisfied with Rabbit Ears' explanation.

"We were taken by surprise in the night," Dean said as he came to his full height and wiped mud and slime off his face.

Badger walked over to stand by his side. He sported a lump the size of a fist on his cheek, and had a healthy red streak across the side of his neck. Kai edged toward Dean and Badger, staying as far away as she could from the five Blackfoot men.

"She is Cree. I heard her speaking," a formidable-looking man said. His topknot stood high on his head, and his cheeks were painted with black streaks. He was as tall as Dean, and just as muscular.

"She is my wife. We have been traveling for many moons. She is a translator for English and Cree," Dean explained in the Blackfoot tongue.

"English," another said and spat in the grass, as if the word left a bad taste. "You are traders? Scouts?"

The man wore a distinctive beaded shirt and leggings. He was shorter than the tallest man, but had a commanding face and an impressive necklace, made of what Dean thought were probably wolf claws.

"Yes. Both," answered Badger.

"This man says he is a Kainah, but his language is like a white man's," another accused as he glared at Badger.

"He is Kainah, a member of the Bloods. That is true. We have been away for many years. Badger has lived with the White Man most of his life. We have much to trade and many stories. We ask to travel with you to your village to speak with Chief Running Fox."

Badger had been trying to learn to speak the language since they made the final decision to come to the past, but having grown up with only English, he was struggling to make the sounds correctly. Dean could understand their misgivings with Badger's poorly spoken dialect.

The group of five conversed as Dean and Badger exchanged a look and then he directed his gaze to their confiscated packs. Everything they currently owned was inside those bags, except the Dragonfly ceremonial pipe, which was still being held by Kai. Dean reached over and took the bundle from her. He didn't show it directly to the men, but he noticed one or two of them eyeing it warily. It was some form of proof of who he was, no matter what he sounded or looked like.

Coming to a decision, the warriors told Dean they would take them back to the main village on the Plains. Then they let them collect their packs. Dean, Badger, and Kai followed the Blackfoot braves as they retrieved their horses and gear.

"Where are your horses?" one of them asked.

Dean's hesitation was nearly unnoticeable as he explained quickly. "Lost in an accident."

Chapter Nine

On the trek out of the mountains, Dean noticed the four scalps of the Cree men swinging from the belts of the warriors.

"They were members of a Cree raiding party," Rabbit Ears explained. "After two hands of winters, the Plains Cree continue to send their men onto Piegan land. These four warriors ran into the mountains to hide, but we found them."

"They knew we were in need a of scalp dance," one of the others commented.

"War parties happen less and less," Rabbit Ears continued. "We were anxious to pursue them because this kind of excitement does not happen often, and we all want to mark our coup sticks like our fathers and grandfathers."

Dean knew the war path was a fading tradition. So many people died from smallpox and other diseases, fighting with the U.S. government, and starvation, that battling with warring tribes would soon be a thing of the past. He also understood it was a challenge for many of the men to sit around or hunt for food day in and day out while they were being disrespected by other tribes. During this time in history, the Plains lifestyle was changing rapidly, and the People could do nothing to stop it.

"This story started many winters ago. A band of Plains Cree were paid in guns and provisions to lead a party of Napikwans in search of unusual stones the color of water. The pay must have been very high, for why else would they risk such a dangerous trip into Blackfoot territory? The Cree men warned the white investors of the many perils they would face by crossing Blackfoot country and heading into the mountains of the west. The group was heavily armed, and they made it most of the distance to Salish territory before they ventured too close to one of our hunting parties. When our men found them, the trespassers had desecrated a sacred burial ground while looking for those blue stones. We could not let them go unpunished, so our hunters killed everyone in their camp. White men and Cree."

"The Cree warriors were cursed for disturbing the burial place of our chief, Blackhorn Shield. We do not like to enter the places where the dead are buried. They are foolish to keep sending their men onto our lands. We have no choice but to kill them for their disrespect to the Blackfoot people. The four Cree men you saw this day will not make it back to their lodges. It was their choice."

"The Cree Liars keep trespassing on our land and we will keep killing them," said Lone Elk, the man with the intricate beadwork on his shirt and two of the scalps hanging from his belt.

Rabbit Ears and Lone Elk were the only two men to give their names freely. Dean agreed with the practice of being wary of strangers and not saying your name until trust was built. He was grateful to the two warriors for telling him their names and ties, if only so he knew they were Piegans.

"How did you know the trespassers were after the stones?" Dean asked after he was sure they were finished telling the story.

Rabbit Ears continued as the voice of the group. "Our hunters found purses filled with the stones in the white men's belongings. Traveling with our hunting party was the medicine man, Laughing Eyes. He found an injured Cree girl with their group. He said he was instructed in a dream to heal the girl. She was badly hurt. The medicine man and the girl could not continue to travel with the group of hunters, so they stayed behind. When Laughing Eyes returned to our village, he told what he had learned from her. The girl did not come back with him."

A small sound escaped from Kai's lips, and Dean looked over his shoulder at her.

"What is it?" he asked in English.

She stared down at the ground, hiding her eyes, but Dean had already read the distress on her face. She refused to look up at him.

"Do you need to rest?" Dean didn't want her to get sick from exhaustion, or worse yet, start crying. They had to make it to the village. Once they found his Lynx Clan, they could sleep and eat and relax. Then he could talk with Kai in private.

He hadn't had time to adjust his plans since Kai unexpectedly joined their summer expedition. He needed to make some necessary changes. Staying with the Blackfoot tribe on the plains was the most logical solution. *Look what just happened to them in the mountains*. It had taken all of ten minutes for her to be captured, and she could have been killed. At least in the village there would be safety in numbers, and if they really were being taken to Chief Running Fox, they should have a friend as well.

"Kai? Say something," he tried to coax her.

She fell further back from the Blackfoot warriors and their horses.

"I have some pemmican or dried apricots. Would that help?"

He got a glimpse of tears running down her cheeks.

"I can't say right now. Leave me alone."

"I'm sure whatever she has to say will only make things worse. Women can lay it out there just enough to make you feel about as small as a flea," Badger said.

"Go on ahead," Dean dismissed Badger with a wave of his hand.

Badger shrugged, glared at Kai, and kept going. Rabbit Ears and Lone Elk had been walking their horses next to Dean, but now they mounted their ponies after seeing that Dean wanted to speak to Kai alone. The riders passed Badger along the trail heading over foothills of endless rolling green grasses and flowers of every color. Patches of scrub and groves of trees lined the hills while ravines and coulees cracked the surface of the land. The Piegan men kept their pace slow so as not to leave the others too far behind, but the group was spread far enough apart that no one could hear what passed between Dean and Kai.

"Damn it, Kai," Dean said, running his hand over his scalp. "This isn't how it was supposed to happen. I'm sorry, but you're going to have to play my wife."

She stopped walking. Dean watched as she swiped her knuckles across her eyes.

"It's for your own safety," he said. "You probably can't believe this, but I'm ninety-nine percent sure we're currently living in 1868."

Kai looked up, and their eyes met at last. Dean was fairly certain that his head was about to explode — that is if Great Spirit granted wishes to irate Cree women.

"No. That isn't possible."

"I don't understand how you managed to fall into this with us. This is a F.U.B.A.R., Kai. Right here, right now. Do you know what that means? Fucked up beyond all recognition."

She blinked at him.

"Listen, I'm going to do everything humanly possible to get you home safe as soon as the next new moon comes around."

When she didn't respond to any of his words, his reasoning hiccupped with misunderstanding and doubt. She didn't believe him, was his first thought. *How could she?* There wasn't one logical explanation for where they were or how they had gotten there. Hadn't he himself denied the truth of the medicine pipe for years? *How could he explain the God of Night and the Void?*

Kai skirted around Dean and followed Badger and the others. As she passed by him she lowered her tone to a threat. "You will take me back to Trevyn, or I'll find my own way."

Warblers and flycatchers darted in and out of the willows along the creek banks. Snakeweed and rabbitbrush dominated the rocky slopes and gravel banks, while wild flowers sprang from the grass everywhere under their feet. The bitterroot flowers were a constant reminder of Dean's homeland both now and in the future. The phlox, lupines, sagebrush buttercups, milkvetch, and all the rest were so numerous that it became a blur of endless color, growing over the prairie. The white peaks of the Backbone of the World rose like giant tipis resting on top of the grasslands. It was a view he'd seen since he was born, and yet right now it only served to remind him that the world would survive the next one hundred and forty-four years. *But would they?*

He had to make right what he'd done to Kai by dragging her into all of this, albeit unknowingly. Dean felt the weight in his chest like an anchor of guilt. It sank straight to the bottom of his soul, reminding him of his pain from Ellie's death. He was responsible for changing Kai's path, and that could irrevocably alter her son's life. Trevyn needed his mother. It would be Dean's fault if she didn't return to him.

As the sun dipped below the mountain peaks to the west, the village with nearly a hundred tipis came into view. Badger stood at the top of a gentle slope, waiting for Dean and Kai to catch up. The braves rode ahead, making their way down the hill to their home. A young boy ran up to the returning men, greeting them a gapped-toothed grin and exuberant chatter. Dean and Badger stared wide-eyed at the view. Kai stood alone; silent and expressionless.

Dean gave Badger a long moment to absorb it all. Beneath the infinite azure sky, the river snaked through the grasslands like a wet, black ribbon. Most of the lodges stood open to catch a summer breeze. The smoke from the cooking fires rose above the camp, while children played or helped prepare the evening meal. Women and men alike hauled water, wood, or rode their horses throughout the village. Dogs ran in packs or sniffed at pots of cooking food. In the distance, Dean saw herds of horses dotting the plains while the herdsman watched over them with dutiful attention.

Badger grinned like he'd just been given the birthday present of a lifetime. Dean had almost forgotten how to smile until he saw his friend's face.

"Don't wet yourself. We still have to find the medicine man of the Lynx Clan and Chief Running Fox. We could be turned away."

"Even if they do, at least I've seen this with my own eyes."

"Let's go," Dean said, and they started down the hill.

They stopped just outside the village near the river, and Lone Elk quickly returned to lead them to a guest lodge on the edge of the camp. He asked if they would stay near the tipi until the medicine man, Laughing Eyes, had come to visit. Inside, they found a small stack of wood and a blackened fire pit in the center. The inner lining had been taken down for the hot weather and was folded neatly on the ground. The lodge looked like it had been used recently, but no other residents were sleeping there.

Dean and Badger shed their heavy packs and picked places for their sleeping rolls. After spending the entire day on foot, after a sleepless night and an unforgettable morning, food and rest were foremost on Dean's mind. He dug out some of the provisions from his bag and looked around for Kai. She had entered the lodge with them, but was now nowhere to be seen. He decided to let her have a moment alone, and then he would see if she was ready to eat.

A scratch near the door's covering preceded the entrance of an elderly man with silver hair and a round face. The lines around his mouth and eyes were etched deeply into his burnt umber skin, but warmth radiated from his golden brown eyes. Laughing Eyes had come to speak with them. Dean's first question was to wonder if he was a descendant of this man. His own eye color was so similar that it couldn't be a coincidence, but he had never heard of Laughing Eyes in his family tree. *Perhaps the medicine man was a great-cousin or uncle.*

"It is good to see you, Dean. Did Two Eagles journey with you?" the medicine man asked.

"He did not. Last winter, he traveled to the Sand Hills."

"I see you have cut your hair in mourning. I was afraid you would say it was because of Two Eagles. I am saddened to hear of this news."

Dean knew that his shaggy hair would look like he was in mourning. He'd always worn it short, but after he and Badger started making plans for this trip, he started growing it out. His haircut fit the current situation well. He should be in mourning over his grandfather's passing. It was okay that everyone here would know of his loss. But if he was being honest with himself, he'd been too numb to feel most of the pain from the loss of his grandfather.

Dean acknowledged Laughing Eyes' words with a nod. "Two Eagles was a respected man, and will be missed by many." Then he gestured for the elder to sit with him and Badger.

The medicine man laid out a piece of leather, and then placed a fur bundle on it. Dean smiled and reached over for his own bundle and laid it next to its twin. With knowing glances they compared bundles and then smiled at one another. It was the same Dragonfly medicine pipe.

"How is that possible?" Badger asked.

"I don't think there's a good answer to that," Dean said. "If you think too hard on it, you'll only make yourself crazy, like a vexed dog chasing its tail."

"Right," Badger said dubiously.

"We are happy to have you return to us," Laughing Eyes said. "We had many good stories to tell after your last visit."

"It has been many years. I too had many good memories after my visit. I was very young then and remember good hunting, many dances, and horse racing, but not much else."

"I missed much of the excitement because I was needed to sit in council and society meetings for much of your grandfather's stay. I am sorry to tell you in the many years since you and Two Eagles visited, we have not heard or seen anything concerning your mother or father."

Dean held himself in check as he processed what he was just told. It was not even close to what he was expecting. The shock overwhelmed him enough that he couldn't respond. *His mother and father? Was that the reason they had come before? And why was he not told?*

"We must have a council with Chief Running Fox and the others so you can share your news with us."

"I would like that. We have much to share with the South Piegans."

"Because you are of the Lynx Clan and holder of our sacred Dragonfly pipe, I ask to speak openly with you now in private, before the other chiefs and medicine men hear what you have to say."

"Of course," Dean said. "I value your experience on all matters regarding our travels through time. I am afraid that I will not be as respectful as my grandfather was in your ways and will make a fool of myself, unknowingly."

Laughing Eyes gave them a kind and patient smile. "You are doing well right now, Dean Wolfsblood of the Lynx Clan. We are lenient with outsiders who do not know our ways." He looked at Badger without really looking at him and then refocused on Dean. "There are many here who remember you from before. I think they will help the others adjust to your differences."

"Thank you for your kind words. We have one more traveler with us. She is my wife and a Cree. If there is any reason she should not be here, we will leave first thing in the morning."

"Your wife is welcome here and there is no need for worry as long as you are among our people."

"She is in need of women's things. Hers were lost during the journey."

Laughing Eyes looked around the small lodge, taking in our couple of blankets and little else. "I believe the women will bring all that you need for your lodge while you visit with us."

"There is much hardship coming for the Aamssáápipikani and the entire Siksika Nation," Badger said. "More loss of land. The annihilation of the buffalo will come in the next fifteen winters."

Dean tried to interrupt Badger by shaking his head at him. *This wasn't the time.*

Laughing Eyes said, "You come to warn us of many things we already know. I will hear you and then consult with the other medicine men. It is not always wise to know what is coming. Our chiefs will have to decide whether or not to listen to the advice of outsiders."

"But if you can be prepared, then won't it help you for the hard times?" Badger implored.

"You have to try to see it from their eyes," Dean said.

Laughing Eyes looked at them both and added. "I know who you are and where you are from, but many of the chiefs see a fast talking white man in Blackfoot clothing. It has always been a challenge for the Lynx Clan to keep the Dragonfly pipe. It may be a benefit to know what comes for us in the future, but it is also a difficulty. Information that holds little importance to you may be seen as having great value to us and your urgent matters may feel small in this time."

Dean had tried to explain much of this to Badger already. The past couldn't always be changed in the ways someone from the future wanted it to change. Listening to Laughing Eyes, it was easier for Dean to see how their words could easily fall on deaf ears or be misinterpreted.

Badger swallowed the harsh truth and leaned back with resignation. Dean suspected his friend wouldn't give up until he had his say to anyone who would listen. It was becoming increasingly obvious to Dean that Badger's lack of mastering the Blackfoot language was a good thing.

"You have a good sleep this night," Laughing Eyes was saying. "Tomorrow night, please join me for an evening meal in my lodge. We will smoke and discuss all that you have to share with the Lynx Clan."

"Thank you," Dean answered. "We will be honored."

Laughing Eyes' smile reached his eyes this time, showing them the reason for his name.

"Thank you," Badger echoed.

The elder rose, collected his bundle, and left them alone in the lodge.

"I can't believe he won't listen to my warnings," Badger said in English.

"He is listening. You have to be patient, Badge. See us from their viewpoint. Time travel is no different for these people. Most don't believe the story of the Night God is true. Only a few know. Be cautious here," Dean warned. "Scare them with too much talk, and no one will listen to anything you have to say."

Dean watched Badger's knee bounce up and down with pent up excitement. He stopped vibrating as he noticed Dean studying him.

"It's hard for me to be the waiting cottonwood seed. I'm more of a barking dog."

"Go for the seed," Dean said as he put his pipe bundle on his bed and grabbed a strip of jerky and his canteen. "I'm going to find out what happened to Kai."

Chapter Ten

How had this happened to her? Kai needed a moment to breathe. With Dean and Badger constantly at her side, she felt like a captive. In many ways she was, she thought as she wandered closer to the river. It was a nightmare, the likes of which she hadn't experienced in years. Only this nightmare had the added bonus of being her new reality.

She wanted to rinse her hands and face in the water and hoped that a dose of cold river water would refresh her mind. Her feet throbbed from wearing Badger's shoes and she made a mental note to acquire or make moccasins as soon as possible. Soaking her blistered feet may do her some good as well.

Kai noticed the children running and playing around her. Some watched her with curious glances and others were too involved with their games to give her more than a fleeting glance, but she wasn't worried about the kids. It's the fact that she was a Cree woman, in a camp full of Blackfoot people that had her nerves prickling. They were warring tribes, and had been for a century or more.

She watched the ground for plantain growing near the water where it liked to thrive. The crushed leaves would be soothing and healing for her blisters. Finding only a small specimen, she passed it by and kept looking and found a patch of Heal All instead. She plucked a few stems and found a rock to sit on next to the water. Growing right next to her seat she found a larger plantain specimen and picked a couple of those leaves too.

Removing the poorly fitting shoes, and then her socks, she rolled up her pants and soaked her feet in the chilly water and began to rinse off her arms and face. Being all too familiar with the sounds of complaining and whining children from her job at the daycare center, she turned to her right as the noise approached from the willows.

A young girl wrestled a multicolored dog toward the river. The dog thrashed and tugged against its leash, but the determined girl didn't give into the resisting animal. Kai's chest tightened as she imagined Trevyn's immediate response to the situation. She knew if he was here with her, he would be jumping in to help the girl with whatever ministrations she was up to. She held back the tears that wanted to spring up with the thought of her son, and had to remind herself that he was safe with his father and grandparents.

The girl backed up into knee-deep water, pulling the lead rope with all of her strength. Kai watched the resisting, filthy dog and guessed he had been rolling in manure or mud. Maybe both. Then she noticed how the animal held its forepaw off the ground and refused to put weight on it. Even with the injury, the dog was winning the tug-of-war as it made another attempt to either strangle itself or get away. The girl fell down in the river. To her credit she didn't let go of the leash. She jumped back up, soaking wet in her dress, grunting with frustration, but not giving up.

Kai rose from her seat on the rock and approached the girl and her dog. She used hand signs to ask the girl is she would like some help.

The little girl frowned, but Kai thought the look was directed at the dog and the situation more than at Kai. The child answered and tried to gesture with one hand. Kai was able to piece together what she said.

"He is hurt. I made him a special place to rest, but my mother says he can't sleep in the lodge until he is clean."

Kai's talent for learning languages was the reason she was chosen to go with her father and uncle on that final trip out west when she was fourteen. Their family needed a paying job and she wanted to help. The income was supposed to secure their survival for another year. Except Kai's father didn't know he would be paying with his life.

Her experiences speaking to foreigners as a kid were helping now more than she could have ever imagined. It didn't surprise Kai how quickly she was able to pick up the Blackfoot tongue. She wasn't lying when she told Dean that she didn't speak Blackfoot, but there's a difference between being able to speak it and understanding what was being said.

Kai softened her voice and crouched down near the dog. She held out the back of her hand, but the dog was too focused on backing away from the river to pay her any attention. She pointed at the injured paw and gestured to the girl that she wanted to look at it. The girl slackened the lead and came out of the water. Kai used firm hands but made soothing sounds on the animal as she guided him to sit and then lie down so she could examine its leg and foot. She found a thorn and the beginning of an abscess between the pads of his paw. She pointed to the problem as the girl knelt beside her.

Her mouth turned down and sadness filled her rich brown eyes. She said something like, "Sings-to-the-moon is my family's favorite dog. Is he going to die?"

Kai looked down at the manure covered dog and then back at the girl's worried face. She gave her a reassuring smile. The way a child's mind could make a situation completely devastating or completely devoid of interest never ceased to amaze Kai. If life were only that simple, she thought as she took the girl's hand and placed it on the dog's ruff. She gestured for her to hold the dog down and the little girl seemed eager to do as instructed.

As she spread the pads of the paw with her hands, the dog lurched and nearly scrambled back to his feet. Kai put a knee on the animal's chest to help hold him. They were both getting horse dung on them, but they kept the dog from escaping. She used her fingernails and pinched the thorn out of the dog's foot, and then threw it into the bushes. She squeezed the swollen tissue to see if there was a pocket of puss. A tiny amount of clear fluid oozed and then a bead of blood came out of the wound. She didn't think it was infected. She held the leash and backed off the dog. Sings-to-the-moon rolled to his feet and made another attempt to bolt.

"We will wash him," she said as she gestured with her free hand and stepped into ankle deep water.

The girl bounced with joy as she shoved the back end of the dog as Kai pulled him forward. The three of them were soaked to the skin in seconds. The stinking manure washed out of the dog's hair with ease, but clung to Kai and the girl. They giggled as they tried to wash the filth off their hands, arms, and clothes. The girl led the dog to the bank and tied him to a sturdy bush then returned to finish washing herself.

Already drenched from head to toe, Kai decided that bathing in the river was exactly what she needed. She plunged deep under the surface and let her hair flow in the current. When she was cleansed of horse manure and trail dust, she stood and untangled her hair from her necklace. She was so grateful the necklace hadn't disappeared like her pants had. It was the only thing she had from her mother, and she never took it off. She wrung out her hair then stepped onto the bank and let the water pour out of her clothes. As the little girl untied her dog, Kai remembered the Heal All. She walked over and picked it up and brought it over to the girl.

She said the Cree words for healing tea and wash.

The girl looked confused until Kai pointed to the plant and the dog's paw a couple times and made the sign for tea and wash.

The girl said, "Clean like saddle sores," and grinned with joy.

She nodded enthusiastically and tucked the plant into the girl's hand.

The girl skipped away towing Sings-to-the-moon back toward the tipi village.

"You're making friends quickly," Dean said.

Kai spun around and saw Dean watching her from up the bank to her right. She frowned at the thought of him spying on her.

"I thought you could use some food."

She was ultra aware of how transparent her wet T-shirt was, and the knowledge didn't improve her mindset. She also didn't want Dean to know it mattered to her. She hobbled across the pebble-covered beach to get her shoes, socks, and medicinal leaves. She tried to hide her discomfort behind a mask of indifference.

"I am hungry," she admitted.

"That girl just went straight into the chief's lodge."

"That isn't why I helped her," she said.

"I know it's not, but it doesn't hurt."

"Because I'm an outsider, or because I'm a Plains Cree?"

He didn't answer, so she started walking away barefoot and dripping.

"That was nice, Kai. You're all haughty on the outside, but you're kind on the inside," he called out to her.

"Don't start having misleading thoughts about me."

"Spoken like a true, subservient wife."

She stopped at that, and turned to face him. His cocky half-grin at his own joke made her want to punch him. "I will not play your wife. I don't care if they make me a slave, but I will not be a pretend wife."

"Slave it is, then."

She wanted to smash a rock in his face, but restrained the urge. The subsequent humorous twitch at the corner of his lips made her bite back the next threat.

"This game of yours is over tomorrow, Dean Wolfsblood. You're taking me back to that mysterious pond in the mountains, and you will do whatever it is you need to do to make this right."

"It's really not that easy."

She stepped in close enough so that she was nearly eye-to-eye with Dean. "I can't stay here. You heard the story. They kill Crees for trespassing."

"Which is why you're my darling wifey. And I thought you didn't understand Blackfoot."

"I understood enough of the story to know I'm not wanted here."

"For the sake of no one getting killed, can you just try to get along? I spoke to Laughing Eyes, the medicine man of my clan. He said it isn't a problem for you to be here."

"It's a huge problem for me." She began heading back to the lodge, but stopped and added, "Your warrior friends didn't tell the whole story. The Cree have their own version. If these Piegans find out who my relatives are, I'm going to need my own gun."

Dean closed the door flap and lit a fire inside their lodge. The soft glow and crackle of burning wood was more for comfort than necessity. The summer night was cool, but his blanket would be plenty to keep him warm. Two women had arrived shortly after they returned from the river and brought Kai a summer-style dress and moccasins. He gave them a pound of sugar, some of the salt, and one of his knives in return. They also brought blankets, which Kai took as her own, and was now wrapped in them, attempting to sleep in her corner of the lodge. Dean knew she wasn't sleeping well, if at all, but didn't bother her, in hopes that a night's sleep would help improve everyone's attitude.

He thought he wasn't getting along well with her, but when Badger made an attempt to explain what they were doing in 1868, she was even more venomous with him. Badger's tolerance for haughty women was just about nil, and Dean was forced to insert unwanted interference between the two over beef jerky and trail mix.

Dean thought back to his encounter with the bear. He imagined his swift and bloody death would have been more enjoyable than being the middleman between Badger and Kai. Then he told himself that daydreaming wasn't going to get him out of this sticky situation. So far the only solution he had come up with was to ask Laughing Eyes if there was any way for Kai to return to the future sooner. The thought of her son wondering what had happened to his mother was more than Dean could handle. Perhaps they would go back to Dancing Bear's Pond and try for an early return. *Would the Night God allow it?* It was another question for Laughing Eyes, but their dinner with the elder wasn't until the next night. *Could he convince Kai to give him one extra day?*

"I'll ask Laughing Eyes if we can make an early return safely," he whispered in Kai's direction.

She didn't reply or move, and he thought he'd been mistaken that she was lying there awake. Badger snored softly from his blankets, and Dean was envious at the man's ease in falling asleep. They'd been awake for over twenty-four hours since the afternoon before he started the Night Ceremony, but the anxiety over Kai's situation and the excitement of being in the village was keeping him awake.

She rolled over, and Dean saw her doe-shaped eyes on him. The firelight glinted off her irises, and he got that same feeling he'd had before when looking at her. The depth in her eyes didn't match her twenty-odd years. Her shield had more layers of protection than even his own.

"Thank you," she said. "I'm still coming to terms with all that has happened."

"I know it's hard to believe, but you felt it. When we left the future and arrived here. The shift through time. The blanket of the void."

"I did feel it," she admitted. "It would be a lot easier to believe I was dreaming, though."

"You can think of this place as a dream," he said as he stared up at the smoke hole. Stars shone through the gap as he went on, "But you if you die here, you won't wake up, Kai."

She cleared her throat. It was a small sound that blended with the crackle of the fire.

"Good to know, Dean. Thanks for the heads-up."

He suppressed the grin at her sarcasm. "Aren't you tired?" he asked.

"Yes."

"Me too, but I can't sleep either. Will you tell me the Cree version of the story of the gem hunters?"

She rolled over onto her back and raised her knees. Her chest rose and fell with deep breaths. He scooted over closer to her and the fire. Not close enough to touch her, although the thought crossed his mind that she could use him as a pillow and he wouldn't complain, but Kai came across as the kind of girl that didn't want to be casually touched, especially by him. He had not forgotten the way she clammed up at Kinder Place when he'd brushed her arm.

"It will help me understand your worries," he prompted.

"I'll tell you what I can," she said, keeping her eyes on the ceiling of the lodge. "It started before the prospectors came to the Plains Cree. Many men in the Red Hawk Clan and the Long Robes Clan were too fond of whiskey. Some traders knew how to take advantage of the situation, and soon the men had traded away too many furs for little in return. The clans were starving. The men were unsuccessful in hunting, and people were going to die during the coming winter because they didn't have enough food stored away. When the men sobered, they were angry with the traders and went after them to be paid their fair share. They didn't return, and later the wives and elders found out that all were killed. With few options and too many widows and children, the surviving families joined the Many Bear Claws clan. *My clan.* They were starving and desperate, and the following winter was one of the worst in anyone's memory. The chiefs and men did all they could to feed everyone, but still many people didn't survive."

"I'm sorry, Kai. There are many similar stories for the Blackfoot people, too."

He watched her close her eyes. Her hand rose to her throat where she toyed with her necklace. He had noticed the same necklace on her at his cabin and was glad she didn't lose it during the journey. He hoped she hadn't lost any other valuables.

She continued. "When a group of prospectors came in the spring, traveling from the northeast, they were at first turned away, for fear that they were bringing more alcohol, but they had none, and instead brought gifts like blankets, cooking utensils, and food. They said they were headed west in search of gold, but when the men noticed the blue and green stones on the earrings and necklaces of some of the people, they offered to pay a fortune in guns and bullets and rations if the men would show them where the stones had come from. It was risky. They had to travel across Piegan lands into the mountains, near Salish country. The chiefs decided it was worth it because the guns would help them hunt, and the food was so badly needed."

"So they took the job as scouts for what? Sapphires?"

"Yes. Sapphires. My ancestors also knew where there was gold, but they didn't share that information. It was far from home and a dangerous trip, and they didn't take the prospectors until the food was in the camp."

"And what about the Cree girl that Rabbit Ears spoke of? Why did they bring her in the first place, and what happened to her? Do you know that part of the story, or should we ask Laughing Eyes?"

Kai turned her head away to stare at the side of the tipi. Dean noticed her stalling to answer, and waited to see if she would continue.

"The Cree continued to search the Blackfoot land for the missing girl when they could. She was the daughter of an important chief, and had a special gift for finding precious stones. She carried a pouch of the gems and gold nuggets that would make anyone rich if they could find it. The few people that were left of the three clans needed the wealth to survive. They barely did. Many more of my ancestors died when the guns were never delivered as promised. The entire expedition was killed except for the girl. Rabbit Ears said she died. My people never knew what happened to her. I guess Laughing Eyes is the only one who really knows."

"I'll ask him tomorrow if I get a chance. Then you can tell your family how the story ends."

"That won't happen. I don't talk to my family," she said.

"I thought you lived with an aunt or something," Dean said trying to understand her meaning.

"My aunt? Yes, I can tell her. She married a Blackfoot, that's why I live around here, rather than up north. But there's no one else."

"What about your parents?"

"They're gone," she said flatly.

Dean felt the hollowness in her last statement. She was good at hiding most of her emotions, with irritation and anger being the exceptions. But Dean was observant. When he wanted to, he noticed a lot about people. He also paid attention to what people didn't show or wouldn't say.

"I never knew my parents," he said, thinking that maybe if he shared something personal about himself then it would help her relax around him. "A strange thing happened earlier this evening. Laughing Eyes told me that my grandfather was here searching for my parents in the past. I can't believe he never told me he was looking for them. All those years I lived with him, and he never said anything about my parents, other than they were in the Sand Hills with our ancestors. I suppose that's why I'm not sleeping. That, and trying to figure out why the hell you popped into our trip with us, and how we're going to send you home."

She looked over at Dean, then up at the sky through the smoke hole. "Before I smelled your fire, I saw that same bear. It's almost like he led me to you. It gives me a chill remembering how your pipe landed at my feet."

"It's a messed up world we live in when even the bears are screwing with us."

"It makes me think Great Spirit has plans for me that I don't know about, or agree with."

"Yeah," he huffed. "I know what you mean."

Dean added a stick of wood to the almost smokeless fire and then laid a branch of balsam on top to add the sweet incense. The talk of the Great Mystery made him want the sacred smoke.

"Now that you know, are you going to search for your parents?" she asked after another minute.

"You're my first priority, Kai. Then, I don't know what. Badger and I had plans, but now, I'm not sure what's going to happen."

"Were you even planning on going back?" she asked.

Dean laid back on his blanket adjusting not only his body, but also his mind. He wasn't used to talking about himself. His usual M.O. was to turn the conversation around, or just make a joke. He found it unsettling how open his mouth was in the middle of the night, in a world so unlike the one he was familiar with.

"It crossed my mind more than once. Badge and I considered the possibility that we wouldn't return and we're okay with it, but we planned on going home after a month."

"Dean?"

Her whisper was even lower, so Dean leaned over to hear her better.

"What is it?"

"Trevyn is with his father for a few weeks. He'll be back a few days before the next new moon."

Dean chewed on the new information and then said, "I'm glad he's not missing you tonight."

The second time you've lost everyone you love, you think, *this can't be happening again*. Denial becomes a dam in a flooding river of devastation. Days pass in numbness and before you know it, life is continuing on around you. Somehow you've survived, and even started rebuilding a new reality. The horrible stories of your past become something to talk about like it didn't completely shred you to pieces.

But the third time you lose everything important in your life, you begin to see the circles closing around you in a stranglehold. Like the sun and moon chasing each other, for eternity. *The days of light and the nights of dark*. It was endless, and made you feel small and alone as you waited for the sun to come back out. Kai started to believe that night won every round. Her life kept being involuntarily thrust into endless dark days, devoid of any sun.

She lay on her side with her back to the fire, and pulled the blanket up to her neck. The sound of Dean's blankets rustling made her think he was finally settling for the night, too. When she was fourteen she'd lost her entire family, except for an aunt she had never met. She barely made it through her school years, and longed for love and a need to have a family of her own. She devoted herself to adjusting to her new life and getting a good education, but marriage tempted her, and the idea of starting a family won out. Then divorce happened, and the separation caused feelings that were almost worse than death because her ex had survived, but he wanted nothing to do with her. She didn't want Gabe back, either. Their divorce was a good thing, but it stung, and left her feeling alone again. It was Trevyn that kept her from drowning in despair. His constant need for her. His precious voice and face, always looking to her to fulfill his every need and want. Her son was her biggest motivator to make a good life for herself. To not let her loss and defeat define who she was. Her five-year-old needed her for his basic survival, but she needed him for her sanity. After all she had been through, she wasn't sure she could live in a world without him.

Knowing that normalcy and a simple life were never going to be her destiny, Kai had the foresight to make plans for any unexpected future that may fall on her or Trevyn. Now she only had to make sure those plans would come to fruition, whether she was in the past or the future.

Chapter Eleven

Dean woke up to the sound of someone singing prayers to Morning Star, welcoming the coming of the day. He peeked out the door, and it was as if the Sun answered the prayers of his neighbor by rising above the eastern edge of the world and splashing streaks of light through the village. Dean and Badger were eager to meet and greet the people and to begin the talks with the important men and the chiefs. They dressed, ate dried fruit, and drank black coffee. Kai nibbled on some of the food, but rejected the coffee.

"Come with us," Dean said, as Badger opened the door flap.

"I don't want to."

"You can't stay inside all day."

"I can."

"I'd feel better if you stayed in sight, so will you walk with us?"

"No. I'm not feeling well."

Dean gave her one last look and frowned at her obstinacy. He tried like hell not to pay too much attention to the way she looked in her new deer-skin dress. It made her fit in to the time period perfectly, and by wearing it, she somehow looked even prettier than she normally did. He ducked out of the door, frustrated.

Badger left a pile of his gear next to his bed and then shouldered his pack and followed Dean.

"She'll be fine. Maybe she'll soften up if she stews for awhile," Badger said.

His bitterness toward her was already old. "Give her a break, man."

"You're hot for her, aren't you?" Badger accused as he practically glared at Dean.

"More than the pea brain next to me," he said.

"You know why I never married?"

"I'm sure you're about to tell me."

"Women are trouble. Top to bottom, inside and out. I don't need it, or want it."

"Chief Running Fox has three wives," Dean pointed out as they stretched their legs and unconsciously headed northeast from the village, out towards the herd of horses.

"He must be a very wealthy man."

"Must be," Dean agreed.

"I don't know how you could afford one wife."

"I barely could," Dean admitted. He wanted to shut down this line of conversation.

He didn't have to though, because Badger went back to discussing Running Fox. "I can't imagine why any man would want more than one. All of your problems would be magnified. And multiplied. God, it would be unbearable."

"You know you're an imbecile, right?"

"Not when it comes to women. I'm much smarter than you think."

Dean glanced at Badger from the corner of his eye. His friend may be able to memorize the entirety of world history and execute a mission on foreign soil, but Badger had some twisted social views.

"Spend one minute paying attention to the work the women do. They raise the kids, prepare the food, and take care of everything for the lodges, including making them. They tan the hides, and then make the clothes. Having a second wife means an easier life for both of them."

"You know, you're sort of like a wife," Badger said, giving him his sly look. "Always nagging me and telling me I'm wrong. I've read the books. It's not that much different here for women than it is at home."

Dean's tolerance for jackass-ism — an infliction Badger suffered from daily — was a quart low this morning. Having only had about two hours of sleep was most likely the cause, but it could just be that Badger was always an asshat, and Dean was just now opening his eyes to the fact.

"Don't give me that look. You worship the ground I walk on." He looked down his nose at Dean and added, "And you should, too."

Badger didn't say it aloud, but he was referring to an incident in Afghanistan when Badger caught a coordinate's correction that Dean had missed. It saved their squad from entering an area laced with landmines.

"We need some ponies," Badger stated, mercifully changing the subject.

They made it to the crest of a rounded hill with a view that stretched endlessly to the southeast. To the north and northeast were sweeping bluffs, rising from the land like monolithic platforms that effectively shielded the valley filled with horses. Other early risers tended their animals. Herd watchers sat on their mounts or rode the perimeter of the valley. Dean watched one rider lead a string of ponies into the village.

"Do you still want to try trading weapons for horses?"

"We have to have them if we want to make good time finding livestock for sale and be able to make it back in four weeks. And don't tell me we're not going to do this now that the woman is with us," Badger said with critical expectation in his voice that Dean was going to deliver unwanted news.

"When the time comes, just let me do the talking," was all Dean said in response.

"Hey, look over there. That's a nice one," Badger said, pointing to a sturdy, long-legged paint.

Dean appraised the animal. *It was a fine looking horse.* It could easily be one of the tribe's most valuable buffalo runners, but Dean didn't admit it. Instead he said, "Don't get yourself scalped by running off at the mouth. Especially before we have a chance to show what we're bartering with."

"You and Kai must be sisters," Badger grumbled, and then ducked out of the way as Dean threw a fist at him.

Kai did some pacing around the lodge before deciding to have a look inside Dean's travel pack. She knew it was an invasion of his privacy, but she shouldn't even be there in the first place. In her mind, the injustices evened out. Nothing inside the large leather bag interested her particularly. Supplies mostly. Useful things like knives and a mess kit and a compass. She inventoried the food supply and sniffed at the packets of dried plants. She noticed the leather-bound book and was about to thumb it open, but changed her mind about crossing that particular line of privacy. As curious as she was about her time traveling subjugator, she respected him enough to leave it alone. Kai eyed Badger's pile next and was equally unimpressed. She was considering what to do next when someone scratched on the door.

She opened it and stepped outside. A slender woman wearing two shiny braids in her hair and necklaces made from bone beads and shells stood there, waiting for her. The little girl from the day before was next to the woman, smiling and fidgeting. She held a box made out of rawhide.

Kai smiled at the girl and then brought her attention back to the woman. Kai assumed she was the girl's mother. She tried to keep her face humble and friendly.

The woman used sign language and spoke Blackfoot at the same time. "My husband is Running Fox, the head chief of this village. He is grateful to you for healing his best dog. This is a small way to show our appreciation."

She turned to the girl and took the box from her and then held it out to Kai. Kai took the gift and set the parfleche inside the door of the tipi. She said with her hands, "I am honored to help the dog of the chief of these people."

The woman smiled at Kai.

"I thank you and your husband for your kindness in allowing me to visit the Piegans."

"We are honored to have such a well-trained healer and translator come here. My name is Lark-in-the-grass and this is my daughter, Sipi Sootaa."

Kai believed the girl's name translated to Night Rain. "That is a very pretty name," she said. "I am called Kai. I am glad to use my healing knowledge for any person, or dog, in this village. Thank you for the generous gift." She gestured to the parfleche and then added, "I am most grateful for the clothes."

Lark-in-the-grass' eyes crinkled with pleasure. Her smile was small, but genuine. "You are invited to the evening meal and smoke this night at Laughing Eyes' lodge. My husband would be glad to meet you."

Thank you, Kai signed again, and the woman and her daughter took their leave.

Kai went back inside to sulk about the invitation. Now that she told Dean about Trevyn being with his father, they both knew that they weren't headed back to the mountains today. The information had slipped from her mouth. She couldn't let Dean keep suffering from her omission. He didn't want her there with him as much as she didn't want to be there. *Tonight's dinner will be awkward.* She wanted to avoid lying to these people, but she felt that maintaining the ruse might be the only way to not get herself killed or make enemies during their stay.

She reached away from the blanket where she had been sitting and grabbed the rawhide box. She opened the lid and looked down at the gifts. Inside were strips of dried meat, blocks of pemmican, and a smaller rawhide container full of service berries. There was also a leather sheath with an antler-handled obsidian knife. She pressed her fingers to her brows, covering her eyes in an attempt to hold back her rising emotions. The clothes, blankets, and the parfleche were perfect, but now she felt indebted to these strangers.

Kai napped until Dean and Badger returned to the lodge. The fire was out, but the warmth of the day had begun to heat the inside of the tipi.

"It's going to be hot today. Should we roll up the sides of the lodge like the others?" Badger asked.

Kai noticed he had stripped off his shirt. His chest was narrow, but ripped with muscles. He had tattoos on his arm and a Marine logo on his back. Gena's attraction to Badger wasn't for nothing. Unfortunately, he opened his mouth and ruined the visual appeal. *At least for Kai.*

She too had thought that the day was going to be hot, but she wanted the privacy and had left the tipi closed up on purpose.

"That's your job, isn't it?" Badger said to Kai. "The women take care of everything domestic here."

"Stop it, Badge," Dean warned.

"She better try to fit in or she'll ruin everything."

Unable to dignify his remarks without unleashing her hatred of him, she rose and moved to the door. "I'll be going with you to Laughing Eyes' lodge tonight."

"Good. And don't worry. You'll be fine."

"I'm going for a walk."

"Do you want me to go with you?" Dean offered, thinking of her concerns about being Cree in a camp of South Piegans.

"Not particularly," she said and left.

"You've chased her off again," Dean said as he noticed the new addition of the parfleche.

"She shouldn't be here."

"Well, she is. Get over it."

"She's lying to us about something. I don't trust her. And she's too damn good at hiding behind that face of hers."

"She is good at that," Dean agreed. "But you're wrong. She cleared the air between us last night while you were asleep. Back off already."

"I think you're the one who's wrong about her. All I'm saying is, don't trust her with your life."

"And yet she has to trust us to keep her alive and get her back home."

"We don't have to," Badger said coldly.

"Man, you need to cool it with Kai."

"She distracts me. I don't want to talk about the *complication* any longer. Now that we've reached a deal to trade the guns for the horses and saddles, we can start figuring out a way to convince the tribe to add livestock to their horse herds."

"That's right. Stay focused, Badger. We have twenty-seven days, and counting."

Kai's sudden need for a walk had everything to do with putting space between her and Badger Lowell. She didn't want to be surrounded by these strangers, but it was a better option than planning how best to poison Badger. She knew how, but she didn't want her mind in such a sinister place. *How was it possible for someone to needle his way under her skin so deeply?* Kai liked to stay reserved and distant when it came to other humans. It's not that she didn't enjoy being around people; she just knew all too well that becoming attached led to pain and eventual separation. She had learned that lesson early in life, so she was hesitant to let anyone get to know her. Her friends were chosen with care. Everyone else was held at a distance. Maybe that's why Badger reminded her of squatting in the briars. *He was too close for comfort.* Prickly in every wrong place.

Not wanting to draw extra attention to herself, Kai headed away from the village, toward the butte overlooking the valley. From the top, she looked back down at the tipi town. She watched the river bend around the cuts in the riverbanks. The water shimmered beneath the summer sun as it carved through the grasslands. In the distance, a grove of trees and tall shrubs swallowed the river, and beyond that, the rolling vista extended on and on until the sky was the only thing left to be seen.

Kai turned back to the mountains in the west. She loved them and hated them. It was because she had ventured into them that this had happened to her. The temptation of berries and spring water had brought her terror and a trickster bear. *Why couldn't she have just stayed inside the truck?* Gena would have come back for her. Kai was sure her friend had returned by now. *Was a search party looking for her a hundred and forty-four years in the future?*

"We will change your name to Frowns-for-her-future," a man said, suddenly by her side.

It made her scowl deeper.

"Aha," he grunted as if confirming he was correct. "The mountain is not your enemy, Kai," Laughing Eyes said as he stared at the glacial capped peaks.

"They are," she said, and signed with her hands at the same time. "They changed my life in a bad way, like an enemy does. Taking a person away from her family."

"The hardest difficulties in a life are the ones least expected."

"I think trouble finds me in every direction I travel to, and it is always difficult."

"You cannot change who you were born to be. You can only change how you think about yourself."

Part of Kai wanted to drop the wall she had carefully built around her. She wanted to find a way to believe life wasn't out to get her, but her past was always too close to her present. She stared at Rises to the Sun Peak and tried to hold back the grudge she felt against the way events in her life had unfolded.

Laughing Eyes continued, "Do not fear your challenges. Great Spirit knows what should and should not fall into your path. When you are an old woman, you will see that every difficulty led you to a better place than where you had come from. You take what you have learned in this place and bring it to your next place."

"Your wisdom is far ahead of where I stand. I can only see the separation of what I have lost."

"Did you lose something?" he asked.

Kai stood still and stuffed her emotions back where they belonged. *How could this man understand what she had been through?* She thought their perspectives were so entirely opposite that she couldn't answer. Besides, she was fairly certain it was a rhetorical question anyway.

"I will learn from you something new," he asked her. "Tell me what it is like in the future. What will you share with me that I should know?" He settled onto his heels and watched the mountains with her.

"Life is as much the same here as it is different. Family, food, shelter, clothing have the same importance, but the way you acquire these things is vastly different. Some things are easier and some things are much harder. People are the same. Some things never change."

She watched the elder for a change in his expression, but he only stared into the distance.

"I have a son, but no husband. It is the reason I need to return home as soon as possible."

"Your son is alone?"

"He is not alone. He will be taken care of, but I need to be there with him. He is small and will not understand my disappearance."

Laughing Eyes nodded understanding of Kai's dilemma. "There is no replacement for a mother."

"No, there isn't." She paused and studied his distinguished profile against the summer backdrop. "Can you send me home, Laughing Eyes?"

"Traveling with your companions by the same way you came will be the safest path, Kai. Your son needs you to come to the correct place and time. Angering the God of the Void could bring harm to your family."

She was afraid of this answer, or one like it, and now she knew she would have to wait out the month with Dean and Badger. She felt defeated, and now even more depressed after speaking with the medicine man of the Lynx Clan.

The older man must have sensed her distress, for he said, "We speak more. Come. I will give you a medicine plant to heal spirit sickness, and you will tell me more about the future."

Laughing Eyes walked down the sloped side of the butte, heading for the river, and let Kai decide if she wanted to go with him or not. Without hesitation, she followed the medicine man toward the cottonwood trees, and began to share her thoughts about what it was like living in 2012, compared to 1868. If they could find the plant he mentioned, then perhaps she would even begin to feel better.

Service berries and huckleberries were served as refreshments before the main course inside Laughing Eyes' lodge. A stew of buffalo meat, nodding onion bulbs, and other root vegetables were cooked in a large pot over the fire. Running Fox, the head chief of the village, and his first wife, his sits-besides wife, Lark-in-the-grass were in attendance, along with Lone Elk, one of the hunters that had found them in the mountains. A prayer of gratitude, coupled with the request of long, healthy lives for the people and their children was said by Running Fox before they ate.

The chief then took a small piece of food and buried it in the ground by his feet as a way to give back to the earth, and everyone at the party did the same. Two other women, sisters of Lark-in-the-grass, helped cook and serve the food. During their dinner, Dean learned that Lone Elk was also a medicine man. Not as skilled or renowned as Laughing Eyes, but he was there to listen and learn. After the stew was eaten, Dean gave Laughing Eyes and Running Fox each a thick knot of tobacco. The tobacco was passed around and smelled with appreciation. The anticipation to try the new variety was evident all around the group.

Dean gave Lark-in-the-grass the rest of raw sugar and some of the salt he had brought. She looked pleased and thanked Dean for the rare foods. Badger gifted one of his knives to the chief and then shared famous quotes with them. He wrote them down on sheets of paper from his journal and gave them to everyone in attendance. It was a novelty. They particularly liked the words from the Great Father in the East, Abraham Lincoln, who had only three winters earlier been assassinated. It was these words that captured their attention the most, *"I leave you, hoping that the lamp of liberty will burn in your bosoms until there shall no longer be a doubt that all men are created free and equal."* Badger's gift had high entertainment value to their hosts. Dean translated the verses four times before they moved onto a new subject.

Then pipes were brought out, and the smoking commenced.

"You are pleased with your new horses?" Running Fox asked.

"It was a fair trade. I am very happy," Dean said.

"What you do not know is that Kills-many-bulls was recently asking the trader about acquiring a new colt pistol of the same kind you brought," Lone Elk said.

"It would have been good to know that before we completed the deal," Dean said, giving Lone Elk a playful frown.

"If you would have waited but a few moments longer, I would have gladly told you as Kills-many-bulls has been very difficult to trade with recently."

"I see that you still have bad feelings over your past dealing with Kills-many-bulls," Running Fox said to Lone Elk.

"I am feeling much better about my dealings after today," Lone Elk said with a grin.

Dean said, "Now I understand why you secured such a good bargain for our saddles, harnesses, bags, and blankets." He looked to Running Fox and added, "We are outfitted like very rich chiefs, thanks to Lone Elk."

They both looked to Lone Elk as the man puffed on the end of his short pipe. Satisfaction and humor showed in his eyes and in the twitching of his lips.

"The horses were already traded for, but I arrived in time to make sure Dean and Badger had good saddles," Lone Elk shared.

Running Fox and Laughing Eyes both looked pleased about Lone Elk's help. Dean was also more than grateful for the assistance. He hoped he could gift the animals to Lone Elk when the month was over.

"We will be leaving the village soon to take care of necessary business. Which leads me to one of the reasons we have come to visit your camp. I have an idea that I think will benefit you and your people, if you will permit me to share it with you."

The couple of sentences spoken from Dean on a more serious topic caused the women, who had been smoking with the men, to rise and take their leave. Business would be conducted with only the men.

"If Kai could stay. She may have something important to add since she travels with us," Dean said.

"Yes. I agree, if it pleases her," Running Fox said.

Kai sat back down on a mat on the lodge floor.

A scratch on the door flap interrupted Dean from starting.

Laughing Eyes called out, "Oki!"

A tall native man wearing white man's rough travel clothes stepped inside. His braids were long, his face was mature but not elderly, and his nose had an impressive hooked curve. He removed his hat and waited to be invited to join the group.

"John Winters. You have returned early. We are glad to see you. Will you smoke with us?" Laughing Eyes said, and gestured to the willow backrest that Lark-in-the-grass had been using.

Dean, Badger, and Kai watched the visitor as he took his place by the low burning fire.

"We have much to celebrate this night it seems," Running Fox said to Dean, Badger, and Kai. "John is a scout and translator of high esteem in the Blackfoot territory."

"It is good to be back with friends," John said as he accepted a pipe and smoked.

His words were sincere but it was clear that something troubled the man. His face looked haggard with worry lines around his eyes and tightness around his mouth.

Kai rose and stepped out of the lodge.

Dean wondered if she only needed a personal moment, or if she was finished socializing for the night, even though she was asked to stay. He was genuinely surprised when she returned a few minutes later with a dish full of stew.

She handed the food to John Winters who accepted it with thanks. Then Kai took her place on Dean's right, like a Piegan wife would. She was so fast in picking up the customs and the language that Dean wanted to ask her where and how she had grown up. He added it to the list of things he was curious to know about her.

"I can see you have something you would like to share with us," Laughing Eyes said.

"It is so. I do not wish to interrupt this night, but since I am leaving again in the morning, I wished to have council with Chief Running Fox."

"It is a fine night to smoke and relax with friends. I am glad you came to us. This is Laughing Eye's clansman, Dean Wolfsblood, his wife, Anna-kai, and their travel companion, Badger Lowell."

Running Fox's accent on the English name, Lowell, came out slightly choked, and Dean thought the distortion he heard was probably much the same way the others heard Badger try to speak Blackfoot. Dean snuck a glance at Kai, surprised that the chief used her full name. She had never mentioned it to him.

"You may speak openly in front of everyone here, as we are all trusted friends."

John Winters sat his dish aside and took a deep breath. He rested his hands on crossed legs and frowned before he spoke.

"There is much happening in the far east and south. There is still reconstruction after the war, and this keeps the White Father very busy. But what troubles me is the talk of men shooting the buffalo and only taking their hides. Sometimes they do not even take that, but leave the buffalo to rot upon the ground. The trains are killing many buffalo also, and there is talk of a new train coming this way in a few more winters. With more and more homesteaders moving to the Snake, Crow, and Salish territories, the hunting grounds continue to grow smaller and smaller. They travel in long wagon trains, as far as a man can see. They fill the towns, searching for their gold dust. They have made deep grooves in the prairie that will never grow back over with grass because they never stop coming."

John paused and looked at each of them in turn.

Then he said, "Some of these homesteaders and gold seekers eat the buffalo, but there are men who shoot them as if it were a child's game. These men are the reason I sit here with you. I saw whole buffalo lying dead in the grass, three days ride south and east from this village, and came to speak of it. I know many are traveling to the Sun Dance camp, but I will tell all the villages I can as I continue on my way to the white man's town of Helena. I am finished."

The pipe was passed as the men and Kai took their time to think over the new information. Badger all but elbowed Dean in the ribs with his agitation. What John Winters shared was much of the same information that Dean was already planning to say.

Finally, Running Fox broke the silence. "This is information that I will share with all the chiefs. Are the Snakes continuing to fight in their war with the soldiers and homesteaders?"

"I have heard that many more Snakes and soldiers have died in the last four moons, but it is coming to an end soon. Too many have died, with no resolution on either side."

There was another silence and then Badger said to Dean, "Tell them what Colonel Dodge said."

Everyone's attention turned to them as they waited for Dean to translate. It was difficult to say aloud, but this was one of the reasons they had come.

He stiffened. "There is a Colonel in the White Father's army that said these words: 'Every buffalo dead is an Indian gone.' It is documented. This murder of the buffalo is happening far to the south in a place they call Kansas. There are men shooting the blackhorns as fast as they can. It is a travesty that in the end will be as bad as, or worse than, the red sickness and the pox for the Siksika and Piegan people."

Laughing Eyes said, "This is the same thing your grandfather has spoken of. We would like to believe the promises made to us by the government agents, but you say the devastation is still headed to us."

"There are good agents and many bad ones. It is of great importance to not rely on outsiders and prepare as best you can so our people will not go hungry," Dean tried to convey the seriousness of the coming situation with every syllable. "When the buffalo are gone, the Blackfoot tribes will suffer horrendously."

"And you have a new way for us to avoid the coming hardships?" Running Fox asked.

"I would make the suggestion that you acquire many sheep and whitehorns. Add them to your herds of horses. The sheep and cattle will graze alongside your horses, and your herdsmen can watch over them at the same time. It is not one answer that will save the People from suffering, but this idea could save lives."

"I have heard that the Dine people keep sheep on their land," John says. "The meat is not as tasty as buffalo or our big horn sheep in the mountains, but it is better than starvation."

"The sheep's wool can be used for making warm blankets or will be good for trading. The cattle can be bred to make large herds that will keep you in meat for many winters. The whitehorns and the sheep are not as sturdy as the blackhorns. Extra care must be taken during the coldest storms of winter. If you keep them gathered together in a sheltered location, like the horses do naturally, they will survive the freezing temperatures."

"We will have to have a council with the others before a decision can be made," Running Fox said. "It sounds like we may want to try to keep these animals. Is it not a concern that our dogs may find them good for eating, more than our people will? How many of these sheep will we share with the bears, wolves, cats, and coyotes before they become a burden to us? There is much to consider with this new idea."

"You are correct in your concerns about animal attacks, but there is not a lot of difference from caring for your horses," Dean said.

"The dogs could be a problem, but I have seen trained dogs protect sheep from wolf attacks," Kai added.

"That would be a better use for the packs of dogs running around our village," Running Fox said with a look of appreciation at Kai's insight.

Lone Elk handed the pipe, bowl first, to the Running Fox. The gesture with the pipe signified the man's role as chief. Running Fox laid it down in front of him and then addressed everyone in the lodge. "It is almost time to move the village for the Sun Dance. I will call a council of all the chiefs and share this distressing news from John Winters and my guests. You are all invited to travel with us to the Sun Dance encampment."

"I will not attend this year. I have made a commitment in Helena and will not be back before it is over," John Winters told them.

Laughing Eyes and Running Fox turned to Dean, Badger, and Kai.

"We accept your invitation, but we are also traveling. We will come to the Sun Dance if we can return in time," Badger managed to say in only slightly broken Blackfoot.

"This year's Sun Dance is hosted by the Little Plume Clan, and will be on the north side of Antelope Butte," Laughing Eyes told them.

"I understand that you will consult the other chiefs before making a decision, but we do not have much time to accomplish many tasks. If we have luck purchasing sheep and cattle in the forts or the towns, will you accept them as gifts for the Piegans?"

Laughing Eyes answered first. "Running Fox cannot make this decision alone, but I am not a chief, and I will accept the animals under my care if the others do not want the responsibility."

"It is kind of you, Laughing Eyes, to take this on. We do not want to cause distress in your village. Our prayers to Great Spirit are that the People live long and healthy lives."

John Winters stayed while talk continued of trespassing hunters, mining, wagon trains, and the clear cutting of the forest around the mining towns. Dean and Badger shared how the local history plays out over the next century, and did not hold much back. They were cautious not to sound outlandish to their hosts, and stuck mostly to topics that Mr. Winters could confirm.

As the night progressed into the late hours, John Winters took his leave with the need to be settled after a long day of travel. Kai, feeling the stress of the journey and the lack of sleep catching up with her, bid the men goodnight, thanked Laughing Eyes for a nice evening, and went to her lodge. Lone Elk and Running Fox also left for the evening.

With only Laughing Eyes, Dean, and Badger remaining, the last topic to be discussed was the Dragonfly medicine pipe.

"Kai has come on this journey with Badger and me by mistake," Dean said.

Laughing Eyes placed some of his own tobacco mixture into a pipe that they had not yet used. He took a small tool made of bone and tamped the tobacco down inside the pipe's bowl. With a twig set alight in the glowing embers of the fire, he lit and smoked the pipe, letting the puffs of smoke waft around him before he spoke. "How do you know she is not to be here with you?"

"I do not know for certain," Dean admitted.

Laughing Eyes passed the pipe to Dean. Compared to what they had smoked earlier, this mixture tasted bitter and seared his throat.

He let his lungs clear and then swallowed before saying, "A bear visited us during the finishing prayers of the Night Medicine ceremony. I was certain the bear was sent to us because we had angered the God of the Void. It was confirmed to me when the bear swatted the pipe from my hands. Kai picked up the pipe and we were brought here together. She has a son who needs her. We would like to know if there is a way that she can take the path back before the next darkening of the moon. I am finished."

Laughing Eyes closed his eyes and sat back against his willow backrest. Dean took the moment to reflect, as it appeared that Laughing Eyes needed time to think. Badger fidgeted in a nondescript manner that was not entirely obvious, but made Dean feel anxious nonetheless.

They exchanged a glance, and then Badger left to go relieve himself. Laughing Eyes came back to the moment and added a fir bough to the fire, sweetening the air inside the tipi. At the late hour, the temperature outside was cool against their bare skin, but inside the lodge, the warmth radiated from the coals just enough to take the chill off.

"Do you believe Kai is your first concern while you are here in this time?"

"I thought it was so, but the way you speak makes me think that I am missing something important."

"That may be," he said and his usually smiling eyes seemed to change in the low light of the lodge. He looked somber now. "The spirit of the bear sent Anna-kai with you. That is clear to me. I would like to think more on this situation before saying anything further. It is your heart, Dean, that needs healing."

He stared at the smoke rising from the fire. "My heart has been wounded. It cannot be repaired."

"Your doubt in the healing path has led you to drink the white man's water."

"It shows that clearly to you?"

"I see the signs on you," Laughing Eyes said.

Dean didn't want to believe it was so obvious. "I quit drinking alcohol two moons ago." *Would he always have the 'signs' of someone who drank too much?*

"That is a struggle which you may battle for many winters. If you fight hard enough, you will win."

Dean couldn't look at the elder. His shame was staring him in the face.

"Before your journey home, you come to me and I will heal the sickness that lives in your heart. This will ease your battle with the white man's drink."

"Like you, I must think on it before I can say any more." Dean didn't want to commit to a healing ceremony yet. He was feeling better about his past, and he was proud of himself for resisting beer over the last ten weeks, but he wasn't sure he could totally let go of everything yet.

Laughing Eyes sucked on the end of his pipe and then exhaled a long stream of smoke. "I know Anna-kai is not your sits-besides wife. She will make a good wife for you one day, but you must both be free of haunting spirits before this will happen."

"She will not be my wife. We are too different."

"You look at her like she is already yours."

"Looking is not everything."

"First you look. Then you imagine her in your furs. Then you become her husband."

Dean tried not to smile at Laughing Eyes' simple and accurate account of finding a wife.

"You said we are both in need of healing. This may or may not happen."

Laughing Eyes looked at Dean as if to say, *of course you will be healed.*

Dean sighed and then said, "Kai is like finding the sacred paints along the river. One must dig through many layers of earth to find the true colors beneath."

"You understand her well, Dean. She understands you."

"I think I have just scratched the surface. I'm not sure I should dig any deeper."

"What you say is true of most women. If you give it time, the rain, the wind, and the changing of the moons will expose what is beneath the surface. Perhaps you will be there to see the colors. Perhaps the colors will run into the river for no one to see."

"I don't know if I can wait for her through the seasons, or even through one moon. When I am home alone, it is a struggle for me."

He swallowed. Alone at home was when his mind turned against him. It was when he thought about his old life and when beer became an easy option.

"A woman in your lodge would cure this problem," Laughing Eyes said with a wink.

How had their talked turned to this? He asked the question he first intended. "Is there a way to take her back before the next new moon, Laughing Eyes?"

"The spirit of the bear guides her clan. If the bear wants her here, I would honor him."

"She has a son."

"Kai has told me this. The risks are great, Dean. The God of the Void may take pity on you. He may not. Would you risk a young mother's life for an early return?"

"I would not take that risk."

They smoked in silence for a time then Laughing Eyes said, "Your Kainah friend has a strong name."

"He does," Dean agreed.

"Many healers carry that name with them. They force the healing into their patients and make the sickness leave the body. It is good to have an aggressive healer so sickness does not grow strong roots within the body. It is not so good when the aggression is turned toward harm and malice."

Dean had not ever thought of Badger as malicious. He had strong opinions that he openly shared, but Dean always thought Badger was an honorable and reasonable person. Laughing Eyes passed the pipe once more and he smoked it as he thought about Badger. He was enjoying the pace set by his host for their speaking time. There was no rush. No need to be asleep because of an early drive to work in the morning. There were no clocks here. The sun and moon were the only timekeepers, and Dean fully appreciated the lack of pressure inside the lodge. The tobacco they smoked seemed to be clearing his mind in one sense, but also fogging it. He was aware of the subtle change coming over him, and thought it was relaxing him further.

"He has a strong personality that matches his name. It drives him to succeed in battle, and he has a clever mind as well."

"It is a worthy combination that will earn him many coup and a long life," Laughing Eyes said. "His thinking may be the harm behind his strong animal spirit. He would make a more useful healer."

"He knows nothing of plants or healing the spirit. He is a trained warrior where we live."

"That is unfortunate," Laughing Eyes said. "Tonight we dream on it. Tomorrow will bring answers. If no dreams come, the Sun Chief will guide us."

>><<<

"I don't know what you think you're up to, but you'd better come clean before one of us gets killed."

"Get your hand off me!" Kai said as she ripped her arm free from Badger. "I don't have to tell you anything I say or do."

She started back to the lodge, unsettled by having been seen speaking with John Winters, and because it was obvious Badger had followed her to question her in private. If Badger could read the sign language she had been using, she'd be up to her eyeballs in accusations.

He reached for her again, this time not letting her slip out of his grasp. He towed her roughly away from any lodges and deep into the night's shadows.

With his face close enough for Kai to feel the moisture from his breath and smell the tobacco on his skin he said, "Dean might be interested in knowing why you were asking about the town."

So maybe Badger knew a few signs after all. Either that or he lied about not knowing. *How much had he seen?* Shortly after leaving Laughing Eyes' lodge she noticed the scout, John Winters, talking to some men by a campfire. She went to her tipi, but her thoughts kept nagging at her so she left again and went to find John and asked to speak with him. The light had been low and flickering. She had wanted to be clearly understood and made sure her hands were seen in the amber glow. Badger must have been looking closely to see her signs. The other men around the fire were not so rude as to look upon a private conversation, but that wouldn't stop Badger.

"I could slit your throat in the middle of the night while you sleep," she said with a chilling calmness. Her free hand slipped down to the handle of the knife tied at her waist. She was bruising beneath Badger's grip, but she wouldn't back down.

Badger narrowed his eyes and then flung her arm away with distaste. "I won't have you jeopardizing my plans because you can't keep your mouth shut. Did you tell that man anything about us?"

"What would I say to him? That I've been kidnapped from the twenty-first century by an asshole and an alcoholic?" She moved away from him and wrapped her arms around herself.

He snorted at her remark then hissed, "Then why were you making the sign for the town?"

She raised her hands in the air and signed, *I hope a herd of buffalo tramples your ugly dog face*, and then she watched his reaction as she recrossed her arms.

He sneered. "Dogs?"

"Get away from me, or I may make good on my threat."

"I knew the Cree blood in you would show itself sooner or later. You're well known for being a bunch of backstabbing, thieving liars."

Kai slapped his face. She was done with this. *Done with him.*

Badger didn't return the strike like Kai expected, but the hatred in his eyes glowed hot, as if a lodge fire burned inside him.

"Go ahead and slap me again. Make sure your husband sees it. I'd like to see how the wives are punished here. And Dean whipping you would be just the kind of entertainment this place could use."

"Shut your fucking mouth," she said as she raged far beyond rationality.

"I think one of the men over there saw what you just did. Morning may bring a walk of shame through the village with you leading the parade."

He sounded so pleased with the idea that Kai almost gave in and slapped him again, or better yet, kicked his balls all the way up to his teeth where he could choke on them. She held back and gritted her teeth until they ached. Having to pretend to be Dean's wife was the pinnacle of absurdity in this whole nightmare. *She didn't have any other choice though, did she?* She was obviously not a Blackfoot, while Dean and Badger were. *What other story could they have told that would explain why a Cree woman was traveling with them?* She didn't want to be a pretend captive. Of the two of her traveling companions, Dean was by far the only reasonable option she had. If she had to act like Badger's wife, she would slit her own throat on the spot.

"I'll find out what you're up to. You can count on it."

"Don't think I can't see through you. Is Dean in on it with you?" she said, and lifted her chin. "I don't believe he is, but maybe he'd like to know what you're really up to."

"Nice try, you conniving shrew. You don't know anything about me."

Kai caught the tiniest flinch of uncertainty at the corner of his eye. It gave her the confidence to keep going. "I've seen your type before. Bent on righting every wrong ever done to us Natives. Revenge for our sickening history. Murder for every last General and whiskey-pushing trader. You're not the first destroyed man I've ever seen. It only took until we arrived here for me to see what you're really about."

Hatred exploded behind his burning glare. Kai wanted to run. *What was she saying?* He could kill her and dispose of her body in the river. Instead he settled himself, squared his shoulders, and taunted, "You sure know a lot about it, don't you Anna-kai?"

Chapter Twelve

With the dawn came the disappearance of Badger and Kai.

Dean opened his eyes and saw a cold fire and an empty lodge. His body was up and moving before his mind could catch up. Rolling his blankets into a jumbled pile he stared at the barren sleeping places where Kai and Badger had been when he had come in last night. Not only were their beds missing, but so were Kai's new parfleche, and all of Badger's belongings.

Could he really have slept through their waking and emptying the lodge? And the dreams he'd had. Even now his mind was half-filled with visions of buffalo lying dead on the prairie and burials of great chiefs among tree branches.

He nearly tumbled out of the lodge as his rifle caught on the door and threw him off balance. The saddle and tack in his arms might have made an interesting cushion to land on, but he corrected himself and stayed upright. His neighbor, whom he had not yet had the chance to be introduced to, watched him with part suspicion and part humor in her eyes from next to her morning cooking fire.

He asked, "Is there a boy to help me retrieve my horse?"

Damn Badger to hell if he took his horse, too. But he thought not. Badger may be an arrogant bastard, but he wasn't a thief, and the trading that happened yesterday was fair for the both of them. They had even split the difference in acquiring a horse and bridle for Kai.

The woman smiled, set her utensil aside, and walked into another lodge. A gangly teen-aged boy appeared from the door flap of a painted lodge. He jogged over to Dean carrying a length of rope and a horsehair bridle. He was bright eyed and bushy tailed, at least in comparison to Dean's burning dry eyes and dragging ass.

"I need my horse as quick as possible. Tall bay with a white blaze." Dean ran two fingers down his forehead as he described the white mark on his horse's muzzle.

"I know your horse. Come. I am the fastest horse wrangler in the village."

He let out a sigh as they hurried past the other morning risers and toward the herd.

"Your friends left at first light with John Winters."

Dean looked over his shoulder at the rising sun. *It couldn't have been much more than an hour or two before now,* he thought. *What had he smoked with Laughing Eyes that had him sleeping so hard and with so many dreams?* He knew nothing toxic or mind-altering had been involved. It was only the company, and the environment. He was comfortable here. He had let himself relax, and slept well without ghosts taunting him. The price of relaxing, even for a few hours, had brought him to this. Dean's mind scrambled for answers as he tried not to explode in a rage with the knowledge that he had been ditched. *And by Kai? What in the world would drive those two to leave him behind?*

"Did you see what direction they went?"

He pointed south confirming what Dean already knew. John Winters said he was heading toward Helena.

The boy whistled a distinctive, sharp call and a pinto mare came running straight out of the herd to her rider. He fed her something green from his hand and slipped the bridle over her head. Gripping the base of her mane, he jumped on bareback and took off at a trot into the wide valley of horses. The boy's hands worked at a lariat as his legs directed the horse. True to his word, he retrieved Dean's bay stallion within minutes. Dean was no slouch when it came to horses, but he knew when to be impressed by another's handling skills.

The boy dismounted, grinning wide and bright. Dean clapped him on the shoulder and shook his head in appreciative disbelief. "Best riding I've ever seen," he said.

"That was nothing. You should come to the Sun Dance and watch the games. There you will see fine riding."

"I'd like that. If we return in time, I will watch for you."

"I am called Catches-many-horses." His smile spread wider. He didn't boast or act prideful, but Dean could tell the boy had confidence. He held the lead rope so Dean could saddle his mount.

"I am grateful for your help," he said, and handed the boy one of the knives he brought for trading.

The boy accepted the gift with awe in his eyes at the steel blade. It was a generous token of appreciation for something Catches-many-horses would have done for anyone without payment.

"Safe journey to you," he said as Dean settled into the saddle.

"May Great Spirit favor you in the games," he said, and clicked his tongue as he urged his horse forward.

Leaving the village behind, he saw Laughing Eyes standing at the top of the butte above the village. His arms were raised to the great Sun Chief. He held his fur-wrapped medicine stick above him. Dangling feathers caught the morning breeze as he sang to the Above Ones and to Wind Maker. Dean knew that the medicine man was asking to keep the summer storms away so he and his friends would have clear passage to the south. Dean felt gratitude toward Laughing Eyes, and added his own pure thoughts for a safe trip to Helena and back.

With the sun on his left, Dean rode hard until his horse had sweat running down his shoulders and flanks. The animal needed time to cool down. Dean slowed and then stopped so the animal could drink from a creek. He swung down to fill his canteen and eat a few bites of dried meat and cranberries from the stores in his backpack. He'd forgotten to bring the packhorse and hoped Badger had her. After long gulps of water, the horse raised his dripping muzzle, sniffed at Dean, and then attempted to bite clean through his side. Dean jumped back with only a slight nick in his shirt.

"What was that for?" he said as the horse threw his head to the side, lips quivering like he was trying to tell Dean about his distasteful buckskin.

He jerked the horse's bridle and brought the horse's eye to level with his own.

"We're together in this for many more miles, so no horsin' around."

Not a willing participant, the horse snapped at Dean's collar and earned a swat on the nose. His not so faithful steed pulled back, nostrils flaring and snorting with contempt, but the beast didn't bolt. As Dean decided his horse's name should be Man Eater, he remounted the wicked beast, staying respectfully aware of the location of the animal's teeth.

"Just what I need. Somebody else who wants to bite my head off."

Man Eater agreed by whinnying a chest-rumbling *halloo* from the creek side. In the distance, an answering neigh told Dean he'd found his deserters.

He spotted five horses and three riders heading south across the prairie. As far as he could see to the north and south, foothills climbed to the mountains in the west. Rivers and streams cut passages through the landscape, with occasional draws and ravines to add depth and variety to the miles of grassland. A group of antelope paused from their grazing to watch Dean and Man Eater trot past.

It was close to mid-day by the time Dean found them. He was already too warm in his leather shirt, and wanted to take it off. He saw that Badger already had, but he wanted to catch up with the group first.

John Winters rode in the lead. A wolfish-looking dog trotted alongside him and his horses. John's tall-crowned felt hat stood out against the blue sky and the mushrooming clouds that formed over the peaks. Badger's buckskin gelding fell in behind John's packhorse. Dean understood why his friend had chosen the animal. They looked comfortable with one another already because the animal was strong spirited like Badger himself. He was leading their sorrel packhorse. Dean reaffirmed his choice in her as he watched the strong legs and sure footing of the mare. She should be a dependable animal for their month long journey. *If Man Eater kept up the biting, he might trade horses.* Kai brought up the rear, riding the chestnut paint mare they had selected for her. The mare was of even temperament and well broke, with older but healthy-looking teeth, and was perfect for just about anyone who didn't need too much excitement. As Dean approached, he watched Kai. They had only been able to acquire two saddles, so she was riding bareback and using only stirrups and a bridle to control her horse. He had been planning to offer her his saddle, but it looked like that wouldn't be necessary. Her seat on the horse looked natural. Kai once again surprised him with her easy adjustment to life in the nineteenth century.

As he rode closer, she noticed him first. There was no shame or remorse on her face for leaving him behind. She only turned back around and faced forward. Dean didn't even see her mouth move to let the others know he was coming.

He reached for his rifle contemplating knocking Badger off his horse with the butt end of the stock.

Before he said or did anything rash, Badger greeted him. "Glad you decided to join us."

John Winters looked back at Dean with steady eyes and a calm understanding of the situation. He spurred his horse forward, increasing the distance between Dean and Badger.

"Are you?" Dean asked, feeling his blood pressure rise.

"Hey. It isn't my fault you were sleeping like the dead," Badger said, instantly on the defensive.

"What are you saying? Why did you leave me?"

"We tried to get you up, man. Ask her if you don't believe me." He waved a dismissive hand toward Kai.

Dean barely glanced at Kai. This was between him and Badger. After all of their planning, Badger shouldn't have left the camp without him for any reason.

"I knew you'd catch up if you wanted to be here."

"What sane person does this?"

"Someone who doesn't want to lose his only guide. John agreed to let us ride with him, and he was leaving this morning."

"You have it all figured out, don't you?"

"Of course I do."

"And what about you?" Dean threw back to Kai. "You couldn't wait for me, either?"

She gave him the cool glare that said everything and nothing, all at once.

"Get your breechclout out of your butt and get over it. You found us before lunch, just like I knew you would."

"Assholes are made of badger skin, you know that?"

"I've been told that's the case."

Dean ground his jaws, pulled Man Eater to the side, and fell back. Man Eater, displeased with the rough steering, twisted his head around and tried to bite Dean's leg, but his rider was already getting used to the horse's antics and missed the nip from those long teeth. The fickle horse only served to increase Dean's irritation. He spurred the animal in the ribs and drove him farther away. Plenty of distance between him and Badger right now would do everyone some good. They had many more days ahead of them, and grudges would only make life miserable. *He needed to cool off, both mentally and physically.* He stripped off his shirt and tucked it into his saddle pack along with his aggravations.

Their shadows upon the ground were but small puddles beneath the noonday sun. Dean watched the play of light in the different grasses as they waved in the breeze. He watched for the next stream or river, or anticipated what lay over the next rise. His mind continually compared the landscape surrounding him with what he knew of home: where a road would later be, or a ranch, or how many trees had grown in the next century. He noticed an entire section of pine forest along the Big Horn Creek that didn't exist in his time.

Hours passed with little or no conversation. No one seemed to mind individual solitude amidst the group's trek. The steady rhythm of hooves against ground and the rocking sway in the saddle worked on Dean until all he could think about was how his body would look after being molded into the unfamiliar shape of the saddle. An upright, bow-legged toad came to mind, but that was probably being generous. It had been years since he'd spent an entire day riding.

John Winters appreciated the quiet. He liked the efficiency of these travelers. No one asked to stop for a break, and they kept pace with him well. He noticed they had an odd manner of speech and dress. They appeared to be of the People, but they didn't match his version of any Native group he had ever seen. Being a scout since he was a young man, he'd seen just about every tribe and many varieties of whites, even some Chinese, but these three he could not place. John didn't mind the differences and wasn't being paid to ask questions, so he kept these thoughts to himself and stayed quiet. Trading with Badger for a Colt revolver was his payment to take the three to Helena. *He was pleased with the arrangement.*

Eager to make Helena in four or five days, they rode until just before dark, and then found a place to camp. Dean checked the horses, avoiding the front end of Man Eater, and decided they were faring much better than he was. Badger looked as stiff and sore as he felt, while Kai and John appeared none the worse for wear. He wondered if Kai was better off because she didn't have to break in a saddle, and contemplated riding without one the following day. As Man Eater raised a rear leg to kick the packhorse standing perilously close to him, he decided that riding the stallion bareback would likely be suicide. He threw out the idea as he led Man Eater away from the others and hobbled him alone, next to the stream.

They ate some roots Kai had dug up and roasted in the coals, along with some strips of smoked buffalo. It was settling comfortably in their stomachs when John offered his tobacco pipe and a story.

"Two young warriors set out to hunt antelope so they could have new hunting shirts made of the soft skin. It was during the red moon, and a good time to hunt antelope. They found a group grazing near the base of the mountains, and one of the young men readied his bow and arrow. As he was about to make his kill, his friend yipped and howled like a coyote. The antelope ran away before the first arrow flew."

The three of them listened to John Winter's story as the fire sizzled and whispered of buried moisture inside the wood.

"'What was that for?' the young hunter asked as he turned angry fists on his friend. 'You made me lose my shot.'

"The other hunter answered, 'The antelope is too easy to hunt. My mother can kill one with only her skinning knife. I want mountain cat fur to keep me warm in the coming winter. Let us go into those mountains and kill one. The whole village will know what great hunters we are if we bring a big cat home.'"

John paused to take a smoke from his pipe. Dean knew that boasting was a sure fire way to have your world explode in your face. He waited for the story of the two young hunters to turn for the worse.

John went on. "The young hunter had prayed to the Sun for success in killing an antelope and he wanted the meat and the skin, not fur from the cat.

"The boastful friend said, 'We are not far from Many Caves Rocks where mountain cats have always lived. Have your antelope skin this winter while I keep warm in the furs of the big cat.'

"The foolish young brave mounted his pony, howled like a wolf, ensuring that the antelope continued to run farther away from them, and then headed for the rocky slopes in the distance. The young hunter was angered by his friend's actions, and afraid that Great Spirit would punish them for turning against what they had prayed for. But he was loyal and valued his friendships, so he followed his friend toward the mountains.

"When they reached the cliffs, they had luck and found the tracks of a big cat. Leaving their horses behind, they followed the prints and discovered a recent kill. The remains of a deer lay a shallow place within the rocks. Knowing cats would return many times to eat their kill until it is gone, they were very excited that they would only have to sit and wait for the cat's return. The young hunter began to think that Great Spirit had smiled down on them after all. The two braves found a good position so they could see their horses and have a view of the deer carcass. With arrows ready, they waited for the mountain cat, but it did not return.

"As night came closer, a group of Salish riders rode out of the forest. They spotted the two horses and recognized the painted marks on the horses as being Southern Piegan. The men approached with caution and were ready for battle. The two hunters knew they were outnumbered and would likely be killed and that their supplies and horses would be taken.

"The two Blackfoot hunters tried to defend their honor and scrambled to change positions. They shot at the Salish to protect their horses, but they were too far away for much accuracy. The mountain cat then appeared. The cat jumped onto the boastful young hunter from a rocky perch above their heads, and bit through his neck, causing instant death.

"The other brave shouted out in surprise, and let an arrow loose on the cat. It shot wide and only angered the beast. The cat hissed and swung his claws at the young hunter, ripping the bow from his hands. He backed into the rocks and pulled his knife as the cat advanced. He thought that Great Spirit had tricked him into the tight spot and was punishing him, so he began to pray for pity and forgiveness. He inched to his left and felt empty space behind him. The hunter wedged himself into the crevice, knife slicing the air in front of him. Then he heard yells from the Salish men and saw arrows flying toward the cat. The mountain cat retreated and leaped onto a boulder, and forgot about the young brave hidden inside the cave.

"The night was cold and lonely, but the young hunter stayed hidden until morning, not wanting to be taken or killed by the Salish. He believed that Great Spirit had spared him. With shame heavy in his heart, he had to return to his village with no horses, no weapons, no antelope, and no friend by his side.

"During the first night of his walk home, he slept in some long grass next to the river and had a dream. His dead friend appeared, and said, 'I am not allowed to enter the Sand Hills until I kill a mountain cat. I need its fur to stay warm in the winters of the Sand Hills. You should come back with me to Many Cave Rocks, and then we will share the new fur.

"Disturbed by the appearance of his ghostly friend, the brave said, 'I will not return to Many Caves Rocks with you, for surely I will also die, and then I will be denied access to the Sand Hills like you.' The young hunter left his bed in the grass and ran all the way back to his village."

John finished his story and leaned forward to add a piece of wood to the fire. He said, "The boastful young brave still hunts at Many Cave Rocks for his cat. He is a ghost in the Shadowlands, and many people say the ghost of a big mountain cat prowls through the rocks, taunting him with its yowls and hisses."

John Winter's dog whined from somewhere in the dark. A long, low whimpering, for no apparent reason. Chills crept over Dean's scalp and down the back of his neck. He raised his canteen and guzzled some water. He had heard other stories meant to scare the daylights out of children, and adults too. But in the flickering firelight, the tension around Badger's eyes and in his shoulders was worth hearing this one again and again. Dean thought Badger looked like the ghost had just whispered secrets in his ear.

Dean held back the teasing remarks and said, "Many Caves Rocks are the ones we passed before sunset?"

"That is the place," John answered, and then lit his pipe.

Kai pulled her blanket tighter around her shoulders. "You can hear the cats if you listen closely," she said while staring at Badger. "They come down here to the creek for water if it has been a dry summer."

He gave her an icy glare, which made Kai perk up more than Dean had seen all day.

"Badger is a smart man if he wants to stay away from the ghosts of the dead," John said. "It is an old story, but I will not be hunting cats in that place."

"I won't be, either," Badger said. "The only hunting I'm going to do is for the black space behind my eyelids. Goodnight."

"Don't let the ghosts keep you awake all night," Dean threw out to him, and watched Badger's jaw stiffen.

"Same to you," he said. Badger laid back, feet to the fire, head on his saddle pad, and wrapped in his blanket, leaving the conversation.

John followed suit, and a minute later, his dog appeared from the hidden depths of the night, curled up next to his legs, and closed its yellow eyes.

Dean looked at Kai, but she wouldn't meet his gaze. He wanted to ask her why she didn't wait for him this morning. *Why she was being so quiet? Did she need anything?* He didn't ask. He thought she wouldn't give an honest answer in front of Badger or John, anyway.

"Do you mind sleeping out in the open?"

"It is what it is," she said as she lay down on her side with an arm curled beneath her head. "The trees are nice."

He looked at the lofty canopy of branches over their heads. He'd never been here before, but it was still so familiar. Many summer nights growing up he slept outside beneath the trees. He liked that the brightest stars still found their way to him through a thousand leaves.

"Only when it becomes dark enough can you finally see the stars," he said, thinking of something he once read. It seemed to fit Kai's somber tone.

"But it only takes a few clouds to block their light."

"They still exist, Kai. Even if you can't see them, or won't look for them."

"I guess we see what we want to see."

Chapter Thirteen

Uninterrupted wilderness for miles on end filled the next day's ride. It was as if the four of them were the only people left in the world, and Dean liked the feeling. As the hours grew long, he began to think about a fire and an evening meal out of the saddle. Then John Winters lifted his curved nose and pointed to an overlook.

"The herd has moved," he said.

In Dean's opinion, only the vast and immeasurable ocean was comparable in the way his soul was affected by the sight before him. Their vantage point from horseback along the rise allowed them to take it all in. Thousands of buffalo were scattered across the valley below. Most of the animals had their heads bowed to the grass. Calves nursed from their mothers or romped with their friends, kicking up dust as they raced over the fertile prairie. The animals were at ease as they drank from the river or ate the lush, sweet grass that grew along its banks. The sight of the beasts grazing beneath the cloud-dappled sky and the musky smell of animals and manure and trampled earth planted a memory within him. One to keep, like the way his grandmother saved flowers tucked between the pages of her books.

Dean thought about the sketchbook in his bag. How he would like to camp here and spend the evening capturing the lines of their broad shoulders and wide skulls. The swish of buffalo tails and the angles of stone as the buttes dropped to the valley floor. The sweep of the curling river, and always the light and the shadows as the Sun danced over the land. *The scene would make a fine drawing.*

"Did you hear that?" Badger asked, interrupting Dean's moment of peace.

All he could think of was how he could hear hooves clacking against the river stones, or the massive, hairy bodies shifting about, or the way they snorted like his Uncle Robert when he had a head cold. "Hear what?" he asked as he turned in his saddle to look over at Badger.

"I heard it," Kai said, and reined her horse to move away from the overlook and back down the slope they had ridden up.

"Shots," Badger said, and angled his chin to the southeast.

Dean blinked and directed his focus toward the direction that had Badger's attention. They heard two consecutive shots. They were distant, but distinguishable. He couldn't see the source from their distance, and the herd didn't sense the alarm. *At least not yet.*

"Rifles."

"There's more than one shooter," Badger said.

"Probably. Let's go," Dean said, and took the path to follow Kai.

Seeing a herd was on his to-do list while they were here, but it wasn't a necessity. He felt fortunate that they had found one on their way to Helena. If their errand went smoothly, maybe they could even manage a hunt before they had to be back to the beaver pond below the Thunderbird Peaks in twenty-five days.

John Winters had continued riding at a slow pace while they watched the herd. He said that by tomorrow they would reach the Sun River. Today they were on reservation land. Dean looked around him at the expansive countryside and thought it was a confusing injustice that if they had arrived five years later, they would no longer be on Blackfoot land. He could only imagine what the natives thought about the continual division of property lines. It was as intangible as trying to sell the air, which he supposed the government would do if they could figure out a way to profit from it. Under the guise of the greater good, of course.

While catching up with John, they heard another round of shots echo over the plains.

"I'm going to see who it is," Badger said.

"Stay out of it," Dean warned.

"It's probably a hunting party."

"Why go nosing around, then?"

He shrugged and waggled his brows. "I'll find you later." Badger loosened the straps around his rifle and laid it across his lap before riding east toward the sound of gunfire. "Unless you're a lucky S.O.B and I get lost," he said over his shoulder.

"Crossing my fingers," Dean said, and held up his right hand, fingers crossed, but making sure his middle finger stayed slightly more erect than the others.

Badger appreciated Dean's sentiment with a smirk and then kicked his pony into a gallop.

"Now's our chance to cut and run," Kai said from atop her horse.

He couldn't tell by her flat expression whether she was serious or not, but if he had to guess, he would say she wasn't kidding. "Is that what you told Badger yesterday morning?" Dean threw back at her.

"Do you want me to say yes? That I was trying to get away from the single person who has the ability to get me home to my son?"

"You're a mysterious woman, Kai."

"Don't ever forget it."

Dean actually saw a shimmer of humor around those lovely lips, but he also noticed the warning embedded in her eyes.

Stopping for the night did not bring Badger's return, as Dean had hoped. They had been riding southeast, looking for a shallow river crossing, and found one about two hours after Badger had rode off to find the source of the gunfire. The buffalo herd was so large that from the top of the last hill they rode over, they could still see some of the animals moving in a northerly direction.

John Winters picked the camp location, saying he had used it many times in the past. Dean agreed it was a fine location, with available firewood from some old pines and good wind shelter behind the dogwoods and the bank of the river. It also meant that Badger wouldn't easily find them, especially in the dark. *Where was he?*

"I'm going after him," Dean told Kai and John. "If I can't find him fast, I'll come right back and he can join us in the morning."

John stopped unsaddling his horse and said, "I ride when the sun returns. I do not wait for you."

"I understand," Dean said.

The dog that John called Philip, which sounded more like he was saying "Fed Up", looked at his master and half howled, half murmured agreement with the new situation. Philip turned his golden gaze to Dean, and all but nodded for him to get out of there.

"Coming with me or staying here?" he asked Kai.

"I'll ride a bit longer, I guess," Kai said, turning her horse and the packhorse to follow Dean.

It didn't take too long for them to back track and find the problem. *The view wasn't pleasant.* From a distance, they could see the dark fur mounds of bodies lying scattered around the base of a fifty-foot rock wall.

Knowing he was running out of daylight, Dean rode Man Eater at a gallop, straight to the hooves of the dead buffalo.

The scene was wrong in every way he could imagine. *Where were the hunters? The women butchering? Anyone?* He tried to make sense of it as he counted the carcasses. At least fifteen mature animals, and three calves. He looked at the steep cliff above and briefly wondered if the buffalo had jumped, but the tracks in the trampled earth showed they had been cornered and shot. They had all bled out. Every one of them had bullet wounds, including the young ones. And yet there were no guards watching out for predators during the night. He saw no fires to indicate that anyone else was around.

He looked for Kai. She watched him from twenty yards back. He circled Man Eater around and headed north past the bodies, following the tracks of surviving buffalo. Kai followed behind, not voicing her opinion of what she saw.

Three more carcasses littered the way. Four, if you included a still-struggling calf. It had been shot in the hind quarters, and was unable to stand, but had not died. He had to keep his composure as he climbed down from the saddle. The baby flailed against the ground, its front hooves clawing the dirt and ripping the grass in an attempt to rise and get away from Dean. Blood matted its fur and flies took advantage of the free meal. Its breath was labored. The fear in its eyes tore Dean to pieces. He sent a prayer to Great Spirit to give him strength.

Dean had prepared for this trip and what he wanted to do, but now decided he didn't want to be here anymore. Any relaxing thoughts or feelings of peace were now extinguished. Great Spirit, Sun chief, Napi, all of the Above Ones knew he had killed before. *A warrior fought for his tribe.* Dean signed up at age eighteen to defend his land, his home, and his people. He could put personal feelings aside and execute orders given to him. It wasn't personal. It wasn't pleasant. *It was a job.* By the time he had left the government's war, he wore honor in the form of badges on his chest and stripes on his shoulder.

"And Plato said, 'You should not honor men more than truth.'" It wasn't until he was out of the Marines that he let himself feel the legitimacy in the quote, taught to him by his grandfather.

Dean pulled the trigger of his pistol and put the calf out of her misery.

Seeing the body relax and go limp should have eased his tension, but his training kept him sharp and alert. The Marine in him wouldn't let him do anything but complete the mission. *Find Badger and destroy the enemy.*

He remounted Man Eater, avoided a bite on his shin from the surly horse, and looked for where the shooters must have been. They had cornered these animals. It wouldn't be hard to find their location.

They rode out of the gulch where the buffalo had been driven and Dean pointed so Kai could see the vantage point on the hillside. Then he steered Man Eater to the site.

A rocky precipice atop the hill had a clear view of the narrow valley below. The location had become the final resting place for two anonymous buffalo hunters. He looked at their bearded faces and pink skin, and knew Badger was the shooter. One lay face down, shot in the back. The other one was askew in the grass, gripping his rifle, and had been shot in the throat. Dean hardly stopped to inspect the corpses. There was nothing he could do for them. Finding Badger was his first priority.

He looked at the possible lines of fire, and then rode toward the most likely position that Badger had ambushed these two men from.

He found horse tracks across the hill and behind some tall brush. It's where he would have fired from if it had been him instead of Badger. Deep divots in the ground showed where a horse had galloped away, downhill and to the south.

"They went that way," he said to Kai with a nod in the direction. "Go back to John Winters. If I'm not back in the morning, stay with him. You can trust him, and pay him anything he wants from our trade goods to keep you safe."

Feeling his urgency, Man Eater snorted, pranced in place, and fought against Dean as he gave the orders to Kai. Dean loosened the reins, and they were most of the way down the hill before she answered.

Because Kai was leading the packhorse, she was unable to travel as swiftly as Dean, but she kept them moving fast enough to not be left totally behind. She caught up to him at an empty campsite about three quarters of a mile from the shooting. She slid off of Mayberry and began a closer inspection of the wagon, bed rolls, and camp sacks.

"Go back," Dean said.

"I'm not leaving you. Tell me what you're thinking so I can help."

"Look at the fire. It's still warm, and their stores were left out. Someone was here. I followed Badge's tracks and found another set. They were headed this way. I think whoever was here saw Badger and started shooting. Badger's horse isn't shoed. His tracks are easier to recognize. He didn't make it this far."

Dean moved to a trampled area in the grass where there were fresh piles of horse manure. He stared at the ground then pointed.

"Pretty certain whoever was here followed him, or made a run for it."

Kai squinted into the darkening horizon. "We're running out of light, but I think that's another body out there," she said, grimacing into the distance.

Dean stared hard and saw what could be a man in the grass. "Get on that horse and go back to John Winters, Kai. This isn't a game."

"I know it's not. And you know what else I know? If Badger is injured, I'm the closest thing you have out here to a doctor."

He felt the muscles in his back bunch with frustration as he jumped back onto Man Eater.

"If you get shot..." he started to say but couldn't finish. *It was unthinkable.* He jerked his horse's bridle too hard, and Man Eater reared in protest. Nearly falling out of his saddle, Dean leaned forward and fisted the reins. His horse stayed in high gear, and they raced off toward the next body.

Kai did a fast once-over of the camp. She took a canvas bag filled with food, a knife lying by the fire, and left everything else behind. *Dead men didn't need to eat.* She didn't have any guilt in taking it, but she wasn't foolish enough to steal anything that could implicate her later, either. The knife was simply made, just a steel blade in a wood handle. It could be useful, or dumped easily if someone questioned her about it. She galloped after Dean.

She saw him pause long enough to check the body on the ground to make sure it wasn't Badger. As he headed southwest, she followed, having no need to stop and look at another dead body. She's seen too many already.

Becoming a nurse meant she would help the living, and that's where her training stopped. Cree superstitions about being near the dead ran strong through her clan, and she couldn't ignore them. These men, whoever they were, needed to be put to rest, but Kai certainly wasn't going to be the one to do it. Let their families provide a proper burial, she thought, even though she knew the wolves, buzzards, and coyotes would most likely take care of them first. Their spirits would have to find their own way. She wanted to get far away from them, fast, before the spirits realized that she was nearby.

Dean felt hyper-vigilant as he followed the trampled grass, shrubs, and roughened ground of a fleeing horse and rider. The body he passed had a gunshot across the ribcage, leaving a bloody tear in his shirt, but the killing blow had been a stab wound to the kidneys. He looked at the unmoving chest of the white man, appraised the damage, and kept moving. The day was settling quickly into night now. The moon was beginning to turn toward its first quarter, but it was still holding back much of its light. If he didn't find Badger soon, it could become a very dark and painfully slow search.

He couldn't lose Kai, either. The headstrong woman wasn't turning back to stay with John Winters. Aware of her following him across the open stretch of the plains, he tried to keep one eye on her while inspecting the dimming landscape. The buffalo must have crossed this area earlier today, because the earth was now stamped with a million hoof prints. With the sun long fallen behind Three Sisters North and Slategoat Mountain, the gray light had nearly faded to charcoal black. He strained to see the circular divots of horse hooves among the cloven shaped buffalo prints. He had to slow way down, and Man Eater flicked him with his long tail like a whip, urging him to pick the speed back up.

Dean's mind created a map of the territory they had crossed. He imagined the river where John was camped in the valley, and estimated it to be about an hour's ride west and a few degrees south. Dean was heading south now, and he wondered if he'd reach the river before finding Badger. If he lost the trail at the water's edge in this light, he would be forced to wait until sunrise to resume the search.

He checked for Kai and saw her far behind him. He clenched his teeth. *She should have gone back when he told her to.* As he turned back around, he noticed off to his left the craggy shadows of stunted evergreen trees and thick brush. Pieces of the puzzling pursuit locked into place like he'd been given the key to a map in his head. He knew if Badger was still alive, he'd gone that way.

Slowing to nearly a stop, he signaled with his hands for Kai to stay back, and then let her know that he was going over into the trees. He waited to see if she would obey this time. She pulled up on her horse and actually stopped.

He entered the growth of scraggly trees and watched for signs of Badger, his horse, or anything suspicious. Then he heard the tumble of water over rocks, and he realized a branch of the river passed through there. With his hearing muffled from the flowing water, his other senses became heightened. He and Man Eater picked a careful path around a thicket of brush, and almost landed on top of a rifle holding stranger.

Both parties were equally surprised. The man took aim at Dean's chest. Dean didn't bother raising his hands in surrender or lifting his weapon. He saw the intent in the man's eyes, like death was the only acceptable place for any intruding Indian. He dove off of Man Eater as the burst of exploding powder shocked his eyes, and the deafening blast reverberated in his bones. Man Eater cried out and reared, his hooves slashing the air wildly. Then the horse countered by bucking and charging forward, toward the attacker. Unfortunately, one of Man Eater's rear hooves caught Dean's upper leg as he was wrestling free of the brush he'd landed on.

"Arrrrgh!" he screamed as Man Eater's missile-propelled hoof collided with his tender groin.

Breath was stolen from him as shock and pain hit hard. His mind tried to ascertain whether or not Man Eater had just relieved him of his family jewels. He was too distracted and slow to stop the next attack. Human flesh slammed into him. His base instincts to stay alive kicked in, and he gripped his attacker, forcing them both to roll out of the bushes and across the rocky ground. Meaty hands pulled and slammed into him. The blast of a gun sent a shower of broken stones and dirt into his face. He jerked his head back reflexively to avoid the debris kicked up from the gunshot and missed a fist colliding with his face. He swung, nearly blind from all of the rolling, into the blur of the oversized body. His fist finally connected with a scratchy jaw but the man didn't relent.

"Your head is about to come off your shoulders," Badger yelled.

Dean was too busy protecting his own face to see where Badger was standing, but he knew he was close.

"What's stopping you?" the man taunted back.

Dean started to believe he was fighting a giant. He couldn't make any progress at releasing himself from the man's grip. The next thing he knew, his body was being swung around and an arm wrapped around his neck, crushing his windpipe.

"Let go of the stranger, and let's finish this," Badger said.

The man spit a gob of bloody mess on the ground, letting Dean know that he'd gotten at least one good punch in.

"You're both as dead as those buffalo, half breed. I'll snap your friend's neck, and yours after."

The man started to drag Dean toward his own fallen gun. Dean finally got a clear look at Badger, standing slightly downhill by some twisted pines. Badger shot as the man tried to bend down and retrieve the pistol. He aimed at the man's hand, because Dean was blocking most of his attacker's body. The bullet hit the revolver's grip instead of the man's hand, forcing the gun to fall back to the ground. Dean kicked the man while trying to tear his arm away, but the attacker only grunted and tightened his hold as they both stumbled forward. Dean could barely breathe, and he knew he would black out soon. He lashed out with his heel and connected with a shin, but the man must have been made of stone, because he didn't even flinch.

"Kill him and you're a murderer. You'll hang for it," Badger tried again to secure Dean's release.

It didn't work.

"I'm not under any pretenses you're gonna let me walk away from here. Besides, no one will care if there's one body or two," he growled as he backed into some scruffy bushes. "I'll either be the one riding out of this or I'll be meeting my maker."

He pulled Dean down to the ground again, searching for the cast off pistol. Dean wondered where the rifles were. *His or his attacker's?* Badger stared into Dean's eyes as if he were trying to tell him something. In the dark, he couldn't tell if it was a command to react or to play along. Dean didn't understand anything in that particular moment, other than his need for air and his unrelenting will to survive.

The buffalo killer fumbled to pick up the gun. Dean knew that with only one arm restraining him, this was his best chance to fight and break free. Black spots clouded Dean's vision as he began to lose consciousness. The man was fast for his size as he sprang back up and aimed it at Badger. Dual shots rang out. The first was a blast from Dean's own revolver, in the man's hand and aimed at Badger. The second was a flash from Badger's gun, fired toward Dean and his attacker. He didn't know where Badger's shot went, but the pressure on his neck eased just as he watched Badger fall to the ground.

Dean whipped around to tackle the man, but he was already turning away from him. Kai stood behind them in the bushes. Then Dean saw the knife stuck in the man's back. Dean threw his entire body into the man just as the stranger pulled the trigger again, primed to shoot Kai.

"No!"

Dean landed on the knife handle. He felt it sink farther into the man's flesh. Badger surged forward and Dean heard the cock of the hammer just before a bullet penetrated the man's skull.

"Who is that?" Kai mumbled.

Badger sneered. "A worthless son-of-a-bitch, buffalo hunter."

"Holy Creator, you're...you're shot," Kai said.

Dean rolled off the dead man, and she watched as he and Badger inspected themselves for damage.

"It's not the first time," Badger said. "May be the last, though."

Kai's body shook so hard she thought she was going to fall down. Managing one step at a time, she made it as far as the feet of the dead man and then she collapsed in a heap upon the river stones.

"Well, this is perfect. Not a one of us is worth a crap," Dean said as the numbing weight of the situation sat on his chest like an elephant.

"It's only my arm. I was kidding," Badger said.

"Good. Then go find Man Eater and let's get the hell out of here before we're all hanged."

"Who's Man Eater?" Badger asked with confusion while he toed the dead man with his moccasin, as if checking to make sure there were no residual twitches of life.

"The teeth with four hooves that left me on the ground and kicked me in the nuts for good measure," Dean said.

She watched Dean force himself onto his feet. He looked around for his missing horse and guns as Badger knelt down and did a more thorough check of the body.

Kai felt shock threatening to engulf her like a shroud. "I'd like a vote," she said in an attempt to stay present.

"Yeah. What's that?" Dean asked.

"Wake me up."

"Sorry, sweetheart. This isn't a dream," Badger said.

"If you're here, it must be a nightmare."

"We might want to start putting some distance between us and this buffalo killer. He's also military, or a law enforcer of some kind," Badger observed as he held up a document of some sort.

"We're dead, aren't we?" she added.

"Nope. Someday we'll travel the path to the Sand Hills, but not tonight. Now get up before we see the crossing to the other side before we're ready."

"Since you put it like that, I guess I don't have much choice," Kai said, and rolled over onto her hands and knees. The ground felt sure and steady under her palms. She clenched the gravelly loam and dug her nails into it for reassurance that it wasn't going to fall out from under her the moment she stood up.

"She can sit her pretty ass here all night, but I'm out of here," Badger said. He whistled a call to his horse and started heading to the river.

Dean and Kai watched as Badger ducked into the brush. Then Dean helped Kai to her feet. His groin was awakening from its blessed state of numbness left after the horse's kick. Leaning heavily on his good leg, Dean was unsure if he was helping her stand up or if she was helping him stay up. Grinding his molars, he guided them away from the body.

"We're going to be fine, Kai. You'll be home again soon. Cuddling your kid and baking cookies."

He saw incredulity mixed with a low tolerance for bullshit pass over her features. He clamped his mouth shut and steered her in a new direction. It didn't matter where, as long as they moved away from the dead man.

Seconds later, she yanked free from him and started off in the opposite direction.

"I could have chosen my words better. Come back, Kai."

"I can't decide which one of you is worse."

He could see her shaking her head.

"It's like you both take turns pulling your head out of your butt to say something completely asinine, and then you shove it back up there again for safekeeping. Get over yourself." She trudged over the rough terrain and finished with, "I'm going to get the horses."

Dean watched her pick up the fallen rifle, and then heard Badger approaching from behind. He was riding the buckskin and towing Man Eater. With ears pinned back and mouth champing, his horse looked ready to dismember the buckskin or Badger. Possibly both. Dean hobbled over to them before any further bloodshed or accidents occurred.

With only starlight to see by, it was impossible to inspect the full extent of Badger's wound. Dean could tell that his shirt's sleeve was black with blood, down to the wrist. Over the musky smell of dried sweat on them and the horses, he picked up the unique copper scent of spilling blood as well. His stomach clenched and he had to suppress the rising bile in the back of his throat.

"Get your arm wrapped up. Then we'll head for the mountains."

It was a tossup whether walking or riding was the most effective way to make Dean want to lie down and die. *Then there was Kai.* As they rode, she reverted back to her silent stoicism. He could be mistaking her impassivity for the disbelieving regret and shock of ending up with two assholes in 1868, which is what it probably was. But beyond everything else, it was the image of Badger slowly slipping into unconsciousness that made Dean dig in his heels and push forward, putting his own pain on hold.

The crisp outline of white-capped peaks against the star-spattered sky led Dean west as the group trudged over and through evergreen covered hills until they were safely buried in the forest.

"Where did you get that?" Dean asked as he studied Kai from his seat on the ground.

"It was inside the bag of food supplies we found," Kai said as she held up a bottle to the firelight.

"Did you take anything else?"

"The knife that saved your life."

Dean swallowed her remark like it was a jagged horse pill. He got a sixth sense type of feeling that Kai was here for more reasons than any of them could name. "Can I see that?" Dean asked, holding his hand out to her.

She withdrew the bottle and lifted her chin. "I thought you stopped drinking."

"I'm not going to drink it," he said with equal parts irritation and defensiveness.

"Well if you do, I'll put you out of your misery and shoot you dead."

"If I had known that's all I needed to do, I would have started drinking hours ago."

She tossed him the bottle of liquor, apparently not caring if he caught it, or if it smashed on the ground. He uncorked the brown glass bottle and sniffed. The fumes of grain alcohol singed his nose hairs. Human instinct made him pull back from the fumes, but the urge to take a swill of the poison almost made him tip the bottle up to his mouth. He pushed the cork back into place. His leg ached and his heart began to pound from the knowledge that the contents of the bottle in his hand could help ease the pain. *All of his pain.* Setting the alcohol down against the stack of wood, he rose from the ground and limped toward the horses.

"Where are you going?" Kai asked in alarm.

"To answer nature's call."

Dean circled around the hobbled horses and leaned against a tree until the urge to vomit subsided and his heart rate returned to normal. He was never one to drink hard alcohol, but the smell had gone straight to his limbic system and awakened every dormant need he ever had to drown his emotions in a bottle. He breathed deeply until body and mind were in check. He was fairly certain forever passed by flinging insults and antagonizing him while he regained self control. It seemed like eons passed before he returned to their campsite and found Kai leaning over Badger, the brown bottle in her hand.

"He won't drink it. It's against his religion."

"It's not for drinking," she told Dean with uncontained irritation.

"Badger. Wake up," she said.

Badger had collapsed on his bedroll the instant he had been told it was all right to get off his horse. After taking a little time to settle the horses, remove their gear, and start the fire, Kai was now allowing her nursing side to come forward. She scooted to the side so the firelight fell across his face. Then she pried one of his eyelids open with the pad of her thumb.

"Wake up!" she repeated with a stiff poke to his forehead with her finger.

"So were you absent from class the day they talked about bedside manners?" Dean asked.

She knew Dean was just being himself, but his remark increased her agitation. She chose not to respond.

Dean cleared his throat. "Can we work on him the way he is? Get it over with while he's out?"

"I wanted him to feel it," she remarked bitterly.

"And you think *we're* the jerks."

She graced him with a venomous glare and then turned her attention back to her patient.

"I'm going to have to cut this sleeve off. Unless you want to help me pull it over his head?"

"Cut it. The less movement the better, right?"

Her nostrils flared with repugnance over the whole situation as she untied the knife at her belt and moved into position over Badger.

"Can you come over here, in case he wakes up?"

Dean moved to Badger's other side and watched Kai slice the sleeve at the shoulder seam. Badger moaned as they worked together at peeling the soaked and sticky leather off of his arm.

"He's lost a lot of blood," she said, despair coloring her words as she examined the wounds. "I need better light."

"Should we wait until morning?"

"I have to at least try to clean it. Infection is as much of a concern as the bullet inside him."

With grim determination, Kai continued to explore the damage. She poured water from a canteen over the dried blood to rinse the skin. When they realized that the bullet had ripped through the flesh of his arm and passed into his chest, the state of Badger's condition became more understandable.

A small entry wound glared at her like a beady black eye from the side of his left pectoral muscle. She used more water to clean the blood, and then sliced the top of his shirt open, exposing most of his chest.

"I can't find an exit wound. There's only the cut across his arm and the hole here." She pointed at the spot by his armpit. "We're going to have to roll him over just to check."

When they didn't find any wounds or blood on his back, they returned him to his original position. Badger whimpered and his eyelids flickered, and then he went still once more. Kai palpated the area with the pads of her fingers. She stopped and closed her eyes when she felt a lump as hard as stone under Badger's skin. It was only about three inches from where the bullet entered. Nestled against his ribs under his pectoral muscle, Kai pushed and prodded, disbelieving what her hand was telling her.

"Feel this," she said, and placed Dean's hand over the lead inside Badger.

"That's crazy. Can we leave it inside of him?"

She shrugged with uncertainty. "I think I can get it out with my knife." Worry lines creased Kai's face. She pressed her lips together and tried to steady her shaking breath.

"Tell me how I can help."

Kai looked down at the knife lying on the blanket. The obsidian blade was perfect for what she had to do. The volcanic glass would make a precise scalpel. The only problem was, she didn't know if she would make a precise surgeon. She had never cut anyone open before. Now, twice in one night. Killing the buffalo hunter was for obvious reasons. Plunging that blade into his flesh and knowing when it nicked the rib bones would be in her memory forever. She shuddered, remembering the feeling.

Taking the knife in her hand, she looked up at the sky for the constant star. It was right there. In the north, just as it always has been, and always would be. As long as she had the eyes to see it and the heart to feel it shining from the vast unknown, she could keep going. Its steady light helped still her trembling hands.

"You have to hold him down," she said with bleak resolve. "No matter how hard he tries to move."

"Sure. Whatever you need. Believe me when I say I've seen worse."

"I can't believe I'm doing this." Kai picked up the bottle of alcohol and pulled out the cork. She rinsed off the black stone blade first. Then she held the bottle over Badger.

"Umm..." she stalled.

"Just do it. I'll make sure he stays still."

The imminent pain of alcohol searing raw nerves made Kai hesitate and start with the water instead. Great Spirit knew she had no love for Badger, but she couldn't knowingly inflict this level of torture on anyone without some hesitation. She rinsed his arm again and then poured water over the chest wound. Dean found a spare shirt to use for bandages and began to tear the cloth. When Badger's skin was mostly clean, she picked up the liquor bottle and Dean pinned his friend to the ground.

"Hey, man. We're fixing you up now. Hang tight and it will be over in two shakes."

He nodded to Kai and she poured the alcohol onto his chest where the bullet was buried. Knowing she had to do this without hesitating, she began to make the incision. Badger woke up roaring and started thrashing against Dean. Kai yanked the blade away right before it sliced Badger open accidentally.

With his good hand, Badger groped for the knife at his side. Dean had already moved it out of reach.

"Stop it! Stay still. She's helping you," Dean said in his friend's face.

Only because Dean was larger was he able to restrain him.

"Keep her away from me!" Badger voice was hoarse and his eyes were insane.

"You have a damned bullet stuck in your chest. We're taking it out."

"Like hell you are." But even as he said it, he stopped fighting. The weakness from a long day and a serious injury had stripped most of his strength.

"Bite this," Dean said as he placed a knife sheath in front of Badger's mouth.

Badger raised his head and clamped down on the leather. His eyes met Kai's and she leaned forward to finish what she'd started.

"You can drink the alcohol if you want. There are two bottles."

Badger grunted and it sounded like a no to Kai. Then he squeezed his eyes shut.

Kai's cut was shockingly deep through the dense muscle tissue, but she didn't stop until she knew she was right above the bullet. Sweat poured out of both of them. Badger growled around the knife's sheath. Blood instantly filled the new wound, impeding Kai's view of the bullet. She used the tip of the knife like a probe and pried the lead upward. At first it felt stuck, but then she caught an edge and worked it loose. Moving as quickly as she could, she eased it upward until she could reach inside the incision with her fingers and pick the bullet out.

With the first revolting act completed, she continued to perform the truly horrific next. Before thinking about it too much, she set the knife and bullet aside and grabbed the bottle of alcohol. She poured it over the fresh incision, making sure the liquid got down deep into the cut. Then she did the same to the entry wound, and the gash on his arm.

Badger's body went rigid as every muscle contracted with unimaginable pain. He screamed as he clenched down and nearly bit through the thick leather sheath. He lost consciousness as the alcohol finished dripping over his arm. Dean looked nearly as stiff as Badger from the exertion of holding him in place.

"Press this over the cut to stop the bleeding," she told Dean as she placed a square of torn shirt over the incision.

"I have dried plants," Dean mumbled. "I mean, I brought medicines."

"What?" Kai asked as she moved to tie bandages around Badger's arm.

"I forgot about them. Inside my bag. I have comfrey and geranium root powder. There's a bunch of different ones."

Kai closed her eyes and took a deep breath in an attempt to let her nerves settle. When she looked at Dean again, it was with fresh eyes. *He had useful medicines.* She didn't admit that she already knew that the supplies were inside his pack, or that she had also forgotten about them.

"I'll get them." She set the strips of cloth aside and rose to retrieve the herbs. "These are good. I can make a poultice. In the morning, I'll sterilize the bandages and we'll redress his wounds. I was planning to search for some fresh plants tomorrow, but I may not need to now. Maybe I can look for something to ease the pain, unless you have that, too?"

"No, nothing like that. I'm off alcohol, remember? Painkillers are in the same class of banned substances."

"It's okay." She scooped out some of the powdered roots and crumbled dry leaves and packed them over Badger's cuts. "We need to make sure that he stops bleeding and then we need to rest, too. We're both exhausted."

Kai used lengths of cloth tied together and wrapped them around Badger's shoulder and under his arm, creating a dressing for the chest wounds. Finally, she dribbled water from the canteen over the herbs and cloth until everything was soaked through, and then finished tying the bandages.

"You're right. We're all tired," Dean said as he moved around Badger and sat down on his bed. "This trip has gotten messy. A new day will help clear the cobwebs and I'll be able to think again."

"It's going to take more than the sun to put my head back together," Kai said as she emptied the last of the canteen over her hands.

"No one said anything about your head needing repair."

"Believe me, it does." Kai wiped her hands on a patch of long grass and then looked around at their hastily thrown together camp.

"You're doing better than the two of us. Look, I don't think I've really apologized for dragging you into this. I'm sorry. You shouldn't be here. I shouldn't be here. The risks involved with time travel aren't worth getting my friends killed over. I—"

"Stop, Dean. Don't say anything else. It wasn't your fault. I went looking for you."

"It was my truck that broke down."

"Great Spirit must have wanted me here. Laughing Eyes said he dreamed of me. I—I don't know what to think."

"Just blame me for everything. It's easier that way."

Narrowing her eyes with suspicion, she said, "Now you're sacrificing yourself for my well-being. I'm responsible for all of my own mistakes."

"I was just giving you an out, Kai. The medicine pipe is in my care."

She eased down onto her blanket and pulled the corner over her lap. "Then make sure it brings us home again."

"I will," Dean promised. "No matter what else happens, you will see Trevyn again."

Chapter Fourteen

Dean was unhappy about Kai's plan to search for willow bark and fresh food by herself, but she assured him that she would be fine. They decided it wouldn't be good to move Badger yet. Dean wasn't moving so well, either. There hadn't been any signs of humans all morning and Badger was in need of clean bandages and a poultice change. Dean finally relented and let her go because they needed water. Kai insisted it was best that the men stay together, guarding against wild animals or anything else unexpected.

From a small hilltop next to their camp, Kai looked to the treetops. A group of towering pines and spruce trees were not far to the southwest. Gigantic trees needed plenty of water, so she rode toward them, stopping periodically to listen for the trickle of a flowing river or creek. She hoped that finding a tributary coming down from the peaks wouldn't be too difficult, or take too long.

Her instincts were correct, and she found a stream minutes later. She dismounted and let Mayberry and the packhorse drink their fill. She looked around at the mature trees, made mental notes of the different plants growing by the stream, and thought about bringing the other two horses here later so they could drink as well. All around her, the forest was alive in green splendor. Birds sang with cheerful exuberance, and the butterflies and gnats flittered around the summer blooms, catching sunrays with their wings. While the horses were content grazing on a patch of grass, she began searching in earnest for edible plants and willow.

As if Great Spirit took pity on her, there was a large balsam root plant with its spear shaped leaves and yellow flowers nearby. She squatted down to dig it up. There were so many different uses for the plant that she started dividing up its parts in her mind. The leaves were for eating, but the roots — another great source of food — would make an excellent immune stimulating tea. Badger could drink the tea to help him fight off infection. Kai glanced around for more, but didn't see any. More Heal All would be useful if she could find it, but willow bark was what she really searched for. It would act like aspirin for Dean and Badger's pain relief. Moving along, she picked some wild mint to add flavor to the teas.

A group of poplar trees shimmied under the morning sun. The trees were called Metoos by her people, and she longed for a healing salve made from the winter buds. Trevyn should learn the tree's importance, she noted to herself. Then she was hit with the overwhelming fear of never seeing her son again. It slammed into her and ached inside the marrow of her bones. The need to hear his voice, and see his vivid smile, almost brought her to her knees. They were a team. There was no way to measure the depth of their connection. He was part of her. If she couldn't get back to him, she couldn't live. It was that simple.

She stopped searching for plants and pressed her palms over her eyes, forcing herself to calm down. *She would return to Trevyn.* Kai let her hands drop. She needed to continue searching for the willow bark, but had lost her focus. Turning back to the horses, she decided to wash in the stream before going back to the campsite.

After putting the plants into a saddlebag and filling the canteens and water skins, she led the horses downstream. The clear mountain water had formed a pool in front of a natural dam of tumbled boulders. A dragonfly hovered at the water's edge, and tiny trout kissed the surface in hopes of catching their breakfast. The silver gleam of a darting fish surprised Kai as she dipped her toes into the water. Her nudity didn't bother her, but the fact that her nakedness made her think of Dean, did.

Their morning conversation came back to her then, word for word and achingly poignant. It was while they finished eating service berries and the pan bread she'd made from the pilfered flour and lard.

"Stop doing that," Kai had told him.

Dean stopped staring at her and gazed at his moccasins.

"I know what you're thinking, so cut it out."

He shook his head and Kai didn't understand the meaning of it. It only confused her more.

"I've caught you looking at me like that before. You think I have a stone where my heart should be. You think I'm cold and uncaring, but I'm not. I'm a survivor. So you can keep those wretched looks to yourself."

It was never overt, but she knew he watched her sometimes, and he needed to stop. She couldn't take it any longer. The way he looked at her made her nervous and edgy.

His still said nothing, simply running a hand over his scalp.

"You're so wrong it makes me want to laugh," he said at last, glancing up quickly and then away toward the eastern horizon.

The dawn had brought slashing rays of sunlight into the camp, bending around tree trunks and striping the earth in long shadows.

"Then what? Do I have manure on my face? Are you silently making fun of me? Do you think I enjoy stabbing people or pretending to be a surgeon? Because I don't. I didn't sign up for this excursion. And what happened to the plan of camping out for a month?" Her temper had finally found release, and Dean was on the receiving end.

"You're uptight, you know that?"

"I am not!" She knew she was, but she couldn't pass up the chance to spite him. She stood up and started walking away from the fire.

"I was thinking about how pretty you are when you smile," he said to her back.

"Well, don't."

"And how you would be if you weren't stuck here with me. I was wondering what makes you happy, and if I've ruined your life and taken away any chance of finding that happiness."

"Dean, stop."

"So, don't assume that I'm condemning you for being brave. I have nothing against you, Kai. Your fearlessness inspires me. And I have never thought you were a cold person, because I've seen you with your son. He's lucky to have such a strong mother."

Tears began to pool around her eyes. *How dare he bring up Trevyn?* It only made her want to hate Dean more. But in the moment, it didn't seem to matter that he had drug her back in time. It didn't matter that she was stuck there on the edge of the Backbone of the World, waiting for Badger to wake up and heal, or die. Dean had somehow worked his medicine on her spirit and wedged himself into her life. She cared what he thought, no matter how much she tried to deny it. She would never let him know just how much she was affected by those golden flecks in his eyes when she saw him watching her.

Then Badger had croaked, "You're making my ears bleed over here. Release the damned tension and screw each other already. Then you can break up or get together."

Dean and Kai simultaneously gawked at a bleary eyed and wincing Badger. He was struggling to raise himself up.

"Shut your stupid hole," Dean said, and went to help his friend.

Kai started to saddle and prepare her horse. She was desperate to clear her mind. Then she had argued with Dean about their need for fresh medicine and water.

Her mind returned to the present as she skimmed the surface of the pool with her palm creating ripples that were swept away with the current. She started with her arms, scooping the icy water over her skin and letting it trickle back into the stream. Goose flesh tingled her skin in protest, but she didn't stop. The chance to wash away dirt, sweat, horse, and dried blood outweighed the discomforts of freezing. Torso and legs were next. As her hands brushed over her legs she remembered Dean again. While she was cooking earlier she'd covertly watched him inspect the bruises he'd received from Man Eater and the burly buffalo hunter.

His upper thigh would take weeks to heal. The contusions and swelling were some of the worst she had ever seen. Conversely, his calves and quads were probably the hottest she had ever seen and his tight six-pack was certainly drool-worthy. Kai shut her eyes, willing herself to deny the attraction toward him. He may be a hunk of muscle with a cute face, but he was also a drunk with a dark history, and had issues that were beyond fixing. She wouldn't want to be judged by others for her own family history, but she also knew what it could do to a person. Willingly inviting that mess into her life was asking for trouble.

Feeling pressured and stressed by her own thoughts, she knelt down in the water and leaned forward, drenching her hair. With the shock of cold, all she could do was focus on breathing through the chill and combing her fingers through the long strands.

Kai rose and brushed her hair straight back. She breathed in the warming mountain air and turned around to find a strange man pointing a bow and arrow at her chest.

"Clear your head of her already. She's messed up. You don't need that drama."

"Tell me why I put up with you," Dean said as he searched inside Badger's traveling gear for a shirt.

"Women," Badger scoffed. "She's dangerous. Can't you see her cold eyes? Hot body or not, that one's a psycho."

"That psycho removed a bullet from your chest."

"About that," Badger said, and winced. He adjusted his position, attempting to stretch his back while straightening a leg. "Don't get shot out here. She's a far cry from a combat medic. I might have chosen death if I knew she was going to get her claws on me."

"She did fine," Dean said. "Badge, what's this?"

Dean held up the small brown leather journal. It was open and he read a random entry.

"My notes," Badger said. "I've been studying since we decided to take this trip."

His face was hard and his eyes flat as he watched Dean.

"Looks like you've been researching long before we ever started talking about the medicine pipe."

"I've always wanted to know about where my parents and their parents came from."

Dean felt a defensive wall creeping up around his friend and paused to look at him for an extra long second.

"Pass me my shirt," Badger said, and stretched out his good arm.

Dean stuffed the journal back into the bag and removed the shirt. It unrolled as he handed it over to Badger. A corked vial fell onto the blanket.

They both looked down at the powder-filled tube.

"What's that?"

Badger picked it up and tucked it into his hand and out of sight. "Prussic acid," he said.

"Don't blow smoke up my ass. I know what that is and I bet I know how you came by it. I've worked for gold mines before, too. Tell me why you're carrying a vial of cyanide?"

He raised his gaze to Dean's. Stiff jawed and eyes hard, he said, "Being prepared is the first rule of any new assignment."

"What assignment are you on that I'm not a part of, Badger?"

The growing disconnect between the two friends widened as Badger decided if or how he would answer the question.

Badger attempted a smile. It came across as strained and vicious. "Man, you never know what's going to happen out here. It's no different than any other undercover mission. Have a way out, no matter what."

Dean didn't buy the explanation and remained silent. Badger dropped the sly manipulation and proceeded to change shirts.

"You want help with that?" Dean asked.

Badger was struggling to remove what was left of his buckskin shirt.

"No."

Dean glanced back into the pack. A thought occurred to him and he asked, "Are you related to the Wrights? I saw the names and birthdates in the journal."

"Stay out of it," Badger said as he wadded up the ruined leather.

There was clear warning to his tone but Dean didn't back off. It made him want to get to the bottom of this before any other surprises surfaced.

He sat down by the fire and adjusted his leg to ease the pressure on his upper thigh. It wasn't easy to find a comfortable position, and he ended up with one knee bent and one leg askew. Badger pulled his clean shirt over his head and used only one sleeve for his uninjured arm.

"Out with it," he started. "I brought you here, and you're going to tell me everything from the beginning. Now."

"There's nothing to tell."

"Why is your mom's name at the bottom of that family tree? Who are the Wrights, and why are you so defensive about this?"

"I told you to drop it."

"I will not." Dean set his jaw and steeled his gaze. "You say I'm your friend, so be one. We've been through more absurdity together than most people can ever imagine. You're not leaving me in the dark now."

Badger closed his eyes for a moment. When he opened them again, Dean was well aware of the seething hatred in his dark eyes.

"This doesn't have anything to do with you or our time in the desert. I told you, I needed to be prepared for any situation that may come up."

"You're planning on poisoning someone. All those names and dates in your book. Who is Hubert Wright?"

"I'm not saying anything else."

"I'm not buying this load of garbage."

"I'm not selling squat."

"Who is he?" Dean asked through gritted teeth. The name in Badger's book had a date of birth and Helena, MT. written next to it.

"Give me a drink, man. I'm parched. And some breakfast wouldn't be turned away, either."

Dean wanted to smash Badger's teeth, but instead he handed him the pan bread that Kai had made and a skin with last of their water.

"Semper Fi, asswipe. When you can't trust your brothers, we're all dead," he said as he tried again to find a comfortable spot on the ground. "You want to be the one responsible for getting us killed? That's your call. You nearly did yesterday. Kai and I will be going back to the village to wait out the rest of the month with the Piegans. I'm not willing to follow through with this operation any longer," he said as Badger chewed in silence.

Dean thought the situation had been handled, and he wasn't going to receive any argument, but then Badger began his story.

"Hubert Wright is the owner of the Mount St. Helena Wright Gold Mining Company. He was one of the first to strike it rich in Last Chance Gulch. We know that the gold runs out after about four years. That's right about now, in 1868. Hubert Wright had a good sense of investment. He owns half of the First National Bank of Montana and is, or is going to, invest in the growing lumber industry, and eventually the family will buy out a copper mine in Butte."

Dean scratched at the stubble on his jaw. Badge grew up in Butte. He waited to hear the connection.

"He's an investment banker, or will be, and his heirs will invest heavily in mining. I guess they couldn't get it out of their system over the next few generations."

Dean picked a berry seed out of his teeth with a fingernail, and then spit it into the fire as he tried to tie it all together.

Seeming to change subjects, Badger continued speaking. "Did you know that my parents were part of a government relocation program? They moved to Denver to be 'urbanized.' Thousands of Natives tried the programs. Most returned home when they ended up starving or jobless or discriminated against. There was no social support for people who had only known the tribal way of life. How did they think they could walk into a white society with open arms and expect to succeed? It was a failure on every level. The job my father took in Colorado didn't pay enough to keep the two of them fed, so they had to move again. He returned to Montana and heard about a copper mine in Butte that was hiring. He managed to get that piss-poor job. I was born a few years later, and then my sister. My father worked his hands raw for those people. When the mine shut down the tunnels and switched to open pit mining, he worked on every truck in the fleet. When there were cutbacks, guess who was fired first? The N-D-N's. White families can't starve, you know? No one cared if another Indian went back to the rez unemployed."

Badger reached for his pack and Dean saw him put the vial of cyanide into one of the inner pockets. Then he retrieved his journal and a knife and placed them in his lap. He flipped his book open and used the tip of his knife to point at passages of his own tight, neat handwriting.

"My father actually held onto his position, but he wasn't much liked. We survived, but we were treated worse than the rodents living behind the baseboards."

Badger looked up at Dean. Hatred harder than granite was obvious in his eyes. Dean always knew Badger had an ugly side to him. He'd seen him shoot the enemy in battle with a total lack of interest. Dean had always thought Badger had the warrior's ability to disconnect from his emotions. They all seemed to have it to some degree. It was a necessity to cope. But now Dean was beginning to think that Badger had no remorse for what he'd done, whatsoever. He didn't want to believe what his eyes were telling him. He wanted to keep searching for some kind of humanity hidden inside his friend.

"Could your perspective possibly be jaded by a few bad incidents? Kids see things a lot differently than their parents do."

"My eyes were wide open. And yeah, my kid-eyes saw things differently than my parents. I saw the fucking truth of how hated my father was for stealing a job from a white man. That's not even the worst part. My dad hated working there. He felt like a slave to commerce and oppression. A slave to a society he never wanted to be a part of."

"Badge, he wasn't alone. Do you know how many people have strong resentments toward big government and big business? You'll find it everywhere in the history of the human race."

Badger gave a derisive snort. "Do I smell a liberal ass kisser sitting here? You know the history of the Blackfoot as well as I do. You know we were nearly annihilated for simply existing. How can you live with yourself? You've had a way to make a change since you were born, and it's only now that you're trying to make a difference. And only after I had to bribe you and buy our passage. It's disgusting what a conformist you are."

"Disgusting, huh?" Dean's temper was thrumming through him like he'd been strung too tightly. Another second of being *badgered,* and he was going to snap. "I've told you. The past can't be altered," he said, fists clenched. "You're a conniving sack of crap for dragging me into this."

"In a few short months, smallpox is going to take out half of the People again. You know it and I know it. Why haven't you tried to save them? Your family line carries the ability to save us, and none of you have tried to make a difference."

"I'm not going to keep talking to a wall about what can and can't happen in the past. And don't assume anything about what my ancestors have or have not done with our pipe. What the hell are you planning to do to Hubert Wright?"

Badger stabbed the open page in his book with the knife in his hand. "In the next twenty years, the Blackfoot population will be about a quarter of what it is now. Starvation, disease, loss of land. It's a never-ending cycle. Not just us. Every tribe will be affected. It's already too late for most of them.

"There are going to be over one hundred sawmills popping up and destroying the forest." Badger looked at his writing and said, "By 1890, one hundred and thirty million board feet of lumber will be cut every year. The forests will be decimated like the buffalo and the People. Trains are coming and slicing up more land, and Hubert Wright is one of the largest instigators of it all."

"You're on a mission of failure, Badger," Dean said, feeling sadness and depression grip him.

"I disagree," Badger said. Stubborn defiance hovered about the set of his shoulders and his stiff neck. "You can stay in your corner and do nothing, but you don't get to tell me I'm wrong."

"Lying and using me to this end is like shooting an arrow in my face. We're done. There's no recovering from this."

Disgust overrode the ice in Badger's eyes. "You're a piece of work. You can't see the deceit staring you straight in the face."

"Don't talk to me anymore," Dean said. "I can't trust you."

"If you're looking at me that way, make sure to use the same x-ray vision on Kai."

Dean clenched his fist at his side. He watched Badger for more lies, but there was no noticeable change on the man's face.

"She's been gone too long," he stated more to himself than to Badger.

"Maybe she ate a bad mushroom."

Dean ignored the jab and climbed to his feet. He stared at Man Eater. The animal wasn't exactly the most dependable companion, but the horse still moved faster than Dean on his gimpy leg.

"I don't like the implication you're making about Kai. She saved your life, dipshit."

"She's pulling the wool over your eyes, but I can see you like cuddling up to that type of irritation."

"Do you ever stop?" Dean yelled as he grabbed the saddle and blanket and moved to his horse without waiting to hear another word.

Kai glanced at her knife lying on the ground next to her dress. It was agonizingly close and yet not close enough to grab before an arrow pierced her body. Her gaze darted back to the stranger. He didn't even notice she was watching his every move. His eyes were locked on her chest. Fury overcame her fear. She wouldn't let any man molest her without inflicting serious injuries. Then she realized that his eyes were focused slightly higher, on her necklace and not her breasts. Her protective instincts soared with alarm. The necklace was the only thing she had from her mother. It meant more to her than anything else she owned and she never took it off.

Feeling alone and at a disadvantage, but not powerless, she waited for him to make the next move. Dressed in a lightweight hunter's shirt and leggings, the symbols and designs he displayed were quite different than the ones Piegans used.

He didn't speak, but used his eyes and pointed with his chin to tell her to get dressed. The scout never loosened the tension on his bowstring as she stepped out of the water and reached for her clothes. When she started to pick up her antler-handled knife, he spoke in an unfamiliar language. She didn't need to understand each word to know what he meant. *Don't touch it.*

Based on the distance they traveled south and west into the mountains, she guessed that she'd found a Salish warrior. *Or he'd found her.*

After she dressed, he lowered his bow and spoke again.

Kai shook her head letting him know she didn't understand. He gestured with his foot for her to kick the knife away. Kai stiffened at the thought of having to give up her weapon. The revolver Dean had given her was still in the saddle pack on her mare. She berated herself for not keeping it in her hands like Dean had warned her to do.

With minimal effort she kicked the knife to the side, not toward her captor.

He said something that sounded roughly like, "Who are your people?" in mixed up Piegan.

All she said was, "Kai Wolfsblood."

He pointed to his chest and then at hers referring to the necklace. "Cree woman?"

She shook her head no.

Kai thought she saw calculating going on behind his eyes and wondered if she was playing her cards wrong. *Why did he ask if she was a Cree?*

She spoke in a loud voice and used her hands to say, "My husband is near. You would be wise to leave me unharmed."

He appeared to take this into consideration, but not whole-heartedly. After a full minute of silence, he raised his bow again and directed her to start walking toward the horses. She let her shoulders droop in fake defeat as she took the first few steps toward the mares. Then she fell to the ground reaching for her discarded knife. The scout was quick to react. Before she could spin around and slash at the man, he was on top of her.

A whimper escaped her lips as he slammed her into the ground. With the wind knocked out of her, the fight was extinguished as she struggled to find her breath. Her hands were yanked behind her back and the man fought to keep her pinned down while he wrapped a strap around her wrists.

Adrenaline exploded into her system. Kai heaved herself backward, trying to throw him off. He slipped to the side, but hung on tight. His hands were fast, and no matter how many times she kicked back at him he wouldn't relent.

When he finally let go, she couldn't move her arms. The scout walked around to look at her from the front.

"Cree princess," he signed with his hands. "The necklace." He pointed at the lump where her necklace was hidden beneath the dress.

She closed her eyes to the sight of his accusatory face and hid in the inner darkness of her mind as ragged emotion threatened to consume her. *Was he was referring to the stories about her clan, or something else? Something she had no knowledge of?*

"Dean!" she screamed.

Halfway through the scream he clamped a hand over her mouth. She bit down and felt her teeth sink into the thick skin of his palm. She tasted the salt of his skin and then he pulled his hand away. She sucked in another breath preparing to scream again, and received a mouthful of dirt, leaves, and forest debris.

Choking and coughing silenced her alarm just long enough for the scout to find a length of rope, double it, and wrap it around her mouth and head. Thrashing proved to be useless against his wiry strength. Her stamina diminished rapidly. Far faster than his did.

From behind, he yanked her to her feet, and then stepped in front of her.

"You come with me," he signed. "Many Bear Claws Cree looking for you. Reward many horses and guns for your return."

She shook her head and tried to answer that he had the wrong person, but it only came out as grunts and whimpers.

"Ride or walk?" he asked in sign language.

Kai quieted her protests and stared at her mare with longing and desperation. *How did she let this happen? Why hadn't she been more cautious? Her daydreaming had brought this on.* She motioned her head towards the horses.

He gave an almost imperceptible nod. Then he grabbed her by the shoulder, forcing her to walk. The warrior kept one hand on her and used his free hand to retrieve his discarded bow and arrow lying on top of a rose bramble. As soon as he released her and turned to untie the hobbled horses, she dug in her moccasins and made a break for it. It was the last thing she remembered before waking up on the ground with three sets of dark brown eyes staring at her.

Lying on her side with hands bound behind her back she watched them without moving. Thankfully, the gag around her mouth had been removed. The three men sat around a cold fire talking, she guessed, about her.

The one who abducted her, signed, "Your husband did not come. Do you lie about who you are?"

Kai remained silent, unwilling to cooperate for the time being.

A taller man with horizontal lines of shells decorating the front of his shirt spoke in Salish, and Kai didn't understand a word of it. The third man, with a broad face and hair cut short on the top but with long braids on the sides, walked over and squatted down in front of her. He reached forward and Kai pulled back. She couldn't go far though, and he had no difficulty reaching into the neckline of her dress and pulling the necklace out. He studied it in his fingers and then let it drop.

"Important chief's daughter wears a necklace of this type. Are you her?" he signed.

Kai shook her head no.

"How did you come to have it?" he asked.

"My mother made it for me," she said in English.

The English threw them off kilter, just as Kai hoped it would. They exchanged looks of confusion mixed with mild concern. Then they continued their talk. Kai wished she knew what they were saying, but as adept as she was with new languages, she couldn't pick out any recognizable words.

Kai squirmed to ease the pressure on her shoulder and to move off of a rock digging into her hip. She heard a rustling in the brush and the snap of a twig behind her. Rolling over to look for someone, there was instant and excruciating pain on the side of her head as it pressed into the ground. Her abductor must have struck her when she attempted to escape. As she paid attention to the painful spot, she knew it was bad. She squeaked with suppressed agony as the stabbing pain in her head caused sparks of light in her vision. When she could focus again she saw the horses, not Dean sneaking up behind her.

As she fantasized about being rescued, the three men stopped talking, having come to some unknown decision. Then her captor and the tallest man loaded her onto her mare. Confused, injured, and outnumbered, Kai didn't fight back. One of the kidnappers held up Dean's revolver and then tucked it into his belt before stepping onto the stirrup and sitting behind her. He untied her, and the second man handed her a water skin. They let her drink, and then retied her hands.

Kai noticed that she wasn't being handled badly as long as she cooperated, but she was also desperately aware that they weren't letting her go, either. She watched as they did a final check of their camp and then mounted the horses. The sun was approaching midday as they rode west, deeper into the mountains, instead of northeast, toward the Cree.

Chapter Fifteen

"I couldn't find her," Dean said as he rode into camp.

"Told you she couldn't be trusted. She probably found John and is on her way to Helena without us," Badger interrupted.

"Why would she do that?"

Badger's lip curled. "Only a woman could answer a logical question with total illogicality. When you see her again, you'll have to ask her."

"You know nothing about women. And I wasn't finished. I found signs that I don't like. Over by the nearest creek, in the direction she said she was going. I would swear there are struggle marks on the ground."

This got Badger's attention. He looked at Dean, not exactly with concern, but a heightened sense of alertness.

"Get up. We're going to track the horses before the signs disappear."

Badger began to rise, grimaced, and then fell back down. His face expressed the amount of pain he was truly in. It wasn't pretty. Dean dismounted, wrapped his reins around the branch of a tree and moved away from Man Eater's teeth.

"I'll slow you down, man. I'm not sure I can hang onto a horse riding much faster than your grandma with her walker."

"Kai borrowed your saddle, too," Dean observed. *Should he leave Badger behind, or risk taking his injured friend along?* Dean was displeased by either prospect. "I don't think you should stay here alone."

"You have to go. I can manage as long as I have water and my guns."

"This is insane."

"If you're not back before I run out of provisions, I'll ride back to the Piegans. We'll meet up there two days before the next new moon, at the very latest. If I'm not there by then, you can take Kai back to her kid without me."

Dean struggled internally as he listened to Badger adjust their itinerary on the fly. It could work, but it was a far cry from what they had planned. "I'll make sure we're both back before you run out of food. It will be today. Tomorrow, at the latest," he said with finality.

"I need another day to rest. Worst-case scenario: if you're not back in three days, I'll head to the Piegan village. If they've already moved, then I'll find them at the Sun Dance camp."

"Okay," he agreed and began to shuffle around their gear so Badger would have enough food, water, ammo, and weapons to hold him over. He ended up leaving most of his own supplies in a heap. He would be back soon enough, and he could ride faster with a lighter load.

Minutes later, he was back on Man Eater, riding southwest toward the scuff marks he'd found near the stream.

Kai was given venison pemmican to eat. It filled her hollow stomach after a long day of riding, but it did nothing to quell the uneasiness in her gut. Hours had passed, with no sign of rescue. The farther they went, the more convinced she became that she would never see Dean again, and would never return to her home in the twenty-first century. *Or to Trevyn.*

The Salish camp sat in the midst of the forest, surrounded by aspen and evergreen trees. It was tucked close to the shore of a midnight blue lake. Hungry fish jumped in search of food. Ripples danced and collided over the surface of the water glinting pewter and gold in the evening light.

Kai observed it all with absent attention. She wanted to run away from these strangers. She wanted them to stop talking about her and shooting covert glances at her like she was a questionable profit-making scheme.

Her current guard was a middle-aged man with a stout build, a paunch, and dour-looking mouth. He was keeping himself busy by knapping arrowheads. A piece of thick buffalo hide lay over his legs, protecting his skin and clothing as he worked to make the edges of stone clean and sharp. His focus was absolute, Kai noticed. She also registered how quickly the man could stop what he was doing and switch his focus to Kai. When she adjusted her folded legs to a more comfortable position, her guard had his work set aside and was on his feet before she settled again. Her thoughts of running away seemed useless. He was bigger than she was by a good fifty pounds. He had a gun, a knife, and a bow and arrow to boot. Kai had nothing, but she stared at a fallen branch a couple of yards away. *She could inflict plenty of damage with it if she had an opportunity to do so.*

The camp contained only men, and she wondered if this was a specialized society within the Salish. Warriors, or hunters? She couldn't be sure. There were about twenty of them. Most were busy with camp activities or were seated around a fire, smoking and talking after the evening meal. Kai had been placed near a small lodge, set away from the cluster of the others.

She cleared her throat and her guard looked up from his arrow point. Kai was careful to move slowly as she raised her hands and signed that she needed to lose water in private. His mouth already so turned down to begin with that she couldn't believe that he could actually frown more, but he did. He folded the leather mat with his arrowhead, the stone chips, and his tools inside, and placed it all on the ground. Then he nodded at Kai.

As she brushed off the back of her dress, she eyed the club-sized branch. Her guard kept a hand close to his pistol, so she let the idea go, and walked away from the group toward a screen of alders. He allowed her a moment of semi-privacy. Kai took longer than necessary and stared at every inch of her surroundings. She saw the dark-veined pink petals of a cranesbill geranium growing near a patch of bear berries. She moved to pick some. She wanted to crush the green parts of the plant and press it to the knot on her head to ease the swelling and pain. Her guard moved to intercept her escape, but halted as he watched her kneel next to the plant.

She narrowed her eyes in a haughty glare and signed, "For head pain. Your friend hit me."

He took a half step back, and let her collect the plant. Kai explored the leaves of the plant with the speed of a caterpillar. She hoped the man wouldn't rush her, and glanced over to see if he was still paying close attention. She was surprised to see him starting back towards the others. It sounded like an argument was going on. With her guard distracted, she yanked the plant by the roots and was just about to make another attempt at getting away when a small pinecone landed three feet from her.

Her breath caught in her throat as she stared in the direction from which it had come. In the soft and diffuse light of the evening she thought she saw a set of light brown eyes and dark hair. Then she blinked and they were gone. *Dean.* It happened so quickly. It could have been a trick of her eyes or she could have seen a wild animal. *Could wishing hard enough cause her to hallucinate?*

Her chubby guard turned his attention back to Kai and he gestured for her to return to the lodge. Kai stared back at the spruce trees where she thought she had seen someone. Nothing but the evergreen branches and their nearly black trunks stared back.

Keeping the spruce trees in a line of sight, Kai sat down on a fallen log and crushed the geranium. The guard took a position nearby, but also closer to the other men. The sound of the arguing continued, and Kai secretly watched for an opening to make an escape. She knew she couldn't run faster than twenty men, and her horses had been taken, but she wouldn't give up yet.

She pressed the leaves and stems to the lump on her head, wincing as she worked it through her hair, down to the sore skin. The lake air caressed the exposed skin of her arms and neck and she shivered. The moisture in the air made the smell of the trees, the grasses, and the ground more fragrant. The tart, sweet pine scent was strong and invigorating, and she used it to breathe in strength and endurance. She had to be ready for whatever was coming next.

The breeze shifted, and camp smoke filled her nose. She was suddenly aware that the men were no longer arguing. Glancing over, she saw the hunter who found her this morning walking toward her.

"You can sleep in this lodge tonight. I will keep watch of you. Do not run again." His eyes moved to stare at her hand holding the compress to her head. "After a sleep, we make our way to the head chief of my people. We will decide how to return you to the Cree." He pointed at the lodge door, expecting Kai to rise and go in.

She shook her head in defiance. Kai wanted to stay out in the open where Dean could see her, and where she could see him if he came to rescue her.

She straightened her back and remained resolute. He grabbed her arm and pulled her up and off of the log. Kai resisted by falling to the ground. He let her drop, and then called to the chubby one.

They stared at her with equal frustration. Kai wondered how badly she would be punished for disobeying. *Was she really willing to find out?*

The guard signed, "She is a no good woman. Why would the Cree have such a high reward for this one?"

The other man signed, "Have you seen the Cree women? This one must be the only pretty one left."

They enjoyed their joke, and Chubby-frowny-face even broke into a grin. Then her captors each took an arm and dragged her to the lodge door, unceremoniously stuffing her inside. They blocked the entrance as she tried to scramble back out again.

The Salish man removed his revolver from its holster and held it up for her to see. Then he settled himself by the door. Kai huffed and stopped resisting. The light inside of the small hunting lodge was dim with the late evening sun. There was a fur lying on top of a mat to sleep on, and that was it. She thought she could wedge herself under the canvas, so she looked for the most likely place to escape. She moved the bedding over to the side of the tipi where the gap between the bottom of the canvas and the ground was the widest and looked over at her captor. He shook his head at her and tapped the revolver with his fingers. Kai sat down on the bed, inwardly fuming over the loss of control of her destiny. It was bad enough being stuck in the 1800's with Dean and Badger, but it had all gotten exponentially worse now that she was being shuffled around by strange men who had even stranger ideas of what was best for her. Feeling desperate and trapped, she made a vow to stay awake and get out of this tipi as soon as possible. If Dean never showed, she would walk all the way back to Laughing Eyes and his Dragonfly medicine pipe. *Surely the medicine man would be able send her home.*

The drumming started after the last touch of daylight disappeared through the smoke hole. The deep, resonating pound of stretched rawhide over a hollow log pulsed over the skin of her tipi. Kai lay down and peered under the edge of the canvas. The flames of the fire reached toward the sky, casting a flickering orange glow upon the shadowed men. They wore feather or roach headdresses, and resembled crowned beasts as they moved around the open flames. She couldn't see the drummer, and thought her view of him was being obstructed by a large tree.

Someone started singing a slow and repetitive song. It rose and fell in a rolling melody, reminding Kai of the hills beyond the lake. The feathered and decorated society men began to dance as the second song started. The new song had a faster beat, and the dancers timed their steps to move with or against the rhythms, depending on what they were portraying. Kai had seen many dances, but none from a society of men only. She thought she might be punished for watching, but she already felt like she was being punished just for being there. When the men were not participating in the dancing, singing, or drumming, they would rest or smoke. Kai's patience was already thin. Seeing these men so relaxed and having a good time infuriated her. And yet, there was always someone sitting at her door. She wondered if the argument she heard earlier was because she obviously wasn't supposed to be there, witnessing the ceremonies. It had to be the reason they were forcing her to stay inside on such a nice summer night.

The dancing and drumming went on for hours. Having promised herself that she would stay awake until she had an opportunity to run, she watched the sliver of moon rise over the smoke hole and contemplated the harsh injustice of time. *There were twenty-three days until the next darkening of the moon. It felt like an eternity of seconds that she would never see the end to.*

Using the fur bedding as a shield to hide her true motives, she scooted closer and closer to the gap she thought she could slip under. As she reached for the gap she was violently wrenched back into the middle of the lodge. She kicked at the man, but missed. He released her and said something she didn't understand. Her attempt at escape hadn't even gotten an arm out of her jail cell.

He signed to her, but she didn't see what he said in the dark. She rolled over, refusing to communicate with him. Then the drums and the song stopped abruptly. Her guard moved to the door with the same silent swiftness he used upon entering, and ducked his head outside.

"What's going on?" she asked in Cree, forgetting herself for a moment and not realizing that she had slipped into her native tongue.

He held up his hand, making the well know sign to be silent. She crawled over to the door and peered around him. He gripped her upper arm, holding his revolver in the other hand. Kai didn't fight. She only wanted to know if Dean had come to rescue her. The men darted into lodges or hid in the shadows, abandoning the fire as they went for their weapons.

Kai heard the horses. A piercing whinny from the east of her lodge preceded an answering snort from a Salish horse tied to one of the tipis.

Riders suddenly appeared at the edges of the firelight. They held their rifles ready atop stamping and blowing horses. Three Salish Warriors, with their breastplates and necklaces gleaming in the firelight and their war bonnets regal on top of their heads, rode off into the forest. Kai heard commanding voices coming from over by the herd, and watched as many of the men found strategic places to surround and stand guard around the camp.

Shots soon echoed across the lake. Then the silence lasted longer than Kai thought it was humanly possible to endure. Her guard never left his position by the door. Stunned by the sound of gunfire and then the ensuing silence, all Kai managed to do was sink down onto the ground and wait for news.

When she heard the whoops and cries of a successful battle, she held back her tears. The men rode back into camp, yipping and howling like excited coyotes. Behind one of the riders was a dark bay with a white blaze down his muzzle. The horse was fighting the tether, and as she watched, she saw him reach his long neck out and bite a chunk of hide off the rump of the leading horse. The hurt animal kicked, but Man Eater was used to this kind of retaliation and pulled back in time to miss the flying hoof. The tether around his neck snapped. The rider hollered as he regained control of his horse. Kai felt mildly triumphant as Man Eater gnashed at a Salish man as he attempted to grab the broken lead rope. After trampling over a different man, Man Eater galloped off into the dark, bucking and kicking to assure that no one else tried to restrain him.

The door flap closed in front of Kai. She pushed it back open and promptly received a painful whack on her knuckles. She yanked her hand away and cradled it against her body, feeling the sting and hoping her ring finger wasn't broken. With the jolt of pain came the awareness that she was no longer in a numb stupor. She ran to the back of the tipi and threw herself down on the ground, intending to squeeze out of the tipi and disappear into the forest, the same way Man Eater had. The canvas was too tight though, and she couldn't get out without digging up the ground. Frustrated that she had wasted precious seconds, she moved to her original spot and tried again. This time, she was rewarded with a blow to her upper arm as she reached out. In her rush to escape, she hadn't looked for a guard outside the lodge. Recoiling, she backed toward the center and held her arm and her sore fingers.

They're not going to let me get away. Closing her eyes, her breath came hard and ragged as she processed the situation. She couldn't give up. Not yet. Kai checked for moccasins this time before squeezing out under the lodge. She saw two sets of feet and withdrew. When whoops and war cries began a second time, she peered under the canvas, looking toward the glow of the fire.

The men cleared a path to the center of the campsite as the other warriors returned. Kai struggled to see through the screen of bodies. Commotion and anticipation was like a fever running high through the men. They danced and called out as the others came into the circle of light. Kai wanted to scream for them to get out of the way so she could see if it was Dean causing the excitement.

Then a narrow space between some men opened up long enough for her to see someone being drug into the camp by two warriors. His tall frame, muscular arms, and his shaggy mid-length hair confirmed his identity. The two men released Dean, and he fell. He was sprawled across the ground, flat on his face.

Kai gasped, and then a primal instinct took over inside of her. She attacked the tipi like it was made of rice paper and toothpicks. She was beneath the canvas, or tearing through it, and was only vaguely aware when the poles crashed behind her. Someone grabbed her, and she lashed out with a ferocious attack to his face while kicking both of her feet. There was a yowl of pain, and then she was free. Kai pitched forward in Dean's direction. Not knowing if he was dead or alive, her eyes searched for any sign of life. She saw him attempt to rise before collapsing again on the forest floor.

"Dean!" she cried as another man came straight for her.

She was a vicious predator; feral and rabid as she punched, tore, clawed, and bit her way to Dean. Kai hurled herself over his body, protecting him from further harm.

Panicked yells and distressed orders were being given, but she didn't understand them, nor could she hear anything coherent over the rush of blood in her ears. She hung onto Dean like a life raft, thinking that if they were both going to be killed, then at least they wouldn't die alone. Time stopped for Kai, and all she could do was hang on. Somehow Dean had become her friend. Her safety. Her insurance to return to Trevyn.

People tugged at her, trying to lift her off of Dean, but she refused to let go. *Then there was nothing.* Stillness in the cool night air. Eventually, she passed out on top of his body.

When Kai came to, she was aware of Dean's warmth and smell next to her. He had a crisp, woodsy scent about him, mixed with horse, smoke, and leather. The aroma mingled with the crushed fir needles beneath them. When she tried to slide away from Dean, she swallowed a cry of pain. Her arm didn't want to cooperate at all. She had to cradle it with her opposite hand in order not to scream in agony. Looking at her shoulder to make sure it wasn't actually ripped in half like the way it felt, she saw the angry scratches and bruises beneath the tears in her dress.

Dean stirred next to her, and his eyes flew open. Their gazes met with simultaneous surprise, shock, hurt, and concern. He broke eye contact first and looked around. She felt his muscles harden in defensive mode. Kai hadn't even gotten that far, but now she viewed the camp. They were still in the same place where the men had dropped Dean, between the fir tree and the fire pit. Dean scooted an inch away, and then pushed himself up so he was sitting by her side. Kai watched their guard yawn as he reached for his pistol. The look on his humorless face was impenetrable. He aimed the gun at Dean's chest.

The sun was making its appearance known somewhere to the east, but the camp had yet to feel its warmth. A blanket of fog hung over the lake, and tendrils of mist crept toward them. Kai managed to pry herself off of the ground with controlled effort and a lot of teeth clenching. She only made it to sitting. Her nails were ragged, her ribcage ached on the right side, and she thought she could have a couple of broken toes. All things considered, Dean looked about fifty times worse.

She watched him take in their surroundings. His eyes, she only just now realized, were like a hawk's. The golden specks making them appear that much more intense and all-seeing. The swelling on the left side of his face and jaw made her want to weep, but it was the fact that she was fairly certain he couldn't stand up that had her even more worried. Then she noticed how intently he stared at the painted lodge across the camp.

Kai turned her attention in the same direction. Two horses stood by the large lodge, and at their heels was a wolf.

"Philip," Dean said.

Their guard didn't shoot Dean for speaking, but he didn't stop pointing the barrel of his gun at him either.

"Are you sure?" she asked.

"Those are John's horses, too," he murmured.

Kai swallowed. The dryness of her throat was just another discomfort to add to the growing list. Dean's gaze was straight and unblinking as he watched the dog and the horses. Kai stared and even began to let herself hope that John Winters had arrived.

Chapter Sixteen

"The Sun Chief has pitied you this day. You paid a small price for your life."

The grudge Dean had been holding since they left the Salish society men was a bitter stink bomb swirling around his aura. Awash in resentment and anger, along with a swollen, bruised, and broken body, he sat on the travois like an invalid, and thought about the days he'd spent in Growler's Tavern, drinking Coronas with lime.

Thinking beer could improve his current situation, he added self-loathing to the long list of his woes.

"How did you find us, John?" Kai asked.

She rode Man Eater, who surprisingly had not tried to throw her or take a piece out of her. John and Kai built the travois for Dean with speed and efficiency. Man Eater wouldn't have anything to do with the poles, so John's packhorse received the extra burden of hauling Dean's handicapped body through the forest.

John had managed to negotiate with the Salish. It had taken half of the day, and cost them Kai's two horses, the saddles, and most of their supplies to secure her and Dean's freedom. After their release, John told Dean and Kai that he knew the chief of the Salish band, and many of the men who were camped there. He talked them out of their plans for Kai and explained how she *was* a Cree woman, but she was married to Dean. That she was a faithful wife, but very mean when angered. Her outbursts, attempts to run away, and attacks on the warriors were only the beginning of their trouble if they continued to keep her from her husband.

Being that Kai had injured three men already, it wasn't too hard to convince them to let her go. They would have to endure a long and dangerous journey to take her home to the Many Bear Claws Cree to earn the reward for her return. Plus, no one was one hundred percent certain that she was the missing daughter anyway, so they had agreed to the trade.

As Dean reviewed John's bargain for their release, he decided that it was a disaster that was difficult to digest. He'd lost his rifle, revolver, mess kit, his blankets, and the coffee. Kai was allowed to keep her women's things, including her knife and the empty parfleche. She claimed that Dean's journal was hers as well, insisting that it was vital to her and of no use to the warriors. The Salish had rounded up Man Eater, but had placed him in a similar category as Kai. *More trouble than he was worth.*

"There is news to tell," John said.

He chewed on a licorice root that Kai had picked earlier when they passed a boggy area near a pond. He spit it out and said, "You killed the buffalo hunters. There was a government man killed with them. I saw a patrol out on the Plains, looking for you."

Dean's gut clenched into a hard, sour stone. "We tried to stop Badger, but we were too late."

"The patrol stopped me to ask questions. I told them I knew nothing. Told them I was on my way to Helena and heard gun shots when the sun was far behind the mountains two sleeps ago."

As Dean rode on the travois, he started to run his tongue around his teeth and then clamped his mouth shut when he felt the pain from one of his many injuries. Then the horse veered around some scrub oak brush, and the travois skidded over a ridge of rough ground. The result of the bumpy ride was that he had to hold his leg so it didn't feel like his pelvis was cracking apart.

His injury from being kicked in the groin had already made riding excruciating, but during the night before, when he was attempting to rescue Kai from the Salish warriors, he sustained even more damage, courtesy of Man Eater. He'd like to report that he had rushed in and killed Kai's abductors. But the truth was, after he spotted her with the men, he started to climb into his saddle, and Man Eater decided that he was no longer willing to be ridden. As

Dean placed his foot in the stirrup, the horse launched like a missile and then stampeded away through the forest. *Apparently towing Dean's one hundred and ninety pound carcass wasn't much of a hindrance to the devil horse.* If it wasn't for the stump that collided with his face and finally tore him loose from the saddle, he could very well be halfway to Wyoming by now. Dean shot the now docile horse a vengeful glare, and then winced as his face protested against being moved in any way. Even eating had become a dreaded task.

"I turned back and went looking for you. I knew the Salish were close, and thought they may have heard the gunfire, too. Many people have heard the story of the blackhorn hunters, and send scouts to watch these white hunters. If the meat is too old, they still collect the hides. I followed their signs, and found the two of you. Where is Badger?"

Dean spoke up, "He was injured, and we left him behind. He is one day's ride north and east of where we are now. If we do not return to him by tomorrow, then he will meet us with the Piegans at the dark of the moon."

John Winters considered the information in silent contemplation as they rode on. It gave Dean time to think as well.

"Is it more important to continue on to Helena or return to Badger's side? I must be in Helena by seven more sleeps to meet with the expedition leader," the scout said at last. He looked to Kai, as if she knew the answer.

To Dean's surprise, Kai said, "I think we need to find Badger before continuing on to the mining town. Badger may need medicine in case a fever has started."

"I agree with Kai," Dean said. "We want to travel to Helena together, or not at all."

Dean noticed Kia avoiding eye contact with him, and the hard lines of tension that had formed around her mouth, but she didn't say anything else.

"Your medicine is weak. You have many bad things happening to you on this journey. Even Philip feels it. I do not like traveling with someone who brings bad luck."

Dean steadied himself on the makeshift seat made from ropes and leather. The truth irritated and stung his pride, but he wouldn't deny it. He listened to the hooves of the horses and the crows cawing from the trees.

John said, "We made an agreement to go to Helena. Now you cannot walk, and have lost two of your horses and your guns. I will take you back to Badger. Then you will go your own way. Find Laughing Eyes, or one of the other great medicine men. They will bring healing. Then you will travel with greater ease."

"You are right, John. I am in need of a medicine man. I will take your advice when we return to the Piegans."

John looked ahead, and so did his dog. They rode for the rest of the afternoon and camped in the mountains. First thing in the morning, they started out again, heading toward Badger. It was slow going with the travois over the rough terrain, but their progress was steady. It was nearing sunset when Dean saw the stream where Kai had been taken. They let the horses drink before crossing, and then continued the short distance to where they last saw Badger. Dean thought they had only an hour or so before it would be dark. Clouds had moved in from the northwest, and it was getting colder by the hour. They would need plenty of firewood to get through the night. Dean was grateful that he'd left Kai's bedroll behind, along with most of their food and other supplies.

When they rounded the small hill and entered the sheltered copse where they had hidden after killing the buffalo hunters, Dean knew something was wrong. It was too still. There wasn't a hint of smoke in the chilly air, or a rustle of hooves from Badger's horse.

"He's not here," Dean said as he peered around the horse to where Badger should have been.

"Do you think he left already?" Kai asked as she brought Man Eater to a stop.

"There has been trouble here," John said.

Dean wanted his gun. It chafed him that the Salish now owned it. The horse stopped walking, and he braced himself against the travois poles and stood up. The pain was there, but he ignored it as his worry for Badger superseded discomfort.

"They are gone many hours," John Winters said as he looked at the cold fire and the remains of the camp. "Philip would let us know if the government men were close by."

Dean hadn't thought about the dog's ability to alert, and the realization helped him relax just a little. Kai slid off of Man Eater and walked over to Dean. She handed him a sturdy branch to use as a cane.

"Same patrol that stopped me," John Winters said as he looked at prints on the ground.

"How can you tell?" Dean asked. He was used to being the one with the intelligence. He wanted to know what he was missing.

"Horse shoes. Boot prints, not moccasins. The only white men in the area are the patrol."

Dean saw it then. The scuff of hard soled shoes and the horse prints were deeper with metal shoes than the prints from their own horses' hooves. He saw how the fire was hastily put out with a few scrapes of a boot to push dirt over it. Kai's blankets were tossed into the brush. Badge's own bed roll was left sitting on the ground, smeared with dirt, and trampled by hooves and boot prints. Badger's pack was gone, and so was the medicine bundle. It was a mistake to leave it with Badger, Dean realized too late. The rush he had been in and the pain in his leg had clouded his judgment. *Now his pipe was gone.*

"Any chance he's still alive?" Kai asked.

"No body," John pointed out, and looked around the tiny campsite.

Dean swallowed and looked for blood or signs of a struggle.

"Would they arrest him? Where would they take him?"

"Could be Fort Benton. Could be the jail in Helena."

"What are we going to do now?" Kai asked as she retrieved her blanket and looked around for their scattered belongings. There wasn't much. Badger's torn and bloody shirt, a broken bottle, and an empty water skin.

"Sleep. It is too late to go farther," John said as he moved to the packhorse and started to settle in for the night.

His dog whined and John said, "Go find your meal."

Philip put his nose to the ground and ran into the darkening forest.

Barely able to walk, Dean hobbled over to Badger's blankets, shook them out, and straightened them as well as he could.

Kai stayed in sight of the men and gathered wood, and then searched the nearby bushes and plants for edibles and medicinals before it was completely dark.

Dean woke up from a fitful sleep when Kai gave him a cup of soup with shredded meat, wild onions, and something green in it. It was so good that he downed it in seconds. It warmed him from the inside, and the pain in his groin lessened. He started to fall back to sleep with the mug still in his hand.

"I'm going to put medicine on your face and leg," Kai said as she retrieved the tin cup from Dean's hand before it fell.

John was generous enough to share his cooking utensils with her and she had immediately started cooking dinner and making a poultice and tea for Dean. Her arm hurt when she moved it in certain directions, but she guessed she was nowhere near the level of pain that Dean was experiencing.

The soup was nourishing and tasty. She had used some of the dried buffalo from John, ground into fine pieces then added some sage and onion for flavor. She had also soaked some willow bark in her and Dean's soup for the pain relieving effects. Now that they had eaten, it was time to clean and dress his other wounds. During their ride she had collected willows and plantain growing by a creek. There were two wild geraniums growing next to their camp, so she would also use them.

John Winters didn't speak much as he shared the soup and then smoked from his short pipe before lying down for the night. He watched Kai prepare the medicines, and then offered her a tin filled with goose grease.

She took it from him and mixed in the mashed plants to make a salve. Kai smeared the salve onto Dean's cheek and jaw and then did the same to his upper thigh and groin. She used strips of Badger's torn shirt, which had been discarded on the ground, to lay over the salve on his leg to keep it from immediately rubbing off. Feeling satisfied that she had done all she could for him, she used some more of the salve on her shoulder and toes, and then finally gave herself permission to stop moving and lie down.

Kai had been cold for the last couple of hours. The fire was warm, but only when she was right in front of it. She had tried to keep her feet close to the flames, but her upper body was freezing. She looked over at Dean, and had conflicting thoughts about how to stay warm through the night. Resolve settled over her, and she picked up her single blanket and went to lay by him. She was careful not to wake him as she rearranged the covers until they were warmly nested inside the combined bedding. The last thing Kai saw before passing out were Philip's gold eyes, watching her from his place next to John Winters.

At daybreak, Kai searched the surrounding woods once more for edible food and medicines. She didn't go far — she'd learned that lesson the hard way — but with the disappearance of Badger and most of their provisions, they needed more food. On the edge of their camp, she noticed something they had all missed the night before. While picking rose hips beneath an old growth fir tree, Kai saw bear claw marks on the tree trunk. She looked up to see how high the bear had reached, and that's when she saw the leather backpack hanging from a branch. How Badger managed to get the pack up in the tree, she would likely never know, but she could imagine Badger throwing the heavy pack with his one good arm when the patrol had gotten close to him. He had been lucky that it had caught and held there. Now she was going to have to get it down. The strap was hanging on a flimsy-looking branch, but most of the pack's bulk rested on the branch below. Neither tree limb looked strong enough to hold her weight, so she was either going to have to throw something heavy into the tree to knock it down, or climb up with a long stick and try to poke it free. She chose option two. By this time she had John and Dean's attention. John joined her, and looked up to see what she was staring at.

"I am too large to make it up there," he observed. "You make the bag fall down, and I will catch it."

Climbing with a shoulder that didn't want to be moved, Kai cowgirled up – as her ex would have said – and hauled herself into the tree. She didn't need the stick after all. Shaking the branches was enough for it to fall into John's waiting arms.

Unpacking the bag revealed that Badger's guns were gone and so was his pouch of gold. Dean wasn't surprised. Badger had his rifle and pistol right next to him when he left to rescue Kai. The other pistols had already been traded away for the horses and tack. The gold however, was a mystery. Dean hadn't given it much thought and didn't know where Badger kept it stashed. Now that it was missing, Dean assumed that Badger must have been carrying it on him.

They were happy to find a couple of knives, some food, and the dried herbal medicines. Most of Badger's personal items were there as well, including his spare clothes, the journal, the cyanide crystals, and a bottle he hadn't seen before filled with what smelled like vinegar. Dean wrinkled his nose at the smell, corked the bottle, and put it back with the food stores. He was relieved to have any of their supplies returned, but disappointed when a more thorough check of the area didn't produce the medicine bundle with his pipe.

Kai was adamant about continuing south to Helena instead of waiting out the month in the relative safety of a Piegan camp. He tried speculating about her motives, but couldn't place them. Since John had to be in Helena in a few days anyway, Kai and Dean decided to continue traveling with him if he would allow it. John said that since he was already paid, he would continue to let Dean and Kai travel with him. Dean prayed to Great Spirit that their run of bad luck was over. He prayed they would find Badger in Helena, and that he hadn't been taken east to Fort Benton.

Despite a cold, drizzly day on the travois, Dean's strength increased instead of depleted like it had the day before. He thought the cause was Kai's medicines and her cooking. She knew every plant for eating and for easing pain. His appreciation continued to grow with every meal and cup of tea she prepared for him. And being who she was, when he tried to compliment her, she only frowned or narrowed her eyes at him before saying a curt *you're welcome*. That was if she said anything at all.

By the second day, Dean was able to ride on John's packhorse. They kept the travois for hauling their gear. On the third day, they left the travois behind and Dean and Kai rode Man Eater together. The horse obviously had an affinity for women, as Kai had no trouble with the surly beast. As soon as Dean approached the animal, he was again avoiding gnashing teeth.

Kai murmured a warning to the horse. "No biting, big man, or he might eat you."

Dean gave her a questionable look.

"He responds to threats," Kai told him.

"No he doesn't," Dean said as he climbed on behind her. "We've talked about the removal of his manhood. It makes his teeth grow longer."

"He hears the mother in my tone," she said, looking over her shoulder at Dean.

"That must be it," he agreed, only half believing it. He thought the horse somehow knew the Cree had been known to eat horses, and that she really wasn't kidding. With her culinary skills and the variety of flavors she added to their food, he would never know if he was eating horse meat or not. He kept these thoughts to himself as they started off on the second to last day before reaching the gold mining town of Helena. He sent another silent prayer to the Great Spirit and the Above Ones that they wouldn't have to resort to eating Man Eater. Deer and rabbits were plentiful. The problem was, he had no way of hunting them. Dean needed a new plan of action, and he needed it fast. He couldn't keep relying on John for meat.

He also really needed to find his medicine bundle. He closed his eyes and breathed. The scent of Kai filled his senses. She had a warm, natural scent like rain in a forest mixed with the smell of a cooking fire. He was getting used to her being near him, and he liked it. He focused on one last prayer, asking that they find Badger and the Dragonfly medicine pipe, both in one piece. A gun would be welcome, too. Until his prayers were answered, John Winters was their savior in more ways than one.

"Strikes-on-the-mountain, the Salish chief, told me a story when I smoked with him in his lodge," John said.

Dean pushed himself up on his bed roll and blinked at the man and dog staring at him from the other side of the morning fire. They were now one day's ride from Helena. They had slept in a narrow valley surrounded by a dense forest. The air was humid and swarming with bugs. Dean was sure the mosquitoes would drain all their blood, but Kai had come through for them once again. She knew to burn fleabane in the fire to produce smoke that the insects didn't like, and she also knew to rub pineapple weed and elderberry leaves on their clothes and skin to repel them as well. They remained pleasantly bug free.

"The Salish say they have heard of a man named Wolfsblood," John said as he slapped at an errant gnat buzzing around the tip of his hooked nose. "He was known as a fierce fighter, with many coup and a brave wife. Strikes-on-the-mountain said he did not believe you could be this same Wolfsblood, because the warrior he saw would be much older than you are. He asked me if you were the son of this other Wolfsblood."

Dean cleared his throat before speaking. "What did you tell him?"

"I said I did not know if there was any relation between the two of you."

"Have you heard of this other Wolfsblood?" Dean asked, feeling his skin prickle with apprehension.

"I have heard a story told, now many winters past, about a Piegan man with a good white man tongue, looking for his sits-besides wife."

Dean kept his face as neutral as John's. *Could he really be telling him about his father and mother? What could have happened to his parents? Why didn't his grandparents tell him anything?* "Do you know what happened to the man and his wife?"

"The story is told that they were favored by the Above Ones. That they turned into eagles and joined the Sun chief."

Dean looked up at the sky seeing the early morning sun brightening the treetops.

"If a great eagle sits before me in the shape of a man, I wish to know how I can serve him," John Winters said, straight faced and humble.

"There is no great eagle inside of me. You have seen the misfortune that I have been through in the last few sleeps."

"Old Man Napi is known to cause trouble in mysterious ways. He has done this since the long-ago times. I do not question the Above Ones for playing their games and tricks."

"Perhaps Napi plays a trick on me. It would explain much," Dean said as he remembered the stories about the old man who created the world. Then he told John, "I have never met my real father or my mother. I do not know if this Wolfsblood warrior is my relation, but I am definitely not the man in the story."

"You have very good white man's tongue, like the other Wolfsblood."

"That is true," Dean said, and paused thinking of a way to explain himself that was honest and believable. "In the land where the Sun begins his journey, many tribes have begun to speak like white men. I have spoken English since I was a small boy, and it is easy for me. You also know the words well."

John nodded with understanding. "I have much practice. The white men trade with me for being a guide into the mountains, and interpreter of many languages. I am most comfortable with the Siksika and Piegan people, but I prefer to live alone or travel. I go where I want to go."

"Sounds like a good life. Better than most people have," Dean said with sincerity.

"Suits me and Philip." He scratched the wolf-like dog's ruff and then said, "Your woman went that way," he pointed up the hill. "Says she will be back before our morning meal."

Dean frowned at the forest. *Why would Kai venture off alone again after the trouble that happened before?* He climbed to his feet, keeping the majority of his weight on his good leg, and stretched his arms and shoulders. Testing his first step, he found that his pelvis was more stable than the day before. The bruises were horrific shades of black, blue, purple and green, but he knew that meant they were getting better. The angry red of inflammation was gone, and he could walk again, slowly, but any walking was better than nothing.

"I'm going to find her before any more Salish do."

"Strong minded women make for the best and most exciting wives," John said with a knowing wiggle of his eyebrows.

"Tell me this isn't what it looks like."

Kai held a flat rock about the size of Dean's foot. There was a hole in the ground in front of her at the base of a larch tree.

She returned to digging and ignored the question.

"Kai, what in hell's name are you doing?"

"Not now," she hissed. "I won't speak here. Can't you see the burial platforms?"

Shocked that he had found her, of all places, at a Blackfoot burial site, he wanted to get her away from there. *As far away as possible.* It was unlucky to disturb a grave. They were risking angering the dead person up in the tree. Of angering Great Spirit, and the Above Ones. The trip was not going well for them already. Kai's intrusion on sacred ground could be the end of them. Any clan members of this person would be offended beyond repair.

"Stop," he ordered. "There could be a chief buried here. We have to leave."

"I saw the robes, and the weapons, and the shield. I know it's an important grave. Now shut up. I'm not done."

"Are you mentally unbalanced? Badger's convinced of it, but I was giving you the benefit of the doubt."

"Go away then," she said as she kept digging.

"John is waiting for us. Let's go before we're both cursed."

"Not yet."

He walked up behind her to grab her shoulder. The whisper of a breeze tickled the back of his neck and he looked over his shoulder, expecting an attack by angered Blackfoot warriors, or a ghost ready to scalp him. His gaze rested on the platform in the tree where a dead body was wrapped in a buffalo robe. He could see the man's spear and painted war shield lying beside him. Trinkets and leather pouches hung from smaller branches around the corpse. If the chief's ghost was really here watching him, he was in deeper, creepier water than he had ever treaded before. He wasn't sure if even Laughing Eyes could cleanse or protect him from this error in judgment.

Kai shrugged out from under his hand and kept scooping away the dirt. The hole was almost a foot deep.

"I'm not kidding Kai. You're asking for serious trouble by messing around in this place."

"Don't say anything else. I want to get this over with and get out of here."

He lowered himself down next to her and grimaced as his healing groin stretched. "What are you doing?" he repeated.

She looked at him with barely concealed patience. "Remember the story I told you? This is the place where there are sapphires."

"How do you know?"

"My father and sister showed it to me before they died."

Dean leaned a shoulder against the gray tree bark and thought about the story she told him.

"You shouldn't even know about it. It's a family secret, but since you followed me and you won't shut up…" She let her words trail off as she put the rock aside and began to clear the dirt with her fingers.

"There's treasure buried right here?" he asked in disbelief, almost rolling his eyes. Badger had seen her craziness and had tried to warn him. *How had he gotten stuck with her? And why was he so damned attracted to her, even with her mental instability and cold shoulder?* She did keep him warm on cold nights, but he suspected it was only for her own comfort, and had little to do with him personally.

She pressed her lips together and focused on the ground instead of answering. Another breeze passed through the grove of trees. With the platform resting ten feet up, the twisted pine tree creaked, and then a branch cracked somewhere in the same tree. The falling limb hit the ground, fifteen feet away from where they crouched. He was already uptight about the location, and now his superstitious side was making him feel like he had fire ants in his pants. He was ready to jump on Man Eater and just say to hell with the whole trip. Staring up at the canopy of branches, he waited for the ghost to show itself, and didn't see Kai pull the wrapped package out of the earth.

He glanced over at her just as she discarded the outer wrappings of rawhide and leather. The pouch inside appeared to be made of thick, tanned buffalo hide. A yellow bear was painted on the outside. *Was it a symbol for Kai's clan?*

Kai untied the pouch and looked inside. He couldn't see what she was looking at, so he watched her face instead. Tears threatened to spill from her lower lids. She swallowed and blinked them away. She used her fingers to prod and search inside the bag and then pulled them back out, empty. Dean could tell there were chunks of something inside, so he waited with anxious curiosity.

She upended the pouch over her open palm and multicolored stones and gold nuggets poured out.

"Holy... You weren't lying," he said, astonished.

She held a small fortune in her delicate hand.

Kai hid her gaze beneath her long lashes and then looked back to the treasure. She shuffled the stones around in her cupped palm. Then she dumped out more gold and sapphires from the bag. The stones varied in color, from different shades of green to pale blue and even indigo. The sizes ranged from half-carat chips to stones larger than his thumbnail. The gold pieces were mostly smaller, but there was still a lot of gold in her hand. It was more than what Badger had brought with him, which was now missing, along with Badger.

"How is this possible?"

She refused to answer as she let the stones and some of the gold nuggets trickle back into the leather bag. She set it down, careful not to spill them, and then reached for a smaller pouch that was tied at her waist.

"Open this for me," she whispered as she passed the little bag over to Dean.

He did as she asked and held it open for her. She emptied the rest of the gold into it and then pulled out a creamy sheet of folded paper. She tucked the paper into the buffalo skin bag and set it back down, then closed and secured the smaller gold-filled pouch onto her belt.

"Are you thinking we can buy Badger's safety with this?"

She squinted up her face and blinked at him. Then she said, "No," like he should know better than to even ask such a ridiculous question.

"Then what do you need the gold for?"

"Stop talking," she scolded. "It's haunted here. If the ghosts know your face and voice, they'll follow you."

He was confused and frustrated with her. He used hand signs to say, "You bring the ghosts to us, woman. It's not my doing."

She flipped him the modern bird and flashed him a taunting, fake smile.

Dean hardened his resolve that he had to wait for her to explain later. He watched as she repacked the buffalo skin pouch inside the wrappings and put it in the bottom of the hole. He helped her push the dirt back into place and then they scattered rocks and needles and leaves so the ground looked undisturbed.

They glanced at one another, and without speaking they knew it was time to return to where John Winters was camped. Dean started to move away from the tree, but when he didn't hear Kai's footsteps following his, he looked over his shoulder for her.

Her fingers rested in the crook of the western larch where the tree was divided down the center, as if two trees had grown together. He watched her fingers slide over something small and smooth. When her hand dropped away, he squinted and saw the curve of a bear claw sticking out of the bark. The color of the claw blended in with the bark with near perfect camouflage. No one would see it unless they knew it was there. Then he saw another claw set to the right, one to the left, and one below. Four claws were somehow embedded into the bark, and the tree had grown around them. He turned back around keeping his face blank, not knowing if Kai was aware that he had been watching her.

When they were out of sight of the burial ground, and far enough away that he could yell without the spirit of the dead hearing him, he let himself speak.

"How long has that been here?"

"I don't know, Dean," Kai said, sounding tired. "Our people don't use the Western calendar in this time. You know that."

"I do. They count by winters, but those claws in the tree can't be that old."

"About a decade, I would guess."

Dean could hear the somber tone of her voice and remembered the tears Kai had refused to shed.

Dean recalled the story of the Cree scouts and the prospectors that were all killed for trespassing and disturbing a grave. "Laughing

Eyes told me the injured Cree girl didn't make it back to the village with him because she died. And that he sent her to the Sand Hills."

"Is that all he told you?"

"Yes. Do you think it was the girl or her father who buried the gold and sapphires?"

"Does it matter who buried it? The treasure brings bad luck. My father and uncle and sister were all killed because of it."

"How?"

"Greed is universal and timeless. It makes people do terrible things. My family was attacked by bad people, who thought they could take what wasn't theirs. My uncle talked too much. He drank too much. He liked to drink with my father. It wasn't a good combination."

Kai stared at the forest while she talked, but Dean didn't think she saw any of it.

They started walking again. Their pace was as slow as a turtle's, and not only because of Dean's injury.

"My father felt like he needed to support our family better. He knew the treasure was there. I guess I'm no different than he is. He wanted to use it to help us, and he was killed for it. Now look at me, I'm using it because I need it, and have no other choice."

"And what was on the paper you put into the bag? Did you write yourself a note?"

"I did. I have to try something, don't I? If I can prevent myself from coming in the first place, then I will."

"That's smart," he said. "Think it will work?"

"I'm here aren't I?"

"True. You've never dug up the treasure since you lost your parents."

"No. But like I said, I have to try something."

"And you took a piece of my sketch paper to write to yourself."

"Yes. I addressed the letter to anyone in my family."

"Do you steal anything you want?"

"It was a sheet of paper. I didn't think you'd miss it."

"Take anything else?"

"No, and I'm sorry. The plan came to me suddenly, when I realized where we were camped. You were asleep. I needed it."

Dean stopped walking and took Kai's hand so she had to stop with him. "What are you doing with all that gold?"

"A similar idea. Only I'm going to write to myself next, and pay a bank to hold the letter for a hundred and forty-four years."

Dean licked his lips and then swallowed. He wrapped his other arm around her and then pulled Kai into a tight embrace with their hands still joined. "That's why you wanted to stick with John Winters so bad, isn't it? He has connections in Helena. I'll help too, Kai. We can figure it out. This has to work."

She nodded against his chest. Kai had blackmailed Badger into paying for her letter to be kept in a safety deposit box. She had found Badger's journal in the tipi, and had read a lot of it. Although she didn't know what his notes with all of the names and dates inside meant, she suspected he was up to something terrible. They had come to a tenuous arrangement, and part of the deal was to keep Dean out of it. She hated using blackmail and being dishonest, but she would do whatever she needed to do to stay in 2012, and sending herself a letter would ensure that.

Since Badger's disappearance, she wasn't sure how she was going to be able to pull this off. Then yesterday she knew exactly how she could pay to secure her letter for her future self. Kai understood that they also needed to live for the next two and a half weeks. Most of their supplies had been taken and they had to have food and protection. The gold could buy what they needed to survive in this harsh and unforgiving place.

She leaned into him with relief as she started to open her past to him. Hiding her true motives had been grueling. Kai didn't know what Dean would think of her plan to message herself in the future, and Badger was against every breath she took, let alone her actually doing something proactive.

Kai believed she couldn't tell anyone about her family's secret hiding place for the gold and sapphires. No one should be exposed to the heartache and demise that the treasure seemed to bring. Even now, she wondered if Great Spirit would punish her for using the gold, but she knew it was her only chance to survive and return to her son.

Dean pressed his lips to the top of Kai's head, and then she pulled back to look up at him. The understanding on his face warmed her, and for a second she forgot to hold up her self-imposed walls.

Dean watched her with his keen eyes. He released her hand and brushed back a strand of her hair, tucking it behind her ear. His fingers trailed down the side of her cheek and lay lightly against the nape of her neck. He wanted to kiss the soft skin beneath his fingertips, where the curve of her neck met her shoulder. But he knew that would be crossing the line. He cupped the back of her neck instead and leaned down just enough to brush his lips over hers.

"You'll be home soon, Anna-kai."

"So will you," she whispered back.

She let him hold her hand as they hiked down into the tight valley, and back to their hidden campsite.

Chapter Seventeen

Kai handed John Winters enough gold to buy a gun, a dress for herself, and other much needed provisions. They also wanted acceptable clothing for Dean to wear into town. She compensated John for his time and for the risks he was willing to take on their behalf.

John sounded confident as he said, "It is no risk to go into Steinmetz and Clarkson Dry Goods. I am a known man, and the trading has been fair. I am a well respected unmarried man. Your generous amount of gold pays me to answer questions about who I am buying the dress for. This is of high concern to me. I do not want the men thinking I have finally found a wife."

"Would that really be so bad?" Kai teased. "Tell them it is a gift for your sister," Kai suggested, and John winked at her.

Kai straightened up their campsite as John rode over the hill toward Helena. They had stopped late the night before in the hills outside of town and found some level ground, surrounded by skunkbush sumac. It made for decent cover, but their proximity to town made her nervous. With Badger having been taken and four dead buffalo hunters lying out on the plains, they had good reasons to stay out of sight. She and Dean were equally guilty of murder. At least that's the way any court would see it.

Kai and Dean's topic of conversation kept returning to whether or not Badger was alive, and if he was, how they were going to help him. She noticed that neither of them brought up the kiss they shared, or how uncomfortable she was anywhere in the vicinity of his lips. She was totally confused about why she let him kiss her, but she had to admit that it was one of the sweetest kisses she had ever experienced. *That bit of honesty scared the piss out of her.*

She needed a walk. She had to trust that John Winters knew the area, but she also wanted to see it for herself and know that no one else was around. Kai stayed close to the tall brush and the scattered bushes near their campsite. The remnants of an abandoned cabin could be seen in the valley to the southwest, but that was the only sign of human habitation. Hearing the meadowlarks, chickadees, and sparrows trill and sing their contented morning songs calmed her nerves. Bees and butterflies flittered around the wildflowers as she wandered back to Dean and Man Eater with an armload of dead branches to use as firewood. She set the wood down and then inspected the water bag and canteen to see how their supply was holding out. She decided they had enough to last the day if they were thrifty with it.

"You could relax, you know?"

"I doubt I can," she said.

"May as well try. John won't be back until late. Possibly not until tomorrow."

She dropped her hands to her sides and decided to stop pretending to stay busy. Planting herself on the blanket, she stared at Dean and waited for him to give her another piece of unnecessary advice.

He had his sketchbook open on his lap and a pencil in his hand.

"Did you change the poultice on your leg? Twice a day is the best."

"I already cleaned it off," he said as his hand sketched with quick and precise movements. "I used the last of the medicine. I don't think it needs it anymore."

"I should probably look at it again to make sure it's healing right," she said with some hesitancy.

Dean thought he heard a cringe in her voice. *Did he repulse her?* He didn't think so. The single kiss they shared was more than pleasant. It had reached into his heart and crafted a memory he wouldn't soon forget. In fact, he was willing to try it again just to make sure he wasn't conjuring the sensations still nestled inside of him. He glanced up from his drawing and saw the grimace on her face. Glancing back down, he stared at the preliminary lines of Kai sitting on top of Man Eater. The sway of Man Eater's back meeting his withers. The mane of black hair lying against his long neck. Kai's single braid draped over her shoulder. He liked that he'd been able to capture Kai's stern expression and still keep her mouth soft and her eyes bright. Man Eater's hidden devil would show in the angle of his ears and the slightly flared nostrils, or so Dean hoped. The animal was nearly as frustrating to him as Kai was. Dean stretched his leg and then crossed it again.

He saw her keeping a watchful eye on him, but avoiding the exact location of his injury. Dean didn't mind the thought of her staring at his healing groin, but then he was suddenly aware of another distinct stirring in the area.

He stuck his tongue in his cheek as if he were trying to remove a piece of stuck food from a tooth and then said, "I can assure you it's much better. Maybe you should keep your distance from my…" He looked down at his crotch and then raised his gaze to hers. "It may be embarrassing for both of us for you to be touching my parts. They're working fine now."

Kai cleared her throat and shifted her eyes away from Dean's. "Great," she agreed with forced cheerfulness. "If you need pain relief, you can just drink the tea."

Since she wouldn't be mixing up a new poultice, and since she was embarrassed beyond belief at the reference to Dean's penis, she turned on the blanket and lay flat on her back. She bent her knees, laced her fingers over her stomach, and stared up at the sky. So she hadn't imagined the sexual tension between her and Dean the last time she had looked at his leg. It was torture for her, but apparently it was for him, too. Relief and anxiety toyed with her emotions equally as she came to the realization that Dean was also struggling with his feelings. The relief was from knowing that she wasn't imagining it, and the anxiety came from knowing that they were going to have to fight it until she could return home. She shuddered as she remembered some of her harsh words and the bitchy things she had said and done over the last couple of weeks. *How could he still like her after the way she had acted?*

Even if he did like her, Kai didn't want the complication of a relationship in her life. Dean's struggles with alcohol and the loss of his daughter were just too many obstacles for one person to overcome. Kai was fully aware that she was also a walking disaster. The two of them together would be a ticking time bomb. She knew it, and she knew that single mothers didn't get the luxury of having quick, meaningless affairs. They weren't worth the heartache or the hassle. She was a mom first, and her young son was extremely impressionable. Trevyn already showed too much interest in Dean during their two-minute exchange at Kinder Place. There was no way she would let her son get attached to a boyfriend, and then yank their relationship apart when it didn't work out.

Kai heard the scratch of his pencil as Dean drew in his book. She refused to look at him. Her priorities needed to stay on track. Get her note written and secured in a safety box, and pray to the Above Ones that they have pity on her and let her future self receive the message before this adventure ever even begins. The loops of time circled around each other, confusing her thoughts about the possibilities and probabilities of her plan actually working, when Dean spoke again.

"If it makes you more comfortable, I'll pretend that I didn't like kissing you," he said as he kept drawing.

"That would be helpful."

"If you want, I can take your letter to the trust company and you can stay here, away from town."

"No. It's my idea, and I think you were right when you said we should stay together."

"Based on what happened the last time we were separated, yes, we should stay together."

"Mmmm-hmmm," she hummed as a red-tailed hawk swept across the sky. "We need to wait for John to tell us what he could find out about Badger. Then we can decide how we're going to commit suicide."

After a moment with the only sound coming from Dean's pencil he said, "I've never met anyone like you before."

"What's that supposed to mean?"

"I don't think I have ever been so annoyed and so intrigued by a person. How do you do that?"

"It's a special talent," Kai said and closed her eyes to the clear blue sky.

"It's not suicide, Kai. We can go to town. John is certain of our safety. No one can connect us to the buffalo hunters, except for John and Badger."

"I meant that whatever John ends up telling us, you'll decide that Badger needs rescuing. Then you'll come up with some testosterone laden plan that is probably going to get one of us killed."

"You really know how to boost a guy's ego, don't you?" Dean said, thinking she wasn't entirely incorrect.

He flipped to a blank page and swept the pencil over the paper making the first lines of Kai on her back with the grass growing around her blanket. A butterfly bounced through the morning air and landed on Kai's bent knee. She didn't even know it was there and Dean stopped sketching to watch it. He decided to add it to the new drawing, quickly penciling its form with wings half open. He wrote at the bottom of the page, *Bringer of Dreams.*

"A man has to do what he has to do," he said glancing up at her. "A woman can't understand unless she is a war woman. Which you definitely are not."

"Stop speaking now before I change my mind about you and allow my animalistic urges to surface."

The black and blue butterfly lifted off of her knee when she spoke and disappeared over the hedges. Dean wondered if it had brought her a dream, and what that dream could be.

"There's a fifty-fifty chance I'll like what you're thinking about doing to me," he said, and smirked.

He watched her place her hand on the handle of the knife tied to her waist and raise an eyebrow.

Kai turned her head, eyes opening to glare at him. "You're tempting me and you really shouldn't."

"I'm stronger, faster, and better trained in combat than you are. If you want to wrestle with me Anna-kai, bring it on. It would be good for you to practice some hand-to-hand techniques in case the Salish think you're the lost Indian princess again."

She closed her eyes again, refusing to look at him. "Insufferable pig," she muttered.

He let out a short snorting laugh and then let it go.

Kai breathed through the urge to dismember him and feed his parts to Man Eater. Smiling to herself, she heard the light brushing strokes of Dean's pencil against the thick cream paper in his sketchbook.

Before she knew it, she woke up, startled that she had actually fallen asleep. The sun was high overhead and her body was warm from its heat.

The gentleman assisting Kai and Dean at the First National Bank of Montana was having a hard time believing the sight before his eyes, or at least that's the impression Dean was getting from the twiggy, pointy-chinned man.

"We would like a signed document of assurance that your bank will perform to the best of your ability the instructions per our request," Dean said. He was trying to speak with some formality, but it was uncomfortable and felt awkward to him. Or maybe it was the period clothing that was making him feel foolish.

Dean was about to seek a third party's assistance from the priest who had accompanied them into the bank. A witness to this man's odd behavior would be a good thing to secure. It was obvious to Dean that the banker had never spoken with a native – a true native Blackfoot – whose English and mannerisms were so similar to his own. Not that Dean considered himself to be anything like this man, but the banker could at least have the decency to close his mouth and blink.

"Is your bank able to assist us, Mr. Henkle?" Kai asked. "We can take our money elsewhere if this is an unattainable task for your establishment."

Mr. Henkle managed to finally snap out of his trance and said, "Yes, ma'am. I think you will find that our competitors in town will not be able to serve you as well as we can. This is an unusual..." He cleared his throat and looked down at the simple wood box sealed with wax on the desk containing Kai's letter to herself and then back up at Kai. "A *unique* transaction. I would like to consult the proprietor of the bank to come up with a fair estimate of the charges we would need to hold your property safe until the year..." He cleared his throat again. "Pardon me. Until the year 2012," he finished.

"Thank you. We would appreciate that," Kai said with her hands clasped in her lap and her spine rigid. Her prim and proper tone of voice and the look of near fright on Mr. Henkle's face made Dean want to laugh out loud, but he held himself in check.

"Before I seek conference with Mr. Thomas, I would like to ask how you will be taking care of the payment."

"As all of the miners in town do. With gold."

"Very good. Excuse me."

Mr. Henkle rose from behind his desk just as a group of men entered the front door.

Dean twisted around in his seat to see who had come in. Seated by the entrance was the priest and Nations sympathizer, Father Martin Connolly, who John Winters had introduced to Dean and Kai. The Father stood and greeted one of the men. They shook hands while two other men dressed in the rougher clothes of working men stood like guards behind a robust, middle-aged man wearing a tailored suit with shining cufflinks, a felt hat, and polished shoes.

"Good afternoon, Father Connolly. Good to see a fine gentleman such as yourself in my humble banking establishment," the well-heeled man said.

"Good day to you, Mr. Wright. Ahh, but it won't be long until the construction is complete on the new building. Then the territory will have its first real National Bank. And a fine building it is, to be sure," the Father complimented.

Dean caught the man's name and instantly thought of Badger. *Was this the Hubert Wright in Badger's journal? The man with investments not only in mining, but also in banking and lumber.*

"Are you here about the supply train coming in to town? My men here have informed me that it is arriving within the week. Your shipment from the diocese in Chicago is guaranteed with this delivery," Mr. Wright said.

"Not to be worrying about the sacraments arriving from Chicago a'tall, Sir. You and your partner, Mr. Thomas, have always seen to the church's needs well. Personal business has brought me to your door this fine day."

"That's wonderful news, Father. Speaking of my partner, will you excuse me while I see what that scalawag is doing behind closed doors? I believe he may want the update on the wagon train coming to town."

"God be with you, Mr. Wright," Father Connolly said, taking his seat.

The other men tipped their hats to the Father and followed Mr. Wright as they passed the main counter. The investment banker pulled out a key from his jacket pocket and unlocked the barred door that led to the back of the bank.

Mr. Henkle had bid his time by the desk, watching Mr. Wright converse with the Catholic priest, but he now hurried over to the group. "Would you like me to inform Mr. Thomas of your arrival, Sir?"

"Yes. Be a good man and tell him I need a word as soon as he's available."

Mr. Henkle's face morphed to one of concern as he said, "A problem, Mr. Wright? Is there anything I can do to assist you?"

"Should have stuck with what I know, Henkle. Mining and timber are where the investments should be. The shipping industry is faulty on every account. It's taken nearly a year for my equipment to get here, and I own half of the damn roads. I'm paying all the damned wages, and meanwhile the gold is buried half a mile under the ground."

The large man thumped his fist on his chest with a cough then continued. "Warn Mr. Thomas that I'm mad as a March hare, and tip him off that it's the damned mud holding us up this time."

"Will do, Mr. Wright. Allow me five minutes to get a dram of whiskey into him, and then come into the office."

Kai and Dean exchanged a look as they sat quietly in their corner of the small bank. The middle-aged, heavyset man continued on about sheep and cattle with his two followers. The hired men attempted to soothe the man by making excuses about the weather, a large herd of buffalo, and a bad river crossing, but Mr. Wright didn't want to hear about any of the problems. He gesticulated and puffed and groaned over hard rock equipment and how the entire mining season would be gone before his cams, pistons, carts, and cylinders had arrived in Helena.

When Mr. Henkle returned to Dean and Kai, Mr. Wright and his two men disappeared into the office. Dean could hear the rumbling exchange through the door, but he focused on what the banker had to say about a safety box and insurance that Kai's letter would be delivered in the winter of 2012.

"Tell me, Father. Was that man Hubert Wright?" Dean asked after leaving the bank.

"Yes. Do you know him?" the priest asked.

"I have heard of him, but we have not met."

"Ah, yes. He is a wealthy capitalist here in Helena and in the territory at large. His foresight in the future of placer mining brings him much recognition. Did all go as you hoped, Mr. Wolfsblood?"

"Yes. I think we accomplished what we needed to. Thank you for your assistance. You have been very helpful to us both. As for the other reason we have come to town. I wonder if you can tell us where these vigilantes are likely to bring their prisoners if not to the jail?"

"Our town changes almost daily since the gold fever struck in Last Chance. Buildings sprout from the ground like the wee mushrooms. Men make fortunes overnight, and lose them the next. The law is a mutable undertaking in the hands of men who see it as their responsibility."

Martin Connolly glanced at Kai and Dean to see if he had their full attention as they walked through the mining town. Horses, wagons, and carriages churned the dust in the street, causing a haze to linger around the wood-timbered buildings that made up the business district. Shoppers discussed the rising price of flour, while miners speculated about where the next big strike would happen.

Dean knew the gold rush was playing out in this part of the world, and that Hubert Wright's forethought into hard rock mining was indeed the way of the future. That, and seeking mining riches in copper in other areas of Montana.

They approached the quaint, single spired Catholic church where the Father lived and worked when he wasn't traveling on his mission trips.

Father Connolly continued, "The mining men are a transient bunch. The laws of God are constant over this good earth, but the governing men in this West region abide by the rules that meet their needs in the passing moment. And if they're clouted off their noggins with the drink, as tends to happen frequently like, then the law is more pliable than was perhaps the fortnight prior."

"You're telling me there is no law, other than by the God watching over us?"

"'Tis' some truth to your words, Mr. Wolfsblood. Currently, Hubert Wright holds much influence over the men in charge of keeping order. He pays them handsomely to protect his investments."

"Mr. Winters informed us that no prisoners have been brought to the jail recently." Dean picked his words carefully. The Father may be sympathetic to the plight of the local tribes, but Dean wouldn't count on the man being lawless. "Can you speculate what may have happened to my tribesman, if he is not sitting in a jail cell, but has been detained?"

Father Connolly frowned as he stared over at the new fire tower on the hill. He shifted his green eyes back to Dean. "Aye, I am thinking your kinsman has joined the Father of Heaven."

"He had a serious injury that I was caring for, Father," Kai said. "It would not surprise me if he has passed from this life, but if he is alive, is there a doctor or infirmary where he may have been taken? I would like to continue my treatments if I could find him."

"The current sheriff is a rough sort. He would not honor the code of the courts to heal your man and bring him to face a judge and jury alive-like. If you would walk with me, we can inquire at the courthouse for your kinsman or any word of him." The Father appeared genuinely distressed by her last words.

Dean said, "I hold much trust in John Winters. He conducted his own search for information and found nothing. However, he mentioned the lawmen have a reputation for holding their own court in private. Where might this happen?" Dean tried again to coax an answer from the man that might be helpful.

Father Connolly blinked a few times and crossed his hands in front of his plain dark suit. He wore a mixture of secular and religious garb that was both practical for living in the western territories and still honored his profession. "The town has woken up to a hanging at the tree by the Methodist minister's home on more than one occasion. It is a reproachful affair to be sure. Many of Mr. Wright's men bunk at Last Timber Gulch on his cattle homestead. These men would know the happenings concerning the law."

Dean filed the information away. This was the first real intelligence he'd received that could help him find Badger. "This tree is here in Helena?" he asked.

"Aye. Walk east from where we stand. Your eyes won't deceive you, for surely you'll know it when you see it."

"We wish not to see our friend hang, Father, but we want to know if it happens so we can tell his family," Kai said.

"Of course," the Father said solemnly. "'Tis' a shame that attendance to mass and confession triples only after a hanging," Father Connolly observed.

Even though the priest's mouth was tight with disapproval, Dean thought he saw a faint twinkle of humor in his pale green eyes.

"Would you care to join me for an afternoon tea?" he offered.

"We thank you, Father, but we should be on our way soon. If I can speak to you on one other matter, it would relieve my mind."

"You are welcome to ease your thoughts with me on any subject."

"Our friend, Badger, was in care of an important artifact which has spiritual and ceremonial significance to my people. Have you ever seen a Blackfoot medicine bundle?"

"I have," he answered. "On my missions into your native lands I have seen these revered bundles you speak of."

"Then you are aware that these articles are as valued to my people as the Catholic sacraments are to your religious beliefs. This pipe and bundle has been passed down through my family for generations. I left it with him when I was hunting, and when I returned, Badger and the bundle were both gone. The pipe would have little value to someone who did not understand what it is, but to me and my clansmen, it is a sacred piece of our history."

"I see on both your faces 'tis of great importance. I will inquire on your behalf, and find out what I can."

They parted ways with an agreement to meet the next afternoon, giving the Father time to find out what he could in regards to the medicine pipe and Badger. Dean and Kai headed east on Man Eater to check out the hanging tree before leaving town for the night.

The gnarled old tree leaned like an old man with a crutch. A nearby log-sided barn tilted slightly in the opposite direction, as if trying to escape the inevitable fall of the dying tree. The surrounding hills were dotted with hundreds of miners' glory holes, where mine tailings had piled up over the last couple of years. The streams running through the valleys had been converted to little more than processing plants. Small shacks and sluice boxes stood waiting to be used or abandoned after falling short of producing any riches. Miners slogged buckets, sacks, or carts of ore as they trudge back and forth over their claims like ants working on a hill. They noticed a few men riding or walking toward the business district, dirty from head to toe after a long day of hard labor. It was the middle of summer, but there was very little green to be seen. Trampled paths over gravel and mud made the land resemble a wasteland, all in the name of the elusive and desirable element called gold.

The sun lowered behind a bluff as Kai and Dean stared at the old hanging tree with mixed emotions and gruesome imaginings. Dean felt certain that Badger's future was intertwined with a rope and the old ponderosa pine. He hoped that the plan forming in his mind for Badger's escape would be a faultless one.

"The tree is long gone by our time," he whispered to Kai.

"It's a beautiful tree," she said. "Old and decrepit, but still deserves respect."

"It's dead," Dean stated.

"It's dying," Kai corrected. "See the green needles? There's life in him still."

He gave her a disbelieving look. *Does she always have to say something surprisingly inappropriate?*

"This tree was here well before any white men. Just because it's been used to hang people doesn't mean it's an ugly thing. The people are ugly. The tree is beautiful. Your grandfather was a war hero. I'm sure he was responsible for a few deaths. He became old and bent, but he was still honored until he died."

How could Dean argue with that? "Even so, I only see ghosts when I look at it, not some noble pine."

She shrugged a shoulder and turned around, looking away from the town, the mines, and the hanging tree.

"The priest is risking a lot by helping you. Why do you think that is?"

"Not everyone in this time is against us, Kai."

"He probably wants to convert you."

"Try all he wants. It won't change any of my beliefs."

"But you'll take advantage of his generosity, and then not subscribe to his preachings."

"The way I see it, he's a believer in doing what's right, and for the most part, so am I."

"How is helping a murderer escape punishment doing what is right?"

"I said mostly," Dean defended. "I can't believe you can stand there and call Badger a murderer. Who stuck the knife in that buffalo killer?"

"Self defense," she said plainly.

"Kai, tell me who the real murderer is. Someone who kills for sport and steals food from thousands of people, or someone who is saving a species from extinction by stopping the cause of the problem?"

She gave him the single shoulder shrug again. "Both. And stop looking at me that way. Badger is paying the consequences for his actions."

"And I'm helping out a friend who has been there for me when we went to war together."

"If you say so," she said.

Irritated by her lackadaisical response, he clenched his fist around the reins and said, "First, we find him. Then, we wait until they try to hang him during the night. We'll take him back, and get out of town as quickly as possible."

"Like that's really going to work," Kai said, the doubt dripping off her tongue. "You don't even know if he's still alive."

"I do know. It's a feeling. Badger is too hard-headed to die. I think they're going to use him to set an example. That's why there's so much secrecy. Father Connolly confirmed it. They like the gore and the surprise of a hanging by night. It keeps the public in order, and cuts out the court."

"I'm not convinced," she said.

"I am. I saw us in a dream with the pipe in our hands. If I have the pipe back, that means we found Badger."

"A dream, huh? Is that how we're going about things now?"

"If that's all I have to work with, then yes."

"Sounds utterly logical, Mr. Intelligence. How about if I point out the fact that you just told me you were going to take back your friend from a group of vigilante lawmen like you were taking candy from a baby?"

"I picture it more like the fox in the henhouse, with a lot of guns."

She rolled her eyes to the sky and took a steadying breath.

"Kai, I'm doing the best I can. Will you lighten up on me for half a second?"

"Probably not. If I let you think you know it all, then what would stimulate your rodent-sized brain into seeing the cracks in your plan?"

"Come on," he said, and clicked his tongue and urged the horse to move. "We're getting looks."

Kai and Dean rode Man Eater west toward the main part of town, and then headed deliberately south. Once they were over a hill and out of sight of downtown, Dean turned Man Eater and skirted around Helena, back up to their campsite in the northern hills.

Chapter Eighteen

Dean went over the plan once more, whether she wanted to hear it or not. Kai stared at the setting sun, listening and wondering just how Badger was going to mess everything up again. Badger accused her of being dishonest, and it was true that she kept her thoughts and ideas to herself until she was ready to share them. She also knew that what Badger saw in her was a reflection of his own conniving manipulations.

She almost felt sorry for Dean. He trusted those around him to a fault. It wasn't right for someone with such a good heart to be taken advantage of by those closest to him. Kai was going to make sure Dean didn't get blindsided again. Badger's journal had hidden motivations in it, she was sure. He was smart enough not to write down any concrete evidence, but she knew he had ulterior motives. She wished Dean could see it as clearly as she did.

They had both read the journal looking for clues or secret messages, and neither of them could pinpoint anything distinctive or telling. Lists of people with birthdates, both white and Native. Historical references, some with dates and others without. Sometimes only a day and month, but no year. Dean suspected that Badger had purposely left out the years of the events that occurred after 1868. A precaution, in case his book was found by a stranger — which it nearly had. Badger's mind was organized and efficient, but also sly. It was obvious to Dean and Kai that much of the important information in regards to specifics was left out on purpose. Dean even found blank spots in some paragraphs or lists where there should have been a date, address, or name. He tried to piece it together with what Badger told him about Hubert Wright. *Had he planned this whole trip to assassinate one man? And why? To rid the world of a single wealthy, mining family?* Bader had also mentioned the booming lumber industry. *Could he really be thinking about saving some stupid trees?* Dean thought there was a lot more behind Badger's motivations. His grandfather was clear with him about not being able to change the major events of the past. Maybe Badger's disappearance was history's way of insuring the web of life wasn't disrupted irrevocably.

John Winters had returned to their camp with his dog and horses to spend one last night with them. His services as a guide were needed for an expedition and he was supposed to leave in two days. John also knew the location of Last Timber Gulch, and Dean took advantage of the last few hours in John's company to leave Kai with their newly trusted friend and go find Badger, if he could even be found.

The full moon darted in and out of the clouds as Dean rode for the ranch. He left Man Eater tied behind a thicket of poplar and went the rest of the way on foot. At zero-stupid-thirty a.m. every creature save the mice, a barn cat, and the owls were sound asleep. Even the ranch dogs, if there were any, were deep in dreamland as Dean took a good look around.

He knew he'd found the right place when he saw Badger's buckskin in a paddock by the barn. He wanted to take the animal back immediately, but he held off. Finding Badge was his first priority, and he couldn't act rashly.

Dean skipped the ranch house and went straight to the outbuildings. The bunkhouse was a rectangular log cabin that looked like it slept four to six men comfortably. He peered through the south facing window, but in the moonlight couldn't see much other than a pot-bellied stove, a table with chairs, and the faint outline of bodies on bunk beds.

Dean knew this wouldn't be where Badger was being held and kept moving around the ranch. It didn't take too long to find a guard inside the large barn, camped on a straw bed in front of a heavy wood door. The back of the barn was windowless, but Dean knew he had found Badger's cell. No louder than a mouse, he used a tap code against the log chinking to send an S.O.S message, and then he waited.

Dean heard the rustle of something large moving inside and tapped out their Marine unit numbers. He pressed his ear to the wall and held his breath. Then he heard the quiet tap of a response.

Three taps for their battalion, and eleven for their regiment.

He tapped the numbers again and then stopped sending messages before someone accidentally heard them.

Dean spent the last few hours of darkness, devising, speculating, and hypothesizing every scenario he could imagine for getting Badger back. Shortly after the rooster crowed, the first of the ranch hands, or vigilantes, appeared from the bunkhouse. Still dark with only a sliver of light in the east, the man stumbled over to the well, pumped a bucket of water, and brought it back to the cabin.

Dean waited within the shadows of the barn, listening to the first of the animals stir in their pens, to see if any other men would appear. When they didn't, he stayed low and made his way to the back of the bunkhouse, where he listened long enough to know that the men were in disagreement over when they should hang Badger. Half of the voices he heard thought they should have already done it, and the other half were anxious to do so the coming night.

"More folks will see him swing on a Sunday morning," one voice said. "Get the whole town talking before Sunday services."

"Look out the window, fool. There's a storm coming in. We're not going to have any moon to work by."

"It's hours away, Bill. We'll be fine."

"We should've been rid of that son-of-a-bitch already. He needs to swing, and I'm ready to do it."

"He's the strangest Indian I've ever seen," someone else said.

Smoke from the chimney floated down around him as it hit the cold morning air and sank instead of rising skyward. Dean heard the clink of dishes or coffee mugs and then more talking.

"Tonight is another official neck tie party, boys. Rain or moonshine. That murdering bastard is going to hang."

Dean had heard enough and slipped away from the ranch before the sun came up. Badger had to survive one more day, and then Dean was going to get him back.

He rode into camp beneath a morning sky the color of old bones. Dean was hopeful that the Above Ones were in his favor. A moonless sky could be helpful for the coming night.

Kai watched him rub down Man Eater and then settle the horse in a fresh patch of grass before offering him some breakfast. He had an entire day to get through before night returned and he could save Badger's sorry ass. Dean ate the food Kai offered and thought about everything that had to be done.

John readied his horses and then said, "Anna-kai and I will go now to buy the extra supplies you request. I have found horses to purchase from the livery. You go see Father Connolly about the medicine pipe. We meet at the upper spring in the direction of the sleeping sun to water our horses."

"You'll wait with Kai until I can meet you?" Dean asked, wanting a guarantee that Kai would not be left alone. The thought of her disappearing again was more than he could handle.

"If you do not return, she will travel with me until I can see her safely with the Piegans."

"I am in your debt, John," Dean said and clasped forearms with the man. "I will be there by evening, but it is good to have a backup plan."

John Winters nodded his agreement while Kai kept her face blank. She wasn't thrilled about having a babysitter at all times, but she could understand it after what had happened to her with the Salish.

After John and Kai left for the town stables, Dean tried to settle down and quiet his mind. He rolled over on his blanket and fell asleep for a short nap before meeting with Father Connolly about his pipe. He dreamed of a tree, and a butterfly, horses, and of Kai.

Father Connolly listened to Dean explain how he had ridden out to Last Timber Gulch and saw Badger's buckskin horse. He left out every other part of the tale, including overhearing the vigilantes and using the tap code to communicate with Badger.

"I'm afraid I could not secure an appointment with the men in question, Mr. Wolfsblood. But tis' no trouble a'tall, you see, as I was needin' to check on the wagon train arriving in town. It has arrived blessedly early. Truth be told, 'tis only half the train. The rest is delayed out on the prairie. Here's what I have in mind. A lawman stands about keeping order when the delivery is being made. We can have a gentlemanly talk amongst ourselves. If he won't speak plain with me, Mr. Wright will surely listen to reason regarding the men in his employ, and the property seized by them."

"If you could explain to Mr. Wright the religious importance of the pipe to the Piegan people, and how it has no monetary value to them, they would have to release it."

"I think that is a fair assumption, Mr. Wolfsblood. Come with me and we shall go about seeing your property returned to youse. I am to leave with the same expedition as Mr. John Winters. If we are to have success in this venture, we need to make haste."

"Your help will never be forgotten, Father. I can't thank you enough."

"Tis' truly an honor to serve God in any way I can. Can I count on you to attend mass so you too can share in the glory of our Father while I am spreading faith through the wild country?"

Dean was reminded of Kai's warning about the priest attempting to convert him. He answered carefully. "Of course, Father. In appreciation of your kindness, when I am visiting Helena, I will come and listen with an open mind to the Catholic teachings."

"Ah, but an open mind is the beginning of a blessed road to knowing the truth of God."

Dean suppressed the rising groan in the back of his throat. The ability of man to believe wholeheartedly that his way of thinking was better than any other man's had been a behavioral blunder since the beginning of mankind. What a novelty it would be to let others live the way they wanted to without the constant injection of unwanted opinions.

Dean looked at Father Connolly and smiled. He was capable of taking his own advice and kept his mouth shut.

The "lawman" overseeing the delivery of the newly arrived merchandise refused to admit anything to the Father. Dean didn't see or hear the conversation. He thought it was best to stay out of sight as much as possible, considering what he planned to do later that night. Father Connolly returned to Dean with lines of tension around his eyes.

"We'll see directly to Mr. Wright," Father Connolly said, and he and Dean left to make their way across town.

"Antiquities belong in museums. Collectors pay high dollar for items like the one you are describing. Who is to say this man of yours isn't going to send it off to a collector across the Atlantic and receive the payment for himself?" Hubert Wright said as he waved a thick hand through the air.

Father Connolly held his hat in his lap and said, "I'll thank you for valuing my honest judgment, Sir. This Piegan person is of fine character and wants what has belonged in his family for generations."

"Assuming my men have the item in question, of which I cannot say, I believe it is the property of the territory to be used as evidence against the crimes for which it was taken."

"You've said yourself that no man has been brought in. Is there reason to believe you may have been mistaken?"

Hubert Wright flattened his vest over his large paunch and sat taller in his leather wingback chair. "My men keep me well informed. I heard of this new slaughter on the prairie. The bodies of the men clearly show foul play. If, and when, my men find the demon who has brought this upon us, I am certain they will give me a full recounting."

"I'm sorry to be the informer of such distressing news, but I have it in good stead that the horse of a kinsman of this Wolfsblood fellow is among your herds at your ranch," Father Connolly continued.

Hardnosed and with cold deliberateness, Hubert Wright said, "Indian ponies are astray everywhere in this country. Without a brand, who is to say which animal belongs to whom?" He laid his hands on the desk and leaned forward. "I was planning to visit the ranch this evening and see to the arrival of the new stock. I will inquire on any recent arrests or the acquisition of any new stock to the work horses. I will send a letter to the church with any news. Though I am in doubt there will be anything left that I haven't already told you."

"I thank you, Sir. May you always be in God's good graces. Good day to you."

"And you," Hubert Wright said as he turned his attention to the papers atop his desk.

Father Connolly rose and took his leave from the offices of the Mount St. Helena Wright Gold Mining Co.

Dean was waiting outside with the horses. He was using the side of the building to shield himself from the blowing rain when the Father reappeared. The weather was indecisive and fickle as it alternated between light drizzles and horizontal drenchings.

As they rode out of town, Dean looked towards the western hills with trepidation, wondering when Kai and John would be at the spring, waiting for him.

"We'll go on a personal call to the homestead at Last Timber Gulch, Mr. Wolfsblood," Father Connolly finally said after they passed the last few businesses on the edge of town.

There was grim determination on the Irish priest's face that Dean hadn't seen before.

"I take it Mr. Wright was less than accommodating?"

"He accommodates his bank well enough," the man said tersely. "As a rector of this territory, the moral decency of the people of this community is my responsibility. I have a wee bit of personal interest in this as well."

Dean couldn't help but wonder what exactly passed between Father Connolly and Hubert Wright, but it obviously didn't go as smoothly as either one of them had hoped. The Father's explanation that a letter may or may not arrive at the church sometime in the future wasn't good enough for him, or for Dean.

After his proclamation, Father Connolly relaxed and inquired about Dean's family and where he was from as they headed to the ranch. The small talk was inconsequential, but Dean humored the man. He thought the Father was genuinely interested, but Dean found it a challenge to answer truthfully without giving away anything that would indicate that he was born in a different century.

As they rode down the muddy wagon tracks leading to the cluster of log buildings, Dean saw a young boy dash across the yard from the barn, straight through the middle of at least three puddles, and then into the house, with one last wide-eyed glance their way.

Father Connolly knocked, and they waited beneath the covered porch of the two-story log house. The front door opened and a handsome woman wearing a light green calico dress greeted them. However, her eyes were the pale blue of a frozen winter morning's sky, and just as chilling.

"What a wonderful surprise to have a visitor on such a dreary Saturday afternoon, Father."

"Aye, it 'tis. Might I be havin' a word with you or himself, Mrs. Wright?"

"My husband is seeing to the new livestock. You're welcome to come inside and join me for coffee as you dry out and wait for him."

She kept her eyes on Father Connolly, and Dean wondered if the invitation extended to him as well.

"If it isn't too much of an inconvenience, I would appreciate the gesture of kindness. And, for my acquaintance as well, ma'am."

"Please come in," she said, stepping aside and directing them to the front parlor. "If you can wait but a moment, I will be back with refreshment."

"Bless your soul, Mrs. Wright. Your invitation is most generous."

"You're welcome in my home anytime, Father," she said as they entered the lavishly furnished room.

The woman said something about the kitchen and as she turned to leave, she whooped, and then said, "Matthew Wright, stop sneaking up on me like that. You're going to give me the fits."

They heard a giggle and then Dean saw the same boy from outside peeking around the woman.

Then she added, "Please keep the good Father and his friend company while I make a tray."

"Yes, ma'am," he said as she scooted around him and gave him a gentle push toward the parlor.

"Good day, young Matthew," Father Connolly greeted.

"Hi, Father," he said as he alternated between staring at the two of them. His eyes finally landed on Dean. Dean hadn't seen himself in a mirror for weeks. Kai said the swelling on his face had gone way down, but he didn't know for sure. When he asked about how the bruises looked, she told him he had the face of a warrior.

"Are you a real Indian?" the boy asked with a mixture of disbelief, awe, and fear in his wide blue eyes.

"I am a South Piegan. Aamssáápipikani. A Blackfoot," Dean said.

He was standing on the wood floor, close to the door so that he wouldn't drip on the beautiful rug or any of the furniture. He was so paranoid about dirtying anything that he felt frozen in place.

"Where's your bow and arrows?" he asked.

"I prefer a six shooter," Dean answered. "Or my Spencer rifle. Have you ever seen one of those?"

"My daddy has one," little Matthew said.

"Is your dad Mr. Hubert?" Dean asked.

He wanted to know if this was the heir to the Mount Saint Helena Mining Empire for multiple reasons. Foremost because of what Badger had told him about this family and their descendants, and also because he wanted to compare the information Badger had written down in the journal to the truth standing before his eyes.

"He's my uncle," the boy said and then added, "I bet he would be all catawampus if he knew my ma let an Indian inside the house."

Dean's eyebrows rose with interest, but he smiled at the boy. "Have you ever seen any Indian treasure around here?"

The boy's eyes widened further and Dean let his smile grow. He glanced at Connolly, wondering if he would object to this line of conversation, but the Father only watched with close attention to where Dean was going with this.

"Like diamonds and rubies? My ma tells me stories about pirate treasure. Do Indians have buried treasure, too?"

"Our treasure would be wrapped up in bear fur or beaver skins. Have you seen anything like that around here?"

"Sure I have. Uncle Hue calls it artic-facts and sells them to bidders back east and all the way across the ocean. It isn't real treasure though," he said as if he had the world figured out. "Just a bunch of old-looking stuff."

"Sometimes the old stuff is the most valuable," Dean said.

He looked up at the sound of footsteps coming down the hall, and saw a man holding an armload of split logs. "Mrs. Wright asked if I could start the fire in here so you could dry up some."

"That would be a blessing, Mr. Pearson. We're soaked through from our ride."

Matthew hopped out of the way as the man walked over to the fireplace. Dean didn't miss the glare of dislike from the man as he passed.

"Matthew, go on and help your ma," Mr. Pearson said.

"But Mama told me to keep the guests company."

"Go on now," he repeated. "She needs helps with the sweet cakes."

The words *sweet cakes* sent the boy scurrying towards the back of the house.

As Mr. Pearson fussed with the kindling, he said to Father Connolly, "Mr. Wright won't appreciate savages inside his house."

"Is that so?"

"Yes, Sir. If he finds him in here, he'll be having words with you."

"I am well aware of Mr. Wright's proclivity toward intolerance, Mr. Pearson. I'll be thanking you for the thoughtful reminder."

The man kept his focus on the fireplace. From where Dean was standing he could see the man's eyes were narrowed with loathing. Father Connolly gave Dean an apologetic smile.

"If you don't mind, I'll be outside checking on the horses," Dean said. He spoke with as much native inflection to his accent as he could muster. He didn't want to give this ranch hand any indication that he was here because of Badger. He heard the men this morning saying Badger was a strange Indian, and Dean suspected it was in part because of the way he spoke. Two Blackfoot men with similar accents would be automatically grouped together.

"You may remain in here with me as long as I am here," the Father told Dean.

Dean gave a polite nod of understanding, but he turned for the door anyway knowing he was at the limit of his tolerance for racism. The fresh air would be welcome, and Dean could clear his head without the haughty looks from the bigoted cowpoke.

As he stood under the cover of the porch waiting for Father Connolly, he heard much of the conversation inside. They exchanged cordialities and talked about the town. He was about to duck his head under the dripping eaves of the porch and check to see if Man Eater had ripped the hide off of the Father's horse when Mr. Pearson opened the door behind him. The man looked him up and down and moved his hand to his pistol grip. His threat and meaning were perfectly clear as he stepped off the porch and stalked toward the barn.

Dean watched him disappear inside the log building. He wanted to go break the door down and take Badger now, but that would be a mistake. Instead he observed the property, making note of the relative quiet and committing to memory any differences from what he'd seen in the dark. There were no other men about. The animals must have been inside the barn and coops, as there wasn't a swish of horse's tail, grunt of a pig, or clucking chicken to be heard. He thought they were probably waiting out the storm. As for the other men, he suspected they were all busy with the new shipment of livestock that had arrived in town. All but this Mr. Pearson, who undoubtedly had been left behind to watch over the prisoner, or the ranch, or both.

The rain was withdrawing, so Dean left the porch and stared at the western horizon as he walked toward the horses. Wispy clouds trailed behind the bulk of the storm, streaking the sky indigo and white.

He was glad he wouldn't have to ride back to town in bad weather, but he was also hoping for cloud cover later in the night. But, he didn't want Badger's hanging to be delayed because of a storm, either. He was figuring out that he could blame the weather for just about any scenario, when Man Eater snapped at him for approaching. Dean greeted Father Connolly's gelding and made sure Man Eater's teeth were out of striking range. Then he covertly surveyed the south side of the house while watching for signs of anyone else lurking about.

He didn't see or hear anyone. Taking a calculated risk, he walked with purposeful strides to the opposite side of the house from where Father Connolly and Mrs. Wright were in the parlor. Given what young Matthew had told him, and the concern on Father Connolly's brow regarding the missing bundle, Dean decided he was going to take the next step toward finding his pipe.

Dean was staring through a window between the narrow gap in the drapes at a furry brown lump when he heard, "What are you doing?"

He decided on the fly that honesty was as good as deceit with a boy of such a young age and turned to look down at Matthew. "Looking for my pipe. It's wrapped with fur and strips of leather. Have you seen it?"

The boy nodded, suddenly looking shy.

"Where did you see it?"

"In the study. I heard Uncle Hue talking about it."

"Is this the study right here?" he asked, pointing at the window.

Mathew's eyes went wide.

"I need it back. Do you think you can get it for me?"

He shook his head and stepped away from Dean. "It's against the rules for me to go into the study without my dad or Uncle Hubert."

"I understand," Dean said. "I wouldn't want you to get into trouble for breaking the rules."

Matthew fidgeted, but looked partially relieved.

"Don't worry. If it's my pipe, I'll get it back. He can get into trouble for taking things that don't belong to him, too."

"He never gets in any trouble. The law works for Uncle Hue," Matthew said with the same tone he had used earlier. *Like he understood the entirety of the universe at seven years old.*

"I have some other Blackfoot things with me," Dean said, trying to ease the boy's nervousness. "Would you like to see them?"

"Yes, sir."

He was showing Matthew the few Piegan items he had with him: the bridle, his beaded clothes, and knife sheath when Father Connolly and Mrs. Wright stepped outside. Matthew ran to his mom, excited to share what he'd just learned about Indians from Dean.

Dean kept his face appropriately blank, but was disappointed to see the Father wasn't carrying his medicine bundle.

On the way back to town, Father Connolly reported that Mrs. Wright would have nothing to do with her brother-in-law's business dealings, legal or not, no matter how persuasive the priest had tried to be. But he was able to confirm that the mining tycoon was expected to arrive that evening for dinner, and would be staying at the ranch for a few days. He was optimistic that Hubert Wright would return the confiscated medicine pipe and send it to the church where Dean could pick it up. Dean's escalating doubts stayed within the confines of his private thoughts. He was sure Hubert Wright would sell the pipe to the highest bidder given the first opportunity. Dean had no intention of letting that happen.

Chapter Nineteen

The wagon squished and slid through the thick mud on the road as it rolled toward Helena's hanging tree. Dean watched the driver of the buckboard wagon and the four surrounding riders approach by moonlight. He was hidden on the far side of the barn, deep in the shadows, as he stared hard into the night, looking for their weapons. It didn't surprise him to find all five of them armed for battle. Dean stayed detached, calm, and confident. He would follow through with his self-appointed mission or die trying. He and Badger had entered into this adventure together, and if death was coming for him, he was going to take the warrior's path to the Sand Hills.

The squeak of the springs beneath the wooden seat of the buckboard protested against every rut along the weather-beaten trail. The men continued through the midnight air in silence, but anyone awake at the late hour could have easily heard the creaking wagon, the clinking of metal traces, or the shifting men in their leather saddles.

Dean held his position, keeping as still as a wild cat before the final killing pounce. He didn't see Badger, but the long, bundled shape lying in the back of the wagon couldn't be anything but his captured friend.

One of the men gave a hushed, barking order. "Take a look around."

Dean stayed low as he streaked out from behind the small building near the tree for the tall bushes he had scouted out earlier in the night. His moccasins and soft, leather buckskins allowed him ease of movement while making virtually no sound. He was inside the brush before the man made it halfway around the barn. Dean crouched and listened for orders or directions from the men.

They must have done this before, as evidenced by their efficiency. Two of the men directed the wagon and its driver into place beneath the thick tree limb. Once in position, the driver and one other man hopped into the back of the wagon with Badger. Someone lit a torch, casting an orange and black glow over the men while they worked at securing the rope on the branch. Another man sat on his horse cradling his weapon in his arms and looking all too eager to use it.

This was the time for Dean to send the signal to Kai. It had been her idea, and Dean admitted it was a good one, but the moonlight had become a necessity for it to work. The storm had passed and the moon was luminous. He prayed to Great Spirit for the timing to work in his favor. If he was too late, Badger would choke to death. Dean silently inched over to the back of the brush. He held up his hand to the sky making sure there was a clear line of sight to the northwest, and that he was catching the moonbeams just right. The mirror flashed three times and he lowered his hand. Waiting, he saw the faint light of a lantern flash four times, and he knew that Kai had seen his signal.

He ducked back into the leaves and branches with his new pistol in his hand and his knife tucked into his belt. Watching these men raise Badger to his feet and lower the rope around his neck sent Dean into a rage like he'd never experienced before. He was ready to shoot every one of these self-appointed lawmen and then hang them from the same tree as an example to the world of what true justice was. He was barely able to hold himself back, but he knew that following his impulses wouldn't serve the higher purpose of freeing Badger, and it wouldn't help Kai's situation, either.

They made a final adjustment to the noose and then the driver stepped back, sat down on the bench, and picked up the reins. The other man jumped down from the wagon. With his hands tied behind his back, Badger would be completely helpless as the wagon pulled away and left him to swing. Dean placed his thumb on the hammer, ready to cock the pistol. If the alarm didn't sound in the next minute or two, Dean would go ahead with plan two and fight them all. One against five.

"Wait," one of the men said.

The driver hissed something that Dean couldn't hear.

"I need to pin the damn sign on him."

"Idiot," someone cursed. "Hurry up."

Dean watched a man hop up into the wagon and pull a folded sheet of paper out of his coat. He stood in front of Badger, apparently attaching a sign to his shirt. Just as the man was finishing, Badger seemed to come alive and thrust his knee upward into the vigilante's groin.

The man hollered and fell back against the side of the wagon groaning and cradling himself. "You fucker!" he screamed.

"Shut up," someone snarled.

"I'll kill you now," the man cried, but didn't rise to follow through with his threat.

"Go. Pull away," one of the other men said.

The driver released the wagon's brake and raised the reins, ready to snap them and move the two horses forward.

Dean hunched in the opening between two of the bushes, his gun raised and pointing at the driver of the buckboard as he waited for the final signal from town.

"Fire!" He heard at last.

"Fire in the Gulch!" Came an answering reply.

A clanging bell rang through the valley and ricocheted over the hills. In seconds, the sound of waking people calling out to one another about where the fire was burning could be heard all around.

The wagon pulled forward as the three men rounded their mounts to face the town center. The man with the bruised balls jumped from the wagon, staggered, and then limped to his horse.

"Round up the brigade, boys! Looks like the bank's on fire. Go! I'll be down as quick as I can."

Smoke could now be seen rising toward the moon in a thin plume from the business district. The four men on horses galloped toward the fire, but the wagon was much slower as it made the wide turn to head downtown. Shouts could be heard throughout Helena. The bell continued to ring from the fire tower. Dean and Kai's plan was working.

Badger swung with hands tied behind his back and gagged at the mouth. The old tree swayed under his weight. It was taking too long for the driver to maneuver the horses around the barn and tree. Dean dashed out of the shrubs and ran like a linebacker for Badger. He took a running leap onto the tree, hands groping for a broken branch sticking out of the trunk about seven feet up from the ground. He held tight and scurried up the bark, using his momentum to drive him up and out onto the limb from which Badge hung.

Dean wrapped his legs and one arm around the thick branch as he reached out with his knife to cut the rope. His groin injury felt like it was tearing him in two, but he ignored it as he heard Badger choking. He hoped like hell he had enough time to free his friend. When a gunshot sent bark and woodchips flying like shrapnel, he nearly fell from the tree. He sawed at the coarse rope until another bullet hit his leg and he slid off the branch and crashed to the ground. Adrenaline coursed through him as he jumped up and yanked his gun out of his belt. He saw a hulking shadow and hurled his body toward his attacker. The vigilante shot again, but Dean's prayers must have been answered, because the bullet disappeared into the night. Dean tackled the man, knocking him flat on his back and clocked him on the head with his gun, hard enough to know one hit would be enough.

He didn't pause to find out if the vigilante was dead, but spun off the man, jumped onto the wagon, whipped the horses into action, and pulled beneath Badger. The unconscious Badger dangled like meat on a hook. Dean stood in the back of the wagon and finished cutting the rope. Badger dropped to the wood planks, and Dean loosened the stranglehold around his neck. Then he cut Badger's hands free and removed the gag.

Trees weren't the most reliable for a hanging. A gallows was the proper way to hang someone, so the victim's neck would snap cleanly and quickly. Badger's death would have been a strangling, which is effective and also cruel. A true hangman knew the difference between techniques and used the one which corresponded with the situation. Dean predicted that the midnight hanging by vigilantes would be hasty and unprofessional, and he wasn't mistaken. Throw in a wildfire — one of the West's most dangerous and all too common threats — and chaos would be easy to achieve.

Dean checked to make sure Badger was breathing before he stole the wagon and drove off toward his horses, hidden a quarter mile up the road.

Finding Kai hidden in the new location, deep within a copse of trees and shrubs, at night, while leading Badger on an unfamiliar horse, took Dean longer than he wanted it to. But, he finally made it. She couldn't have been there very long, having made her own getaway from town, but she had the small campsite ready for them. Bed rolls were laid out, canteens were full, and dried food was plentiful.

They were far enough out of town to have the hills and the narrow valley to themselves, but close enough for them to carry out the plan and return before dawn. Dean jumped down from his horse and hurried to assist Badger. His friend was listless as he lowered him to a blanket.

"Should we risk a fire?" Kai asked.

"Yeah. I circled around the thicket twice and couldn't see a thing. I think we're safe out here, and we need to get a better look at him. And warm him up."

Kai used one of the precious matches to save time and lit her new lantern. As Dean checked himself over, he listened to the rustle of tinder as Kai worked on starting a small smokeless fire for warmth. He was undamaged. The shot that knocked him down from the tree had ripped his leggings, but his skin had barely bled.

Badger's eyelids flickered, and then he was staring up at them. Dean grabbed the canteen and eased Badger halfway up from the bed before tipping it up to his friend's lips.

"All those years of lifting weights at the gym saved your neck, man," Dean said as he helped Badger sip the water. "I always thought it was overkill, but now I take it back."

He noticed the wet trickle leaking out of Badger's mouth, and how pained he looked as he attempted to swallow. Dean wondered how bad the injury was around Badge's neck.

"Damn it, you should know I'm always right," Badger said.

Dean swallowed. The choking rasp coming out of his friend's mouth hurt to listen to. Badger laid a hand over his throat and closed his eyes.

"You burned down Helena for me?" he asked in a croaking whisper.

"Not me. Kai."

"I did not," she said as she slipped in next to Badger's side. "I have absolutely no idea how that pile of rubbish accidentally fell onto my lantern."

"She's a freak. Watch out for her," he told Dean.

"She's completely innocent. I'd swear it in any court on earth," Dean defended.

He was still having a hard time believing just how cooperative Kai was to go along with the plans to rescue Badger. She'd told him, "any means to an end was fine by her," and she didn't mind stirring up a town of miners as long as no one got hurt. It was her idea to sneak into town unseen and start the fire alone, knowing she could control how and where it might happen. Dean hated the idea of them being separated, but the reward outweighed the risks.

"Did anyone see you?" Dean asked.

"No, but they heard me when I started screaming about a fire by the bank."

"Was the building on fire?"

"Not when I scooted out of town. Just the barrel and wagon in the alley where the oil rags were. I was careful about the details, but I don't give a shit if the whole ugly place burns to the ground. Dirty, greedy miners and the businesses that keep feeding them don't deserve an ounce of my pity."

"Well then. Now I know where you stand," Dean said.

Kai glared at Dean with grit and insolence written on her face. "Not a one of them cares about anything other than making money."

"Except for the good Father," Dean added, just to goad her.

"The church is on the opposite side of town," she supplied.

"Maybe the wench isn't so bad after all," Badger said.

"And you—" she said, turning her wrath on Badger. "Shut up and let me look at you. Chances are, by the rope marks on your neck, you're going to suffocate before the sun comes up unless we figure out how to keep the swelling down."

Dean and Badger blanched simultaneously.

"That's right. If his larynx, esophagus, and all the surrounding tissue swell up, he won't be able to breathe. Keep a cold cloth around your neck and we'll see if you survive. I'll do what I can, but I'm not making any promises."

Dean blinked at the reality check Kai had just delivered and then mentally reassured himself that her medicines fixed his own injuries up in a hurry. When Dean had major swelling, her mix of leaves, flowers, and roots, had worked like magic. Faith would have to be his sustaining power for the next few hours. It was all he had.

Dean and Kai alternated between watching Badger through the rest of the night. By morning they needed to refill their water supply after using a continuous cloth soaked in Kai's medicinal infusion, or in plain cold water to help keep the inflammation down. Dean left to fill the canteen and water bags in a nearby creek, while Kai worked at preparing a meal of strained soup and mashed berries for Badger.

When Dean returned, he found Badger sitting up with his journal lying next to him.

"How bad is it?" Dean asked.

Badger opened to a page in the back of the journal and wrote something down. He held it up for Dean to read.

Probably should have let me hang last night. Save us all a bunch of misery.

"What? And miss out on all this fun?"

I'm dying anyway. Check out my gunshot.

Dean had noticed Badger being extra careful with his arm and shoulder. He glanced at the shoulder in question, but couldn't see anything significant because of Badger's shirt.

"It's infected. There are signs of blood poisoning," Kai said from her place by the fire.

"No there aren't," Dean said in automatic defensive mode, without knowing what the truth actually was.

It's no good, Badger scribbled on the paper.

"Can we get some antibiotics in town?" Dean asked Kai.

"I don't think they've been invented yet," she said.

Badger wrote, *They haven't. Doesn't matter. I'm ready to die.*

"Cut it out, Badge. Kai knows what to use. She kept my leg from getting infected."

"I'm already using the pipsissewa and Echinacea from your pack and some Old Man's Beard. It's the strongest meds we have, but I have no idea if they will work."

Badger started to shake his head, but the pain and stiffness stopped him.

"We start riding north tonight. We'll find Laughing Eyes and use his pipe to return to our time," Dean said.

He wanted to retrieve his own pipe before leaving Helena. He'd thought about the consequences of traveling with Laughing Eye's pipe from the past, and wondered about the effect he was going to make on any other travelers over the next one hundred and forty-four years, but he couldn't come up with a better solution. If it had life altering consequences, then so be it. He'd deal with them. *They had to go home.*

"If we can get Badger back to our time, he has a greater chance of surviving," Kai said.

"Kai, whatever you can do to keep him alive, please keep doing it. Maybe we should leave right now," Dean suggested.

Badger's pencil moved across the page. *They will be looking for us. We can't risk moving in the daylight.*

Dean set his jaw and scrubbed his fingers over his scalp with frustration knowing that Badger was right. If they had any chance of making it back to the South Piegans, they were going to have to travel at night.

"Then you need to gain as much strength as possible today. You're not dying, and you *are* coming with us," he said with finality.

Badger's face was hard and his eyes distant, but he returned a single reluctant nod.

"If we take Laughing Eyes' pipe, doesn't that mean that your parents won't have one to travel with, Dean? It could mean that your entire future will be totally different."

"I can't dwell on what might happen," Dean said as he looked in his saddle bag, not wanting to see either of their faces. Kai's line of thinking made some sense. If he took the pipe from this time to 2012, then there wouldn't be one in the 1980's when his parents disappeared into the past. *But where would his current pipe exist if that happened?* "I'm not even sure how it's possible for the two pipes to exist in the same time. We have to do what we can right now, and that's all."

"Maybe Laughing Eyes can send us forward through time without actually having to take the pipe with us," she said, not able to let the subject drop.

Dean sucked in a breath. "Why would you say that? Did he tell you he could?"

She shrugged and turned her gaze to the glowing embers of the fire. "He's a powerful medicine man. We talked about time travel on our walk. I think he's capable of more than we will ever know."

"Either way, we have to get Badger home. And you, too. The timing is just about right. Eight or nine days to find the Piegans. They're farther north now for the Sun Dance camp, so we'll need two to three days to get back into the mountains." Dean glanced up to the sky, even though the moon was nowhere to be seen. He knew they had thirteen days until the new moon. "We'll make it."

Dean spent the final hour before sunset checking the snares he had set earlier in the day. Fresh meat would add variety to their diet and it gave him something to think about other than the constant worry of what he was up against.

He caught one rabbit and was wondering if Kai would cook up something mouth-watering with it, or if he should just roast it over the fire. Then he walked into their campsite and saw a vital missing element.

"Where is he?"

Kai opened her eyes with reluctance. She pushed herself up from her blanket and looked at the empty place where Badger had been most of the day. She gave Dean her typical shrug of indifference.

He laid the snared rabbit down on a rock near the fire ring and left to check on the nearby horses. They were hobbled deeper into the tight valley, near enough to hear, and completely hidden by the leafy shrubs, but Badger's horse was missing.

Returning to Kai two minutes later, he said, "Badger took off again."

"Let him go," she said. "How many times should you risk your life for that idiot?"

If Dean was on edge before, he was now walking a razor's edge between outrage and murder.

He cast an accusing glare at Kai. "Why didn't you stop him?"

She turned her back to Dean and began to roll up her bed.

"I have almost everything ready to go. Do you want to cook that now, or wait until we stop again?"

"Damn it. Answer me, woman!"

"Wow. What's that smell?" she asked sticking her nose in the air. "It reeks like an asshole around here."

Dean's jaw felt like it would split from the pressure of grinding his teeth so hard. He managed to say through tight lips, "Did you see him leave?"

She turned cold eyes on him. "No, I didn't. I fell asleep. I guess making medicines and keeping the swelling down all night and day finally wore me out. How could I have let this happen? Oh Great Spirit, this is all my fault. I am a terrible woman. I deserve to be punished."

Her sarcasm irritated him like being bitten by pestering horse-flies. But, he brushed it off and said, "I'm sorry. I'm frustrated. I'm also going after him. He can't be that far."

"Of course you are," she said, and unrolled her bed to lie back down.

>><<<

Dean found Badger exactly where he thought he would. On the way to Last Timber Gulch, Hubert Wright's family ranch.

He forced him to pull up. "Stop right now, or I'll give up your position. Right here, Badger. I'll shoot my gun until every last gold-fevered miner or damn cow wrangler in this county knows you're out here."

Badger took a moment to consider, and then they rode into a wash behind a grove of willows where he finally let Dean hear it all.

"Do you remember when I told you about my mom getting really sick? And her fever dreams?"

"Sure. That's when you found out about the Dragonfly medicine pipe."

"Yeah," Badger said with a sneer. "What I didn't tell you, or anyone, is that was the day I also found out that my mom was raped by the owner of the mine where my dad worked."

Dean looked down at his hands. His mind went blank and stopped functioning correctly as he tried to process what Badger had just said. He wasn't sure how to respond to something so personal and violating. Badger grabbed his knife handle from the leather sheath hanging on his belt. He slid the steel blade back and forth over his leggings, as if cleaning off nonexistent grime as he talked.

"She was hired to clean the business offices at first. It was perfect for her, and helped our family have a little extra cash. They really liked her, or so my father said. Then she started cleaning the owner's home. That's where she was raped and got pregnant. My father was furious about her quitting her job. He threatened to leave her if she didn't tell him why. She used the excuse that her pregnancy was fragile or some shit. He never knew I was a bastard. I guess it's a good thing I look so much like my mother."

"Wait a second. Are you telling me Hubert Wright is your great-grandfather?"

"Two times great," Badger said. "There won't be any descendants from his filthy bloodline left. I'm here to see to it."

"She told you this?"

"I heard enough when she was fevering. I can put two and two together."

"You don't know for sure," Dean whispered. He looked in the direction of the ranch. He couldn't see the house, but it was less than a half mile away. "What if you're wrong? What if your dad really is your real dad?"

Badger put the knife back in its sheath. "I'm ending this tonight. The Wright family has caused incredible damage and harm to Montana, to my family, and to who knows what else. You've said it yourself; the man is an arrogant, greedy son-of-a-bitch. He's going to pay with his life for starting this domino effect of false superiority and destructive wealth."

Badger's gaze met Dean's, and then he dashed out from behind the cluster of branches and headed toward the shadows of some cottonwood trees. The horses were tied, so Dean followed quickly behind him.

"You were never planning to return to our time, were you?"

"It is what it is," he hissed in the dark. His voice creaked, and the more he spoke, the worse it sounded. "I'm a walking dead man. I honor my mother this night. She deserves it. You were a damned good Marine once. Stand with me, and let's end the blight these people spread."

Dean clenched his fists at his sides. "There's a woman and kid inside that house. I'll give you one last chance to ride away free."

"Freedom," Badger scoffed. "Freedom died the instant Europeans landed on this continent."

"I'm not debating this with you again. Beat the dead horse all you want, but Kai and I are out of here. You can't change the past, Badge. I've told you over and over."

Badger didn't hesitate when he started jogging toward the ranch.

Dean followed because he couldn't stand to leave Badger behind. He couldn't keep up because of his leg. Running was excruciating, but he kept going anyway. When he neared the ranch, he looked for the most undercover spot and thought of all the years he had worked side by side with Badger. *Where would Badger do reconnaissance from?* He veered left and crouched in a low spot with plenty of tall grass and some sumacs. Badger was little more than a stealthy breeze as he dove into the grass, ten feet from Dean.

"You're insane," Dean said.

Seventy-five feet of open space lay between them and the west side the house.

"You don't think I can change things, but I already have," Badger hissed in the dark.

Dean raised his head and scrutinized the moonlit house and the outbuildings.

"Can you smell it?"

Dean smelled the sudden increase of smoke in the air. He thought it was stronger than a regular chimney fire should smell.

He looked to the sky for rising smoke against the backdrop of stars and saw the haze drifting from the far corner of the barn.

"You didn't," he said.

"Kai's a smart bar wench. Thank her for giving me the idea."

Before Dean could make his next move, the door of the bunkhouse slammed open and men rushed into the yard.

"Horse barn's on fire!"

"Someone wake up the Wrights!"

"Not again!"

"All hands to the fire buckets!"

"Pearson, get the animals out!"

They watched a man race to the house and burst through the front door hollering about a fire in the barn.

"Now I change history," Badger said as the same ranch hand flew back out of the door of the big house and sprinted to the barn.

Dean steadied his nerves. His training told him to back Badger up and complete the mission, but his gut wanted to knock his friend over the head with his pistol and haul his butt out of there. Badger believed he was a good soldier, and likely on the outside he was, but Dean had been out of that life for a few years, and he didn't want to live with that mentality any more. Unfortunately, the scene before him was happening fast, and he needed to react even faster. His military training blended with his need to prove he was a worthy warrior and instincts took over.

"Orders have changed, Badge. Back me up or not. I'm going in to get my pipe."

Without exchanging words, he could feel Badger's energy shift from the two of them standing at odds to working together as one.

They listened to the men shouting from the barn. An orange glow could now be seen as the flames grew on the backside of the log structure. Dean didn't think it was a coincidence that it was the same side as where Badger's jail cell was located. Horses whinnied and called to one another while pigs screeched and snorted. Cows bawled as they were shepherded out of the barn. The yard was filling with confused animals while people began to trickle out of the house.

The first was a tallish man that Dean didn't recognize, but he was issuing orders so Dean assumed he must be Hubert Wright's brother. Then Dean saw Mrs. Wright leading Matthew off the front porch. Her hand stayed on the boy at all times. Her grip tightened around the blanket wrapped child as he pulled to get away, insisting that he could help fill buckets. In her other arm was a swaddled bundle and Dean wondered if it was a baby.

Hubert Wright's paunchy form was next as he made his way out of the door and toward the burning barn. Sparks were shooting into the sky and the frantic atmosphere of the ranch escalated with the stomping hooves of the upset horses, the chaos of panicked chickens, and the hollering of the men. The night breeze picked up, and Dean knew it would fuel the flames and send sparks drifting in whichever direction Great Spirit led them.

Dean set his eyes on the back of the house and motioned his intent to Badger with his hands. They spaced themselves only seconds apart, dodging behind the shrubs, and then dashing across the open side yard for the back door. With the distraction of the burning barn, Dean was optimistic that no one would see them.

He forced the locked door open with a well placed kick and then waited, listening for anyone inside the house. When he was sure it was clear, he said. "My pipe should be in the study."

"Bastard," Badger rasped.

Dean positioned himself in front of his friend's weak side and pointed toward the hallway across the darkened kitchen. He watched Badger nod and then they moved with silent steps deeper into the house. He was hyper-aware of the muffled animal sounds and the yelling coming from outside of the open front door, but Dean stayed focused on finding his pipe. He tried the knob on the second door to his right, where the study should be, and it clicked as the metal latch released inside the jamb.

"Close and lock it," he whispered as Badger followed him.

The room was almost pitch black. Dean used his memory from when he spied through the window to make his way over to the wall and felt for the drapes. He pushed the heavy fabric open and let in a miniscule amount of starlight. It was just enough to see the bulky shadows of the heavy desk and the chairs around the room.

"I don't see it," he said to Badger. "It was on the desk."

Groping across the surface of the desk did not yield the medicine bundle. He tried again and still nothing. Then Dean began to search the rest of the study. When he saw a lumpy shadow on a high bookcase shelf, he grabbed it. The beaver fur beneath his hands was all the reassurance he needed to know he was doing what was right to preserve, maintain, and respect the honored bundle.

"Got it," he said, and then he heard Badger unlocking the door.

A tiny creak to Dean's left made him flinch and he shifted defensively away from the sound. He pointed his gun in the direction and then stepped toward the door after Badger.

"Who in God's name is inside my house?"

The noise must have been a door opening from a side room. Dean hadn't known it was there.

The blast of a rifle going off lit up the room with a flash and then the wall plaster shattered behind Dean. He dove to the floor and shot his own gun at the intruder. There was a yell and then a clanking thump as something heavy landed on the rug. Dean thought he had hit the man's rifle and knocked it out his hands.

"Thieving arsonists, show yourself!"

Dean heard the large man scrambling to retrieve his weapon as he crouched next to the desk, cocked his pistol, and looked for Badger. It didn't take but a second for him to hear his friend's spitting sarcasm.

"Mr. Wright, we're so honored you've decided to join us," he said. "You already tried hanging me and that failed miserably."

Dean saw Badger's outline against the study wall.

"My gun is on you," Badger lied, having lost both his guns when he was captured. "Move away from the rifle."

Badger's voice ground like broken glass, but it was stronger and more forceful than Dean thought it should be, given the circumstances.

"Get out of my house. How dare you!"

"How dare you! Greed is a loathsome mistress, but you, you take pride in destroying everything you see. Families. Forests. The ground beneath your own feet if there were gold in it."

"With pride, I take the wealth of the land to build cities you cannot dream of. Ignorant soulless heathens such as yourself will never understand civility and commerce."

Badger moved forward and Dean took the opportunity to rise from his hunched position. He spun around to aim his gun on Mr. Wright.

"You'll never get out of here alive," the man said with his hands raised.

"Should I shoot him or do you want to do it?" Dean asked Badger.

Badger was fidgeting with something in his hands. He couldn't tell what it was, but he heard the clink of glass.

"Get out of here right now," Badger ordered Dean.

"No. We're leaving together."

"You don't want to see this. Go!"

"What's that smell?" Dean asked.

"If you're refusing to leave then keep the gun on him, while I tie him up," Badger said as he set something on the desk.

Badger took a coil of rope from his belt and moved toward the large man. Dean stayed by Badger's side, gun aimed at Mr. Wright's face, wondering what the hell his friend was up to. He didn't like any of this, but he wouldn't leave his buddy behind.

Hubert lashed out at Badger with a meaty fist and then attempted to tackle him. Badger was ready and easily countered the heavy man's moves with a swift and lithe duck and then knocked the big guy over. Ol' Hue banged against the corner of the desk before crashing to the floor.

Dean held himself in check as he watched Badger take full control of himself, regardless of his recent injuries and his greatly impaired shoulder and arm. As Hubert Wright grunted and started screaming for help, Dean became aware that the sickly sweet burning smell was growing stronger.

Badger was on Hubert Wright's back wrapping a rope around the man's mouth and tying his hands.

"Let's go!" Dean said.

The study door slammed open. The stranger took one look into the room and fired. The window next to Dean exploded. Glass shards sprayed in every direction. Dean shot back and saw the man dive behind the doorframe.

Badger grabbed for whatever he had placed on the desk, and then frantically shoved it in Hubert Wright's face. Dean watched him tear the rope out of Hubert's mouth and then pour something from a vial over the man's face and lips.

"The suffering you've caused stops now," Badger hissed as he stabbed his knife into the man's side. "Rot in hell."

"Now!" Dean yelled and grabbed Badger by the back of his shirt.

With the medicine bundle tucked under his arm, he crashed through the broken window, dragging Badger with him into a tumbling downhill roll. Another shot deafened him, but he kept moving. He used momentum to keep them rolling through the grass, and then back onto their feet, towing Badger along like a pile of raggedy bones.

"You know the difference between me and you?" Badger asked.

Dean looked down at a stranger. His friend had changed to someone unrecognizable. The bitterness in his eyes was as clear as the snowmelt trickling down from the highest mountain peaks. Icy. Unforgiving. Following its own path. Badger had hid it from him all along, but now as his friend lay dying, he let it show.

"You see the good in people and I don't."

His voice sounded like he had flint chips stuck in his throat.

"There are men in this world who don't deserve a second chance, or even a first one." Badger put his knife to the hem of his shirt and cut it until he had a decent length of fabric. He began to tie the strip around his thigh. "I've stopped the Wright family lineage. And I'm still here. What do you think that means, Dean?"

"That you were wrong. That you couldn't have been the product of a rapist. Your father was your blood father."

"When you get back, check the birth records for my existence. Maybe I exist here but not in the future," he said. "You know what, brother, I don't care if I was mistaken about who my father is. My parents have been honored."

Through sheer determination, and under the cover of night, they had escaped from the ranch and made it back to the horses. Then they had ridden over a few hills and down to a dry creek bed when Badger asked to stop. They knew they were being pursued, even with the fire burning in Last Timber Gulch. Badger had slid out of the saddle and collapsed on the ground. Dean was anxious to put as many miles as possible between him and the ranchers, but Badger refused to stay on the horse. It was then that Dean saw the dark stain on Badger's legging. Dean could hardly stomach seeing it. Badger had been a human target since they had first arrived in this time.

"I won't say that you're wrong. If it were my mom, I would kill to save her, too." Just thinking about his mother and what he would or wouldn't do to have a chance to meet her gave him empathy for Badger. "I'll lift you back onto your horse. We have to keep moving."

Dean thought he saw a sneer on Badger's lips.

"This is the last time I'm going to tell you, asshole. I'm not going back."

"Want to arm wrestle me over it?" Dean said with an obvious hint toward Badger's nearly useless arm.

"They'll be coming soon," Badger wheezed.

Hearing the strain in Badger's voice made Dean clear his throat and suppress his own cough. Now that they had stopped, he was suddenly aware of how hard it was for him to take a deep breath.

"What did you do to Wright? Why am I feeling so weird?"

Badger gave a half snort. "Stabbed him in the kidney."

"Explain the smell, Badge. Why am I feeling sick?"

"I gave him a dose of his own poison. If you mix cyanide with something acidic, like vinegar, it makes a deadly gas," he said almost conversationally. "I hope they all choke on it."

Dean looked up at the hillside they had just ridden over, half expecting to see the outline of riders coming for them. He wondered if the cyanide gas was going to kill them, too.

"Stabbing him wasn't enough?" Dean quipped, as he reached down to help Badger up.

Badger pulled away so Dean couldn't touch him. "His son and his grandson's mine will kill a hundred and sixty-eight people in a mining accident in 1917. The poison his family puts into the ground and in the water is unforgivable and immeasurably devastating. I wish I could have shoved arsenic down his miserly throat, too."

"What if you've committed suicide for nothing? What if I was right all along, and you can't change the past? Did you consider it at all?"

"There you go again. You and I see the world in different ways. Go away, Dean. Take that silly girl back to her son. I know that's all you've thought about since the minute we got here."

"Damned if you're not a brainless jackass," Dean said as he stared at Man Eater. Badger was right about Kai. She had thrown a wrench right at his nuts for coming uninvited. It wasn't her fault, and it wasn't his, either. "She couldn't be ignored."

"You need to save people, Dean. That's why you started drinking so much after your daughter died. You couldn't handle the fact that you couldn't save her."

Dean's fist landed solidly against Badger's jaw. It happened without any conscious thought, and he was left staring down at his friend sprawled on his side. Badger eased himself up with his good arm and stared down the gulch. "Bastard," Dean said, and walked away before doing something else regrettable.

"You're right. I am. I don't regret it. I kill other bastards, too. It's the perfect way to get even for hating yourself. Now go back to Kai, before they find me," he garbled as he tried to stand. He wavered, but didn't collapse.

Badger's strength and willpower to see this thing through was commendable, Dean thought as he watched him. How much blood had he lost? How was he able to keep going? Dean could see and feel the fever in him. His eyes were sunken and heat radiated out of his body when he had pulled him away from the ranch and to the horses. He should be in a hospital, and yet somehow he kept moving. *Facing death with a roar of rebellion would be Badger's way of leaving this earth.*

Dean glanced at the hill behind Badger, wondering if there was any chance that the Wright men wouldn't find them.

"I can't see Kai again. She ruined everything. I thought once we were here, you'd join my cause, but she's been too much of a distraction."

Dean breathed through the unsettling restriction in his chest and tried to ignore the toxic headache he felt from the cyanide gas.

"She kept you alive. And she would keep doing it, too, if you would get up and come with us," he said through clenched teeth.

"I think I hear something. Get on that demon horse and go back to the Piegans."

Dean took the few steps back to Badger. Their eyes locked in the darkness of the shadowed valley. *He hated this.* He couldn't leave Badger or Kai. But Badger refused to leave, and Kai wouldn't make it on her own. He had his pipe, and all he had to do was make it back to the Dancing Bear's Pond in the mountains above his future cabin and wait for the new moon to perform the Night Medicine ceremony.

"I'm not going with you," Badger said again.

He glanced up at the hill and then back at Badger, the knowledge of impending capture urging him to keep moving before they were found. "After I get back, I'll do the research and see if you've changed our history." Dean reached for his belt and then pressed his pistol into the dying warrior's hand.

Badger took it and said, "I don't need you anymore. I can finish this on my own, but Kai's son needs her."

Badger's last words hit the heart of it all. *Kai couldn't get lost in the past.* Her son would be left behind, like Dean had been by his own parents. And Dean knew the other side of the coin, too; the unbearable heartache of losing of a child. If he could save Kai and her son from that misery, he would. He had to.

Badger was attempting to rid the earth of unworthy men, while Dean wanted to save those he cared about from experiencing pain. Part of the reason Dean had agreed to this whole time travel game was to save the kids, the parents, and his cousin, Gena, from the misery of societal pressures. Badger's money would keep Kinder Place open and affordable.

"Damn it, you're right about me," he admitted to Badger. "I'm saving a few families, but you're no different than I am, except that you're trying to save generations of anguish."

"You finally caught on," he said and then shifted his attention to the hill. "They're coming. Don't say anything else. Your parting kiss was enough. My jaw aches like a bitch. It's now or never, brother."

Dean clasped Badger's forearm and said, "There's no greater honor than dying in battle. Hiyah, brother!"

Dean turned to Man Eater. He could hear horse hooves pounding the ground from somewhere to the south. With haste, Dean released a saddle pack and tossed it over by Badger's feet.

"Ammo," he said.

"I hear it's a great time of year to visit the Sand Hills," Badger joked as he grabbed the pack awkwardly and moved into a position with a clear view of the hill.

"So it is," Dean agreed as he swung into the saddle, pressed his heels into Man Eater's ribs, and disappeared.

Chapter Twenty

"Today ranks number one on my list of the most abysmal days of my life," Dean said as he paced in circles.

"Don't worry. I was careful. And you were right about the other priest. He was willing to help us."

"I can't believe I let you go into town alone, again."

They both felt that the fewer people who saw her, the better, so Kai had ridden into Helena before the sun had come up. Dean needed to a new weapon and shells for their protection, but also for hunting. It was midday by the time she had returned. She had made remarkable time in getting back to camp.

"I told you I would be fine, and I am. It went off without a hitch, and I was extra cautious."

As he looked at her, he tried to settle his nerves by telling himself she was safe, but they refused to cooperate. He was on edge, and there wasn't much hope for coming down. "Is Father Connolly gone like he said?"

"He is. I told the other priest our story about how my brother was too ill to come into town to buy the supplies, and that's why I was there. He was a little hesitant, but he did it. I'm sure it's only because of Father Connolly's trust in you."

"I don't know what I would have done if you didn't come back," he said and shook his head. "He purchased the rifle without question?"

"He didn't like it, but I told him our family would starve without it."

"Hmmm," Dean said, trying to envision Kai persuading a priest to buy a gun and ammo.

As he rode away from Badger the previous night, he never heard any shots. Throughout the morning, he continually wondered if Badger would come riding up, but so far there had been no sign of him.

Dean led Kai to the new spot he had scouted for them to spend the day. It was close to where they were camped before, but deeper in the valley. The bushes were denser, the scrub oaks more mature, and inside all of the greenery was a hidden spring and small stream. Getting the horses through was the difficult part, but they had managed, and now the four of them were concealed as well as they could be.

Kai hobbled her chestnut-colored mare on a patch of decent grass near the water. They decided to wait out another day there, and then leave during the night. The pair now had ten days and eleven nights to make it to Dancing Bear's Pond by the dark of the moon.

Dean inspected his new rifle and shells and was grateful it wasn't a musket with powder and balls. Some conveniences of modern life, such as weapons, made Dean appreciate living in the twenty-first century. Going back to town had been a huge risk, but they both had wanted the security of having a gun for their journey back north.

"Did you stay in the church while he went to the mercantile?"

"I did. He agreed that I should stay out of sight too, since I was without a male companion."

"Did you get any news in town?"

"They're talking about the fire at the ranch, and Hubert Wright's death, but nothing about murder or the break in. Everyone is still trying to recover from the alley fire by the bank. That's what the Father told me."

"No talk about the hanging?"

"Nothing."

Dean thought on the news for a long moment. Did they want to keep Badger's escape from the hanging quiet? He was sure it was an epic failure on the part of the vigilantes. Maybe they didn't want to promote their incompetence. Dean was mildly relieved he didn't kill the hangman, for surely if a man's body had been found by the hanging tree, there would be plenty of gossip, and a territory-wide manhunt, too.

Kai looked as exhausted as Dean felt. Adrenaline alone must have been keeping him going. Every shift of the wind, or unexpected flutter of a bird, had him envisioning that they were being discovered, killed, or taken prisoner. He had seriously worried that he would shoot Kai for returning to camp, but he didn't, and she had made it back to him undetected by the vigilantes.

"Your ex-husband must have been a complete idiot."

"What are you talking about?" she said as she rearranged the new supplies.

She appeared annoyed. He was pleased that his comment had gotten under her skin. It encouraged him to continue. "You're strong. Smart. Capable of anything. Your cooking is the bomb and you're a caring and amazing mom. He had to be a loser to let you go."

He watched her flush with embarrassment, and then turn away to hide her face.

"I'm thanking you, Kai. For taking these risks. You shouldn't have to, and yet you do it willingly. Not many men could accomplish what you have."

"I need to get home. Anyone desperate enough will do desperate things," she said as she fussed with her bedding, brushing away the leaves and debris. "So who gets to sleep first?" she asked.

"You."

"You need it more than I do."

"Doesn't matter. I can't sleep."

He watched her cover her mouth with the back of her hand as she yawned. "Okay."

Kai stretched out on her back, not bothering to change out of her town clothes. Dean still preferred the way she looked in her buckskin dress. Then he noticed that her hair and face looked damp. She must have rinsed off in the stream after hobbling her horse. He decided that he needed a dip in the spring as well. He found the soap and then waited until her eyes were closed and her breathing was slow and deep before he undressed and splashed cold water over his skin and washed the grime away. His hair felt matted with dirt and knots. He scooped water with his hands over his head and body until he felt back to himself, inside and out.

With the rifle resting by his side, Dean sat on his blanket and sorted his remaining gear. Then he reread Badger's journal, looking for anything he had previously missed. He thought many of the names of the people belonged to members of the Wright family, but Badger often used a first or last initial instead of a full name. He was also careful about dates, and seemed to have a code that only he could decipher. Dean couldn't stop wondering if Badger was alive or dead. He dwelled on his mixed feelings of betrayal and desertion over what he'd done the night before. Even with the knowledge that there was no other choice, the weight in his chest over leaving Badger behind was going to be with him until the day he died.

Dean finally settled into drawing a picture of their horses, dappled with sunlight while nestled in the shrubs, with the stream running near their hooves. It helped pass the time, even though his paranoia refused to calm down.

Kai awakened after the sun dipped low over the horizon and they were blanketed deep in the shadows beneath the branches. Dean had packed everything but her bed, and was just about to wake her up when he saw her watching him. They needed a trace of useable light to get the horses out of the narrow dell.

As they left the oak grove behind, she looked at Dean and smiled. It was unexpected, and gave him the tiniest amount of hope that they were going to make it back with time to spare.

"I was so tired, I forgot to tell you the good news."

"While you were sleeping today, you actually woke up from your nightmare, were rid of me, and Badger was just a furry, obnoxious nuisance that you ran over with your car?" Dean offered.

"That sounds pretty good, but no, that's not it. I really do have something to tell you."

He raised his brows and waited.

"I used the last of the gold to buy a herd of sheep, two herding dogs, eight heifers, and a bull. Father Smithson assured me that when Father Connolly and John Winters returned, they would receive the message about the animals belonging to the South Piegans. I think John will know what to do. He was agreeable to the original plan about bringing the Piegans the livestock to help supplement them through the hard times to come."

Speechless, Dean blinked at Kai. He stuck his tongue in his cheek before saying, "Where did you... I mean, how did you find them?"

"Well, apparently the barn at Last Timber Gulch burned down last night, and they didn't have room for the new animals that had just arrived there by wagon train. The animals were being held in the livery yard until they could be moved. With all the upset, someone authorized them to be sold immediately to the highest bidder. I put in an offer that couldn't be refused, or should I say, Father Smithson did."

Dean dropped Man Eater's reins and wrapped his arms around Kai. This woman never stopped amazing him. He allowed his heart to open a crack. It was the first time in years he'd felt something other than a dull ache or numbness, and he clung onto to it. Onto her. Moments of pure lucidity had been on the brink of extinction for Dean. He had been dwelling in the past – his personal past – for too long. He had been living like that since his daughter became ill. But now, he actually felt hopeful for a future.

He became suddenly aware of the feel of her back beneath his hands. The curve of her lower body as it dipped in and then swayed back out. First it was his arms as he felt the warmth through her dress, and then the rest of his body awakened to the realization that the full length of her was pressed against him. She fit, he thought. *She fit perfectly next to him.*

His breath stilled and his pulse quickened, realizing how comfortable it was to have her in his arms. Once his body was aware of her, his arousal was instant and unwavering. He knew she sensed the shift between them. There was a sudden and awkward stiffness in her body. He expected her to pull away, but she didn't.

"Let's give this a chance," he whispered to the top of her head.

His fingers skimmed up her back, and he let his hands rest on her shoulders. He thought he felt a shiver pass through her, and it increased the rising heat in his blood, warming him all over. He suppressed his desire to lower her to the ground and take her in grass and leaves, beneath the sunset sky. There was no way he would take anything from her that wasn't given willingly, be it her thoughts, emotions, or her body. He could ignore this attraction as long as she could. *Or at the least, he could pretend to.*

Kai gripped the back of his shirt as she looked up at him. He was expectant and nervous, but also hopeful. She raised her hands to the back of his neck. With slow, careful movement, she pulled his head down to hers. Willing, ready, and eager, he placed his mouth on hers and let instinct guide him. He explored her mouth with soft and tender caresses at first, being cautious to not let his primal needs take control. It lasted an achingly beautiful few seconds before she deepened the intensity. Her fingers splayed over the back of his neck and into his hair as she pulled him closer to her. She nipped his bottom lip before opening her mouth to him. Tongues were meeting, tasting, and lightly sucking in a teasing dance that sent Dean over the top. His hands roamed over her back. He gripped her waist, holding her firmly against him as his other hand explored the side of her ribcage to the swell of her breast.

He felt her body lengthen against his touch, and a tiny moan escaped from deep in her throat as he received a hint of what was under her dress. He let the side of his hand brush back down over her curves and rest on her hip as he refocused on her mouth. An involuntary groan rumbled through him, and then he was sealing a promise between them as he pulled back. He kept her close, resting his cheek against her hair while smelling her unique scent. A mix of earth and grass, sage and cedar. A hint of campfire smoke. It was a warm and inviting smell that made him want her like he'd never wanted any woman before.

She rested her forehead against his shoulder, hands on his chest. "I can't give you an answer. Not yet. Maybe not ever."

The kiss hadn't fully extinguished inside him. It was still zinging through his blood, and he was damned afraid of where it was going to finally settle. Right in the root of his manhood. He didn't think he could speak coherently just yet. He took a few deep breaths, filling his lungs with her, with the scrub oaks, and the horses, and then sighed.

"Your eyes will open, Kai. Someday. The way mine have just now. Waiting will hurt us both, but we're not strangers to pain and longing." He stroked the top of her head and ran his palm down her long braid. "Promise me, you won't let regret win."

He felt her swallow. She wouldn't hand out promises lightly, and he knew he wasn't going to receive one right now.

The dark was encapsulating them, and it was time to start moving.

"Please don't die before I decide."

He barely caught her words because she had spoken them so softly. He squeezed her tighter. "Having something to live for changes everything. I'm not going anywhere."

With no little reluctance, he released her and retrieved Man Eater. Dean interrupted his horse from ripping out tufts of grass and was rewarded with a snap of teeth at his arm. Used to the horse's antics, Dean yanked his hand away and then snaked it back to grab the reins just as Man Eater lowered his head to take another bite.

"Your horse likes me. I wouldn't mind trading if you want to ride Opal," Kai said as she led her mare away from the low branches so she could climb on. "It would save me from having to make up another batch of bruise balm after he finally gets his teeth on you."

"I like you too, and you're not riding me, either. I think we'll suffer in silence together."

The decision to ride west and then north was a tough one for Dean. Badger was taken by the vigilantes in the foothills, almost due north of Helena. It was risky no matter which way they went, so Dean chose the route that had the most places to keep them concealed. He also knew it would be slower going with more obstacles than staying out on the prairie, but it was the most logical solution to ensure their safety.

They were silent as they rode past a recently clear cut forest. The devastation by moonlight was humbling for Dean. The unwanted slash was everywhere. It was a wasteland of branches and needles. Wagon ruts and erosion had caused black gashes in the landscape where it would take decades to heal, if it ever did. A fox appeared among the wreckage. It stopped and looked at them with its yellow eyes, then pattered off through the never-ending graves of tree stumps. Even though they stayed at the edges of the cut forest, Dean could see hill after hill of tumbled landscape. He tried to picture what the area looked like in 2012, and all he could recall were rolling hills. Now he could clearly see that a forest was meant to cover the land as well.

Mining in the 1800's needed timber. The influx of people to Montana in such a short amount of time meant no forest would be left unmolested. Dean had read the stats in Badger's journal. He knew that the coming copper mines were going to be the most destructive to the forests, using up to a thousand cords a day in their smelters. Badger wrote that by 1890, there were going to be over a hundred lumber mills in operation. He believed that Hubert Wright was a vital link in the cataclysmic chain of destruction. In the midnight hour, Dean didn't know if he was staring at thousands of acres or hundreds of thousands of acres of clear cutting, but he knew that the latter was coming. Badger's need for revenge for his mother and to be an environmental savior was starting to make more sense to Dean now.

Finally, Dean and Kai left the wasteland behind. They rode down a grassy slope, toward a crooked stream at the bottom of an open valley, when Kai said, "The Salish and Kootenai get the worst of it."

"I learned about it in eleventh grade history. The settlers didn't think the Natives had a need for lumber, so they didn't consider it stealing, even though it was obviously cut down on rez land."

Kai continued, "There were attempts to sue for illegal timber cutting, but the railroads were, I mean, are going to be," she corrected herself, "too powerful. They're invested in the local banks, which are also owned by the territorial governors. A perfect recipe for corruption. So the land, and the people who lived on it, lost, and no one could do anything about it."

"Then apocalyptic fires and wind come through here in 1910 and cleanse the land of what few forests are left."

"The end," she finished.

They were silent as they listened to Man Eater and Opal drink from the creek. As Man Eater raised his dripping muzzle, Dean steered him upstream, and Kai followed.

"Do you think Badger was wrong for wanting to stop him? I mean, the man was a mining magnate, had invested in one of the largest banks in Helena, and is, or was going to start copper mining in a few short years. He had to be partly responsible for what's coming."

Dean contemplated the question before answering. Kai didn't know the part about Badger's mom. He didn't think he should be the one to tell Badger's story.

"Men have been killed for less. Badger's motivations were honorable to him."

"But what do you believe? Was he right or wrong?" she pressed again.

"What I've said all along. You can't change the past. He was wrong for thinking he could. He was wrong for trying, and for lying to me. And he was right for fighting for something he believed in."

"So you'll find out if he succeeded when we get home."

"I might look it up when we get back," he said.

"If he was my friend, I would, too."

They left the valley and reluctantly rode over open hills. Preferring to stay in the cover of evergreens, they headed still farther north and west, toward the forest. Dean stayed alert, but the farther they traveled with no sign of pursuers, the more his energy began to wane.

Dean played mind games to keep himself awake. He watched the sky. The Seven Persons as they made their nightly path through the universe. He watched the North Star, Orion, and Lyra. He had a silent conversation with The Night God, asking that he and Kai would have a successful and safe journey home. When he heard a wolf howling in the distance, he thought his prayer was being taken into consideration by the Great Mystery. When he could think of nothing else to carry him through the long hours of the night, he irritated Man Eater. He coaxed his horse into a trot then stopped abruptly. He steered him in directions he didn't want to go. The horse wasn't happy with this nonsense, and it helped Dean stay vigilant by watching for Man Eater's revenge. The laying back of his ears. The quiet stillness of the brute's large body, just before he reared or swung his head around to bite Dean's leg.

The games didn't last long enough though, and Dean's adrenaline boost finally left the territory, possibly the entire continent.

"How far have we ridden, Dean?"

The sound of her voice broke the monotony of horse hooves, and he sat up a degree or two taller, feeling more attentive. He looked over his shoulder, then ahead to the peaks rising to meet the stars.

"Maybe twenty miles."

"We have a hundred and fifty to go." She practically whimpered this bit of trivia back at him.

"We're doing well, Kai," he assured her, even though he'd like nothing better than to fall into a heap on the ground and stay there until someone built a road north. "No one is shooting at us, and we haven't lost any of our gear. Great Spirit smiles on us."

He thought he heard her sigh, and wondered how tired she was after sleeping all afternoon. He'd been awake since... He'd lost track, and felt a flash of insanity as his mind couldn't recall when the last time he had slept for more than a couple of hours. Then he remembered. It was days ago and it had been restless, full of disturbing dreams about Badger hanging from a tree.

"We'll stop at first light," he said. "You're in charge of finding us a good camp, Kai. I can't be trusted right now. I'm sleep-driving."

He heard her mumble something that sounded sarcastic and biting, and he smiled to himself. She would find the perfect spot.

Chapter Twenty-one

With no sign of pursuit over the past few days, Dean felt he could risk the noise of firing his rifle. He wanted fresh meat, and the flock of turkeys that had just scrambled through the brush not twenty yards from them would be good eating.

Kai had seen the birds too, and she looked eager when Dean picked up his gun and hurried to stalk them.

When he returned, he carried their lunch by its feet.

"Do you know how to cook a wild turkey?" she asked as he neared their campsite.

"I bet you do," he said with a hopeful smile.

"Give it here," she said, and took the bird from him.

He watched her remove the majority of the wings with her knife and then make a small slice near the tail and pull off the entire skin, feathers and all. She gutted it, and then they had fresh poultry ready in minutes.

"How do you know so much about living off of the land?" he asked.

"It's how I grew up," she said as she laid the bird on a stone and looked up at him. "Should we take the time to stew it, or should we roast the whole bird over the fire and then gorge ourselves?"

"Did you camp a lot, or were you raised by wolves and bears?"

She gave him a look of annoyed impatience at his questions.

He decided to change tactics. "We can take our time today and stay the night here. I don't think anyone is following us. Then tomorrow we can start traveling during the day instead of at night. What do you think?"

"I think this turkey will taste good with cattail shoots, onions, sage, and choke cherries."

"Tomorrow it is, then," he said as his mouth began to water at the thought of a real meal and not the measly handfuls of trail food they had been living on for the last few days.

"How can I help?" he offered.

"Hmmm," she considered. "You've done your part already. You shoot it, and I'll cook it."

"Sounds like the deal of a lifetime."

She smiled and stirred the fire. "I don't mind, you know."

"Mind what?"

"Living out here. Sleeping outside. Traveling by horseback. It would be better if we didn't have to worry about the Wrights and the vigilantes following us, but it's not so bad."

"I don't mind it either," he said. "But I could use a hot shower now and then."

"Do you have hot water at your cabin? I noticed you don't have electricity."

"I have a generator if I want to use it, and I also have a wood burning hot water heater. I appreciate a few modern conveniences, even when I'm by myself."

She filled their small pot with some water and started adding the wild vegetables and herbs. The turkey was already skewered and placed over the coals to roast. "It's funny what people can and can't live without."

"What about you? If you could have anything from our time right now, what would it be?"

"I really don't need anything," she said, and sat back, cross-legged next to her culinary creation.

The sun beat down on her black hair and made it shine. It was a hot day, but it felt good after the cool mountain night.

She stared across the fire looking at the meadow beyond the trees and said, "I wouldn't turn down a real bed, or a pizza, but if I could have one wish granted, it would be for my family to be here with me."

Dean looked off to the north, thinking she wasn't wrong. He would easily give up his life in the future and live here with Ellie. He had mixed emotions about his ex-wife, Marissa, coming too, but if Ellie had lived, maybe their marriage wouldn't have fallen apart. He couldn't picture himself with Marissa now, though. She would never have been willing to move to northern Montana, away from the city and shopping malls, and the convenience of takeout and delivery.

He turned his mind away from Marissa and Ellie.

"Pizza in bed?" he said, hardly attempting to hide the suggestive smirk.

"I said one or the other."

"It would be better the way I'm envisioning it." He looked down the length of her and back up again, unable to help himself.

"Did your dirty little mind see me slamming the door in your face and eating the whole pizza myself?"

"Nope. That's not the way it happens at all," he said, letting his mind think of all the things he would do to her if they were alone in a bedroom.

"Well, there won't be any pizza ever again if we don't make it back," she said, and shut down his tantalizing fantasy for good.

"We're about three days away from the beaver ponds, and have six days until the new moon. I think we're doing all right."

She pressed her lips together and stirred the food.

When the meal was ready, Dean dug a small divot in the ground by his foot and placed a choke cherry and piece of the cooked turkey in it. He covered the offering with dirt and then they ate the incredible feast with minimal conversation.

Dean thought that Kai was even sexier outside, surrounded by the woods and nature, than in his imagination, but he didn't say so. She had told him she would let him know if and when she was ready. He would wait for her. He had a strong feeling she would see how well they fit together soon.

The day of rest was sorely needed for all of them, horses included. Kai collected food and taught Dean many of the plants she knew. He calculated and planned the last part of their journey as the horses grazed in a lush valley. They needed to head east for at least half of a day, and then turn north again. The mountainous terrain to the north was becoming too extreme to travel safely with the horses. He had been vigilant about staying alert for pursuers, or anyone else, but they hadn't run into a single person so far. It helped ease the tension some, but he knew the threat of the unknown wouldn't leave completely until they were back in 2012.

Kai and Dean felt fully rested for the first time in weeks as they left the valley and rode east. By midday, Dean was acutely aware of the change in the weather. The temperature hadn't changed much, but the occasional gust of wind blustered and shook the forest, then whipped uphill and disappeared. Thunderheads were accumulating over the peaks, and Dean thought it looked like much more was brewing than an afternoon shower.

They rode out into the open from under the forest canopy onto a bluff, high above the plains as the first thunder rumbled. It was still miles away, but the black clouds rolling in from the west were moving fast.

"Let's head for those rocks," Dean said, and pointed to the far side of the vista where massive boulders could be seen jutting out of the hillside.

They trotted across the meadow looking for shelter. The horses quivered beneath them with the increased anxiety of their riders. They paused at the top of a massive stone outcrop that dropped down to a lake far below.

"We can't get down from here," Kai said. "We have to go back, and then try to get around."

The horses wouldn't make it over the jutting spires and crags in front of them. Downhill to the east, the rocks became cliffs and ledges that tumbled down to meet the water.

"Look over there," Dean said, steering Man Eater uphill toward the trees.

It was rough and uneven ground where the edge of the forest met the rocks. Dean spotted a game trail, and it led them around and down, along the base of the stones. Beneath the tree limbs the shadows were deep, the moss and ferns lush, and the rocks were slick with lichens. The charcoal clouds overhead growled and grumbled, as if protesting against the mighty climb over the peaks and the following descent on the other side. The storm seemed to have reached the summit at their back, and was now striking with bolts of lightning and claps of thunder. The sky began to spit pieces of frozen rain, and Dean knew it was time to take cover.

They made it down into the forested valley close to the western edge of the lake. Dean wanted to stay away from the stream in case of flash flooding. Ahead of them on the right, the woods opened up to a small beach that backed up against the boulders. He thought the cliffs were too open to the sky, but then he noticed a shallow rock overhang where he and Kai could crawl beneath. On their left there was nothing but forest and the stream that fed the lake, and on the other side, the valley rose steeply once again.

"Get off and grab everything you can," he said as he dismounted Man Eater.

"Here?" she asked as she raised a hand to shield her face from spattering sleet.

"We have to leave the horses under the trees. It's the best we can do."

She squinted against the weather and slid off of Opal. She tied the horse to a tree and then grabbed all of her gear. Dean ran over to the rocks and set his bags and bedding under the overhang. A flash of lighting startled Kai into a jog to catch up with Dean, but the thunder that followed made her heart skip a beat and her adrenaline pump.

She didn't set her blanket roll and bags down next to his. The spot he chose was more exposed than just settling down next to a tree trunk by her horse. She scanned the prospective trees and saw Dean hacking off the branches of a fir tree. Realizing what Dean was doing, Kai changed her mind and tossed her bags and blankets over to his. She grabbed her knife from her belt and found another tree to cut branches from. The sleet was turning to hail, but it was small and soft, like tiny snowballs. They had a large pile of branches in just a few minutes, and they rushed over to the rocks and built a hasty lean-to.

"Get in," Dean said as the pieces of hail grew in size and started to sting when they hit their skin.

"Where are you going?"

"We need a few more branches."

She frowned, and then winced as she was struck by a ball of hail on the cheek.

"Hurry," she said as he darted across the tiny beach back into the trees.

Kai climbed behind the screen of branches and felt instant relief to be out of the pinging hail. She kept her eyes peeled for Dean, but couldn't see him through the narrow opening they had left as a door.

To her relief, he returned quickly and stacked more of the soft-needled branches against the wall they had built and then slipped inside, pulling a thick branch in place behind him. He half crawled and half scooted over to a place where he could sit up without hitting his head on the rock ceiling. He ran a hand over his head, brushing the hail and sleet from his hair.

"There's nothing like a mountain storm," he said as the downpour increased to a roar.

The branches shook and the needles vibrated with the beating they were taking, but almost no hail came inside. Kai thought the forest was falling down around them and wanted to cry for the poor horses. She jumped when a clap of thunder shook the ground beneath her.

"Easy there, soldier. It'll pass soon," he said, and tried to straighten his leg. There wasn't enough room to stretch it out, so he bent his knee and looked around at their tiny space.

"I'm fine," she lied, and then grabbed for her heart as another *boom* threatened to split the rock over her head.

"You're actually afraid of something?" he teased.

"No I'm not," she replied, a little too defensively.

"Yeah, I can tell you're loving this right now."

"The lightning is closer than I would prefer."

"Uh-huh," he said.

The hail was already beginning to lighten, but the storm wasn't. The lightning seemed to be centered over them, and the ice was now being replaced with rain. Kai shivered and leaned into the granite.

"Well, I can't squat like this for very much longer. Do you think you can help me spread out the blankets?"

She looked at the pile of gear squished against the rocks and grabbed the bedrolls.

Dean saw how unsteady and pale she looked and leaned over to help her. As soon as they had the blankets flat, he said, "Lie down."

She looked hesitant, and then started to move over to where he was sitting near the end, closest to the exit.

"Come on, Kai. We've done this before. You've got goose bumps, and I need to straighten my leg."

The rain was heavy outside, and they would need each other to stay warm, especially if it didn't let up through the night.

"You look a little too happy about this," she said, and crossed her arms over her chest.

A flash lit the inside of their shelter and was almost instantly followed by another rattling *boom*. Kai practically threw herself down and huddled against the bed. Dean slid over and stretched out behind her. He placed his back to the branches and reached over for the saddle bag that held their spare clothes. He pushed it under their heads to use as a pillow then covered the two of them with the top blanket. He tucked it in snugly around them, and then wrapped his arms around Kai.

"You wouldn't take advantage of a frightened woman, would you?" she murmured.

"Wouldn't dream of it," he said as he tried to get comfortable and realized that with her this close to him for the entire night, he wasn't likely to get any rest at all unless he seriously rearranged his brain. Her smell, her softness, her warmth; it was definitely keeping parts of him awake.

"Scouts honor?"

"Whatever you want, Kai," he mumbled. Then Dean said near her ear, "Ksiistsikómiipi'kssii, great Thunderbird, have pity on us for the sake of Kai's small son. Let your trail of lightning move far away from this place."

"What are you doing?" she asked when a break in the thunder allowed her to speak and be heard.

"Asking the Thunder God to spare you."

"Do you think he listens?"

There was a lull in the crashing sky as if his prayer was being answered. "It doesn't hurt to try to appeal to the Gods."

She glanced over her shoulder at Dean to see if he was joking or serious. "The Cree have their own stories of the Thunder beings. Tell me your version," she said as the next bolt of lightning lit up the sky and reflected off the stone with eerie flashes. She shivered and tried to bury her head into the saddle bag.

He tensed, squeezing her tight until the cracking sky settled. "He lives in a massive cavern on the side of Chief Mountain. When he leaves his stone lodge he becomes a bird with feathers of every color like a rainbow, and his talons are the color of spring grass. His beating wings make the sound of a million drums and the lightning trails behind him as he crosses the sky."

She let out a deep breath and then inched in closer to him as another rolling *boom* tumbled over the mountain.

"And sometimes he steals women."

Dean felt Kai stiffen again.

"Not helping," she said flatly.

"Don't worry. As long as you're in my arms, he can't get you."

"Are you making this up now?" she asked, doubtfully.

"Nope. Everyone has heard of Thunder. He is a bad person and roars in the mountains and crashes over the prairie. He has no appreciation for the cliffs, the trees, or of man. He will strike down anyone and crush them."

"How is this supposed to help me relax?" she asked.

"Just listen," he said. "In the long-ago times, a man and his wife were sitting in their lodge when Thunder struck. The man fell back as if he was dead, but he awoke some time later, and rose to his feet. He looked all around for his wife but she was gone. He knew Thunder had taken her.

"He wandered away from his lodge, mourning the loss of his wife, and he spent the next four days thinking about how to get her back. He asked all of the animals if they knew where Thunder lived, but no one knew, or they were too afraid to answer. When he came across a wolf, the wolf said, 'We would not go looking for the home of the one we fear most. We can run from all of our enemies, but from Thunder there is no hiding. He strikes us down and we do not get up again. Go home to your people and do not search for the dwelling place of that horrible being.'

"The man did not take the wolf's warning and continued searching for his wife. He traveled unknown distances until he reached a peculiar lodge made all of stone. He quickly discovered he had found the home of Raven chief.

"The chief of all the ravens invited him in and fed him a meal. After he had eaten, the Raven chief asked why the man had come. He said, 'I am looking for Thunder's dwelling place. My wife was taken by him and I will have her back.'

"'Are you brave enough to enter the lodge of that despicable person,' Raven asked. 'He lives close to this place. His lodge is made of stone like my own, and inside are the eyes of the ones he has killed or taken away. He takes out their eyes and hangs them from strings inside his home.'"

"Dean! Why are you telling me this?" Kai asked, and pinched his arm.

"Ow," he said, and flinched. "Shhh…you're interrupting. Now be quiet, so I can finish telling you the rest."

"I don't think I want to know."

"Do you really want to miss the end?" he asked.

"Since I can't leave for fear of being abducted by the sky, I guess you get my undivided attention."

"Okay then," Dean said, and settled back into the story. "The man was terrified and told Raven so. 'I am afraid. No one could look upon such terrible things as hanging eyes and live.'

"Raven said, 'No man can, but there is one creature that Thunder does not scare and cannot kill. It is the ravens. I will give you a special medicine to protect you against Thunder. You will enter his home and find your wife's eyes and make Thunder give them to you.'

"The man took the gifts from the Raven chief and went to Thunder's lodge. When he entered, he saw all of the eyes hanging from strings. It was awful, but not nearly as terrifying as when Thunder spoke and asked the man, 'Why have you come?'

"His voice was dreadful and the man trembled before him, but he would not leave. 'You have stolen my wife and I have come to take her back. I see her eyes hanging from your lodge.'

"'No man enters my home and lives,' Thunder said, and rose from the back of the lodge to strike the man down.

"But the man was prepared to use the gifts from Raven chief and pointed a raven wing at Thunder. The powerful being fell to the floor. As Thunder rose up once more to strike, the man pulled out the antler arrow given to him from Raven chief. He fitted it to his bow and shot it through the wall of Thunder's dwelling. It pierced the stone and let the sun shine in.

"'Stop!' Thunder boomed. 'You have great medicine and you are more powerful than I. Take down your wife's eyes and have her back.'

"The man cut the string that held her eyes, and then his wife appeared at his side.

"Thunder said, 'You know I have great powers. I live here in the summer, but I follow the birds far to the south when winter comes. Here, take my pipe. When I first return in the coming spring, and you hear my wings beating in the sky, light this pipe and smoke it. You and your people will pray to me that I bring the rains that make the grass green and the berries grow large and ripen.' This is how the People received their first medicine pipe."

Dean lay still feeling the rise and fall of each of her breaths. The rain had not lightened, but the thunder was moving away and made the story easier to hear.

"I think you like that story more than I do," she finally said.

"Oh come on. What's not too like? The woman lives, and gets her eyes back." He could feel the scowl on Kai's face without even seeing it. He smiled into her hair.

She shifted and they shared a sideways glance. "I'll give you one more chance to tell me a story that doesn't shed a negative light on women."

Dean scratched his chin. "That may be difficult," he hemmed. "I'll do my best."

They spent the rest of the evening and most of the night sharing stories and debating their difference of opinions. The rain roared, wailed, and eventually whispered against the rocks. Then they drifted off to sleep.

Dean was restless. He wanted to keep moving, but he thought it would be best to let the storm ride out over the plains first. He and Kai had talked for so long during the night that Kai was still asleep, and there was no need to wake her if they weren't leaving yet.

He took his sketchbook out of his bag and left their lean-to. Dean checked on the horses, let them drink from the lake, and then moved them to fresh grass. Satisfied that they were temporarily taken care of, he climbed the rocks above their shelter to an overlook and sat down on the damp stone taking in the view. The departing storm hovered over the foothills like a reluctant traveler unwilling to mosey on down the road. He shifted his attention to the lake. The water was cupped in the bottom of the valley, and sparkled where the sun had broken through the clouds. The shoreline was soggy and littered with debris and piles of hail that had washed out of the forest, and he could just hear the stream running full and fast as it emptied into the lake.

Dean flipped his book open and the page landed on his drawing of Ellie. He stared at his four-year-old daughter's face. Her wide eyes crinkled with joy above her plump little cheeks. Ellie had her mother's mouth and chin, his hair and eye color, but Marissa's long lashes. In his eyes she was child perfection. Innocent and well loved. He let himself think about the future and how Ellie hadn't even been born yet. If she wasn't born, then she couldn't die. Her cancer didn't exist here. It gave him a strange sort of foggy peace over his otherwise turbulent memories about his daughter.

Dean laid his fingertips against the page as if he could feel the softness of her hair one more time. He wished she could see this place. That she could be surrounded with the trees and feel the cool air blowing off of the lake as he taught her how to scramble over the rocks. He ripped the page from his book and moved to the edge of the cliff where he looked out over the water. He found a stone the size of his fist and placed his drawing under it. Ellie could have this spot. He wanted to give her the mountains and the views. His daughter could exist here as yet another memory.

"Is that Ellie?"

He turned slowly and saw Kai looking down at the drawing.

"Yeah."

"Gena told me."

"She would."

"She made me swear that I wouldn't tell you I knew anything."

"I know everyone talks. It's okay." He looked away and stared at nothing.

"Sometimes it gets easier, Dean. And sometimes it feels worse than ever."

"How long has it been for you since you lost your family?"

"Eleven years."

"Do you think we'll ever stop marking the time?"

"No. My sister should be twenty-seven this year."

"And Ellie would have turned six last March."

"Come on," Kai said, and took Dean's hand.

She pulled him toward the other side of the rock pile and led him down an easier way than he had climbed up.

At the bottom, she let go of his hand and took his sketchbook from him.

"Give me one second," she said.

He watched her kneel down and lean in under the canopy of their little shelter. She backed out and walked over to him.

"What are you up to?" he asked.

"I'm starting the day by trying something new," Kai said. She took his hand and led him to the water.

There was a hint of playfulness around her eyes and the ghost of a smile on her lips. Dean was almost afraid to ruin the moment by saying something that would anger her, so he bit the inside of his cheek and went along with her 'something new' in silence.

She stopped in front of him and reached for the hem of his shirt. Dean looked down and watched her slender fingers strip off his clothes.

He stood bare chested in front of her. "Do I get to take yours off next?"

"No," she said simply and reached for the ties of his leggings.

"Fair is fair," he said and raised his hand.

She playfully batted his hand away from her dress. "Wait your turn," she scolded. "I'm not finished with you."

He kept his eyes steady on her face as she untied his leggings and then eased them down. She went for his belt next, the only thing keeping his breechclout in place. He grabbed her wrist, stopping her.

"Are you sure you know what you're doing, Kai?" Dean's voice was thick and he had to work at keeping his breathing steady. It had been sweet torture to hold her through the night and not touch her the way he wanted to. Now she was pulling his clothes off of him.

Her gaze rose to meet his. Her eyes were sure, but her pulse raced beneath her jaw.

"You were really thoughtful last night," she said, lifting her chin. "I know it was hard for you and I know I'm—difficult sometimes. If you want me to stop, I will."

He released her hand and she removed his belt and breechclout.

He cleared his throat. "I think I like this new you."

His clothes lay in a heap by his feet. She took half a step back and shimmied out of her dress.

Dean wanted to reach for her. He ached to brush his hands over her caramel-colored skin. To caress the curves that she hadn't allowed him to touch, but he waited for her to make the next move.

She bent down, picked up the bar of soap that was lying by her clothes, and stepped into his personal space wearing only her necklace. She placed her hand on his chest. Her fingers trailed down his abdomen and stopped on his taut stomach. Every nerve ending in his body came to attention and concentrated on where her hand was traveling to. It was a promise. *A tease.* It made his heart pound. Her other hand brushed down his arm, and she took his hand and led him into the water.

The cold exhilarated them. It thrilled and refreshed. It was freezing, but the heat from Dean's loins kept him warm. She stopped when they were waist deep in the water and her hand moved to his thigh and worked the soap up and down over his leg. She circled over the muscles of each leg and kept her eyes hidden beneath her lowered lashes.

He raised an eyebrow and waited to see how adventurous she was going to get. She stepped behind him and the soap moved down over the back of his knees and then back up over his buttocks to his low back. He felt the water trickle down his back as she worked higher over the muscles of his back and then lower again. Her hand slipped between his thighs and he nearly groaned in sweet agonizing need.

He turned around and grabbed for her hands to take the soap away, but she was quick to keep it out of his reach.

"I'm not done," she said with a devilish smile.

"Woman, I get a turn with that. Now hand it over."

"Come and get it," she said stepping into deeper water.

He dove for her just as she plunged beneath the water. He felt her leg snake out of his grasp. He kicked hard against the gravelly lake bottom, and had her in his arms as she surfaced for air. She gave a little shriek as he captured her and she splashed at him to get away. He wrapped an arm around her and brought her in close, so she couldn't escape. He took the slippery cake of soap from her hand and then went to work on her.

Dean wanted to explore every inch of her, but he started by circling her shoulder and then slid the bar along her collar bone. Her head tilted back, eyes closing, and exposing more of her nape. He placed his lips to her thrumming pulse as he let his hand glide down over the mound of her breast. She was firm, yet her skin was as soft as silk. Her nipples stood erect in the cold water, and he circled the soap around one, then the other. He moved lower over her smooth belly.

"Is this what a thunderstorm normally does to you?" he asked as he let his hand explore her lower back and then down over the curves of her backside.

"It wasn't the storm, Dean," she said, opening her eyes and running her fingers along his spine. She whimpered when he pressed himself up against her to reach the back of her legs without turning her around.

"You enjoy torturing me, don't you?"

"I can't help myself," she said, and giggled. "I'm an awful person. You confuse me and make me want to do things."

"Things like this?" he asked, and lowered his mouth to hers.

He wasn't soft or timid this time. He held her body tightly against his and took her mouth the way he'd wanted to for weeks. His kiss was deep and urgent. He tasted and explored and teased. She rose up on tiptoe and met his need with equal desire. Her hands gripped his back and held him to her. He moved to kiss her throat and she purred and dug her fingers into his flesh. He cupped her breast and murmured, "Still confused about us?"

"Yes. No. Yes." Her last *yes* came out as a moan, as he lowered his mouth to her breast. "It doesn't matter. Just please, don't stop." Her hand glided around to the front of his body, and then down to his manhood.

He groaned against her hot skin. He could feel her heart thumping beneath his lips. He felt her breath catch, and it encouraged him to continue.

Then she said, "Dean, stop."

The tone of her voice alarmed him and her body went stiff. He looked up at her face and knew something was terribly wrong.

"What is it? Kai, what's the matter?"

"Mmmhh," she made the tiniest sound. Her eyes were trained on the shore.

Dean turned his head to look. A man holding a rifle was standing next to their clothes, and another man on horseback was at the edge of the trees.

Chapter Twenty-two

"Where's your friend?" Pearson asked Dean as soon as he and Kai were dressed. He kept the barrel of his gun aimed at Dean.

"I don't know what you're talking about," Dean said as he kept one eye on the man while observing the others.

The three men were outfitted for travel and all were well armed. He remembered Pearson's racist remarks from the afternoon at the Wright ranch, and felt his disgust rise and settle in the back of his throat like a foul glob of hatred. The other two weren't as memorable, but he was sure they were employed by Hubert Wright or his brother.

"Don't play stupid with us. We know you three were together."

"We'll flush him out of these here mountains whether you're alive or dead. Speak the truth, and we might spare your woman," another man said, and then looked up at the rocks, like maybe Badger was hiding somewhere nearby.

Dean was relieved to know that Badger hadn't been caught, but he was also worried for his friend. He tried to inch away from them toward their lean-to where his gun and knife were. Kai stood behind him, and he was careful to keep her shielded with his body.

"Shut up, Sloan," Pearson barked, and then to Dean he said, "Don't you move, or I'll shoot."

Dean stopped. "I'll come in with you. I think I know where he is, just let my wife go free."

He thought working out a deal with these men might be the only way Kai was going to get away. "She doesn't have any part in this."

"Tell us where he is, and we'll think about it."

"No," Dean said. "She goes, and I'll track him down."

"I don't like it," Sloan said.

The third man interrupted. "Look at that." He pointed at their shelter and jumped down from his horse. He walked over to the lean-to and brushed aside half of the branches, exposing their bed and saddle bags. He rummaged through their belongings and took the rifle and the medicine bundle.

"Well, look what we have here," he said holding up the pipe bundle and the gun. "This must be from the shots we heard. And we'll be taking Mr. Wright's stolen goods back."

"Now you're coming in for murder and theft," Pearson said. "That lump of fur is all the evidence we need."

Dean narrowed his gaze on Pearson. "That's a relic that belongs to my people. I suggest you put it down right now."

Sloan sneered while Pearson's jaw hardened. Dean didn't care that he was threatening a man with a gun trained on him. He'd had enough of these vigilante cowpunchers.

"The woman leaves, and then you can do what you like with me. She's also taking that bundle with her."

"He sounds about as arrogant as his weasel friend," the third man said.

"Doesn't he just," Pearson said, looking Dean over as if contemplating what he's going to do about the situation before him.

"Let's use them as bait. His friend won't stay in hiding for very long when he hears them screaming for their lives," Sloan said.

"Round up their horses," Pearson ordered the third man.

The short, scruffy bearded man stamped off toward Man Eater and Opal.

"You're both coming back to Helena."

"There's no reason for her to come. She'll only slow us down."

"You'll do exactly what I say."

"Let her go, and I'll turn myself in."

"Turn yourself in for what?"

"You know what," Dean said, trying to buy them any time he could.

"No, I don't. Tell us exactly what you're confessing to."

"Whatever you say I am," Dean snarled. *Kai had to get back to Dancing Bear's Pond, if not with him, then with Laughing Eyes.*

"Order your wife to pack your camp," Pearson said. "And don't you move."

As they had sloshed out of the lake, Dean had whispered to Kai not to speak. The men were under the assumption that she didn't speak English. Carefully, Dean shifted so she could read the sign language. He spoke Blackfoot at the same time.

"Pack everything," he said. "Escape as soon as you get the chance. Go to Laughing Eyes if we get separated."

She shook her head at him in defiance.

"You will do as I say," he signed.

She gritted her teeth and moved over to their rock overhang, careful not to turn her back on Pearson and Sloan.

"Tell her, if she touches a weapon, I'll shoot her," Pearson said, as Kai grabbed the bags and rolled up the bed.

Dean said in Blackfoot, "I'll give you a signal. Go as fast as you can. I'll make sure they won't catch you."

He saw her swallow and then her eyes shifted to the man leading Opal and Man Eater to the beach. Kai clicked her tongue, and the two horses shifted their attention her way. Opal pulled in her direction. Man Eater was being uncharacteristically docile with the stranger, and Dean wondered if the storm had exhausted his horse.

"Tell her to load them up. Make sure she knows I'll kill you without a second thought, and then take her as a prisoner if she tries anything," Pearson said.

Dean signed and spoke again, "I mean it, Kai. You have to get away from these men. I don't care what else happens."

She did a quick check of the bridles, stirrups, and saddle bag straps. As she secured their gear, she kept easing the horses around and closer to the men under the guise that they were being uncooperative. Kai gave Dean a poignant look and then shifted her gaze to Man Eater, then back to him. He could see her planning something that involved the horse, and he readied himself. The men watched her closely, and the scruffy one raised his gun. Kai was careful not to show her emotions, but Dean was aware of how close Man Eater was to Pearson on his horse.

She let go of the bridles and signed, "Stay alive or I won't ever forgive you."

"She understands, and is willing to do whatever you want," Dean told Pearson.

"Tell her to get on and wait for us while Sloan ties your hands and secures your horse to his."

Dean signed and said in Blackfoot, "They picked the worst time to show up. Do you know how long I've wanted to kiss you like that?"

She shot him a deadly glare and didn't reply. She climbed onto Opal and then looked over at Sloan. When the man was halfway out of his saddle, she kicked her foot into Opal and charged her horse right at Man Eater.

The horse responded exactly as she'd hoped he would. Man Eater reared, slashing the air with his hooves and spun around, right into Pearson's horse. Opal lunged to get away from the panicked animal. She darted into the forest as Man Eater came down and started biting and kicking anything in his way. Kai galloped through the brush and around trees, looking back to watch the chaos unfolding on the tiny beach. Pearson's mount retaliated by jumping out of the way while bucking and kicking back. Sloan and his horse were blocking the path, and the three horses were a tangle of flying hooves.

Sloan cried out as he hit the ground and was trampled on by one of the horses. Dean risked being crushed and dove for his medicine bundle, grabbed it, and rolled to his feet. The third man was close to Dean, but his attention was diverted as Man Eater was headed straight for him. Dean's horse barreled right over the top of him and then kept going. Dean jumped out of the way then followed Man Eater, running for his life.

He had no chance of catching up with his horse, and he knew it would only be seconds before Pearson or one of the others would be on top of him. He turned to a crevice in the rock wall on his left, and started clambering up the stones. Dean could see a place where if he could just get behind the boulders, the men wouldn't be able to shoot him. He made it to the spot behind the rock just as a bullet struck the stone by his foot and sent a spray of sharp chips into the air.

"Kill him!"

"Boyd, you go up and around," Pearson ordered. "I'll get him from down here."

Dean heard the horse riding up the narrow game trail that led to the top of the rocks. He looked up and saw an open line of fire to the edge. He thought he could make it up there by climbing, but then he would out in the open with the man coming for him. Pearson was down below, cursing obscenities, but making his way up slowly. Dean looked for a loose stone to drop on him, but only found some small gravel in a crevice. The stone was solid here, and he was running out options. He grabbed the gravel anyway and threw it around the edge of the boulder, hoping it was aimed for Pearson's head.

Dean left the partially sheltered spot and started climbing up and over in the hope that he would find somewhere else to hunker down, or make it to the top, ahead of Boyd and his horse. He wasn't sure if Sloan was back in the saddle, but had the feeling that the man was still on the beach, injured from being trampled.

He quickly realized that he was now even more exposed. Pearson saw him, wedged himself securely in a crevice, and fired at Dean with a pistol. Dean ducked, and gravel flew around him. Dean was in a worse place than before, and it was nearly impossible to make some of the holds while also holding onto his medicine bundle. He inched over to an open and sloped rock, gripping the tiny ledges and bumps in the rock with his fingertips and toes so he didn't tumble to his death.

Then he heard someone above, and looked up to see Boyd glaring down at him. Dean started edging down instead of up.

"I see him, Pearson. You want me to kill him for you?"

"Take him out!"

Dean felt like an insect scurrying for cover. All of the rocks near him were tall and wide, or flat and long, with no caves or crevices large enough to hide in. He looked down the length of the sloping rock he was on and noticed it ended over the top of nothing but air. He was stuck with nowhere to go, and was about to be shot.

Boyd's eyes were ruthless and filled with hatred. Dean moved to the very edge and kept trying to think his way out of this. He couldn't abandon Kai. He couldn't disappear on his grandmother the way his mother and father had. *He had to return to both of them.*

Dean watched the vigilante lawman take aim with his pistol.

Then he turned and jumped.

He hit the water, and at first wasn't sure if he had survived or not. Then he was fighting to reach the surface, struggling to breathe. His head was above water, but his lungs wouldn't work for him. The impact must have knocked the wind out of him. *Or worse.* He forced himself to stop panicking and started treading water until he could breathe. The medicine bundle was still clutched in his hand. He tucked the heavy, wet fur under his arm and swam one-armed, closer to the rock wall. Neither Boyd nor Pearson could be seen from his vantage point, but he knew they were up there, somewhere.

Dean stayed along the cliff walls and swam until he found a place to rest on the rocks that was out of sight of the rest of the lake. He waited there for hours, never hearing anyone. Just before dark, he lowered himself back into the water and started swimming again until he reached the shore on the east side of the lake. He found the outlet and slogged downstream staying low or crawling on his hands and knees through the brush. He stayed alert, listening for any sign of pursuit, but never heard or saw anyone. It was fully dark when he climbed out of the water and lay beneath some dense shrubs, passing out from exhaustion.

Dean awoke at daybreak stiff, sore, and surprised he hadn't died of hypothermia during the night. He listened to the morning and heard the chirp of grasshoppers and a robin singing about finding its breakfast. He eased himself up and peeked out of the brush.

He was alone in the valley below the lake. The grass was tall, and the bushes and shrubs even taller. The waterway meandered east out of the mountains, and Dean could see that the valley soon tapered into a narrow canyon. He thought it looked too rugged for Kai to travel by horseback, so he started moving back toward the lake and slightly north in the direction they had been originally traveling. He hoped Kai was safe and that he could track her. He sent a prayer to the Above Ones that Pearson and his men didn't have the same notion and had already found her.

Dean stayed concealed as well as he could in the undergrowth until he reached the trees. He followed along the base of an east-west ridge, and had found the single set of horse tracks by mid-morning. The hoof prints led up the slope in the direction he had wanted her to go.

Dean was panting and sweat poured down his back as he jogged up the steep incline. He was pushing himself past the limits of his endurance. His stomach had shut down the night before, after the hours of swimming and treading water. He told himself he was fasting and reminded his body that it had endured worse during his time fighting in the war. He was determined to find Kai and get her back to the beaver pond below the Thunderbird Peaks at any cost to himself or his health.

He crested the ridge and temporarily lost her tracks in the carpet of evergreen needles. He searched the branches for any broken or bent stems, or horse hair stuck to the foliage, and found her trail once again. From what he could tell, she had changed direction more than once. She was moving east, then doubling back, and then finally had hit the trail headed northwest into higher ground.

Then he noticed the extra set of prints. He panicked at the sight of them and started running. *Did Pearson find her? Would he take her captive in the hope that it would flush him out?*

He stayed on her trail, jogging endlessly over the forested hills as his panic rose. For the most part, the ground was still saturated from the storm, and the hoof prints showed easily in the leaf mold and moss, allowing him to keep a fast pace.

He didn't know how many miles he had covered, but Dean was on the verge of collapse. He needed water, and told himself that he would stop at the next stream or spring. There had been no sign of struggle along the trail, and that eased his mind enough to allow a quick rest.

The forest thinned as he approached a meadow. She had gone around it, staying under the cover of the trees and he followed the path she had taken. It led to a section covered with flat shelves of rock. The prints were nearly impossible to find over the stone, and he had to search for the slightest brush mark of hooves in the pockets of gravel or sand. He spotted a trickle of running water over the rock, and made himself stop tracking Kai long enough to follow it to its source. It could be runoff from the passing rain, but it could also be a spring. He had to find out, and drink what he could.

The water seeped out of a crack under a massive stone. Dean laid on his stomach and put his mouth to the source, drinking until he felt satisfied.

He heard the clack of stone against stone and bounced to his feet, staying in a crouched position, ready to attack. He heard the sound again and whirled around. It wasn't the sound of tumbling stones but of horse hooves against rock. Kai sat atop Man Eater, with Opal tied behind them.

"You're okay?" he managed to breathe out as he rose to meet her.

She gave a hint of a nod. He noticed the strain around her eyes and the smudges of dirt on her cheek. *Kai hadn't had a good night without him either.*

"Pearson and his men?"

"I haven't seen them."

Her nerves were shaken, he thought, but he saw relief on her face as she swung down from his horse. Her foot touched the stone and Man Eater snorted and pulled away, his hooves stamping. Kai grabbed for the reins, but Man Eater snorted and reared. Opal yanked her head away and backed up as Man Eater darted to the side.

"Whoa there, big guy," she said, and tried again to gain control. "What is up, you dumb horse?"

Dean rushed over to help, but Man Eater was too fast as he bolted. The lead rope tethered to Opal snapped, and the two horses were headed to the woods before Dean or Kai could restrain them.

"Stop!" Kai yelled.

"What the hell was that about?" Dean was saying as he suddenly became aware of the chills running up and down his arms. He looked at his skin and saw the gooseflesh. Then out of the corner of his eye, he saw a dark shadow moving toward Kai.

"Move!" he screamed and ran for her.

She had her hands on her hips and was staring after the lost horses, looking perplexed and pissed off. Kai glanced over her shoulder at Dean and he saw the confused look on her face and then the stark terror when she saw the bear charging at her.

Dean waved his arms and roared. He wanted it to be a false charge. He wanted to frighten the bear with his screams. He wanted to save Kai from being mauled. When he intersected them, it felt like he had been taken out by a battering ram. His skin was ripped open as he was knocked off his feet. Then he felt himself tumbling and crashing against the unforgiving stone. His back wrenched and cracked, and then his head hit the rocks. Then Dean wanted absolutely nothing.

They had gotten so close to succeeding. *Why had Great Spirit led them all the way here only to fail now?* The bear had stopped advancing once Dean rolled down the mountain, broken and defenseless. Kai didn't even have a chance to think about the bear during her frantic flight to rescue him. But the bear had lumbered off and left Dean bleeding from his head and back. Kai was talking and making sounds about how he wasn't going to die, but Dean wasn't sure if he should be grateful for the knowledge. Dying would have been easier than living with the constant reminder of his failures.

All he was certain of, was that he couldn't move. Pain was everywhere, and it wouldn't stop.

"Wiggle your toes," she ordered.

He obliged.

She said, "I don't think your spinal cord is damaged, and your head could be a lot worse."

Dean would like to swear an oath that his head was split open just like the sky when it cracked with lightening, and that Kai was just trying to make chicken soup from chicken shit. Between the combination of feeling like his head and back were both shattered, he lay helpless, and even the effort of speaking was too much.

She stayed with him until the bleeding subsided, and then left to search for the horses.

As Dean slipped in and out of consciousness, he was aware of a new sound, and wondered if it was Kai or if the bear had changed its mind and returned to finish him off. *He felt like he deserved it.* They had escaped the vigilantes and were only a day and a half's ride from Dancing Bear's Pond, only to be set back yet again.

She tucked the medicine bundle up against Dean's side, and murmured, "Here you go."

He placed his hand on it reassuringly. The feeling of the fur brought the image of the bear's massive arm into his mind. Then Dean fell into the blackness once more.

The sound of heavy paws and the click of long sharp nails against stone brought him part of the way back. He felt a snort of warm breath on the side of his neck, and then something nudging the back of his shoulder. He was certain he was about to be eaten or clawed or beaten. Dean tried to turn his head and face his attacker, and that's when he felt the first chomp. Pinching, stabbing pain attacked his upper back. He flipped over, fist flailing and landing on the stone, missing his assailant completely.

He heard another huff, and pried his eyes open. His vision was blurred, but he could make out the hoof of a bay horse as it pawed at the rock. Man Eater's muzzle lowered to nip at Dean's hair, and he reached up just in time swat the horse away.

"There you are," he heard Kai accuse.

From his position on the ground, he saw only the lower half of her body walking over to him.

Dean tried to focus, but his eyes wouldn't cooperate as well as he wanted them to. He thought he saw her lead Man Eater away, and listened to her scold him.

"Get away from him, you fiend. Where have you been? You never abandon your rider. How dare you scare me that way?"

He heard the horse blow some air and then watched the hooves disappear from his line of sight. Dean blacked out while warning signals went off inside his head. His inner sirens screamed at him to get up and hide from Pearson and his men, but he couldn't. All he could do was ignore the torment inside of his own head as he succumbed to the numbing dark.

She didn't know how bad his back was, but suspected it was broken somewhere in his lumbar spine. He also had broken ribs, and a concussion. Kai had spent the rest of the day wondering if Dean was going to die before her eyes. Her concern for him outweighed the fact that they weren't going to make the new moon's window unless Dean could ride. She was acutely aware of the three and a half days they had remaining until the dark of the moon.

The heavenly bodies were always present in her daily life, yet over the past month, every night, every passing hour even, had become of vital importance. That was, until Dean had been attacked by the bear. Suddenly Kai had experienced a hundred and eighty degree shift in what mattered to her. Surviving, whether it was in

1868 or 2012 was her first priority. That was the only way she could return to her son. Even though Trevyn needed her, he could live without her. He had his father and grandparents to care for him, and he had the sun to play beneath and the moon to watch him sleep, with or without her. Dean's state of near death was changing her perspective, and it frightened her.

Kai's entire day was spent making sure Dean continued to breathe. She washed the cuts from his fall and from the bear claws as well as she could, made a poultice with the few plants she could gather in the area, and then stayed by his side. Man Eater was back, but Opal had not returned. Kai wouldn't wander too far away from Dean with the bear around, and her horse had all the medicines inside its saddle bags. Kai considered using a travois again, but without the right tools, or any strips of hide, sinew, or rope, she couldn't make one.

Evening came, and Kai started a fire. They had some food packed on Man Eater, but Dean refused to eat and only drank some water. The bear didn't reappear, but Kai kept watch all through the night.

The next day went much the same. Kai ventured a little farther in search of food, medicinal plants, and her horse, but had little success in finding anything useful. They slept on fir boughs that she had cut and brought over to the rocks. Dean hadn't improved at all by the next night, and was probably worse.

The following morning, Dean shocked her when he woke and started mumbling about the moon. He began clawing and pulling himself up. As if Man Eater's loyalty had finally been given, the horse whinnied and pawed at the ground in unison with Dean.

Half conscious and barely able to move as his wounds began to bleed again, Dean insisted that he could make it to the Night Medicine ceremonial place if Kai would help him onto his horse. It tore her to shreds watching him struggle through the pain, but she agreed that they had to start traveling again if they wanted to try to make it in time.

Chapter Twenty-three

Kai nearly collapsed beneath Dean's weight, but somehow she held her ground and lowered him to the grass next to Dancing Bear's Pond.

The ride had been excruciating for Dean, and Kai wasn't sure how he had managed to make the last leg of their journey. It had been hours of constant, unimaginable agony. The only highlight had been the evening before when Opal had nickered softly from the forest and then appeared at their side. The horse still wore her bridle, and their supplies and blankets were tied securely in place. She could treat Dean's injuries a little better with the returned medicines, but she felt like it might be too late to make much of a difference.

Kai knelt in the cool grass and felt Dean's forehead. He was warm to the touch, and she thought the worst of his cuts were infected. She wanted to make him some tea, but wasn't sure how much time they had. She rose and returned to Man Eater to retrieve the medicine pipe.

She heard the warning slap of a beaver tail on the surface of the water, and glanced over at the rippling pond. The animal was nowhere to be seen, but Kai noticed the large lodge where the beavers lived. She tilted her head to listen for the sound again, but only heard the trickling fall of water over the beavers' damn. The air was moist and gnats swarmed around the fringes of the shore. Kai used the back of her hand to wipe the sticky sweat and travel grime from her forehead. The last few days had been grueling, and challenged her in ways she had never known before, and it wasn't over yet.

"I'm supposed to take a sweat before I start," Dean said, scattering her thoughts.

Kai looked over at him, noticing how badly he was listing to the left, and about to collapse. "There isn't a sweat lodge here and we don't have what we need to build one," she said.

"I don't know how this is going to work."

"I'm going to do the dancing," she said.

"You'll have to. Let's hope the Night God allows it."

The weakness in Dean's voice scared her. She moved to his side, and placed the bundle in his lap. Then she helped him lie down in the grass. He was stiff with pain and tension, and she kept her hands on him in the hope that it would help him relax.

"What time do we start?" she asked.

"In a couple of hours," he said.

His body started trembling beneath her hands.

"Rest now," she said quietly. "I'll wake you when it's time to begin."

>><<<

Kai collected punk wood and snapped off the dead lower branches of the trees for dry tinder, and then started the fire. She picked some cedar and mountain sage to burn for its spirit medicine, and then woke Dean.

At first he refused to be roused, and Kai was near panic at the thought that he'd slipped into unconsciousness. She had no way of knowing how bad his head injury was, and she also worried that he had internal damage to boot. The grizzly bear was just too large, and no human body could take that type of beating without serious harm, not to mention the previous injuries he had already sustained during their journey to get here.

The appearance of the bear had been her fault, but she couldn't explain exactly why. It was true that she was a member of the Many Bear Claws clan, *but what did the bear want from her?* It felt like the past was conspiring to keep her at any cost.

If the bear got his way and the ceremony didn't work, she planned on riding to the Piegans and begging for help. She wondered if they had made a vital mistake by waiting this long to get Dean to a medicine man. *Should they have ridden straight to Laughing Eyes or any of the other great Piegan healers?* Dean didn't want to. He was set on returning to the ceremonial place.

His eyelids cracked open. She watched his eyes roll back in his head and then disappear behind closed lids once again.

"Dean, it's time."

He groaned, and Kai reached over to cup his cheek. His skin felt even hotter than before in the cool night air. He tried to push himself up, but then he fell over. She eased him up and wedged Badger's backpack behind him. It contained the few belongings that she wanted to take with them, including the journal and Dean's sketchbook. She hoped the horses would be found by someone and taken care of, but that was out of her control if they actually made it back to their time.

Dean began to loosen the leather ties of the medicine bundle. With the severity of the pain in his head and back, and the incredible challenge to stay focused, this small task was quickly becoming proportionally overwhelming. Kai sat down next to him and took the bundle of fur into her lap. She released the tedious knots and carefully handed him back the wrapped pipe.

He laid it out with the bowl facing west. Then he arranged the feathers to lay flat. Next he took the pieces of various animal furs and the leather pouch of smoking mixture and placed them around the pipe to honor the four directions, the Above Ones, and Below Ones.

"Sit on my left, Kai," he instructed. "Honor all of your ancestors and the God of Night and the Void with only pure thoughts. Think of the place you wish to return to. Hold the vision of Trevyn in your mind while we do this."

"I will," she said.

Seeing the pipe while sitting beneath the stars gave Dean a temporary strength. He filled the pipe bowl with the sacred mixture.

With the pipe in his left hand, Dean took the small balsam branch Kai offered him and he leaned forward to light it in the fire. He breathed in the smoke, and winced from the pain in his ribs, but his mind cleared enough to make it through the first few rounds of prayers without too much distraction from his aching body. He handed the pipe to Kai, and she smoked, and then passed it back to him.

Encouraged, he continued with the prayers for the long and healthy lives of his family. Then he started the prayers to the Night God for his and Kai's safe journey home. The prayers turned to songs. Kai rose and began to dance by the fire. It was a woman's dance, and different than the ones he was taught by his grandfather, but she was beautiful and graceful, and her tempo matched the songs. The singing continued, and he repeated the melodies until he was completely lost in the sounds. Dean imagined his cabin with the pond out on the prairie. He saw the river southeast of his house. He pictured the home of his grandparents, where he grew up.

He rocked in place as the rhythms flowed out of him. Kai would need to hold onto the pipe with him after two more rounds, and then it would be up to the God of Night and the Void to see them safely through the passage. He didn't know if they had done enough. He didn't know if skipping the sweat lodge would change the ceremony too much. In the original story, the warrior didn't sweat before accidentally going back in time. *Could he and Kai be granted a pass for this part of the Night Medicine?*

He sang the second to last chorus, and was about to motion to Kai to hold the pipe. She knew to watch for his cue, but he didn't get the chance to signal her. Pain ripped through his torso, and he grunted. The pipe fell from his hands as he grabbed his stomach and collapsed sideways.

"Dean!" Kai called, and threw herself down next to him.

The pain stole his breath. He was rigid with the searing burn inside, and he clenched his jaws and tried to endure the stabbing fire in his back, stomach, and kidneys. He couldn't pinpoint where the throbbing was centered. *It was everywhere.* He heard the scream leave his body, but felt disconnected from it. Something terrible was happening inside him.

"What is it! What's wrong?"

Her voice was distant. She screamed his name. He heard her telling him to answer, but he was powerless to do anything other than lay in the indescribable darkness of agony.

He thought he heard her singing the last song. In a remote corner of his subconscious, he pictured Kai pressing the pipe into his hands. She was crying and singing over him. Then even that image faded and Dean was farther away than even his subconscious could travel.

Kai kept Dean's hand clutched under hers against the stem of the Dragonfly medicine pipe. She saw the pain on his face, and it had undone her. Rivulets of tears streamed down her cheeks. She knew she should have insisted he go straight to his people instead of back to the pond. Her mind imagined the worst. His organs rupturing, hemorrhaging inside his body, systems failing. Everything shutting down. She wished she knew what was really going on inside his broken body. She wanted to take him to a real hospital, a doctor, a surgeon. He needed anesthesia. No medicine man of this time could give him that.

"Don't go. Stay with me," she pleaded as she gave up on the song.

Nothing had changed. They were still sitting by the same smoldering fire while Man Eater and Opal grazed nearby.

"Great Spirit have pity on him. He's a good man with a good heart. Night God, send us home where he can receive help. Please," she cried, and pressed her face to his shoulder.

His breathing was shallow and she sat back up. She slipped her fingers under his jaw to feel his pulse. It frightened her more than his weakened breath. His heartbeat was thready and irregular.

"I'll do anything you want. Just keep him alive," she begged to the unseen gods. Tears poured from her eyes. "Please live, Dean. I choose you. I want to be with you. I'm not confused about us anymore," she finally admitted. The vulnerability of opening up to him scared her to her core. Especially now that his survival was so uncertain.

"The God of the Void thinks you belong in the place you were born," a voice said in Piegan.

Kai's head whipped around and she saw a shadowed figure standing past the circle of firelight. Men and horses stood even deeper in the shadows behind him. Laughing Eyes stepped forward so she could see him.

"You're really here?" she said as she wiped her fists over her eyes to clear her vision.

"I had a powerful dream about a bear. It threw Dean Wolfsblood from the top of Woman Strikes Mountain. When you did not come to the Sun Dance, I knew I would come find you."

"We tried the ceremony, Laughing Eyes, but Dean is so sick. He doesn't have the strength, and I am just a woman who knows nothing."

"You are a strong woman, Anna-kai, but you are correct in some ways. The Night Medicine is for warriors of the Lynx Clan to perform."

"He's dying. Please help us return to his home."

"Tell me with detail how he has come to be so ill."

"He shielded me from a bear attack. He has injuries on the outside, but they are worse on his inside. That is why we must go tonight. In the future time, there is great medicine that can heal him," she signed, and used the broken Blackfoot that she knew.

"A bear brought you here, and now takes from you the journey home. You listen to this bear, Anna-kai. He knows you belong here as I know you do."

"I don't care that I was born here. My home is in the future now, with my son."

"That is a strong argument you make, but the Above Ones are insisting that you stay. On my journey from the Sun Dance, a fierce storm kept me from arriving here. This is why I am late. You stay with me this time, Kai. Dean travels alone to his time."

"We both have to go back! Dean won't survive by himself."

The older man looked around as if now realizing that Badger wasn't with them. With his feathers in his hair, silver braids hanging down past his shoulders, and his fur and bear claw collar around his neck, Laughing Eyes had a striking profile in the flickering glow of the fire. With kindness always his eyes, it was easy to trust the medicine man, even as supernatural power emanated from him. Kai knew from her own experience just what the medicine man was capable of.

"Badger wanted to stay behind in Helena. I have to go with Dean if he has any chance of surviving. You sent me through time when I was fourteen winters, and I know you can do it again. It's even more urgent this time. I am begging you to have pity on me. On us. And on my son."

"You are not like all women. You are the lost daughter of Many Bear Claws chief. You should not be able to travel with the Dragonfly pipe, and you do. You have a mother in the North. She is sad for you the way you are sad for losing your son."

"I am grown. My son is still young. We are running out of time. Dean will not last long in this condition."

Laughing Eyes shifted his wise and clear gaze to Dean. His frown deepened, and then he closed his eyes, as if seeking council within himself. When he opened them again, the deep lines of his face were relaxed.

"If the Night God allows it, I will send you to your boy, Anna-kai. The great bear may punish me, but I will take that fight for you to be with your child. You tell your son about Laughing Eyes the Many Faces Man. If we meet again, you will tell me of this great and powerful medicine in the future time."

"I will," she said, and choked back a sob.

She leaned over Dean and placed a tender kiss on his cheek. "Stay alive. Please stay alive. We're going home."

She heard a high pitched shrill, and looked up to see Laughing Eyes blowing his eagle bone whistle. The other Piegans who had come with the medicine man moved around the clearing. Kai counted four men. She could see them tending the horses and unpacking their bags to set up a camp. One man looked familiar, and she thought his name was Lone Elk. He moved forward, holding the other Dragonfly pipe bundle while a second man tended the fire.

Laughing Eyes removed a beaded leather bag from a thong at his waist and opened it. He reached inside and pinched some of its contents, then held it up to the sky. He spoke a prayer, and then put the sacred medicine into the flames of the rekindled fire. He repeated his action four more times, and after the last pinch of his sacred mixture, he placed it in the ground. Lone Elk sat down near the fire ring, and when Laughing Eyes finished his prayers, he took the pipe from him. Then Lone Elk began to sing. The song was similar to Dean's. The rise and fall and the tone and rhythms were the same, but it sounded vastly different in another man's voice. The old medicine man filled the bowl from another beaded bag and then he lit it with a fire stick and smoked. Kai stayed next to Dean and waited for instructions.

The memories of the days and nights she had spent with this man all those years ago came back to her like the storm she had endured with Dean. It was a sudden onslaught, meant to knock her down so hard she couldn't get back up again.

The terror of that night when the white men turned on her family members and the other clan members couldn't be forgotten, and yet she had somehow blocked out the fear attached to those memories. The level of deception and lies had been unfathomable to her naïve, young mind. Kai had been brought along with the expedition because of her ability to translate English, Cree, and sign language. She had begged to go on the trip since her sister was being taken as a guide to find the best stones. Gem hunting was something Nadie was exceptionally skilled at. Her sister didn't like these men, but their uncle had insisted that she was the best, and would bring good luck at finding the sapphires. Kai received permission to travel with the group. Her mother didn't cry, but Kai knew how upset she was to have both of her daughters leave their village. Kai never thought for an instant that she wouldn't see her mom again. She even thought she was proving what a useful woman she would make for a future husband. Her foolishness as a young girl astounded her now, but she wasn't capable of doing anything different at the time. She had only been fourteen years old and her wants in life were so vastly different before that journey into Blackfoot territory.

The fortune hunters had turned against their guides once they found out where the land of the sapphires was located. They attacked at night, killing her father and uncle after getting them drunk.

Kai and her sister had been the only women in the group, and she had survived by chance. Her stomach had been upset from eating a disagreeable meal for dinner. Awaking late in the night, and embarrassed that she had to be sick, she snuck away from the camp and found a private place in the forest. She heard the grunts, clashes, and the screams as the men and her sister were slaughtered by the investors and prospectors. She hid in a tree for the rest of the night praying to Great Spirit that no one would notice she was gone.

As the sun rose, the group of drunken white men boasted about what they had done. Kai listened in horror as they made their plans. They were going to scalp the men and make it look like a warring tribe had done the killing. They couldn't stop talking about how rich they were all going to be. Little did they know that Blackfoot hunters were nearby, and that the same fate they had given to her father was about to fall upon themselves.

The sapphires were located near the burial place of a very important chief. When the Blackfoot braves saw the dead Cree and the white men desecrating a burial ground, it didn't take any convincing to kill the intruding enemy.

Thinking her sister was dead, Kai had gone berserk when she watched Nadie being dragged from the canvas tent they had been sleeping inside.

She must have made a sound, because one of the warriors saw her, and she was forced down from her tree. When Laughing Eyes noticed her, he told them of the dream he had and they let the medicine man take charge of her and her sister, who wasn't dead after all.

Nadie had been hit her on the head, but she was strong, and still alive. Barely. Laughing Eyes said he would stay behind and heal her, and that the other Blackfoot men should continue with their hunting expedition.

Kai had knowledge about plants that healed wounds, and she helped Laughing Eyes as much as she could, but her sister wasn't getting better. On the fourth morning after the attack, Kai had awakened at the first light of the day with a bear sniffing around her body. It was a large grizzly, and she thought she and her sister were going to be eaten. She lay perfectly still as the animal smelled her hair and chest, and then walked around her legs and sniffed her sister as well. She had been too frightened to move.

The bear took its time exploring the girls, and then had shuffled away, leaving them unharmed. Laughing Eyes told her that after seeing the bear, he knew how to help her and her sister. He explained that he had a medicine ceremony that could send Nadie to a place far away to receive healing. He was told by a bear in a dream the night before that he would use the Dragonfly medicine pipe and the Night Medicine ceremony to send the girls to a land where she would be healed. He told Kai she must travel with her sister to help her, and to speak for her when they arrived. When he woke up and saw the bear in their camp, he knew that the Night God had sent the bear to make sure it was so.

Laughing Eyes sent Kai and her sister one hundred and forty-four years into the future that night. Only Nadie didn't make it.

When the forest shifted around her and she was overcome by the black void, she had been totally alone. Her sister didn't travel with her. She had no idea what had happened. All she knew was that she was by herself.

When Kai returned to 1868 with Dean and Badger and saw Laughing Eyes in the Piegan camp, she had to know what had happened to Nadie after she had traveled forward through time. She forced herself to wait until she could speak to the medicine man alone. She received her answers when she walked with him along the river. Laughing Eyes told her that he performed the Night Medicine ceremony exactly the way he had been shown in his dream. The ceremony had been slightly different than the way he had been taught, and had attributed the differences to honor the bear and accommodate the Cree girls. He did not know that Kai had gone forward into the future instead of back until she told him a month ago on their walk next to the Piegan village. He confirmed to Kai what she already believed about her sister. She had died. Laughing Eyes sent her spirit to the Sand Hills instead of letting her become a lost spirit in the Shadowlands.

Kai held onto Dean, suddenly feeling the overwhelming fatigue and stress of the last four weeks and the crushing emotions from her memories, as she watched Laughing Eyes complete the ceremony. The rise of the suppressed memories made her ache to go back in time and save her and her sister from ever leaving on that fateful journey. She knew it would never happen. Nadie was gone. That part of her past could never be changed.

She shook herself and focused on Laughing Eyes as he danced with precise steps and moved in her direction, while Lone Elk sang the travel songs. His shoulders and arms swayed and flowed with the tempo as his legs and feet carried him with a measured cadence until he was standing in front of her and Dean.

"Smoke, and then ask the God of Night and the Void to carry you home."

He placed the pipe in her outstretched hands. Lone Elk continued the song, now chanting in low tones. As Laughing Eyes lit the pipe for Kai, he began to sing a complementing refrain so the voices layered over one another.

Kai remembered what to do now. She breathed in the burning mix of sacred plants and then turned and exhaled the smoke over Dean's body. She silently prayed to the Night God for a safe journey, and asked Great Spirit for safety and protection from all harm for her and Dean.

Laughing Eyes took his pipe back and held it up to the midnight sky. Kai reached for Dean's hands, placed them on the stem of his pipe, and then held them with her own. She trembled, remembering how her sister's hands had been limp and cool to the touch, and how she had slipped away in the void during the fateful journey Laughing Eyes had sent her on. The song went around and around, circling and infusing the air until she was dizzy with sound and shivers ran up and down her spine. The pipe smoke from Laughing Eyes wafted around her, and she breathed it deeply into her lungs and let it fill her entire being. Kai repeated the silent prayers and looked to the stars overhead. Only she wasn't looking for the stars, but the blackness in between, into the depths of the unknown, and into the vast and infinite all. *Take me to Trevyn. Take us home.*

Kai opened her eyes, and the song humming in her skull had vanished. There was no warmth of the fire at her side. The Piegan men had disappeared. Dean lay before her in the grass with the hiking pack at his side. She was still gripping his hands under hers, against the pipe's stem, which lay across his body. She wanted to cry out, or get up and scream, or run down the mountain, or collapse against Dean's chest and sob with relief, but she didn't do any of these things. Kai had to stay calm. She had to keep a level head, and figure out the fastest way to get Dean the medical help he desperately needed.

"You young ones are never content to accept things as they are," an elderly voice said.

Kai craned her neck to see who was speaking. At first she thought she was mistaken about returning home when she saw the old woman, wrapped in a Hudson Bay blanket, standing near the low-roofed hut. Then she remembered that the small building didn't exist in the past she had just left behind. Neither did the three four-wheelers, or her best friend, Gena.

"Always wanting what to change the parts of life that can't be changed," the woman continued. Her voice was jagged in the predawn hours, but rich and full of life and experiences that Kai could only imagine. "What lives in the past should stay there, where it belongs."

Kai barely caught these last words as Gena stumbled out of the building, shrieking, "Kai! Where have you been? Rosemary said we had to come back up here during the new moon, but I didn't think we'd ever see you again."

Kai rose to her feet just as Gena latched onto her.

"Are you okay? You've been missing for weeks."

Gena blabbered on and on in near hysterics, not letting Kai actually answer, but Kai finally asked, "Who's Rosemary?"

"My great aunt. Dean's grandmother," Gena answered as if this was obvious, and looked at the elder. Gena stared at Kai, her face filled with confusion and concern.

"My grandson," the old woman said as she knelt down next to Dean. "What has happened to him?"

Kai swallowed the choking lump in her throat and pulled away from Gena. She lowered herself down next to Dean and his grandmother. "Possibly his spleen or appendix has ruptured. I…" she stumbled over her words. The emotions, the weight of them all: helplessness, vulnerability, pain, fear, terror, confusion, were overpowering her at last. She was broken into shattered pieces that didn't fit together anymore. *Who was she? How had an innocent fourteen-year-old girl acquired a time traveling life?* "He needs a hospital right now," she said and the tears began to fall again, leaving dark tracks on Dean's torn and stained buckskin shirt.

A warm blanket wrapped over her shoulders and Rosemary squeezed her tight. "The Night God would not have brought you two back only to let my strong grandson die before me. Dean is in good favor with the Above Ones, Kai. He will be all right."

Kai leaned into the woman and shook. She was vaguely aware of Gena talking into some kind of radio. When they loaded her and Dean onto four-wheelers, she was both aware of and separate from the situation simultaneously, as if she was watching everything happen from Morning Star's point of view.

The ride in the Flight for Life helicopter was a whirlwind of excitement and noise, but all Kai could do was keep her eyes on Dean. She noted every moan or wince of pain, and the misery on his face as he briefly woke and then blacked out again. He had become something more than her life raft back to 2012. He had inserted himself into her consciousness. She needed him to live like she needed air. Kai couldn't understand this delusion, but it felt real to her. If Dean didn't make it, she wouldn't either. It would break her forever, and that scared her beyond all reason.

Two days later, when Kai received word that Dean was being moved from the ICU to the regular patient ward, she left the hospital without a single word spoken between them.

Chapter Twenty-four

"Mom, badgers and coyotes hunt together like best buddies. They eat..." Trevyn squinted with concentration as he looked up at his mom, trying really hard to remember the trivia he had recently learned about badgers. "They'll eat anything. Rabbits, squirrels, worms, prairie dogs, cats, bats, rats, muskrats—"

Kai smiled patiently at her son's enthusiasm, and then placed her palm over her son's mouth before he could continue.

He pulled her hand away and spoke loudly so the entire group standing outside the daycare center could hear, "They'll even eat each other! Can you believe that? Badgers and coyotes will kill and eat each other." He waved his hands in the air to emphasize his shock at this disloyal behavior.

Kai clapped her hand over his mouth again and fixed her eyes on Gena, who was unwrapping a brand new wooden sign. Lowell Kinder Care Center. Named after Badger Lowell, for his financial donation, which allowed Gena and her mother to buy the building and save it from closing its doors forever. A ten-inch badger with its brown and white striped face was carved and painted on the sign as the center's new mascot.

Gena ripped the shiny red paper aside and wore a smile brighter than the sun. She said a few words about the daycare, how happy she was to finally own the building, and how much she loved all the kids. Then she thanked all the parents for coming to the grand re-opening celebration. She invited everyone to come inside and see the changes she'd made, and waved an arm for the group to follow her.

Kai's attention was only half focused on the present. She was all too aware of Dean standing somewhere behind her right shoulder.

His truck had rumbled into the parking lot just as she and Trevyn were walking up to join the assembled parents and children for the unveiling. It was everything she could do not to look at him. *Dean was off limits.* Of course she'd heard about him anyway from Gena, but Kai said little to nothing in return when Gena gave her the latest report on her cousin and his health.

Kai had blocked out all her feelings about what had happened during the thunder moon and their trip into the past. She had gone back to work, not at Growler's Tavern, but at the daycare, and had spent every free minute spoiling Trevyn, and not thinking about 1868, her lost family, Badger, or Dean. The only part about the trip she allowed herself to reminisce over was in sharing stories with Trevyn about Laughing Eyes. She would keep her promise to the medicine man, even if her son never knew the Piegan elder was more than a story.

She was about to usher Trevyn into the building when she heard, "Look Mom, it's Dean, the bareback rider."

He was out from under her hand and running up to Dean before she could stop him.

Kai turned around and saw him in his Levi's and T-shirt. He hadn't cut his hair short after their return and it was even longer now. It shone under the sun like a raven's wing. She swallowed hard. Her shoulders sank in defeat, and she walked over to retrieve her overjoyed son.

By the time she reached them, the two were already deep in conversation about Dean's close encounter with a real live badger out on his land.

Dean finished his story and then said to her son, "I really need to give this to Ms. Gena." He held up a plain envelope. "It's important that she gets it, but I'm not sure I should go inside right this second and interrupt her special moment."

Trevyn jumped up and down. "I'll do it. I can give it to her."

Dean started to hand the envelope over, but held on when Trevyn went to take it. "I need someone I can count on for this job. Do you think you can handle it?"

"I know I can do it, Mr. Dean! Mom says I'm a trustworthy kid."

"You're a good man, Trevyn," Dean said appreciatively.

Trevyn snatched the envelope from Dean's fingers and ran inside the childcare center.

Kai waited until her kid was inside and out of hearing range. "Seriously?" she asked, already annoyed with Dean that he had so easily gotten her alone.

"I didn't think you would want him to hear us talking," he said as his eyes searched hers.

She looked at his ear — his ridiculously cute ears — so she didn't have to see the desire hidden in his golden brown eyes. "I don't. I don't want to talk at all."

"We could skip the talking and go back to what we were doing before the vigilantes found us," he said, and took a step closer to her.

She could smell him. It was his naturally warm scent, like sun-heated pines and water rushing over the stones in the river.

"Don't." She raised a hand to hold him off.

He hesitated then asked, "Why wouldn't you return my calls?"

"I told you why. I don't want to talk."

"Kai, we were there together. I may have been mostly unconscious when we returned, but I know I heard some things clearly. You don't have to hide anything from me. I know who you are."

"I'm not hiding. I just don't want to be involved with someone like you."

"What's that supposed to mean?"

"I can't be with an alcoholic," she said coldly.

Dean stuffed his hands in his pockets. "I'm glad to hear it, because I'm not one. I haven't touched alcohol for months. Not one drop for months. That is one thing I have to thank Badger for. That jarhead bet me I couldn't give it up, and there was no way I was going to let him win."

Kai lifted her chin. She wasn't willing to give an inch. She couldn't feel vulnerable again. Her strength is what held her up. It's part of what made her a good mom, a woman who could endure any hardship and still come out on top.

He softened his tone. "I also remember what you said before Laughing Eyes saved our hides, Kai."

She took a step back and started to turn away from him.

He risked touching her and took her hand gently, holding her fingers so she wouldn't leave.

"I didn't die. I have time. We have time. You don't have to see me if you don't want to, but don't shut us down because you're afraid of losing me. I'm right here."

She lightly squeezed his hand. That was exactly why she couldn't get involved. She was afraid. She was afraid to even look at him.

"We went through it together, Kai. You're not the only who was screwed up by traveling to the past."

She stared over his shoulder, feeling suddenly ashamed by her selfishness. "You almost died. The bears were my fault. And I'm sorry for that, and I'm glad you've stopped drinking. I shouldn't have brought it up. It was a low blow. You're doing great. I can't tell you how relieved I am to see you recovered from the back injury, and everything else. You look..." she stalled and licked her lips as she actually made eye contact. "You look amazing." She shut her eyes. "I'm not worth the hassle, Dean. Badger was right. I'm messed up."

He squeezed her fingers and then let go of her hand. "Let me decide if you are or you're not, just don't hide. We have something between us. It's real, and undeniable."

She felt suddenly raw. *Exposed.* Kai wanted to shut it off, close herself down and ignore her feelings, but she knew she had seen the same things inside of him. They both understood pain and loss. They both understood loving and losing. She bit her lip. "I'm pretty good at denial, you know? I like to turn off my emotions and pretend they don't exist."

"I know you do, but that's going to change."

He smiled at her. It was sort of shy and bold at the same time.

"So now you're going to change me?" Kai crossed her arms over her chest, but she felt a lightening somewhere in her spirit.

"I am. I already have, and I know you like it." His grin spread.

"I do not, and I'll make you truly miserable if you try."

"Oh, I'm counting on the misery," he said, reaching up to brush her cheek.

She rested her face against his hand for one achingly sweet second and then tried to pull away.

Dean took a chance and cupped the back of her neck, and then bent down to steal a kiss.

She resisted for all of a millisecond and then gave in. She had missed him, and what was the point of denying it any longer? She wanted to finish what they had started at the lake as badly as he did, and they both knew it.

He kept his hand resting gently against her neck as he leaned back and said, "Unfortunately, we're starting this relationship with something you may not want to know, but I'm going to tell you anyway."

"I don't know, Dean. You're pushing the limit on what I can endure as it is."

"Before I say anything else, I need to know if you ever received your letter to yourself."

She shook her head. "I think it may have burnt with the fire that I set. You said over and over, we can't change the past. The entire bank didn't burn down, but there was some damage, and it's the only explanation other than that the letter was lost over the years."

"You could still get it, or it could still be in the bank. What about the letter buried with the sapphires?"

"I haven't checked. Nothing's changed, so it doesn't matter if the letter is there or not."

"And you're the one who originally buried that pouch of gold and sapphires by the larch tree, aren't you?"

"Yes, and I hung my father's bear claw necklace on the trunk. I didn't want anyone else to have them. Those stones caused my family to be killed."

He paused, looked down at the ground and then back into her eyes. "I went to church in Helena."

"That's a long drive for a church service."

"The Catholic church. To make good on my word to Father Connolly."

She waited, knowing he was going to drop a bomb on her.

"I checked out the historical records while I was there."

Kai took a deep breath and let it out slowly.

"I found Badger. Actually, it was a record of his death. The Diocese in Helena has recorded the lives and deaths of the citizens for centuries."

"Are you're sure it was him?"

"It said, 'Badger Lowell. Born   – Died May 1872. Tattoo marks on body. The words, *Semper Fi* written on deceased's back.'"

Kai wasn't sure what to say. She didn't want to think about the past now. It was too full of heartache.

"I have to go back to Helena and look some more. I'm going to compare what is written inside Badger's journal to what I can find in the historical archives. Maybe he did change history. I'm going to find out everything I can."

"And then what? Are you going to go get him? Are you going to try to find your parents?" She could hardly stand listening to what was coming out of her mouth. She didn't care about Badger Lowell and his crazy scheme to rid Montana of a capitalist mining magnate while saving the Blackfoot Nation from unfathomable hardships. *Or did she?*

"I don't know, Kai. But if I ever do go back, I'll be sure there are no bears around."

Other Works Available:

An Angel Falls series

Death Lies Between Us #1

Angel Dreams #2

Haunting Me #3

Book #4 coming soon!

If you enjoyed reading *The Night Medicine*, please help spread the word. The greatest compliment you could give is to write a review at your favorite online retailer, share with a book club, or recommend it to a friend!

A Note From The Author

Great care and endless hours of research went into writing a historically accurate account of life during 1868. I did however take the liberty of using an artist's license to create a world where time travel is possible. The Dragonfly medicine pipe and the God of Night and the Void are complete works of my imagination, as are the characters in this novel. All references to herbs, medicinal plants, field medicine, and wild foods have been written to the best of my knowledge. However, any information in this novel regarding wild crafting should not be used as a reference guide. The reader should always consult a physician or expert in matters relating to his/her health. Any errors in this novel are mine, and may or may not have been written purposefully.

About The Author

When Jody isn't navigating the terrain of her imagination and writing it down, she can be found exploring the wilderness of Colorado with her family, or in the kitchen baking cookies & brownies - and then trying not to eat them all. She's passionate about continuing to learn and reads anything and everything that catches her interest. Jody is a full time mom, a Reiki master, and has taught Hatha yoga for over a decade.

Death Lies Between Us, book one in the *An Angel Falls* series, is the winner of RomCon's Readers' Crown award for best Paranormal Romance in 2014.

Jody A. Kessler invites you to stop by her website and see what's new at: www.JodyAKessler.com. You can also connect with her on Facebook at Jody A. Kessler, or on Twitter @JodyAKessler.

For updates on future releases you can sign up for the newsletter.

From the Author:

I would like to say a special thank you to my family, friends, beta readers, Jim McLaurin, Sonya Writes, and fans for their continued support. I couldn't do this without you.

75871305R00200

Made in the USA
Columbia, SC
20 September 2019